PRAISE FOR *A CONVERGENCE OF SOLITUDES*

"Refracted through the lens of Quebec's years of turbulence
and hope, *A Convergence of Solitudes* tells the truth
about the world: there were never only two solitudes,
but many. By gathering us all, atoms of light, Anita Anand
has focused the blazing beauty of our richness and
possibility, transmuting us in our yearning and our pain
into shining creatures of love. This may be the essential
story of our place and our time: the world, once and always."
—ELISE MOSER

"*A Convergence of Solitudes* is an ambitious novel structured
as a double album and focusing on two different families.
Over the decades that their stories unfold, members of
both clans grapple with solitude in its myriad forms.
The novel paints a multicultural portrait of Montreal as
characters converge on the city from around the world:
India, Vietnam, England, Ireland. Fans of seventies prog
rock will catch the sly references to Quebec superstars
Harmonium. Anita Anand has created an impressive opus."
—NEIL SMITH, AUTHOR OF *JONES*

A Convergence of Solitudes

a novel

Anita Anand

Book*hug Press

TORONTO 2022

Library and Archives Canada Cataloguing in Publication
Title: A convergence of solitudes : a novel / Anita Anand.
Names: Anand, Anita, 1962- author.
Identifiers: Canadiana (print) 20210367210 | Canadiana (ebook) 20210367245
   ISBN 9781771667449 (softcover)
   ISBN 9781771667456 (EPUB)
   ISBN 9781771667463 (PDF)
Subjects: LCGFT: Novels.
Classification: LCC PS8601.N28 C66 2022 | DDC C813/.6—dc23

The production of this book was made possible through the generous assistance of the Canada Council for the Arts and the Ontario Arts Council. Book*hug Press also acknowledges the support of the Government of Canada through the Canada Book Fund and the Government of Ontario through the Ontario Book Publishing Tax Credit and the Ontario Book Fund.

Canada Council   Conseil des Arts
for the Arts   du Canada

ONTARIO ARTS COUNCIL
CONSEIL DES ARTS DE L'ONTARIO
an Ontario government agency
un organisme du gouvernement de l'Ontario

Canada

ONTARIO | ONTARIO
CREATES | CRÉATIF

Book*hug Press acknowledges that the land on which we operate is the traditional territory of many nations, including the Mississaugas of the Credit, the Anishnabeg, the Chippewa, the Haudenosaunee, and the Wendat peoples. We recognize the enduring presence of many diverse First Nations, Inuit, and Métis peoples and are grateful for the opportunity to meet, work, and learn on this territory.

for my mother, Kailash Anand

DISQUE 1

Face A

1. Prélude: Six solitudes (instrumental)

1996

"SUNIL, WHAT HAVE you done with my keys?"

Hima's voice reached Sunil in their bedroom, where he was getting dressed. He gazed around, spotted her change purse and opened it. The silk lining was torn, which made a new pocket just big enough to slide a finger inside.

He froze as he felt something like two tiny metal buttons. The bugs! So this was where they'd been all along.

He did not want this to be true.

His finger pressed against one of them, pushed it up through the lining, pulled it out. Relief swept through him. An earring, a small, glittering diamond. He put his finger back in and pulled out the other one.

Hima appeared in the doorway. Sunil gave her a sheepish smile.

"Your jewels, Madam," he said.

She shook her head and disappeared from the doorway. Before the front door shut she called back that she was taking his keys.

And if I want to go out? He did not much enjoy being alone with his thoughts. They could be so treacherous. An idea came to him. He'd call Rani. He brightened at the thought of an excuse to spend time with his daughter.

ON THE BUS returning from the airport, Mélanie glanced at her mother, fast asleep across the aisle. Someone had left a copy of the *Montreal Gazette* on the seat beside her. Mélanie reached over, picked it up and began flipping through the pages. The Letters page. Surprise, surprise. A *Gazette* reader had more to say about the former premier's infamous declaration—blaming the loss of the referendum on *"l'argent et le vote ethnique."* She counted on her fingers. That was almost six months ago. God. Time to move on!

But she was one to talk. Until very recently, she'd spent all her time scouring newspapers from two decades ago. Way too distracted to pay attention to anything happening around her. Her father would be heartbroken. He'd be livid if he knew she'd basically ignored the last referendum. She didn't care. Yes, she did. Maybe her old self wouldn't have. Poor Serge. The tug of regret combining with shock as she recognized Sunil Roshan's face on the Obituary page.

JANE STOOD WITH her back to the wind. She held the line in her left hand, and lifted the kite she'd painted in the other.

There were people walking by in the park, mostly people with dogs. She felt their stares. She was alone, and enjoying herself, and this would always be considered odd. This was the first time she'd ever taken one of her paintings outside. A swirl of vibrant colours. It was the first warm day of spring. There were still patches of snow mixed with gravel on the field. Her last kite had been a giant fleur-de-lys, guaranteed to keep strangers and their small talk away in this Anglophone neighbourhood. As she let the wind catch the kite, she wondered why she had never done this simple activity with Mélanie when she was a child. The top lit by the sun now. The pull of the kite, its strength always surprising.

HIMA WAS RE-LEARNING. Needing to wear warm socks at night. Waking up to an empty bed, eating breakfast alone. At the grocery store now, training herself not to fill her cart with food she'd enjoyed with Sunil. The cashier was the woman from two buildings over who had suddenly started talking to Hima when she'd returned alone from the hospital. She'd noticed the ambulance.

"I feel so bad for you," this woman was saying as she placed Hima's items in a bag. "It was the same for me. Such a shock. Some wives are more prepared for the death of their spouses. They get to witness a slow decline."

The implication being that those wives were the lucky ones. What is lucky about having to look after a sick person? Hima felt impatience for this woman, and cut her off, shaking her head and waving her hand in her face. She walked down the slope to their—*her*—apartment, with careful, heavy steps to avoid slipping on the black ice. Irritable now, the cashier's words still in her head, causing trouble. Her legs wide apart, shifting the weight of the bag in her arms. *A slow decline.*

It was a shock, yes, of course it was, but her life had not been stable for a long time, always up and down. As she turned the key in the lock and entered the front hall, she prepared for the stillness that would greet her. She was horribly lonely, but she had been lonely for a while. It was just a matter of degree.

THE GOB OF PHLEGM in his bathroom sink. His bedroom blinds askew.

Downstairs, in the kitchen, the cutlery drawer pulled halfway open. Funny, Serge hadn't noticed any of this when he came home last night. A remnant of a dream, a baboon with its lower lip out in a pout, the sight of the open drawer resonating now. Other signs gradually registering as he prepared coffee: yesterday's newspaper on the kitchen table, and not in the magazine rack. Fingerprints—blue ones!—on the surface of the stove, a ball of pasta in the garbage, a saucepan and a plate with remnants of the same noodles in the dishwasher. Imagine: explaining to a journalist that he always washed his dishes by hand, a changed man now. Really.

Fastidious about keeping the blinds straight.

Yes, really.

That gob of mucus in the sink is not mine.

His heart leaping, falling, much too heavily, like blows but from inside his chest. Hope, followed by the abject fear of it. A memory of Mélanie's face, contorted with bitterness, spilling and slurring, that last time she was here. *Serge*, she'd said, instead of *Papa*. Where was she? Close? Eyes darting around the room, but no, of course she was not hiding in a corner of the kitchen.

A possibility, though, of forgiveness? Of starting over, like in a brand-new country, tabula rasa. The excitement pressed against his ribs, wrapped his stomach in this hard, frozen soreness. Must calm down. Up the stairs to his bedroom. His heart still pounding. But a slow climb, like an old, old man.

Facing the framed picture of Shiva on his bedroom wall now, slow inhale, exhale, dropping to the maple floor, crossing his ankles to land in the lotus position. Half-closed eyes, preparing to receive whatever the universe was planning to send his way.

ON THE WAY to Hima's apartment, Rani tried not to think about the last time she had been on her bicycle—her heart pounding, her head buzzing with a kind of manic energy. Rob believed she was grieving normally. Even if she told him what she had been up to that night, he would have just blamed it on the pills. But she would keep this story to herself. She imagined Mélanie saying, in an aggrieved tone, "At least you know who your parents are. You can always say 'I'm like that because of my father.'"

Was she like Sunil?

Is this how it starts?

2. Samskara: Suite en quatre mouvements (Suite in Four Movements)

i. Aux quatre vents (In All Directions)

1975

THE SCHOOL PICTURES had arrived and were handed out. The same photographer did the rounds of all the schools Rani had attended. You took the pictures home and returned with money if your parents agreed to buy them. Some parents couldn't afford them. Others, like Rani's, could but objected to spending the money, didn't even bother to take the pictures out of the plastic sleeves.

"Do you want a class picture, Rani?" the teacher asked. "I have an extra copy."

Rani accepted it, and remained seated, studying her new classmates' faces, silently matching names to each. The fifth time she'd changed schools. Would she even be here for grade seven? Some of the kids stood up at their desks, shouting, gleefully pointing out each other's stunned stares and dorky smiles.

Such a relief to have arrived at this particular school only last week, too late for Picture Day. This year there would be no moment of mortification and shame as her eyes fell on the shit-stain in the bottom row.

RANI WAS ITCHY. And the blouse was not just uncomfortable: it was *weird*, bright purple with a lot of fussy gold embroidery and little round mirrors sewn into it. It had come in a parcel from her mother's family that Uncle Krishen and Aunt Thérèse had carried back from India. Hima had made her wear it to school, and now to visit their relatives, insisting that her aunt Thérèse would love to see her wearing it.

Well, yeah, she was right about that.

"*Que c'est joli! Venez ici, mes amours. Venez voir la belle blouse de votre cousine.*"

Rani's young cousins came running over—they looked so much like two pairs of twins—and here was the familiar rush of pure envy. None of them had to be alone at school in strange clothes covered in little mirrors. But as Thérèse continued to compliment her blouse, Rani relaxed, and even stopped itching. She noticed something: unlike her mother, Matante Thérèse genuinely seemed to enjoy children.

Rani's aunt was a hippie, and apart from children, what she loved the most in the world was everything that was Indian. She outlined her green eyes in kohl, wore a nose ring, dressed in brightly patterned salwar kameez. Today, even ankle bracelets. The house was full of incense, Indian cushions and rugs, sitar music. Thérèse was the opposite of all the other white people Rani had ever met. She'd even married Uncle Krishen, whom she called "Balamji," "Chéri" and "Beloved Husband." Rani's cousins looked vaguely like their father but with lighter skin. The girls' hair was in French braids, and the boys had Beatles haircuts. This afternoon, dressed in matching wine-coloured jumpsuits their mother had knit, they looked like a children's rock group. Chattering together in French. Rani forced herself to join the conversation now and then, even when she had nothing much to say. She knew her cousins had no idea how happy she was in this alternate language reality, where she sang "Au clair de la lune," chanted "Violette à bicyclette" and learned the French names of flowers, berries and insects. It was like one long game she knew was too childish for her; at twelve, she was too old. But, still, she sang and ran around in the woods behind their house with them, greedily absorbing their language, enjoying this break from the rest of her life.

THE SCHOOL BELL rang, breaking the silence. Friday, finally. Rani watched her classmates jump out of their seats, cheering, forming pairs and little groups as they went outside together. One girl was saying to another, "I have a lot of new friends because of Hebrew School but I hate them all." If only this girl could somehow trim those excess friendships from herself and glue them onto Rani. Rani took her time packing her school bag, zipping up her coat. The important thing was that nobody should notice that she was alone. Maybe someone was waiting for her after school, a friend; nobody would know yet that this would be impossible.

When the voices had faded from the schoolyard, she walked toward the main doors, by the principal's office, rather than the side doors that the kids were supposed to use. She could probably stay in the building until after dark if she liked. She'd never get in trouble; it was as if she were invisible, as if she were the one who was colourless. She opened the door slowly and peered out. She didn't see anyone there. Nobody left to chase her down the street shouting things.

She resumed the daydream that played like a never-ending TV series in her head. Her name was Samantha; her sister's, Stacey. Their mother stayed at home, made normal, odourless food, and each kind of food fit cleanly into a section on their plates. Her eyes were green, Stacey's blue. They had to be careful about sunburn.

"RANI," UNCLE KRISHEN said, following her as she stepped off her bicycle and walked it to the back of his house. "I have a favour to ask of you."

"Sure!"

"Just speak English when you're here."

"Oh!" Rani said. Her heart sank. She looked at her uncle's handsome face. The habitual teasing expression wasn't there.

"I always speak to *you* in English," she said, propping her bike up against a tree.

"And that works, right?"

"What? Yes, of course." Rani normally enjoyed their conversations. Maybe because she was older than his kids, he talked to her almost as if she were an adult herself. He was younger than her parents and, although he had immigrated here after they had, he seemed less foreign, better adapted.

"So just speak English to your cousins, all right?"

"But they always speak French."

"That's the problem."

"Speaking French is a problem?"

"I want to put them in English school."

"Why?"

"To broaden their horizons."

Rani felt dismayed. She liked spending time in their alternative reality. Anyway—

"I wish *I* could go to French school."

"Why would you want to change again?" he asked. "You're always complaining about changing schools."

Now this was really disappointing! If she talked to him, it was because she'd imagined he was somehow on her side.

"Anyway, you're not allowed to go to French school," Krishen said. "You have to be baptized."

"Why are *your* kids baptized?" Rani said, repeating something she'd heard her parents say. "You're not Catholic."

Krishen shrugged. "For Thérèse. It wasn't about religion. Actually, it was so we could send them to French school. But I've changed my mind."

What about her? Rani felt a pang for her aunt.

"So I can speak French to my aunt?" It seemed to Rani that Matante Thérèse would appreciate her efforts.

Krishen waved his right hand dismissively. He said something in Punjabi that she couldn't understand and walked into the house.

LIBELLULE. POMME D'API. *Martin pêcheur.* There were so many words that Rani learned from Matante Thérèse that she had never learned in English. Her aunt had made a pie with the *mûres* they had all picked that morning. She had explained how to tell them apart from the poisonous berries. She put the pie on a lace doily and asked the kids to go pick some flowers to make a *beau bouquet* for the picnic table. The kids went running off in all directions, *aux quatre vents*.

Rani's cousins gave her a doubtful look as they all arrived back at the table.

She looked down at her flowers, which were not neat and pretty like theirs. The ends were scraggly and full of dirt.

"Who told you to pull the flowers up by their roots?" they asked her, one after another.

She didn't answer. She didn't know. She could not admit that she, their older cousin, had never learned how to pick flowers.

"I DIDN'T COME here from India so that my daughter would go shit in the woods," roared Sunil.

Rani wondered if her older brothers had ever wanted to go to camp. They probably wouldn't remember, if she asked them. She wasn't really surprised to be turned down. And who knew if camp was really the answer? The children there would probably all know each other. It would be like school.

"Sunil," said Hima. "Watch your language." She said this in their own language, but Rani understood.

"What an idea, though," said Sunil. "We don't earn salaries so our kids can sleep outside!"

Rani did not tell her parents the reasons she wanted to go to camp, the embarrassment she kept experiencing at her cousins' house. There was something wrong with the way she was growing up. She thought of her science teacher talking about how animals adapted to their environment. Well, it wasn't very "adaptive" to be going to an English school in a place where most people spoke French. And her parents really didn't know anything about their environment, beginning with the names of insects. Her parents called all insects *flies*.

It wasn't their fault. They were from the other side of the planet.

They'd sent her older brothers to boarding school, so maybe camp had never come up.

But her father's answer rankled all the same. What salary was he referring to? He hadn't worked in years.

AT HER COUSINS' house, watching them from the entrance to their playroom, not sure where to stand. She was almost a teenager, only a few years older, but a lifetime in child years. She wandered over to the living room, where Thérèse was fiddling with the TV channels before settling on a concert.

What *was* this music? A thrill went through Rani from the first few notes. The beginning of the melody, the guitar and bass, and then this voice, the voice of a man who sounded like he was about to start crying. In French. But French from right here, not France. She dropped down next to her aunt on the sofa. At home, nobody ever thought of switching to a French channel. Words at the bottom of the screen named this revelation: *Sensibilité*. She whispered the syllables to herself.

The lead singer was smiling, but he had the saddest eyes ever. And a strange kind of beauty, like Jesus, all skin and bones, long hair, wispy beard and loose floppy clothing. Probably exactly the kind of charisma that Jesus must have had. The warm smile he wore even more beautiful because of those eyes, with their dark circles, and that voice, so naked and raw, as if he was in pain. Love, his face said, love for the people. The music moved from a simple folk melody to a rising, crazy, emotional, symphonic climax, singers from other bands joining him on the stage, creating an instant choir.

The man with the vulnerable voice kept smiling as he sang, and the smile was so big and kind that she began to fantasize that it was for *her*, that he was smiling at *her* through the TV screen. But of course, it was for Québec, for *l'indépendance*, for *le pays*; he was shouting now and the people in the audience were whistling back at him like a huge flock of ecstatic birds. This was all about a dream, a dream of a beautiful country where they would be free. She wished she could be in that audience, warmed by that loving smile.

RANI WAS WHEELING her bike out of the garage when her father came out and put his hand up to stop her. Her mother's head appeared in the window. She called his name, and they began speaking a mixture of Punjabi and English.

He turned back to Rani and gave her an apologetic look.

"What?" said Rani.

"This weekend isn't a good time to go see your cousins."

"Why?"

"Well, you see, the family is splitting up."

"What?" Couples split up. She had never heard of families splitting up.

"Oh, you know. They had all those fights…"

"Uncle and Matante Thérèse did?" Rani thought guiltily of the last time she had spoken to Uncle Krishen.

"The whole family. The girls sided with your uncle, the boys with their aunt. So now your aunt is leaving with the boys. The girls have decided to stay with their dad."

Rani was stunned. She thought everything in that family was so much better than hers. And now it was cracking down the middle?

"Fights about what?"

"Ah, I think stupid things. You must have heard...TV channels, schools, French-English stuff."

ii. La fuite (The Escape)

1977

SHE TURNED AND asked why they were following her, and they repeated her question back, but with an Indian accent. She felt humiliated and angry. She didn't sound like that. They laughed nastily, frightening her. They were coming up to the strip mall. She could cut into the record store. Or would they follow her inside? No. She went to the back and absorbed herself in studying the liner notes on a Sensibilité album. Her eyes fell on the lyrics to a song called "Fuite"—*escape*—and someone, maybe Serge Giglio himself, had written in swirly handwriting above the typed lines that this song in particular was "*Pour toi, mon amour.*" She read and reread those four words, her heart beating loud in her chest, from excitement now, not from fear.

A tinkle as the door opened. She glanced up. Shit, they were here. Not moving, just lurking in the doorway. But a store employee was walking toward her now, smiling, asking her in French if she wanted to listen to the album. She said she would love to. A rush of joy, just to be speaking French.

Since Matante Thérèse had left her uncle, she'd keenly missed their conversations.

Of course, she *had* the album. She listened to it all the time. She had *all* of their albums. But she accepted the headphones offered to her. They cushioned her ears, wrapped her in the warm sound, blocked everything else out. It was like she'd accepted a new head, one in which only music played. She turned and faced the back of the store, let herself be absorbed by the sounds of Serge's twelve-string guitar, let the bass hum through her body, here was Serge's soothing voice now.

Dusk by the time she left. Purple sky, a bit of fuzzy light from the baseball park across the street. Nobody waiting for her. She supposed they'd heard her having a conversation with the guy in the store in French, about a French record. Disconcerting for them, almost as if she'd performed a magic trick.

HIMA WAS EXHAUSTED. Chopping onions, ginger, garlic. Making dough for the chapatis. Sunil was always there with her, but he was exhausting too, in his own way. Their daughter said they should just order pizza or something, like other people. She claimed that fried onions and cumin seeds gave her indigestion. Difficult girl. Who exactly did she think she was? The boys had always been too hungry to complain. They wolfed down anything. No fuss.

"Why should we order pizza?" Hima said. "Are we Italian?"

"No," said Rani.

"And are we just 'other people'?" Sunil said.

"No, of course not," Rani said.

Hima picked up on the sarcasm, was pretty sure Sunil missed it. *No, of course we're extraordinary, especially you.* But for Hima the issue was different. As a daughter, Rani should be helping prepare the meals with them. She should be helping, period. And she should learn to cook food from her own culture. Otherwise, what was she? She pictured two wavy dashes: approximately equal. This was followed by a minus sign.

"Why do you spend so much time listening to music in your bedroom?" asked Sunil. His eyes showed genuine concern. "Is something wrong?"

"Why would something be wrong?"

"It's just, *beti*, it can't be healthy!"

Hima saw that Rani was rolling her eyes now.

"And what *is* this French music you are always listening to?" Hima said.

"It's Québécois," said Rani. "It's from here."

"Québécois," repeated Hima. "You are Parti Québécois now?"

"All we need," she continued, when Rani didn't answer, but then stopped. She saw, in her husband's expression, that he was far away. She reached out and touched his shoulder. *Come back here, you.*

And then, to Hima's amazement, the girl was at the door, putting her coat on, walking outside. The gall. All this cooking, and she wouldn't even deign to eat with them.

"Hey, where do you think you are going?" Hima said.

"I feel like riding my bike."

She feels like. Hima felt dismayed.

She turned to her husband, who was just smiling benignly now. *Aren't you going to do something?*

"Ah, at least she is not spending the whole day in her bedroom," said Sunil.

SUNIL PICKED UP the giant plastic bag from the floor of the bedroom closet and was about to head out the door when he caught Hima's withering look. He turned around.

"What now, Your Majesty?"

"It's a little late, that's all."

"You think she'll be in bed?"

"No, of course not, Sunil. She's a teenager."

"Then what?"

"All this."

She rose from the bed and spread open the top of the plastic bag, as if to show him the things he'd bought. A white pup tent, decorated with cartoon Dalmatians. A bright pink sleeping bag. A pink Thermos. She gave him a questioning look.

The plan was to fill it with hot cocoa, so Rani could warm her hands by holding it in the night. He'd go out and check on her, maybe sit inside the tent and listen to the crickets.

But Hima was right. Crickets would not compete with this Western music his daughter listened to. Not at all the music that his office mates used to listen to, with the scandalous but crystal-clear lyrics: *She wore an itsy-bitsy-teeny-weeny-yellow-polka-dot-bikini.* This music was more complicated, at once darker and sweeter, mostly instrumental but nevertheless very alien. He went and stood at Rani's door and listened, made out a few French words: *Dis-moi qui je suis.* Tell me who I am. He hit the door a few times. The music obscured his first knocks, so he hit the door louder a few times, and then gave the doorknob a tentative half-turn. Another. A glimpse of her rising from her bed, her eyes open but unfocused. The low neckline of her t-shirt, the small, round bumps. He blinked, looked away and then looked back. Her face, entranced.

"What is it, Dad?"

"That is what I was going to ask you."

"What?"

"What is this music that you play over and over?"

She looked blank.

"It's just... music," she said, bending over the stereo receiver and turning the volume down a few notches.

He met her eyes as she looked up at him. He held her gaze, but could not think of what to say. He watched as she slowly straightened, balling her fists, frowning. How to tell her that he was just trying to be a normal father, expressing interest in the things she enjoyed. Worrying a little. Nothing over the top.

That temper of hers. An angry sigh as she went over to the turntable and lifted the needle from the record. She sat back down on her bed. Her face said, *Are you happy now? Why are you still standing there?*

This sulky mood was normal, of course it was. And Hima was right about the little tent, the child-size sleeping bag, which he suddenly realized was too small. But there was something else, something he feared, a sort of blind gleam in Rani's eyes, something he'd seen before.

iii. Neige folle (Crazy Snow)

1978

A COLD, BRIGHT blue winter day. Rani on her way to school on cross-country skis. Suddenly whizzing up behind her: another body, slightly smaller than hers, also on skis, crashing into her back, knocking her down.

Rani and the other person lay panting in the snow, him on top of her back, at first. A long moment. Then, he rolled off into the snow and lay beside her. They both stayed there, not speaking, completely winded from their falls. He looked about sixteen as well; smaller, though. She didn't feel afraid, just intrigued. What would happen next?

She didn't recognize this boy and guessed that he went to the French school before he said anything.

"Bonjour."

They continued to lie panting, and she watched the breath emerge from their mouths in the cold air. He did not apologize for knocking her down. Instead—what was this? The boy brought his face close to hers. Maybe for a kiss. *Yeah, right!*

But he did kiss her. And she let him, and even kissed him back. *Someone actually kissed me. It's happened. Someone thinks I'm okay. Maybe it's because he's French.* Then he got up and asked her to follow him. She sat in the snow, her legs and skis stretched out in front of her, and gazed up at him. In something like a state of shock, she felt herself shake her head. He shouted, "T'es belle. Je t'aime!" She found some words; she told him that she couldn't follow him because she had to go to school. He laughed and told her again that he loved her, and suggested that she accompany him to *his* school. She got up on her knees and reached for her ski poles, feeling scared for the first time, but then, looking at him, not scared again. He was so small. He stuck his ski poles in the snow and stood, searching in the pockets of his puffy ski jacket. He pulled out a pen and quickly waved it at her, smiling, before writing something on a piece of paper. He scrunched the paper up into a ball and threw it to her. She removed a mitten, and held it in her mouth as she began to pull the paper flat: it was just numbers. She rolled it back up into a ball and tucked it into the pocket of her coat. As she put her mitten back on, it slowly dawned on her. *A phone number.*

He asked her where she lived, and she pointed to her house. He told her he'd come by that evening. Then with a push of his ski poles, he created a cloud of white powder and then disappeared into it.

After a moment, Rani came out of her daze and continued on her way. Softly singing along to the Sensibilité song that was playing in her mind. Did *he* like the band too? Yes—suddenly, she was sure he did. A possibility occurred to her, amazed her: life, *her* life, could be wonderful, not something pointlessly heavy to be trudged through. Someone actually wanted her, the way people wanted each other in love songs and school buses and maybe later, when it would be time to match up with someone and have a family, something like this but less crazy could happen to her. This was just the beginning. Eager now, about what would happen next. In any case, what had just happened meant that there was hope.

WHEN RANI CAME home from school that afternoon, her parents were in the kitchen preparing supper together. Her mother sifting through lentils with her fingers, picking out the tiny, rough stones. The dough already prepared for the chapatis, a few cups of whole-wheat flour in a pot because there was no bowl that was big enough, because in this house, of course, another bowl meant excess. Why have both pots and giant bowls? This is how her parents thought, because they were crazy.

Rani watched as Hima set the lentils aside and turned her attention to the chapati dough. Adding a cup of white flour to the pot, then drops of water. Pulling off her rings, setting them on the counter. Mixing and finally kneading with her hands. Hima had a full-time job; why did she have to do all this as well?

Sunil was sitting on the floor in a white undershirt and a pair of tennis shorts, cross-legged, a large slate-grey stone mortar in his lap, grinding cumin, coriander and mustard seeds with a huge wooden pestle, a *dunda*. It was the size of a baseball bat, and the crudest thing she could imagine. Long strands of Sunil's straight, jet-black hair fell over his forehead. His eyebrows were much too long; her mother always nagged him to trim them, but his only concession was to comb them so that they didn't stick up or even fall straight down over his eyes. His undershirt failed to hide the black, hairy mat on his chest, black strands poking out from his armpits. *Ugh.* His arms and legs covered in it too.

Hima asked Sunil if he would be finished with the dunda soon and he said, "Yes, ma'am." Rani sniffed; Hima turned and looked up, spotted her slouching in the doorway. Their eyes met.

"Go wash your hands and come help," Hima said.

Rani looked at the clock. *Great, just great.*

Hima, hands full of dough, used her chin to point to the counter, where Sunil had cleared a space and set down the dunda. Rani put down her schoolbag, washed her hands in the kitchen sink and wiped them with a tea towel. She began sprinkling the counter with white flour. Then she stood next to her mother, reached her hands in the pot, pulled out a handful of the sticky, rough-textured brown dough, and patted it between her hands to make a small ball. She worked slowly but made sure she breathed in a way that expressed that she was completely disgusted and couldn't wait to scrub her hands clean. When she had made ten of these balls, she gave one last deep sigh. She made a quick and faltering attempt to wipe the sour expression off her face as she told her mother that a friend was coming over.

"Fine, go wash up."

But would he show? She looked out the window of her bedroom, imagining the boy on skis, stepping out of the woods behind her house.

She came back downstairs and studied the scene in the kitchen, thinking of how it would strike a white person. Her parents passing a thick wooden stick back and forth, using it as both a pestle and a rolling pin, as if those tools had not been invented. Something that looked like a hollowed-out rock on the floor. Her father, his hairiness, his thin white undershirt.

She felt in her pocket for the precious slip of paper. She studied the number and finally dialled it. She told the boy she would meet him at the park instead.

HE WAS SITTING ON a bench next to the deserted skating rink, a pair of gloves beside him, rolling a miniature, crumpled looking cigarette between his fingers. When she approached, he put it behind an ear and stood up to kiss her. His breath was sour, but his lips were warm, and he was here, here for her. It was a miracle! They didn't speak. He sat back down on the bench and invited her to straddle him. She lowered herself onto his lap and marvelled at how comfortable she felt, how well their bodies fit together. She removed her own mittens and then plucked the thing from behind his ear. She wasn't sure if it was a cigarette or a joint, so she turned it in her fingers and brought it close to her nose. He told her she looked sexy when she did that, and so she did it again. They grinned at each other. He told her his name, Benoît, and asked her hers.

She closed her eyes. Ready, go! They kissed, their hands in each other's hair.

Quick steps pushing through the snow, rushing up. She opened her eyes and her father was there, a coat open over his undershirt, hairy and mad.

"Rani!"

Sunil bawled her name, like a child calling his mother. *Ugh*.

But she didn't move. She kept her arms around Benoît's neck and squeezed her eyes shut, trying to disappear into this other reality.

"Rani, c'est bien toi?" Benoît asked.

And then her father lunged at them. They untangled from each other and tried to leap from the bench, but he was already there, hovering over them.

"Ça va," Rani said to Benoît. She repeated the words in English, staring at her father. "It's all right."

Sunil wasn't in that Indian-father rage he could get into sometimes. Or if he had been, he had already popped out of it, into that other thing.

He indicated to Benoît to take off his watch. Benoît gave him an uncomprehending look, but slipped it off and held it out to him, clearly afraid.

"What is it, Daddy?"

"I just have to check something," he said. He moved a few feet back and stood under a street lamp. Subdued now. Had the situation been normal, this voice would be considered normal.

"Not this again," Rani said. But at least he'd calmed down.

She turned to Benoît, and said, "C'est correct. Il va juste vérifier le numéro de série."

Checking serial numbers. He did this with appliances and bicycles too. He compared these serial numbers to license plate numbers he'd jotted down, sometimes pulling over on the road to enter them in a tiny notebook he kept in the pocket of his trousers. Benoît half-lay on his back in the snow beside the bench, propping himself with his elbows, an alarmed stare on his face. He held his hand out as Sunil returned the watch. Rani studied his wavy brown hair, his wide brown eyes, his freckled nose and especially his full, sensuous mouth. She knew she would never see him again.

ANOTHER MOVE. AS soon as Rani crossed the threshold of her new classroom, new insults that she could not even repeat, much less report to her parents. Not that it would have any effect. Younger, it had been "chocolate face." Her parents had laughed at that, suggested she call them vanilla. Sixteen now, she knew it was no use, they'd never just pick up and move again because of the hell she was going through at school. She was just a thing they put in the car with their suitcases and houseplants. They never asked if she was making friends. She wondered if this was an Indian thing or a crazy thing, that all they wanted to know was why she was doing better in Typing than Math. Did she think they wanted her to be a secretary? That's what they asked. Rani wondered if her brothers were nagged like this. No—they could just be good at typing. It didn't occur to her parents that her marks had nothing to do with what they wanted, just as where they lived, what school she attended or was pulled out of in the middle of the year, had nothing to do with anything she wanted.

She stood glaring at the latest configuration of their living room furniture, and at her parents behind their newspapers.

"I hate it here. The people at this school are the worst ever."

"Oh well," her father said. "There are good and bad people everywhere."

He spoke in such a bland voice. Was it the pills or the voices in his head distracting him that made him like that? She felt a rush of anger that these voices had so much more sway with him than her own.

The kettle began to whistle in the kitchen.

"Yes, good and bad people everywhere," she said, raising her voice above the piercing noise. "I bet you think they're right here, don't you, all the good and bad people, in this room right now?"

Hima shot her a glance: *Bas.* Enough. Rani said, "Fine!" but continued to stare at her father as her mother got up from the couch and went to the kitchen to make tea. She felt the venom in her own look. *Here, you think someone wants to poison you? I'll spare you the trouble of trying to figure out who it is. Look. I'm right here.*

As if a poisoned dart had landed on her arm and all the poison was spreading to her head, to her heart. She had to stop this hateful feeling; her father looked so bewildered and pitiful. He turned to her just as she was letting the fierceness fall from her expression, as if he'd sensed everything. Sharing this sad, bland look. Two tears dropped from her eyes and she gave them an impatient swipe. He patted the space on the couch that Hima had vacated.

The heat from his body, his smell of Brylcreem, these were things that remained constant and comforting. She noticed a photo album between them on the sofa. She picked it up and moved closer to him.

"Wanna see a bear?" he asked.

She was pretty sure she had seen these photographs, all black and white, before. There were sharp portrait shots of Indian relatives she had never met, pictures of her sweet-faced mother at her wedding, looking like something awful was about to happen to her, pictures of Sunil's family, all thin and humbly dressed, the women in plain, pale fabric, the men in either cotton tunics or creased Western shirts with the collars unbuttoned. There was a picture of Hima, somewhere in her twenties, sitting in a sari, singing and playing the harmonium.

Looking at her dad now, his big worried eyes, the over-sized lashes and eyebrows, his large hairy hands, the baggy skin around the knuckles. She rested her head on his shoulder, inhaled his scent and watched his hands turn the heavy black pages of the album. She tried to feel fond of his hands. She wished she could be a normal girl, one who felt willingly connected to her parents.

Sunil leafed through the photos, pausing here and there to gaze at the pictures of dark faces with heavy eyebrows. Rani vaguely recognized a few now. This one with the little mustache. Harbinger? Could that be his name?

"I sponsored so many of these people to come to Canada," Sunil said. "They don't stay though. They go to other provinces, or to the United States. You know, I tried to make a little community. There were just two Sikh families when we settled here. Those were the only Indians. And they'd been in Canada for a long time. They'd come here from B.C. Their grandfathers were indentured labourers on the railroads. Canada had had these people come over, these Sikhs from India, and Chinese people too. But once the tracks were laid, guess what happened?"

"What?"

"Canada closed the doors. For a long time. Then, they opened them just a crack. I came to Montreal as a student, you know. Then your mother, your brothers, your uncle and all the others."

Rani sighed with irritation. He seemed so proud. Of what? Of being the first that didn't belong, of making a family that didn't belong here either? If she asked why *he* had come here, he would say for the snow. He didn't seem particularly adapted to the cold though. Every winter he'd go outside dressed for fall and come back frostbitten. One time, his ears had turned purple, and then green. They'd oozed with pus.

Sunil found the picture he'd been looking for.

"This is the one. From our road trip."

Her parents had driven across the country, long before she was born. Somewhere in Alberta, off the highway, Hima, elegant in a long camel hair coat, her hair long and curly, bending on one knee next to the car, holding her hand out to two bear cubs.

Rani gasped. She looked at her father, searching his face for some sign that he saw what she did. There was none, no sign at all. She had seen this picture before, as a little kid, but only now did she understand what it implied. She shivered. She turned the page and shivered again. Another reminder of the kind of upbringing they'd had.

"Oh, yes," said Sunil, oblivious. "Here is Arun in the cable car."

This photo was from the same trip, somewhere near Jasper. A boy between two and three years of age sitting by himself in a cable car, surveying the world. He was tiny; he could have slipped under the bar he was holding. In fact, at that age, he would have been small and slippery enough to fall out the side, which was completely open. Rani put her hand over her father's as he was about to turn the page of the album.

"Dad, how come Arun's alone in the cable car?"

"Oh," Sunil answered with a laugh. "You know, sometimes with parents, the mother thinks that one's with the father, and the father thinks he's with the mother. They lose track."

Of course there weren't any photos of the trip Sunil and Rani took to India when she was eight years old. Her father had left their suitcases—containing their clothes and his cameras—on a train.

It's a miracle I'm alive. It was suddenly clear. It would be despite her parents, and not because of them, that she would survive.

iv. Kermesse (A Celebration)

1979

JANE CAME DOWNSTAIRS and tiptoed around the six hippies lying on the living room floor. Did these people just drift in while Serge was playing his twelve-string and singing to himself in the middle of the night? She parted the curtains. There were at least fifty more hippies sleeping in the front yard. They looked young—vulnerable and exposed. They lay together in different shapes, as if trying to spell out a message. None of them had blankets or sheets to cover their bodies, though they did wear scarves, which made them look vaguely European; these and their faded, loose cotton pants and dresses billowed in the morning breeze. A scent of patchouli mixed with hashish came through the window; it seemed to come from the tops of their heads. She shook her head in disbelief. Only in Québec. Back home in Britain—and in the rest of North America, for that matter—punk had all but completed its invasion. With its black clothes, piercings and harsh haircuts, punk had made all these people extinct. How much longer could this last?

She went upstairs to the bedroom, tried to talk to Serge, who just groaned and rolled over, smashing his face into his pillow. It was seven in the morning. He had been up until around five, she knew, wouldn't wake until the afternoon.

Jane observed him for another moment and then opened the bathroom door. Something flipped in her chest. A girl she had never seen before was sitting on the toilet, apparently asleep. Bloody hell.

She hesitated. Wake up this sleeping stranger? Being Serge's wife was a liability here; this young woman might not be thrilled to know of her existence. She imagined the girl hissing at her. Should she step behind the shower curtain, pee in the bathtub drain? But then Mélanie was beside her, yawning, rubbing her eyes. Burrowing her sleepy head into her middle now, into the silk fabric of her nightgown.

"Mélanie, love," Jane said, shaking her tiny shoulders. "Do you need a wee?"

"Yes," Mélanie mumbled.

"Tell the girl," Jane said. "Tell the girl to get off the toilet."

Mélanie leaned over and gave the girl's arm a pinch. "Ôte-toé, tabarnac!"

Jane gasped in alarm, almost laughed. The girl let out a little cry and opened her eyes. Jane was relieved to see that she just looked startled.

"OK, man," the girl said. "On relaxe, OK?" She jumped off the seat in a panic and ran out the door.

"Good job, Tweetie," Jane started to say to her daughter, but just then there was a loud retching in the hall.

MÉLANIE STOOD IN the doorway.

"Papa?"

Small and strident, like a piccolo. Serge closed his eyes and raised his chin as if sniffing the air, something Mélanie herself did when she announced she was invisible.

"Papa!"

The child gave a loud sigh. He could *hear* her shrug her skinny shoulders. Her hesitation. Her footsteps now, as she went outside into their tiny backyard. He closed his eyes again. The noisy creak of the swing, her shoes scratching the bark of the maple tree, and then hitting the ground with a slap as she seemed to abruptly change her mind. Running across the concrete slabs, scuffling closer to the back wall of the house, toward the mini-trampoline. The springs under her weight as she bounced up and down. He opened his eyes, looked at his hand resting on his guitar, and finally began to strum along in rhythm with the sound of her landings.

There was this recurring dream he had, of trying to open the junk drawer in the kitchen, but finding it impossible because the handle was missing. Jane, whimsical, quirky, lovely Jane, had installed drawer handles adorned with real pieces of cutlery. The one on the junk drawer was a bladeless knife. In the dreams, someone had stolen it.

Today he had woken from this dream, bid it good morning and then dismissed it, as a yogi had advised him to do. If he just let it, the music would come to him. He sat with his twelve-string guitar, strummed, picked, hummed, made up rhymes about how he was feeling, began a story for Mélanie, and a love letter to his wife. The words and melody just flowed, together. Everyone thought he was hugely talented but he knew he was just a vessel. This apparently magical thing that was happening to him could happen to anyone, if they just let it. And if their families were good enough to leave them alone, because part of the process was working through the night, rising at two in the afternoon, spending the afternoons meditating. He could count on Jane; she'd keep herself... *amused*, making her abstract paintings, never minding whether he was around or not.

A frown formed on his face as he thought of his little girl, her demands that he play with her, watch every little thing she did. "Watch me jump, Daddy!" she was chanting now.

Simply acknowledge and let go. He tuned in to a cardinal calling its mate. He closed his eyes, visualizing its redness. Next, he turned his attention to the wind in the trees, thinking how he could mimic these sounds, going through the instrumentation currently used by his band: guitar, drums, clarinet, keyboard, violin, mellotron, and harmonium.

"WOULD YOU LEAVE me the car keys today?" Jane whispered in Serge's ear as they lay in bed the next day, her arms around the front of his body. "I want to take Tweetie shopping for shoes."

"In the summertime?" Serge said.

Jane didn't know whether Serge was talking in his sleep, or whether he objected to imprisoning their daughter's feet in shoes in June. She waited. Finally, he sighed.

"Yeah, fine, if you can find them," he said.

Jane went downstairs, stepping over the bodies on the floor. The keys were not on the hook by the front door. She rummaged around in the junk drawer, searched under the pile of sheet music on the kitchen table.

Jane counted the bodies on the floor. Three. Plus two on the sofa bed, another on the child futon. No fans this morning, though, just the band. A slight relief. She found a package of rolled oats in the cupboard, but as she was heating up the milk she saw Hugo, who had been on the floor, rise to his feet and, apparently still asleep, go to the piano and begin playing. Jane turned the stove off and stood in the entrance to the living room to watch the room come to life. Marie-Claire woke up, looked around blinking, and then rolled off the futon onto the floor. She sat up in a cross-legged position, her head, and all its hair, forward, buried in her harem pants, listening as if the music were coming from inside her head. The other ones on the floor rose, and the ones on the couch rolled off and picked up their instruments. Daniel went and sat in the corner behind the drum kit and sat nodding for a moment before he gave his cymbal a few light, ethereal taps. Serge came down the stairs in a trance and sat at the edge of the piano bench, facing the others. He began to sing, his voice softly tracing the arpeggio Hugo had been repeating for a while. Marie-Claire slowly lifted her head and joined in, and they began to paint over Hugo's notes with a jazzy melody. *Nananananana*, no words yet. Then Hugo got up and went to the synth and Serge moved over on the bench, played his melody and sang, the first sounds from his throat a cry quickly followed by a moan. Marie-Claire joined in, and they both began wailing. Marc plucked his bass, Yvon blew a few tentative notes on his clarinet, Stéphane cocked his head, listening, before abruptly picking up his bow and scratching a series of urgent notes on his violin. Serge then sat down on the other side of Hugo and accompanied him with his right hand on the higher keys.

Jane walked into the room and sat down on the couch. Mélanie came downstairs and wordlessly crawled into her lap. The band members turned to glance at them and then turned away again. Marie-Claire and Serge with their eyes closed, Serge's eyelids fluttering, his eyes now opening to look across at her. Jane suddenly felt as though she'd interrupted an orgasm. She spotted the keys on the radiator across the room and got up and walked toward them. Serge, still singing *nanananana*, followed her with his eyes as she slid the keys into her pocket and sat back down with Mélanie. He stopped singing for a moment, closed his eyes and began again, intelligible lyrics now beginning to flow from his mouth. Jane made out the phrase. She rubbed her daughter's bare feet. She busied herself with putting things in her purse and nodded her head to the music, pretending not to understand his words. She would make breakfast for Tweetie and they'd go shopping for shoes. "Ôtez mes fers," he sang. *Unshackle me.* The others all joined in, their voices like a rising wave.

"I'M SO AMAZED. We're still surprising each other. The riff Marc played near the beginning, the way it locked in with the piano and the drums. Man, that was powerful."

Jane stood at the edge of the living room, listening to Serge hold forth. The smell of spicy incense mixing with the scent of roses blowing through the open windows.

Serge's bandmates had arrived at noon, and waited two hours until he woke up. Jane had served them tea. They didn't take milk. The girl, Marie-Claire, asked for a slice of lemon. Jane disappeared into the kitchen, couldn't find any, and when she came back the whole band seemed to be arguing about something anyway. But once Serge came downstairs, everything was cool. They were all so enthralled with him, and with each other, such exquisite music they had the privilege of playing.

There was a concept in Indian music, Serge was explaining: certain kinds of pieces were supposed to be played in the morning, the afternoon, and at night. He told them they should think about this, their music in relation to time of day. He said while listening to the tape of the songs they had just been working on now, during the day, they sounded sharper and somehow shinier than their night music. He said he could imagine light coming out of the ends of Daniel's drumsticks, off the strings of his own guitar, the keyboard. At night, he said, everything sounded slightly muffled. But also, he could hear something else.

A pause. Jane knew what was coming.

Their music in relation to history. Its own history, and the history of the Québécois people. Gently breaking free of colonial bonds. A gentle, beautiful birth of a new country, where anything would be possible for their people.

"The magic is still happening."

"It's happening."

"It's gonna happen for la Saint-Jean."

"It's gonna be the most incredible fête nationale in history."

"They're going to coast on this music. It's going to be the wave..."

"They're going to ride it to a *Oui.*"

MÉLANIE WATCHED JANE pull at the hairs of her eyebrows as she stared into Serge's shaving mirror. The bathroom was full of steam from her shower, and Jane kept rubbing the small mirror with her hand. Mélanie tried to see her own reflection in the big mirror above the sink, but that was all fogged up as well. Jane's eyes were like two little blue lights, her hair light brown, her skin as white as soap.

Suddenly something in Mélanie's head, something small but thick, like the plug in the bathtub, seemed to pop out.

"Did you steal me?" she said.

"What?" Jane said. But her face was getting all red.

THE CONCERT FOR Saint-Jean-Baptiste Day—la fête nationale. Their set began in twenty minutes. But how to get to the stage at the top of Mont Royal without the crowd—what a crowd, in the tens of thousands!—converging on Serge? He finally agreed to let his bandmates disguise him. He was slight and long-haired, so sure, why not, let them dress him as a woman. He wore Marie-Claire's canvas sunhat, Jane's sunglasses, a long white tunic, and brown leather boots.

He walked up the hill with the concert-goers, through clouds of tobacco and marijuana smoke, separate from his band members lest anyone recognize them and make the connection. A warm evening; he was overdressed, and the sweat poured as he climbed the hill. As he passed the port-a-potties their odour mixed with the marijuana smoke. A brief wave of nausea, passing now, as he walked on. A breeze stirring the trees.

Les Enchanteurs were winding down their set with their hit, "Nouveau Monde." Some people were clapping to the beat, but many were engaged in conversation, even singing bits of Sensibilité songs. It hit him: Sensibilité were more popular than les Enchanteurs. It seemed impossible; les Enchanteurs, his heroes, the ones who first dared to sing about a new direction for Québec, in Québécois. That trademark sound, that traditional lilt mixed with folk-rock. He listened carefully. Sensibilité were the better musicians, he had to admit, yes, they were the more innovative band. A twinge of guilt. Mostly, though, everything just felt unreal.

Having to wear a disguise. Funny that nobody turned to stare at him. He was sure he looked pretty weird.

The sunglasses were filthy, with slicks of greasy mascara on each lens. Still, he liked how they deepened Montreal's dark blue sky, made it look even more like ink. It was romantic. He missed Jane, who'd told him she was going to leave Mélanie with a babysitter and go for one of her meandering walks around the city. Everyone was out tonight; all the houses must be empty, except for sleeping children and old people. There were so many people right here in the park. He heard someone singing his new song, "Déjà demain," screwing up the lyrics and laughing. People the age he'd been when he'd started Sensibilité. Just kids, he mused, kids without responsibilities dragging them down.

YVES RICHARD, the band's manager, came by with some news. He had received a phone call from Québec's Intercultural Affairs Minister—

"Who?" Serge laughed and pointed his cigarette at Jane and Mélanie, who were finger-painting together on the kitchen table. "Is this about us? Our intercultural family?"

"They are organizing a trip to the United States," Yves said, ignoring him. "It's a charm offensive. They want to invite Sensibilité."

Serge squinted as he smoked. An uncomprehending look.

"The idea is to demystify Québec," said Yves. "To make independence sexy and safe."

"Sexy and safe," Serge repeated, smirking.

"Attractive and not scary."

"For capitalism," Serge said, taking a last drag on his cigarette and quickly exhaling.

He shook his head and stubbed out his cigarette, getting ready to say more.

"Serge, wait," said Yves. "René Lévesque himself wants you to come along. Are you listening?"

He was.

"The minister is inviting you on behalf of the premier. Because you are brilliant and talented. Because your music transcends language. Because you are the best thing Québec has. And Serge, they can book you in a club in L.A. They will pay your way. They'll take care of getting your instruments there. You are not a small band. This is not something to sneeze at."

"René?" Serge was aware of the awe in his voice.

Yves nodded. Serge's eyes widened, Yves imitated him, and they laughed.

"Of course," said Serge. "We'll do anything for René."

THE GROUP FLEW out west. Serge told Jane they had no expectations for the concert in L.A. Before the concert, they went to a record store to promote their albums. It felt strange, he said that afternoon, on the phone; it had been so long since they'd had to do anything like that back home. Young Californians in shorts came into the store, asked what was playing, chatted with the French-speaking hippies, and before the end of the day, all their records had sold out. But Yves explained that the Starwood was a club that usually catered to punk groups. It wasn't clear who would show up.

Jane showed up. Leaving Mélanie with a babysitter, she took a cab to the airport, and arrived at the club in L.A. half an hour before the concert. She watched as the room gradually filled, the lights dimmed and the curtains opened to a stage bathed in blue light. The six male members and one female member of Sensibilité were dressed in white; all of them had long brown hair except for Marc, who, with his blond curls, did not look out of place among all the other angels on stage. As Serge began to strum his guitar and he and Marie-Claire began their raw, wordless vocals, Jane felt what Serge would call *positive energy* in the air. It was unmistakable. This crowd of young Americans was receptive. They were ready for something new. But when the songs began in earnest, and Serge sang a few French lyrics, she felt the energy push back, like a receding wave. This was going to be a disappointment. A beautiful idea that depended on a leap of faith. It *almost* worked.

Backstage after the concert, Serge was shaking his head at Yves's proposal.

"I could write it for you," Jane said.

Yves looked interested, Jane noticed, but not hopeful.

"We're not going to sing in English," Serge said. He'd barely acknowledged her presence.

"All right," Jane said. "I'm just saying."

She thought, *I'll just make myself scarce*, and got up to leave, but then changed her mind and listened from the doorway.

"It's a question of survival," Yves was saying, his tone light, as if suggesting that he agreed with Serge, as if his words meant the opposite, that nothing was actually at stake. "We're too small."

By "we," he meant Québec. Sensibilité was big: they could play to crowds of twenty thousand fans, mostly local cégep and university students. They were surrounded wherever they went. But this would never translate into a viable income for the band. It had seven members. They needed a semi to transport their instruments and equipment. And to sell records in another province, or in the U.S., they would have to sing in English.

"Yes, we are talking about survival," Serge said. "That's the only thing you said that I can agree with. For me, this is about the survival of our culture. It's about our beautiful language, *hostie*, and our musicians and writers and filmmakers. If that makes me political, okay. You know, there were a couple of Italian bands, they started changing all their lyrics to English, and then, like, they just sort of turned into nothing. They sound like everyone else. They're nothing."

Yves didn't say a word, just nodded. He met Jane's eyes, looked down, kept nodding, as Serge said, "I'm not doing it. That's the one thing we'll never do."

"NAMASTE."

An outdoor concert on the grounds of l'Université de Montréal, a warm blue August evening. Rani was self-conscious in this crowd, feeling like a visible imposter in the middle of all the waving fleur-de-lys flags. She envied the other fans. It was like they all knew each other. There was the sour smell of beer, the heady musk of hash and pot. She felt virginal, alien, wished she could jump out of herself, out of her skin, leave her claustrophobic, foreign-looking teenage shell, join this crowd. But how?

And then she saw him.

It was only an instant: he ran up to the stage throwing off his disguise, layers of strange clothing and a comical pair of sunglasses, pausing, gazing in her direction, greeting her— *her!*—with folded hands and a slight bow, and when she smiled, amazed, telling her in a voice she was sure no one else could hear, "Tu es radieuse."

A sharp electric sensation shooting upwards in her chest, buzzing through her body. *I'm radiant. I'm radiating.*

More than that, these words were crucial information: *I'm all right. I must be. Serge Giglio thinks so.*

The musicians quickly tuned their instruments and the concert began to euphoric cheers. The sky was beautiful, indigo. A spotlight scanned the crowd. It was searching for her. It found her. She was floating above the ground, almost riding that beam to the stage. "*Tu es radieuse.*" The words danced around and around. She waited for more messages from him. He smiled as he sang. She smiled back, feeling their eyes lock. Shocks through her body. Her legs felt weak.

Between the first and second song, he started to talk about a trip to L.A. He said it had been a quick trip, but he'd learned something about what was important to him.

The audience was rapt.

"Having a culture, a language, an identity...a country!"

As he pronounced the last words—*un pays!*—the crowd roared and whistled.

"But enough about me..."

Another roar, of laughter.

He asked if there was anyone in the audience who had recently gone on a trip. A few people shouted out answers to his questions.

Rani hadn't been on a trip, but she felt sure these words were meant for her.

He kept the conversation going as the clarinettist began to play the intro to "Un jour, un voyage." He asked about backpacks and train passes and whether Magic Buses were still a thing. He began to strum his guitar.

"That's great. Seriously, everyone should travel. I wish I could go abroad. Someday I will."

As he leaned into the microphone, closed his eyes and began to sing, Rani marvelled that this was her answer. It was as if he'd read her mind, and was offering her a solution. These words were for her. This was her way out. She needed to go on a trip alone, without one of her parents this time. She resolved to save up money and go backpacking someday. She brought those other words back into her mind; she'd never forget them. It was as if he'd painted her some new, radiantly beautiful colour. He loved her too! They couldn't be together; she was too young—but he loved her too.

The rest of the crowd, and even the other band members, fell away as she stood gazing at him. It was just him and her and the night sky. The beauty of the music, the lovely soft deep blue, the gentle breeze, the stars that were beginning to emerge. The spotlight landed on her again. *I'm radiant, I'm shimmering, I'm—*

"Ayoye, tabarnac!"

The angry scream broke into her reverie. She'd stepped backwards, onto the bare feet of a hippie. He and all his friends gave her a fierce look as she stammered an apology.

3. Un jour, un voyage
(One Day, a Journey)

1952

SUNIL UNFOLDED a blue airmail letter, dipped his pen in the blue ink and began to write to Hima, "I have received an invitation to supper at my professor's house here in Montreal. I am the only student he has invited, although I think there will be other guests." He thought of scratching this out and writing, "There is a dinner in my honour at my professor's house" but refrained, because Hima might mock him. Hima couldn't see what he could, that he had special gifts that *others* could see, especially here in Canada. She had tried to stop him from completing his journey here. He had received a telegram at the port in Aden in which she complained of stomach cramps, as if expecting he would just turn around and go back. She apologized later, saying she didn't want to stand in his way. He wrote back, telling her to give all his love to the baby. He was far away, too distracted to hold a grudge. He would meet influential people at this professor's house; perhaps people in the government would be there too. He had told his professor about the book he had written about hydroelectricity, and his professor had given him a knowing smile. *He* knew. Perhaps he had snuck into the room Sunil had rented and read it, and told others about it. It was only natural. Sunil looked around the room. He wondered what his professor's apartment would be like. Not bare and drafty like this room. By the time Hima arrived, he would be able to provide her with the sort of lazy life and opulence she was used to.

He shaved for the second time that day, splashed aftershave on his cheeks and chin, and combed some Brylcreem into his hair. He unhooked and pulled down the ironing board from his closet door, plugged in the iron and inspected his pants for lint, pinching the white fuzz between his fingertips and flicking it away. As he waited for the iron to warm, he sang the refrain of a Hindi song about dreams coming true. He'd have to wear a shabby brown cardigan over his silk shirt; it was freezing outside. He only had a trench coat to wear over these. Nothing to do about that until he received his stipend. He looked out the window at the falling snow. The road and sidewalks were beautiful, glistening and white. The professor and his wife lived in an apartment near the university, a short walk away. He wondered what they would eat. He'd been living on rice for weeks.

A few minutes later, he held on to the railing as he mounted the slippery, winding staircase to his professor's apartment. His hard-soled Italian shoes were no protection against gliding backwards and falling, perhaps breaking his neck. Was this some kind of set-up? Did someone want him to fall? He shook his head at this thought, and prepared his face so that when Dr. White and his wife arrived to greet him at the door he was already smiling, albeit a little unnaturally.

"You must be freezing like that," Mrs. White said as they ushered him inside. "Come in."

The couple dusted the snow off his shoulders and made a fuss about finding him a proper coat. They left him at the door and stood in front of a closet in their hallway, sliding hangers back and forth, nodding and shaking their heads and murmuring. Sunil found this very strange, as he had just arrived. Wasn't there going to be a meal? Dr. White finally pulled a long, heavy coat off a hanger and held it in front of his wife, who made a gesture with her thumb that struck Sunil as obscene. Then they came back to him and urged him to try it on. Mrs. White said she was going to powder her nose and that she would be right back. Dr. White went over to a low table next to the closet, put a record on a turntable and lowered the needle. Sunil peered inside the apartment from the vestibule, which was all dark wood. There were a middle-aged man and woman sitting on the sofa, which looked like it belonged in the last century. Faded paisley tapestry, heavy oak tables, a fireplace. He hoped that someday he and Hima would have an apartment like this, but without all this shabby stuff.

As Sunil entered the room wearing Dr. White's coat, the couple on the sofa stood up.

"Sunil, this is Dr. Cameron. He works at the Allan Memorial. Donald, this is Sunil, a very promising young engineer from very far away, ha ha. Poor lad, he's going to have a hard time understanding all this Scotch."

It was obvious that everyone was speaking slowly for his benefit, although he had no trouble understanding anyone's accent. However, he saw that he was going to have some trouble telling the two men apart. Dr. Cameron looked very much like his professor: bald, white, glasses.

When they sat down to dinner, Mrs. White moved around quickly like a servant. She was even wearing an apron now, over her pretty, bright frock. What was this she was putting on his plate? It was a mound of hot white fluff, but he understood by the comments of the people around him that it was not a dessert, but some sort of potato dish.

It tasted like nothing. Nothing at all!

"How remarkable!" he heard himself say aloud.

One of the bald white men was staring at him with a slight smile from across the table. Sunil tried to remember which one this was. Well, Dr. White wasn't wearing a tie, and this one was, so that was easy enough. Sunil looked at the piece of brown leather that was next to the tasteless potato, and wondered what to do with it. He started to pick it up with his fingers but stopped when he noticed that everyone else was busily cutting it up in pieces using a fork and knife. The two men and Mrs. Cameron used their left forks to lift a piece of the brown material to their mouths, while Mrs. White switched hands after the sawing and used her right hand. They masticated their food, mostly in silence, although Dr. White spoke a little, with his mouth full. Sunil tried to imitate them but this food was even stranger than the puffy potatoes. Hard to chew, a challenge to swallow. He suddenly felt alarmed. What was this? Why were they eating shoes? Why were they exchanging glances as they ate, and excluding him? He told himself that if he didn't drink the wine, he might be all right. He felt he was suffocating. The air in the stuffy apartment, the strange, heavy, bland, indigestible food, the odd way these people behaved. He would leave all this out when he resumed his letter to Hima.

WALKING BACK TO the rooming house, the realization that he was far from home hit him hard. For a second or two his mind had tricked him into expecting that once he'd escaped his professor's apartment, the sights, sounds and smells of Delhi would return. Instead, the streets were silent and deserted, the trees black, the sidewalks and roads white with snow. He missed the colours of India, the riotous noisiness, the smells, which were the smells of life and death and heat and shit. The only thing that reached his nostrils as he left his professor's apartment was a metallic sensation, the smell of cold, only cold.

And he didn't like this new coat. It was at once too loose, because he was so thin, and too constricting, because of the weight of its material. He would not do up all the buttons, even if his hosts had insisted that he do exactly that. Such stupidity: if they had wanted him to be conspicuous, so that he could be more easily followed, then why not leave him the way he was when he had arrived, absurdly underdressed, in his swishy English trench coat? And the card that Dr. Cameron had thrust at him at the door as he was leaving: he found it, deep in the folds of his coat pocket; his fingers grabbed and then twisted its corners, tore and continued to tear at it until he had ripped the damn thing to cottony shreds.

1953

COCONUT CREAM CAKE, balloons and streamers and a band playing "Happy Birthday." Hima looked around. It had been different in India, where she'd felt embarrassed meeting people for the first time with her little boy, without a husband next to her. On board the RMS Empress of France, little girls begged Hima to let them hold Ramesh, and Hima wished them good luck. He kicked his legs and wriggled out of her arms whenever she tried to hold him, and he spent good chunks of his days running wildly around the deck like a dog. He was a handsome, curly-haired boy. Hima felt that when Sunil set eyes on him, she might burst with pride.

Give all my love to Ramesh, Sunil had written in his letters to her. He meant that the love she felt for him, she should transfer to her son. The love she felt for Sunil was different, though. It was more visceral. It had to do with his man smell. His letters smelled of his aftershave, Brylcreem and something else, the smell of his armpits, his hot breath, his groin. She wondered if he washed enough. She remembered, with shame, the times he had embarrassed her by coming to her campus, unwashed and wearing torn, ill-fitting pants. This shame mixed with the shame she felt about her own body and its painful longing for his. He and everything he touched absorbed smells in a way that made it seem he was always there, in his letters, in the presents he sent to her of scarves, cardigans and stationery, and it kept her body on alert. She didn't like this feeling. It made her uneasy, agitated, and guilty for feeling this way. And yet the longing she felt was overwhelming. It carried away and then buried all the warning signs, all the fears and misgivings.

SUNIL HAD FINISHED his coursework at McGill in just a year and was already working as an engineer in Niagara Falls by day, while completing his Master's thesis at night. Even before he'd gone to Canada—a shock that part of Hima's brain would never get over—the truth was they hadn't been together very much since they'd married. He'd spent five months working outside Agra at Bhakra Dam, travelling home every second weekend. This was just as she was realizing what was happening to her, why she had stopped menstruating and why her small belly was rounder, with a deep brown line pointing down from her navel like an arrow, like an exit sign, as if her body saw her own dim grasp of these matters and compensated for it. She herself worried that she would be vulnerable without Sunil during the long months of pregnancy, and after the birth, but the truth was that she'd felt safest, as she always had, at home with her family. The year was one of languor, of watching her brothers play croquet, of embroidering shawls and knitting sweaters and booties for the baby. She played her harmonium on the floor until it became absolutely impossible. Then there were months when she placed it on a table so that she could sit and play comfortably despite her expanding belly. After the baby was born, suddenly there was no time, and when the date of her departure for Canada arrived she reluctantly decided to leave the instrument behind. Her family joked that it was between the harmonium and the baby.

When her family—her parents, and all seven of her sisters and brothers—saw her off in Bombay, tears streamed down her face. Boarding the ship, she felt she was entering prison. There were so many people in her family, and they all had each other. They all waved at her as she wailed in misery, her baby wailing along with her.

WHEN THE SHIP DOCKED and they lifted the giant hatch, it was like being born into a new, frozen world. Hima wore a long woollen coat over a sari, and red fur-lined boots she'd had made by a Chinese shoemaker in Delhi, but the cold still bit her cheeks and her ears. Sunil had written to her that when he'd arrived, unprepared for winter, dressed in an Englishman's trench coat and pointy Italian shoes, the temperature minus ten, he'd immediately come down with the flu. Hima was confused, because when Sunil described this illness, with its fever, weakness, chills and sharp headaches, it sounded like malaria. One of his professors, he'd written, had taken pity on him and given him a proper winter coat. Sunil was lucky that way, Hima thought. Someone always took care of him.

Her heart jumped as she spotted him across the gang-plank, on the pier. He looked remarkably like the other men in the crowd. He wore a fedora and a long coat, woollen like hers, and his skin was paler, almost as pale as everyone else's. So many white people. It was as if she had stepped into an American movie, or a British newsreel. She knew she was conspicuous, with her dark face and gold bangles, the bottom of her sari visible beneath her coat. She held the little boy in her arms. He wore a fur jacket specially made for him by a Kashmiri tailor. Unsteadily, they made their way down the swaying gangway.

"I CAN DO THIS," Hima said, looking around the apartment.

"You've never had to cook or clean before in your life," Sunil said.

"I know," she said. "Doesn't matter. Don't worry."

It couldn't be that hard. She looked at the equipment he'd bought. A squeeze mop and bucket, a rubber sponge, tea towels, dishwashing soap, floor wax. She would figure it out.

"I'm going to need Ajax for the bathtub," she said a few days later, with something like shy pride. Mrs. Abbott, who lived downstairs, and who called her Renée because she couldn't pronounce Hima, had told her that. "And for the cooking, no problem; the landlady gave me the name of this book." She tore a sheet from a note pad. "Just buy this too, please, Sunilji?"

The Five Roses Flour *Guide to Good Cooking*, with the yellow cover. Sunil sighed as he slipped the piece of paper in his pocket. Hima just laughed as he mumbled, "Can't wait to eat more shoes."

She knew he didn't want his princess to have to clean the bathroom, to stand over the kitchen stove heating vegetable oil and frying vegetables, the fumes of the oil getting into her hair and her pretty clothes. But he seemed to realize that he was helpless to stop her. How else was she going to spend her days? And anyway, there would be no servants here. Her dowry wealth amounted to very little in Canadian dollars.

"Let me teach you to cook, then," he said.

"You know," she said, "I can make a rice dish. They taught us at school, in cooking class." She wanted to reassure him. He got so stressed sometimes, about nothing at all. "We learned samosas too."

He gave her a doubtful look. She smiled and shrugged. They both knew that chickpea flour wasn't something that would be sold at the MacDermott's grocery store. Cans and cans of dog food, yes. Cat food. Bird food. But everyday food for people like Sunil and Hima, channa dal, channa flour, spices and creamy milk to make ghee, these were bewilderingly absent. Sunil hated going to that freezing store, which smelled like cleaning products and roared like a giant fridge.

There was a noise now, a rolling-off and a plunk. That would be Ramesh, getting up from his nap. Sunil moved toward the bedroom, pushing past Hima before she could say anything. Hima followed him and stood outside the doorway to watch.

The boy was standing a little unsteadily next to the low cot they had put him in. He blinked at his father, and then put his thumb in his mouth.

"Da Num," he said, his thumb muffling his sounds.

"We're going to have to teach you to talk," Sunil said, scooping the sleepy boy up in his arms. "I'll teach your mother to cook, and I'll teach you to talk. And you will be a most helpful boy. You will clean the kitchen for your mummy."

HIMA STOOD OUTSIDE the room, fists clenched. Sunil looked over his shoulder and waved her away. She reluctantly returned to the kitchen but continued to listen.

"Now say, 'Daddy.' 'Mummy.' 'I am a most helpful boy.' Look, are you an animal? Why can't you talk? Go on. Repeat after me. 'Hello, Da-dee.' Say it."

Why can't you talk? He was completely serious, Hima realized. The odd things he said sometimes. Just yesterday, after running into some neighbours in this building, he had asked her, as they nodded and then continued up the stairs, if they were real. She frowned now, tried to push away this memory, shook her head as if to negate it, one slow shake. She opened a window and stood in the breeze, letting it blow her hair around.

She remembered a conversation she'd had with her landlady the other day.

"Before you start feeling too hemmed in," Mrs. Abbott had told her in the laundry room, "open a window, dear, it helps."

Hima thanked her for the suggestion, wondering how she knew.

"You're very welcome, and oh, here you go, dear, this should help get rid of that nasty smell," Mrs. Abbott had said, as she handed her the bottle of Lysol.

That nasty smell.

"Ginger," Hima said, surprised. "You don't like ginger?" *Well, okay,* Hima thought. *If everyone everywhere in the world were the same, life would be very boring. Sunil and I don't like to eat shoes.*

1954

ONE NIGHT, RAMESH cried and called for her. It took Hima a full minute to open her eyes, to draw the covers on her side of the bed off her body. She asked herself why. Was she sick? Why was she moving so slowly?

It was as if she knew before she got out of bed and walked the two steps to the bedroom door. Knew that her husband had barricaded the door with furniture, and that she was too tired to deal with this. She sat back down on the bed and simply looked at the armchair, which was sitting atop the dresser, which he had put against the door. She got up again, went to the door, looked at the pieces of furniture piled on top of each other, and debated asking Sunil for help.

Ramesh was bawling now. His voice was steadily increasing in volume, as if someone was gradually turning a dial clockwise. She felt she was still just waking up, slowly, as if something in her knew it would be safer not to. Something in her did not want to turn the light on and confront her husband, whom she knew was awake, lying in bed and listening to her move around in the dark. Her son would be safer too, if they just pretended this wasn't happening, and she didn't leave the room.

She lay back down next to Sunil, drew the sheet over her and waited for Ramesh to wear himself out. She listened to Sunil breathe, and it seemed to her that she could hear him thinking. He was unravelling, it was clear; maybe his disappointment had triggered it. Under the terms of his scholarship, he was to return to India after he obtained his Master's degree. He had been hoping to be offered a job at the company where he'd done his internship. He thought he'd made a good impression, but it hadn't happened. He had his own peculiar ideas about that but he no longer shared them with her. She knew why he had given up trying. She had no patience for his mad garbage talk anymore. If he asked her if people had followed her home when she went out during the day, she would say, "No, of course not." If she took the bait, showed the slightest interest in his question, he would launch into his big theory, the big theory of The World vs. Sunil.

The loving Sunil of their courtship had been replaced by this nervous, morose man, obsessed with some unlikely conspiracy. He was not like other husbands. He was not solicitous; instead of helping her with Ramesh, opening doors for her, this was what he did: pile furniture in front of the door so she couldn't get out.

She lay in the dark, stomach clenched, and listened to her son cry himself to sleep.

At last, no more sounds from outside their bedroom; she let out a great gust of air, and finally began to relax. Things would change once they were back in India. She would have an *aya* to look after Ramesh. And she wouldn't have to go back to the male doctor, the hulk of a man with the cold blue eyes and impatient manner who had opened and probed her as she lay on the table, mute with humiliation and shock. In India, mothers had lady doctors, and she missed hers terribly, the smart, educated woman in her lovely saris, always in hues of purple and mauve, her soft scent of rosewater, her gentle touch, her soothing, maternal, Punjabi words. She just could not believe it, that all the doctors here were men. She was so relieved to be going home.

4. Je me souviens
(I Remember)

1974

SERGE FIRST MET JANE at a party in a warehouse in an abandoned industrial district, just south of Little Burgundy. It was a hot August night. The party was a fundraiser for an author who'd had mental health issues since being arrested during the October Crisis of 1970. The author's apartment had burned down.

"Oh, that's terrible," Jane said. "I don't suppose he had insurance?"

Serge noticed that she didn't completely close her mouth after she finished speaking, although she didn't seem to be stoned.

"What kind of artist has insurance?" Serge stared at her. "It wouldn't have helped, in his case. They found accelerant at his place."

"Arson! How awful!"

"No," said Serge. He thought a moment before continuing. "Uh, well, yes, it *was* awful, but in this case, he burnt his own place down. Like I said, he had issues."

"Of course—he would. The poor man! Your government really are such bullies."

"You're not from around here, are you?"

"No, I'm from London."

"Not London, Ontario."

"No."

She didn't volunteer any more. She had red hair and wore an orange-and-brown cape. Serge found it hard to get her to talk about herself; it was as if she understood that she was cute, and that when men spoke to her, it wasn't out of any serious interest in what she was saying. But Serge felt he wasn't a typical man in this situation. Most people recognized him now. How refreshing, a conversation untainted by his reputation.

Nevertheless, Jane remained a mystery that night, while Serge found himself telling her about himself, about his father, an Italian who headed a wedding band, his mother, a pious Québécoise bank teller who had left the family and moved into the woods in the Laurentians. How his interest in music came from his father, but although he had grown up in an Italian neighbourhood, he only wrote lyrics in French, and was committed to the idea of *un pays*. He sang a bit of a song to her about narrow walls coming in on you, telling you it was time to leave. Jane nodded, said she understood.

Serge liked Jane immediately because although she had never heard of him or his music, she was interested in him and his political ideas anyway. And because, unlike other Anglos he'd met, she seemed genuinely curious about his culture, not contemptuous or condescending. She was sweet and earnest, words he had been hearing about himself for several years.

A band that had been playing was finishing their last set, and he asked her if she wanted to dance.

"Dancing brings out my inner prude," she said. "I do it, but it strikes me as outrageously, publicly sexual. I don't understand our culture at all. We don't walk around naked. We don't have sex in front of other people. But we thrust our hips about rhythmically, do it in pairs, and the person we dance with is not even always our sexual partner!"

"What? What culture are we talking about now?" Serge asked. Distracted by her body, how she had used it to mime what she was saying.

"I imagine you must find me terribly British," she said.

He found her insanely attractive. He gave her his best smile. He couldn't think of a thing to say. He enjoyed this moment, as they stood against a wall, sipping their drinks, their arms touching, other people's conversations washing over them.

"First of all," a woman with a Spanish accent was saying, "it's called Turkish Delight, so you know it's going to be something *really* good."

Another group of people was discussing spontaneous combustion, a conversation inspired by a pair of woman's black kitten heels and a lone workboot in the middle of the floor.

"I mean, is it art?" asked a guy who resembled John Lennon. "Or did something really bad happen here?"

An eruption of giggles.

And then Serge's band was setting up, and he had to go, but before he did, he thought of one last thing to say; he told Jane that he liked her accent. A roar of feedback invaded their conversation, making it hard for them to hear each other. He shouted that she reminded him of an English actress, Jane Birkin, but couldn't tell if she liked that.

JANE HAD NEVER been happier. In England she would never find herself in a loft mingling with people speaking English and French in a variety of accents. She closed her eyes and tried to follow the story of someone speaking in a sing-song voice now, someone she understood to be from a rural area, somewhere in northern Québec. She was surprised at how little she could understand. She liked it. She liked all these new feelings, of being lost, vulnerable, unknown.

When her friend Alicia had come to see her off, she'd teased her about how her classy accent would be of no help to her in Québec.

"They'll hate you on sight," said Alicia. "They hate people who even look like they speak English, apparently. It's worse than France."

But it was the weight of her own privilege that Jane was fleeing in the first place. She didn't mind the resentful sneers her upper-class accent occasionally provoked in England as much as the obsequiousness. She'd tried to escape her easy, hateful life by working as an au pair in France, and that is where she had first met Alicia, a hairdresser's daughter trying to improve her status in life by learning a second language. Alicia had been wary of her at first, and then they'd become fast friends. There was something so innocent and guileless about Alicia. Jane wanted to keep her under her wing, always. She'd offered to pay her airfare to Canada, and room and board and anything else—but this had been too much; she'd managed to offend her.

"I need to be closer to my family," Alicia said in a tight voice.

"I see," Jane said. "*I* need to get away."

"What do you need to get away from?"

"Myself, I think."

SERGE INVITED JANE to go for a walk on Mont Royal, long after midnight, when it was deserted and quiet. A rustle of wind in the trees, a whiff of damp leaves and loam, the crunch of their shoes on the gravel path, the sound of their own soft voices.

They searched the sky, hoping to see stars, but the city lights obscured them. When they got to the Belvédère, the east side of Montreal spread out around them, Serge pointed out something that looked like a giant Bundt cake-mould under construction.

"It's for the Olympics," he said. "For the summer of '76."

"Ah, isn't that lovely," Jane said. "We don't do modern very well where I come from."

"And this is for you," Serge said. Jane turned away from the view as Serge withdrew an envelope from the pocket of his jacket, opened it and shyly gave her the photograph that was inside.

Jane took a few steps backwards until she was standing under a street lamp, and then studied the photo, her brow furrowed. It was a black-and-white image of a boy of about six or seven. Serge's smile, but with a few missing front teeth. Moths and flies flitted and buzzed above her, some colliding tinnily with the lamp. Serge had followed her, was standing in front of her, peering down at the photo in her palm. She looked up at him with a slight smile and a quick raise of her thin eyebrows.

"It's me, that sweet little boy," he said.

She studied the picture some more, nodding, and then tried to hand it back to him, but he waved her hand away.

"No, keep it," he said, hearing the plea in his own voice. Could she hear it too? "It's for you."

1975

JANE SHOWED SERGE a song she'd written. She'd been working on it for weeks, dreaming about it at night, tweaking the lyrics in the mornings, sitting at the piano and softly working out the melody while Serge slept. When it was ready, she wrote it down in a notebook, in purple ink. A few more days before she mustered the courage to tear the sheet out and show it to him.

He was sitting with his twelve-string guitar, staring into space. A weak winter sunbeam crossed the room from the window, just missing his face. As she stood in the doorway, she wondered if this was a good or bad time to present her song to him. When she entered the room, he looked up, moved his guitar off his lap, patted his thighs and beckoned her over. His smile changed to a puzzled frown as she handed him the paper.

After a moment, he pointed out that the lyrics didn't rhyme. It was a song pleading for an independent Québec. Not only did it not rhyme, he said, it was in English. Who was going to sing a song like that? It never occurred to her husband that she could sing.

"It does rhyme," is all she said.

"What do I know?" he said. "To me, nothing in English ever rhymes the way I want it to."

Jane thought about this. So *We're fine without your help here* didn't really rhyme with *Everybody's dying to be free* if you pronounced the words with short, clipped French vowels. Fine.

"But sweet, sweet Jane, my love, ma belle chérie, consider working on your paintings instead."

Jane felt anger rise in her. He never even looked at her paintings. Not that she went out of her way to show them to him—they represented something that was hers alone, a precious, deeply guarded solitude—but she *was* showing him this song.

"Or you could pour your creativity into something else. Making babies, maybe."

She grabbed her song from him and stormed off.

Well, of course she knew he didn't mean it, the part about the babies. It was the last thing he wanted. It hadn't happened yet, despite their carelessness, so maybe it wouldn't. He'd thought he was being hilarious. She understood all that, yet she couldn't bring herself to speak to him; she clammed up and didn't say a word for days. Couldn't. She made a phone call to her parents, who lived on a sprawling estate in England, and asked for a plane ticket.

FROM THE AIRPORT, she caught a bus to her parents' place.

In her five years away, England had not changed. The house was chilly and there was mildew on the window frames. Her parents, John and Vera, had not changed either. Her father was pompous, her mother meek; the only things they were—had ever been—passionate about were birds and the stock market.

One morning, scanning the front page of the *Times* of London, her eyes fell on a photo of Ulrike Meinhof, who was awaiting trial in prison. She'd heard her parents murmuring about the case in the kitchen. She sat staring at the newspaper in her lap in the huge, empty, adjacent room they called the parlour. For John and Vera, the Baader–Meinhof gang were a bunch of dangerous criminals. Its members were in jail for bank robberies, which the group had committed to help support their attacks on U.S. military facilities. For her, Ulrike Meinhof was a hero who had tried to call attention to the atrocities of the Vietnam War.

Jane sighed, all day. Why had she felt compelled to come home? She tried to summon back the fury behind this trip. It was useless. There was only an intense longing to return to the home she shared with Serge, which she'd recently decorated with posters of Bonnie and Clyde, Che Guevara, and the FLQ manifesto. She considered cutting her trip short, hitching to the airport and flying home that evening. But she'd have to ask her parents for some money if she wanted to change her flight. Everything would be easier if she had a gang of friends with whom she could rob banks.

Then, that day, her parents had friends over for tea, and her father introduced her to George Helsham, a tall, beefy-faced friend from his days at Eton, a lawyer whose clients included a record producer who worked with many successful rock bands.

"Well, your daughter has a lovely figure, Charles," George said to John.

À propos of nothing.

Jane glowered. Then, as an idea suddenly came to her, she stared into space after it, following it before it ran away. She'd tweak the lyrics of her song, make it about saving the world from American imperialism.

She went to bed excited, the new song on her lips.

The next day, she looked up George's address in the telephone directory, drove the Bentley to his house. Stood on his doorstep in a yellow halter-top and jean shorts, despite the cold, pissy weather. His stupid face peeking out of his living room window, frowning. A maid in a white kerchief, a black dress and a lacy white apron opened the door and she spotted George hovering behind her. His stupid smile.

"Is she a fantasy of yours?" Jane asked as he led her into the living room. Cream shag rug, tapestry depicting Asian peasants in rowboats, a huge bronze vase that could also be an urn. "Do you think she minds, wearing the outfit?"

"To what do I owe this visit?" George said. Trying to express nothing in his face, failing. Silly geezer.

"It's about connecting."

"Really?"

The conversation continued in vague, suggestive language. George would be much too old for what she was pretending to be offering, but of course, the pretence clearly flattered him and made for a diversion on yet another rainy day. As she had expected, by the time she coyly opened her batik change-purse, he was begging her to sing him her song.

He closed his eyes and listened, really listened. Jane felt an ache in her chest, as she pictured Serge.

George held his hand out to receive the sheet of lined paper. He scanned it, said, "Yes." And then he was offering to make some calls on her behalf.

A few moments later, George handed her a turquoise Princess phone, gave her some numbers to dial.

Then he took the receiver from her and she waited—the phone heavy and cold on her bare thighs, both of them twisting the matching cord, poking fingers in its rubber coils—as he spoke to a record producer. They did the same thing three times, with three phone numbers. Because it was George Helsham making the pitch, she was able to score three appointments.

She sold her song, and returned home in a state of euphoria.

SERGE WAS HAPPY to see her. He'd been surprised when she left, surprised again by her triumphant return. She saw all this in his face. He'd missed her.

And then one day a few months later, drinking coffee in the kitchen, she recognized her song as it began to play on the radio. She ran to get Serge and they stood staring at each other with open mouths for a few seconds before whooping and laughing. She knew he understood that since the song was in English, recorded in England, the fact that it was playing on CHOM-FM meant that it was being played by thousands of radio stations, whereas a Sensibilité song might air on a few dozen.

He also correctly predicted that within a year Jane would be collecting ten thousand dollars a month in royalties—a fortune. Sensibilité was a large band, with many musicians to pay. Serge was fantastically famous in Québec, but Jane would be the one with the international hit keeping the couple afloat.

The money gave her new leverage in the relationship. She had no interest in pregnancy or infants; she was firm about this. Having babies wasn't changing the world; it was adding to its burdens. Still, she loved Serge and felt vague, puzzled regret about letting him down. *Was* she letting him down, she wondered? Or was it herself she was letting down? Did she actually want to be a mother? Was she in denial?

A DULL, COLD DAY. Serge fast asleep. Jane called up a friend of hers and Alicia's from their au pair days. Pamela now lived in the States, where she was working at an adoption agency. What were *her* days like? Were they meaningful?

Pamela told her about a couple in Leeds who were supposed to adopt a Vietnamese orphan. The plans had fallen through because the woman found out she had ovarian cancer.

"Leeds!" Jane said. "You mean they're English?"

"Leeds, *South Carolina*," Pamela said. She sounded irritated, as if she already suspected what was coming next.

"Can I have her?"

"There are other couples waiting."

"Can I have her?" Jane said again.

"You have to go through the proper channels."

"How much?"

"You know, you're a rich shit too, Jane. And you complain about *your parents*! The apple doesn't fall far from the tree."

"And I shall write your agency's name in my will."

"Is this what your parents do?"

AND LATER, with Serge.

"Can I have her?"

She was wearing her yellow halter top and jean shorts. Her legs were long and smooth. She exuded health and sexiness. Serge felt happy and wanted to make love.

"Why can't we make our own baby?"

"It'd be French and English," said Jane. "It would hate itself."

"*We* don't hate each other."

She waited. In *her* family, if she waited, she got what she wanted. It was like with birds and stocks. She thought of her parents' serene faces, sitting outside patiently with binoculars, the business section of the *Times* unfolded on her father's lap.

"You want to save the world," he said.

"You make it sound like an accusation."

"Lord give me strength," he said. "I'm an idealist too, you know."

That was why he had so much charisma, so little money. And money *was* power. That was why she was going to win this argument.

"The only reason people have babies is a huge fucking ego trip," Jane said, rolling her eyes.

"It hurts," Serge said. "When you roll your eyes like that." He pointed to the ribs in his thin chest.

She knew he was wondering if she had similarly dismissive feelings about *everything* he expressed, but didn't dare to ask. She wasn't going to soften now. She waited.

"Lord give me the sérénité to accept..." he said after a while. "How does it go again? My mother, always in these dark clothes, fingering her rosary, always saying prayers, like every day was a funeral."

He frowned. "No, but this one... the old men in my neighbourhood got this from AA."

"Poor old geezers," Jane said, her eyes bright with amusement.

Serge began again, got to the part about changing what you can, and paused. "And the wisdom to know the difference," he said.

Jane held his gaze and raised her eyebrows, her lips curling at the edges. Serge shrugged, sank to a lotus position on the bed and held his arms out to her. She joined him on the bed with a bounce; his skinny body rolled out of position.

"Sure, I agree with all that," Jane said. "Except for the part about God. Believing in God is a cop-out."

SERGE WOKE UP an hour before the sun, and only two and a half hours after he'd gone to bed. Beautiful music was playing in his head. He started to make his way downstairs to capture it with his hands, with his twelve-string guitar. Halfway down the staircase he was distracted by the sound of a child whimpering.

He climbed back up the stairs, wondering what he was supposed to do. The whimpering quietened, turned into a soft, snuffling sound, and then stopped. He gazed at the little body lying on the cot next to Jane's side of the bed. The small head of thick, black hair, the little brown fists on either side. He moved back toward the door and the whimpering started again. He froze. He was rewarded with silence. He remembered her little face peeking over Jane's shoulder when they arrived from the airport together, the shy wonder in her lovely eyes. He tiptoed out of the room and descended the stairs again.

The tune had left his memory. He put on his coat and walked outside into early morning. He walked from their house all the way downtown. The sun came up. He thought of the new little girl in his life, her shining eyes. The blue and white of the sky, the promise of the new day. The music from his dream was somewhere in the back of his head, and he tried to bring it back with his steps. He experimented with different walking rhythms. He walked all the way to the Forum. All the way back home. By now, the first song was irretrievable, but other music had taken its place, as hopeful, bright and interesting as the future would be. *Le nouveau pays.* He was sitting in the living room playing the melody on a classical flute when he noticed his wife and his new daughter peering at him through the window from the garden. Jane was pointing him out to the baby, trying to get her to wave to him; she blew him a kiss, and gave him a pretty smile. They wouldn't disturb him, her smile seemed to say; they would wait until the song was done before coming inside.

Face B

5. Rêves d'indépendance (Dreams of Independence)

May 1980

AS SOON AS Rani started cégep, she found a job in a restaurant and began to plan her escape. She opened a bank account at a branch nearby. By the following spring she had already managed to save up two thousand dollars.

It was her life, not theirs. She would find a place to live and then declare her independence.

She spotted an ad for an apartment-share on a bulletin board at UQAM. The idea of living with a university student thrilled her. She carefully tore off a phone number, pinched the tiny strip tight in her fingers and held it until she found a pay phone.

Nobody answered. She scooped up her quarter, walked around the university, went to the bathroom, gazed at herself in the mirror, wondered how old she looked, could she pass? Could people think she belonged there?

Two young women came in, singing and laughing. One of them was wearing blue face paint, a fleur-de-lys on either cheek. They both continued singing in their stalls. The one without the face paint came out first. She glanced in the mirror and then turned around quickly, as if she had seen enough.

Facing Rani now, she sang louder, with more gusto, as if inviting her to join in. But Rani didn't know the words, and she quickly left the bathroom.

Suddenly, in the hallway, a stream of people, as students began to spill out of classes. They were older than her and recognizably Francophone, Québécois. The young men had longish hair and wore light, brightly coloured quilted jackets she'd seen in Indian boutiques, or wool cardigans depicting moose and deer. Most of the young women had brown hair tied in neat ponytails. All wore scarves around their necks. Once in a while they would turn and notice Rani staring at them. Did they know how she envied and worshipped them? Could they guess?

She tried the number again. No one home. She walked outside. Mild spring air, a bit of slush on the sidewalk. *Oui* signs in the windows up and down the street. Independence. Time for everyone to throw off their chains. She stopped in a café and drank espresso, staring out the window. A man went by on a unicycle, a Québec flag in his teeth like a rose.

When she went outside again, the sun was setting and the summer sky was turning effervescent oranges and purples; she walked on as it settled on a deeper shade of blue, setting off the cornices of the buildings. Everything was so charming, not flat and lonely like home. She found another pay phone. A man answered. Her stomach started to churn and cramp with excitement.

Yes, he was looking for a roommate. Actually, he wasn't a student, and he travelled a great deal, so she would have the apartment to herself most of the time.

The place was bright, clean and furnished. The rent was a hundred and eighty dollars a month, and she would pay a little less than half. Five shifts at the restaurant would pay her rent.

This would be the one; she was sure. She ached with anticipation.

HER PARENTS WERE in the kitchen, having a conversation in Punjabi. Hima shushed Sunil, asked Rani if she wanted something to eat. Rani hesitated. Sunil patted her on the shoulder, pulled open the fridge door and withdrew a small plate piled with rice and chick peas. He put it in the toaster oven and pressed a button. He took out a bowl of raita and put it on the linoleum table.

"Are there bits of cucumber mixed in?" asked Rani.

"Yes," said Sunil.

"I don't like—"

"Yes, but they are already there, aren't they?" said Hima. "We finished eating half an hour ago."

As if there is any such thing as suppertime in this family, thought Rani. Sure, they could have supper together on the days that Hima wasn't teaching in the evening, and when her own cégep classes ended before five. But nobody really remembered, especially not Sunil, who was nominally in charge of the meals.

"We can keep you company," Sunil said, and Hima gave a conciliatory shrug.

The three of them stood in the kitchen as it began to fill with the smell of cumin, listening to the tiny motor noise from the appliance.

Rani wondered how to tell them. The last supper.

HIMA HAD ALREADY gone upstairs; Rani was washing the dishes with her dad. She told him she'd been looking for a place and had found one. He went up to the bedroom and told Hima. He came back, looking shaken. Hima had said something strange, he said. She'd said, "I wonder what other life I could have had." Sunil looked at Rani, as if expecting her to explain his wife to him. Rani patted his arm, then stepped forward and hugged him. But what she was thinking of was the suitcase in her bedroom closet, ready to go.

A MILD EVENING, after a long, bright day. Serge and his band members returned from the local community centre after voting to be free. They settled in around the TV, uncapped their bottles of Laurentide and Black Label, strummed guitars, played a nationalist ballad or two, a couple of love songs. They were nervous, upbeat, optimistic. All the poets and artists were for the *Oui*, all the intellectuals, all the progressives, all the cool people. Jane and Serge, the other members of Sensibilité, of les Enchanteurs, Beau Dommage, none of them knew anyone who was against sovereignty. There were blue *Oui* signs in most of the windows. They were already jubilant; they could not imagine defeat.

Jane surveyed the group, awed that a bunch of hippies could get so enthused about a referendum. She studied the faces around her, struck by their earnest expressions. Her mind went back four years, to the concert Serge's band had played in Rimouski the night of the provincial election. They'd had TV monitors tucked up in the corners of the stage ceiling, where the audience couldn't see them, so that they could watch the results coming in. They were giggly with excitement about that vote too, as well as the realization that the band was big enough now that favours like the TVs would be automatically granted. So as they played, they'd glanced up once in a while and their fans were none the wiser. Serge had told her that they couldn't even see the audience. There was just darkness and lots of smoke, a thick, heady mix of pot, hash and tobacco. When it was clear that the Parti Québécois had won, they'd suddenly begun to play their happy hearts out, Daniel attacking his drums, Hugo's hands flying around the keyboard, Serge and Marie-Claire bellowing lyrics, although the song itself, which was about romantic love, meant nothing to them that night.

Jane looked at their faces now. Back in Britain, anarchy was what young people were into. Voting was considered bourgeois. She considered saying this and thought better of it. She had an urge to get away from the group and remembered she had an excuse. She cleared her throat and said she would go up to check on Mélanie.

Mélanie had announced she was sleepy and had put herself to bed unusually early. Jane kneeled next to her daughter's bed and sang an English lullaby, softly so as not to be heard downstairs. She didn't remember all the words, and she stayed there a good half hour, starting over, trying to remember. Did Mélanie have memories of songs sung to her in Vietnamese? The child's eyelids fluttered. What could she be dreaming? Jane sat down on the floor and leaned back against the bed, her head close to Mélanie's.

She woke up two hours later with a start. Something was wrong. It was too quiet downstairs.

As she came downstairs, she glanced at the TV screen. They'd lost.

She watched the hippies' disbelieving eyes filling as they listened to René Lévesque, also in tears, invite them to "la prochaine fois." They all looked as if someone had slapped them hard across their faces. When she sat down, they suddenly started to speak, all at once.

Who were these people who had voted *Non*? Oh, Hugo remembered there was a friend of his, whose father was a policeman. The father said he was going to vote *Non*. More discussion, and then they were quiet again. After a moment, Marie-Claire looked up at Jane.

"What about you?" she asked in English.

The group held its breath. Serge put his arm around Jane.

"Do I know anyone?" Jane asked. "No, I don't know anyone." She wondered if this was how it was going to be from now on. They would speak to her in English. Everyone else in Montreal did. As soon as they heard her accent, they would switch to English. How was she going to ever speak French like them if they kept doing that? She was aware of feeling like she was having her own private crisis, not quite feeling the same way as they did. Fuck it. She switched to French. She swore. A long, twisting rope of religious terms, a list of things you could find in a church.

Yvon abruptly stood up and joined her. He swore at the traitors among his own people who had refused to have their shackles removed. Serge rose to his feet, held his hand up, and the group went silent. He suggested playing some music to blow away the negative energy in the room. They picked up their guitars, bongos, clarinet, and violin. Hugo sat with his hands poised over the second-hand harmonium he'd just bought for twenty dollars. A joint was passed around the room, and even the hippies who never got high sucked at it, desperate for something to soothe their wounded hearts.

In bed that night, Serge cried in Jane's arms. The air coming through their open bedroom window had turned bracingly cold now, and there was a sour smell from the Japanese willow outside. Serge dived deep beneath the blankets; Jane cradled him as he spoke to her breast. It wasn't the people who voted *Non* that he was upset with, he said. It was the people who didn't vote *Oui*.

"I just can't believe it," he said. "I can't accept it. We could have had a country. All they had to do was check a box. All they had to do was check 'Oui.' Where did they all go, all those people who had something to say? What happened? Could they not get up off their asses and go check a box?"

Jane knew that for Serge, the dream of an independent Québec was like a shortcut to utopia. It wasn't anti-anybody. So, according to this view, she and Tweetie could belong in this fantasy. But she felt awkward trying to comfort him; as she held him and stroked his hair the words that came to her to were the words she used with Tweetie. English ones.

"There, there," she said. And, "Never mind."

6. Va-et-vient (Come and Go)

1955

AFTER THEY RETURNED from Canada, Sunil got a job in Delhi, working in the irrigation department for the Indian government. Hima was ecstatic to be close to her family again. Sunil's job paid well, and she had new furniture made. An oak dining table with six matching chairs, a bed with a set of shelves in the headboard where she could put her Noxzema night cream and her hairbrush. She focused on these things, ignored her husband's silence. She continued to be affectionate to him, and knew he was grateful for this, at least.

Hima's sisters and brothers lived nearby, and they often visited, occasionally ending the evening with an improvised concert, everyone singing together.

Hima's harmonium arrived one day from her parents' house. She clapped her hands and squealed like a child when the delivery boy set the box in front of her. She called little

Ramesh over as she unpacked it. She had forgotten what a pretty thing it was. She ran her hands over the decorative carvings, admired the painted designs framing the top. She sat down right in front of the doorway and pumped the bellows, ran her fingers along the keyboard, adjusted the tuning. The delivery boy waited patiently until she remembered to put some coins in his hand.

SHE WAS SITTING on the bed, brushing her hair, waiting for Sunil to follow her into the bedroom, when she heard a voice in the living room. She got up and found him sitting under the lamp, writing notes.

Speaking into the dark.

She asked him what he was doing.

"Immigration application," he said. He didn't look up at her.

She was shocked. These words, delivered so coldly, a stinging slap. But she told herself not to panic.

SHE HAD A SECOND little boy. Sunil barely seemed to notice. But Hima was happy. How relieved, how grateful she was to be back in India, with a cook and a servant who took care of the household chores. She so enjoyed sitting with her sisters, drinking tea and idly watching the children. Life was warm, sunny, familiar, and slow.

She knew that Sunil was restless. He said he didn't like the sweaty office where he worked, with the noisy overhead fans, the lazy people who would take off at lunchtime. One evening he attended a lecture he'd seen advertised in the newspaper on "Energy Needs of the Future." When he returned, he told her of how he had introduced himself to some Canadian engineers who were building a dam in India. He informed them that he was a genius, and offered to show them proof. He gave them his resumé, a copy of his university transcripts, a letter of recommendation, and a copy of his scholarship. Hima laughed nervously as she listened. She imagined his face, solemn and serious, as he told these cold, white Canadians that he was a genius and thrust his pile of papers at them.

"They must think you're quite the kook," she said.

Surely they could see. Sunil waited for his letter and she waited with him; the nature of her waiting, her secret hope, felt treacherous to her.

THE LETTER FINALLY CAME. A job offer from the Shawinigan Water and Power Company, in Montreal. Sunil read it aloud to Hima. He was invited to be part of a group of engineers that would study the possible diversion of the Nottaway, Broadback and Rupert Rivers to the Saint-Maurice River watershed in order to increase output at the company's power stations. He emphasized the names as if he thought Hima wanted to hear them, as if they meant something to her.

"What?" Hima's question was sharp and impatient. "What is this about?"

"Hydroelectricity."

The company was based in Montreal, but the work would take Sunil up north, to James Bay, where there was even more snow. She wouldn't have to follow him, he said; she could stay in Montreal. She stared at her husband. This was everything he had wanted, she saw. This was the ticket he had been waiting for.

"IS THERE ANYTHING you like about Canada?" her sister asked her the next day when she came over for tea.

Hima was silent for a moment as she thought of the long days she'd spent in the apartment with the bottles of cleaning products under the kitchen sink, the occasional glimpse of the landlady, who did not like her, she realized now, and whom she disliked as well.

"Well, there is clean air," Hima said. "And clean water."

"And anything else?"

"No beggars in the street," Hima said. "Everyone is nicely dressed."

But how little these things mattered. She felt as if someone was grabbing her heart, twisting and squeezing it. They sold the furniture again. This time when they got on the ship, they'd packed her harmonium, her sewing machine, and a trunkful of toys and clothes for their two sons.

1960

SUNIL SOON LOST his job in Shawinigan. But before Hima
could allow herself the hope of another return to India, he'd
managed to get another one. And then another. On the first
of December, after he had lost his third, Hima dreamed that
she and her children were on a lifeboat, and the boat was
Ramesh's school. She knocked on the principal's door the
next day and inquired about a job as a teacher.

Mr. Murray looked very harried when he opened the
door but by the time she finished her sentence the creases
in his forehead had disappeared, as if they had been ironed.

"I was praying," he said.

"Oh," said Hima. "I'm sorry to have disturbed you."

"Can you start tomorrow?"

"I..."

She was holding Arun's hand.

"How old is he?"

"Four. But very quiet and so so smart."

"Well, then he should be able to start kindergarten, shouldn't
he?"

She would be teaching fifth and sixth grade Math and something called Catechism.

"You just need to read aloud," Mr. Murray told her the next day as he walked her to her classroom, and so that is what she did.

She wrote to her father, told him of her new job, explained that they lived in a three-bedroom house in the suburbs of Montreal now, with a large backyard.

He wrote back: "This is wonderful news, *beti*. We are all very happy for you and Sunil." There was something like embarrassment, embarrassment and pity for her in those short sentences. Hima wondered if her desolation had been all too clear, between the lines. The job was rather dull; *children were dull.* The other teachers at the school behaved as if they were afraid of her when they passed her in the hall, smiling stiffly, never stopping to talk.

She looked out her window in the evening. Four o'clock, the sun already fading. She had worked for weeks planting a garden all spring and summer, and it had all vanished under an expanse of white snow. The only other colour was a bit of rust, a few sick-looking leaves in a clump at the edge of the driveway.

TWO WEEKS INTO his latest job, Sunil studied the plans. He looked at his watch. Time wasn't moving fast enough. It should be at least eleven o'clock by now. He had started at nine, and his watch said nine thirty. What was going on? He got up and took a walk down the hallway. As he approached the reception desk, his blood went cold. The hands on the clock above Solange's head of orange curls were on the nine and the six. He raced back toward his office, but skidded to a halt at the sound of low laughter coming from Ron Fairfield's office. He peeked through the venetian blinds on the glass door. Ron, Lou and Tom were there, chatting, thick as thieves. And the hands on the clock on Ron's wall were at nine thirty-two! They had been sloppy, too sloppy to cover up this discrepancy.

He put his watch to his ear. There was some kind of bugging device in it. He could tell by the ticking. It was too slow. That might also be what was slowing the clock down.

He felt a hand on his shoulder, and smelled familiar, spicy cologne. He turned around slowly. It was his boss, Alan Schumacher.

"Just knock, Sunny," he said in a friendly voice. "They'll let you in."

Sunny. But Sunil didn't mind. Mr. Schumacher wanted to give him a chance; he was one of the good ones.

Sunil could not contain how he felt. Tears rolled down his face.

"I am so grateful to you, sir," he said, gasping on the last word. His heart pounded, seemed to want to push everything, his whole essence, out where it was visible.

"What?" Mr. Schumacher said. "Why, that's all right."

Wait, why were his boss's lips curling like that? A shock, like a hard slap. That smirk! Not one of the good ones after all. Oh, how dare they! As his boss began to pat his shoulder, Sunil broke away. He walked swiftly to the men's room, pulled his wristwatch off and flung it in the garbage bin.

1961

HIMA MARKED QUIZZES in the teachers' room as Brenda, the school secretary, made herself a cup of instant coffee. To Hima, the bitter smell was like someone putting burnt-toast crumbs up her nostrils. On bad days it gave her nosebleeds. She was the only one who drank tea.

She read over the answers to the division problems she had given her students. Some had shown their work, and others had rather obviously copied answers from each other, but she didn't care enough about these children to make a fuss. She considered giving some of the students extra points for trying. There were those who tried, and those—the scruffier ones, usually—who didn't, and it seemed unfair not to acknowledge this. The bell rang, and she heard squeals and shouts as the kids ran outside for recess. She looked out the window, searching for her sons. She saw Arun emerge with a similarly thin, brainy-looking child, and turn as someone called him. She hoped it was Ramesh, although she couldn't see from where she was sitting. She knew that Ramesh protected his brother from the bullies at school at least as much as he bullied him at home.

"HELLO, HYMA," said Mr. Murray. "Oh, about that form Brenda gave you to fill out?"

"Oh yes, Mr. Murray," she answered carefully. The form was one they had forgotten to give to her when she was hired. It asked for her name, address, next of kin and religion. She had half hoped they would ask about her qualifications. She was proud of the Master's degree she'd done at Delhi University, wished it meant something to them.

"Well, you didn't answer the question about religion."

"Oh," she said. "Didn't I?"

She didn't turn her head, but she could feel other teachers looking in her direction with interest.

She had hoped it would be okay, the part about the religion. The form asked her to tick a box—Protestant, Catholic, or Jewish. She had drawn a new box, written the word "other" next to it.

"Could you...could you just tick a box?" Mr. Murray asked.

"Um," Hima said. "No."

She felt her face grow hot.

"Couldn't you?"

She noticed that he looked uncomfortable too. In fact, he was bright pink.

"I'll—I'll think about it."

BUT SHE DIDN'T want to. She lay awake that night, wondering what had gotten into her. The last thing she needed was another bloody war about religion. Telling the story at dinnertime, she had been aware of her husband supporting her, and her sons' complete bewilderment. They were Hindu? It was practically news to them. Didn't she teach Catechism to the grade twos? Who cared? She was going to lose her job, the boys complained, the way their father was always losing jobs. Why didn't she just tick a box?

Sunil was snoring next to her now. Her mind wandered back to that night almost three months before when he had woken her up and she had been too sleepy to make sure her diaphragm was in place. If she fell pregnant now, it would suit Sunil, who had always wanted a daughter. They could give her his sister's name, Rani—a fond joke they shared. But what if it was another boy? And what would she do with a girl anyway?

"Girls are better," Sunil said. "Girls are *devis*." Goddesses.

And also: "There is a reason for everything."

As far as she was concerned, that was more of his crazy talk.

In the morning, it seemed to her that she suddenly felt very heavy. A fleeting, weakly hopeful thought: it could merely be dread that was weighing her down. She called her doctor's office and made an appointment.

THE BOYS WERE shouting, threatening each other with fratricide by punching (Ramesh, now) and choking (Arun, later, while Ramesh slept). She had hoped that having *two* boys would be like cancelling each one out; they would play together and leave her alone. Ramesh was nine, Arun almost seven. When would this stop? In India, children weren't this much trouble. She searched in her memory for times when her parents had had to discipline any of their children. It wasn't that they had been such angels. She remembered shooing her sisters from her closet, where they would hide, pull her clothes off their hangers, or even, in their cheekiest moments, try them on. But there were ayahs, cooks, servants, private tutors. Her life here was so different from her own mother's, so full of chores that she secretly resented. Impossible to imagine living there now. The boys spoke no Hindi. Their first language was English. They had a second language, French, which they studied at school and picked up at hockey practice. But she and Sunil had stopped speaking Hindi with them when a doctor said it was probably the cause of Ramesh's stuttering.

Maybe the boys would stop fighting if she called them to the kitchen for a snack.

"Boys! Stop it. Just stop it. Come, have some cake."

To her surprise, her sons came running into the kitchen and slid into their chairs. Was it that simple? Just feed them sweets, and they stop bickering. She was too smart for this dumb job of housewife. The solution to every problem was too easy. She thought of that idiot blonde selling lemon Pledge, smiling at her own face in the shiny surface of a table. She caught her own frowning reflection in the gleaming toaster. The blonde might be an idiot, but at least she was bouncy and full of life, whereas Hima found herself about as attractive as a wilted houseplant. She tilted her head and bared her teeth at the toaster as she cut pieces of cake and arranged them on sandwich plates. Such lovely white teeth, such minty flavour. *Colgate tastes—*

The phone rang, shrill and imperious.

"Mrs. Roshan speaking."

"Hello, Mrs. Russian, my name is Sharon. I'm the secretary for the head of Mathematics at Concordia University. Could you possibly come in to talk to us next Monday? Dr. Connolly was wondering if you might be interested in joining the department. We're rather urgently trying to fill a position in September."

"Okay," Hima said, as if she were accustomed to receiving job offers from universities every day.

Sunil had applied on her behalf. She had let him. When you live with a nut you must pick your battles. She'd never imagined he could be right. She kept her left hand on her chest as she spoke on the phone, as if that would keep the emotion out of her voice. But as she put the phone down, she squealed her delight, using another phrase she had learned from daytime TV: *Ya-ba-da-ba-doo!* The boys looked up at her, mouths still working on the cake.

So maybe Sunil had a point when he said that everything happened for a reason. More importantly, she was going to receive an exit pass from this kitchen! She smiled at her sons now, admiring their little-boy beauty, their soft curls and huge eyes. They didn't smile back.

"You're not Fred Flintstone."

"You're not a man. You're supposed to be a lady."

She told them her news. They pouted.

"Why do you hafta work, anyway?"

"Other mothers don't work. You're not supposed to work "

"Dad's supposed to work."

"Yeah, he has a new job."

She glowered at them. Couldn't they ever be happy for her? These Canadian sons of hers, always such experts on how they were all supposed to live in this country. *Try being me. Just come here and try. Come take my place.* The phone rang again. Hima recognized her doctor's nasal accent. She asked him to repeat what he had said although she had understood him, as if she hoped he might change his mind, give her the opposite result. She put down the phone, her face tight. She cut her sons more cake. It didn't matter, she told herself.

And it didn't, not really, not to her. Five weeks after giving birth, Hima went to work at Concordia, leaving their baby daughter with Sunil, who had lost another job.

1980

A MONTH AFTER Québec voted *Non*, Serge was still crushed. Almost four in the afternoon, but he hadn't emerged from the bedroom yet.

"Serge, *viens voir*," Jane called upstairs. "It's Tweetie's report card."

Heavy, dull knocks, a drawer, and then a door opening and closing. Jane wondered if this was a response.

She waited for the sharper sound of clicking footsteps to descend the stairs and cut through the quiet of the ground floor. From the open windows came vague bird chatter, and there was the muffled grey rumble of traffic in the distance. Inside this house, every movement—even the slightest shift of a hip in a chair—produced a loud creak. A *maison patrimoniale*: a plaque next to the front door said so. And although it was one of the rare remaining detached homes in the area, with no neighbours above, below or on either side, it could be very noisy, especially when it was quiet.

Especially lately.

Mélanie, perched on Jane's lap, began to read the words on the blue cardstock aloud, slowly: "Mélanie Giglio, classe de Nicole Leroux, École de la Petite Patrie, 18 juin 1980."

Jane kissed Mélanie on the top of her head, and then rested her chin there for a moment as she scanned her daughter's results.

"Oh my goodness, Tweetie. You're doing so well in everything, especially math."

"That's because I'm Chinese," Mélanie said.

"What!" Jane said. "Who told you that?"

"Everybody," said Mélanie, shrugging. She inserted her small fingers between the bangles on Jane's pale arm and pushed them apart and then back together again.

"Are *you* good at math?" Mélanie asked after a while.

"I'm all right, I suppose," Jane said. "I was never as clever as *you. I* never skipped kindergarten."

She sensed that this piece of information disappointed her daughter. She looked outside. It was turning into a dull, drizzling afternoon. The house was making various discontented noises as if it were crying out for repairs. She gazed around at the mouldings, the stained glass windows, and the walnut cabinets. The expensive maintenance all this beauty required. There was the foundation repair, the new furnace, the French drain. She was the one who paid for everything, and she didn't mind, well, not really. Only... Serge was so oblivious! He just loved telling people that they lived in a *maison patrimoniale*.

Mélanie slipped off her lap and went to the piano. Not yet six years old and already learning to read music; the piano lessons had been her own idea. The girl's awkward grace. Little brown fingers depressing the keys with effort. A short piece her teacher had assigned her, an untitled melody by an unknown composer. The page heading simply read "Overture." Jane listened as she played it over and over. Every time Mélanie made a mistake, she started over from that point, repeated that measure a few times, continued to the end and started again from the beginning. There was something heartbreaking about it. Jane wondered if Mélanie wanted Serge to play with her, if this was her way of summoning him.

After fifteen minutes of this, Mélanie abruptly got up from the piano bench, and went to the kitchen without a word. From the living room, Jane heard the girl emptying her backpack onto the table.

"What are you doing, Tweetie?"

"Homework," said Mélanie.

The stairs creaked as Serge came into view, tying his bathrobe shut. His hair was long and greasy, his body skeletal, his robe grey with cigarette ashes. Jane watched him as he paused to look at something at the bottom of the staircase. He seemed to be trying to make his mind up about it.

It was that beautiful, broken Indian instrument, a harmonium, that had been lying around, the wooden box with the carved holes and the pretty trim. After a moment, Serge sighed and kicked it toward the door. It made a sound like a warped accordion as it moved along the floor.

"Bonjour," Jane said.

Serge grunted. So she began again.

"Good dreams?"

Silence. All his dreams were broken. How to engage him? One more try and she would go to Tweetie.

"You know, I wanted to ask you something. Was it difficult to learn music from your own father?"

Her father-in-law had led an Italian wedding band. Hilarious and bewildering to think that that was actually where Sensibilité had originated. But the question was meant to nudge Serge toward acting more like a father himself.

"I didn't learn like that," he said, nodding toward the sheet music on the piano. "Painting by numbers."

FROM THE KITCHEN, Mélanie could hear her parents' voices, but she wasn't able to make out many words. She wondered if it was secrets. She heard her father shout "organically" three times, between other words. She wondered what it meant. She opened her binder and withdrew the chart with a soft click. She began filling the branches of the family tree with Serge's and Jane's names, and the names of her grandparents. So on one side she was English, and on the other, Italian and French-Canadian. Jane's surprised response had reassured her a little. It couldn't be true, that she was Chinese.

JANE STOOD BAREFOOT in the small unfurnished room off the kitchen, in paint-streaked shorts and a t-shirt, a paintbrush in her hand. She was staring critically at her canvas when the sound of voices made her turn around. There were people peering at her through the window of the side door. Jane walked up to the door, squinted through the glazed window and saw the members of Sensibilité, minus Serge. Jane opened the door and the band poured in like a wave. Marc, the tall blond one, remained crouched in the doorway, blocking the exit. Jane walked backward, stood against the far wall of the kitchen. The musicians smelled like their concerts, of pot, beer, and sweat.

"Where is he?" asked Hugo.

They were pissed off. They must have heard through Yves that CBS, an American record label, had officially offered Sensibilité a contract, if they agreed to sing in English. Serge had refused.

"Look, guys, you know he had his reasons," Jane said.

The band had had enough of scraping by, of playing concerts to thousands of people and yet, still, barely being able to pay their rents. None of them cared about politics anymore. They'd had their hearts broken by politics. It was over for them.

"Where is he?" Hugo asked again.

"If I tell you, what are you going to do? Beat him up?"

"We just want to talk sense into him," said Marie-Claire.

"You can't talk to him."

"Is he here?"

"No, he's at the ashram."

"Nice for him," said Hugo. "Meanwhile, we live with room-mates; my girlfriend works in a meat factory to help us pay the rent. You have this house, you paint pictures all day..."

"You know you're welcome to stay in this house," Jane said, although she was only speaking for Serge. She longed for quiet, yes, to paint her pictures—well, she'd earned that privilege. Well, sort of.

Mélanie appeared, rubbing her eyes. She was wearing pyjamas covered in yellow chicks. Jane put her arm around her, worried she could feel the freezing cold atmosphere. But she just stood, taking in all the people, without interest. Jane scooped her daughter up and turned toward the stairs.

"You're welcome to stay," she said again, over her shoulder, knowing they would anyway. She was tired of this, having to tiptoe around their bodies and those of their fans as she went about her day.

You're welcome to stay. But I don't know how much longer I will.

JANE WAS TRYING to make up her mind about something. She and Serge were supposed to be gaga in love. Everybody said so. Sometimes they would go away, just the two of them, to a motel, to escape everyone else, to *celebrate their love.* Serge also drove her bonkers. Well, he made *everybody* bloody bonkers, didn't he? Marc, Hugo, Yvon, Marie-Claire, the main members, the ones who had stayed with the band since cégep—all of them revered Serge, almost as much as his fans. He was so talented. Anyone who had ever been in his presence, had ever heard him sing and play, felt they had experienced something almost supernatural, and felt forever grateful for the experience. But the fans didn't have to live with him. They didn't have to wait for him to wake up, or show up, or sometimes just say something, the thing that needed to be said. Sensibilité was one unit; she, Serge and Mélanie were another. Serge was the point of intersection. They were like two families with a common husband and father. They danced around each other warily.

"Mama, Marie-Claire's eaten all the Froot Loops and all the licorice," Mélanie said.

Jane looked at Mélanie, slightly startled to remember that she was there. "Yeah, I know, Tweetie," Jane said, stroking her daughter's smooth hair.

Her own hair was in tangles; the word "hag" came to her as she contemplated the man's undershirt she was wearing as a nightgown. Just a few years ago, she could wear anything and look adorable.

"Wait a minute," Jane said. "Who gave you licorice?"

"TWEETIE, COME UPSTAIRS with me for a sec."

The three of them lay together on the bed, and Jane talked the most. Nobody cried. There was a lot of hugging. Mélanie understood from her father's resigned expression that he wasn't happy about this, but he wasn't shocked either; the two of them had already discussed it and made up their minds and whatever she felt didn't matter.

"This way we can all get more sleep," Jane said.

The shock of seeing much of the contents of the house emptied into cardboard boxes. The slight echo within her own bedroom walls matching a hollow ache that didn't seem exactly new. It felt like something remembered.

Serge helped Jane fill the van his group used for their music gigs. They drove across town, into streets that only had houses with sprawling lawns, no apartment buildings at all. Mélanie wore a kangaroo-shaped backpack, sucked her thumb like a baby, and watched her parents carry furniture and boxes into this new house. When Serge finally announced that he was going home, he said "chez moi" and not "chez nous," and those two words finally made the tears come gushing out, for all three of them. He got back into the van but didn't leave right away. He just sat there behind the wheel in the driveway. Mélanie knelt on the mattress in her new bedroom and watched him from the window, waiting to wave goodbye. Eventually, she was too drowsy to continue; she turned away, lay down and fell asleep.

1968

HIMA WAS AWAKENED by a knocking. Her husband was not in bed with her. She listened. She thought she heard someone pressing the keys of her harmonium. Hima realized that the sound had infiltrated her dreams, in which she was back in India. She sat up in bed and listened. No, it wasn't someone just pressing the keys, but also knocking on the wood, picking it up and shaking it. She threw off the covers and followed the noise to the living room.

Sunil was sitting on the floor, talking to the harmonium, as if to a giant telephone. His words were indistinct. He paused and listened, and when he looked up and noticed Hima he merely put his hand up, as if to tell her not to interrupt. She stood in her nightgown, not wanting to look at him. Instead she turned and gazed at a moonbeam falling across the floor from the kitchen window.

SUNIL READ RANI a story about a dark-haired little girl who went to school but never spoke. The other kids and the teacher tried to talk to the girl all day, but she just stared at them, apparently frightened. At the end of the story, they asked her name and she suddenly said, "Maria." Laughter and applause.

Rani cried throughout the whole story, and then asked her dad to tell it again. Which he did. Again. And again. Until the weight of salt water within her eyelids drew them down and she fell asleep, wondering vaguely at her father's patience.

The next day, he was gone. Her mother told her that he had to go away because his new job had made him very nervous. Hima seemed nervous herself, and also very tired. She said they would have to move.

"Because of the bugs in the walls?"

"What?"

"Daddy said—"

"No, because of your dad's job. It's far from here, but he'll be back."

"In a few days, like the last time?" Rani asked.

She felt her mother was better at questions like this.

Hima nodded.

"He'll get another job," Rani said.

Hima nodded again. She was wringing out a dishrag, a slight scowl creasing her face. Rani wondered why she didn't seem to want him back. She watched as her mother left the kitchen, and, moving like a sleepwalker, sat down on the oriental rug in the living room, drew her harmonium to her and began to sing. She sang just one note that stretched and wound higher and higher. She gave a little toss of her head and prepared to place her right hand on the keys, her left on the bellows. Rani turned and walked away as a whine began to fill the room. She wished her mother played something normal, like a piano, something that made happy music you could skip to.

"IN A NORMALLY functioning brain," the psychiatrist was explaining, "a person has an idea, checks it against reality, and only then lets his thoughts proceed. But in Sunil's case, his brain skips that second step. The drugs slow things down so that connection to reality has a chance to happen."

So Sunil's speech, which had always been slow, had become hypnotically so. Which was fine, Hima thought, because he put her to sleep. The pills caused him to lose his desire for her. The psychiatrist confirmed that it wasn't her fault. It didn't have anything to do with her supposedly emasculating status as a university professor. She had lived with guilt since they had come to this country, even though she realized it was nonsensical, one of those things that irritated her about Canada, this belief that if you didn't spend your days doing housework, you were letting everyone down.

It was Sunil himself who had urged her to talk to his doctor, who'd arranged this meeting, now that the new medication had allowed him to trust them both with such a conversation. He told Hima through his doctor that he wanted to stay at the hospital a little longer. She missed him now, sitting alone with this doctor. She dreaded the night, when her arms felt empty, and his absence haunted her dreams. Dreams in which he wasn't there but spoke to her in the way the voices in his own head presumably spoke to him.

"You say that something triggered this," Hima said. "What was it?"

"Well, typically, something happens in late adolescence. There are many possibilities. My impression, from what he's said and you've confirmed, is that he was a very driven sort of student. Sometimes it starts with something like exam stress."

"*Exam* stress can cause a person to lose their connection to reality?"

It was April, and the end of term was approaching. Hima thought of her students, tried to recall any of them with that tormented expression that sometimes appeared on Sunil's face.

"Well, no, remember there has to be a predisposition," the doctor replied. "And there might have been something else. Perhaps a problem with other family members..."

He cleared his throat and waited. Hima realized this was meant as a question, but she remained silent. The last time she'd suggested they visit his family in India, Sunil told her to go ahead, feel free, but refused to accompany her. He said he had no interest in seeing his older brothers, had not forgiven them for their brutality. But she had never seen any of this brutality herself. The only brother Hima knew well was Krishen, who was a few years younger, and who claimed to have never seen it either. Krishen was Hima's best friend in Canada. Once she'd had to barricade herself in the bedroom because Sunil was running up the stairs threatening to slap her. For being a bad wife, which, for Sunil, was about not believing him. She'd called Krishen, knowing that Sunil was listening on the extension downstairs. Krishen had raced over and calmed Sunil down by shaming him. *We don't hit women. Shut up! We just don't. What are you?*

She never told anyone about this; the kids had no idea, and she wasn't about to tell this doctor. She loved her husband, had no intention of betraying him.

"Sometimes some kind of upheaval, some kind of displacement."

Ah.

"Ram," she said, and closed her eyes.

"Sorry, what?"

"Nothing, I was just praying."

"Ah...Is it Ramadan now?"

Hima stared at him. Really! So ignorant, it was amazing.

"We're not *Muslims*. We're Hindus. *Ram* means God."

"Oh," the doctor said. "I see. Sorry."

"Never mind," Hima said. "It's just a thing we say."

She wasn't much of a believer. Praying could not be less crazy than what Sunil did, she reflected, talking to people who weren't there, giving them names, Ram, Krishna, Allah, Jesus. She was a mathematician; she believed in proofs. Another way to look at what Sunil had, she thought, was that almost everyone else had it too. It was just that he was more daring and creative: he made up his own grand, beautiful story, in which he played the central, world-changing role.

1970

THE KITCHEN WAS full of boxes again. Rani watched her mother crush the tablet into a cup of coffee. This would be for her father, who was still in bed. She reached for the small plastic bottle, but her mother batted her hand away from it.

"I just wanted to look at it," Rani protested, but her mother was in one of her moods and didn't answer.

Rani read the word on the label aloud: "Stelazine."

Hima shot her a fierce look.

"It won't work," Rani said.

Another fierce look, a finger pressed against her lips.

Rani understood plenty. She was almost eight. There were so many things that were obvious to her, but were lost on her parents. Why did they keep trying things that had never worked before? Moving again, because Sunil had gotten a new job and her father needed to be close to his new job. But why did he always have a new job? Her mother managed to keep hers at the university. Her mom had tenure, which Rani imagined was a kind of mental toughness, something her father lacked. Arun was in boarding school in Winnipeg and Ramesh was in college in Ottawa. Once again, Rani would have to start over at a different school, as the new kid, and the only Indian kid.

This wasn't going to work any better than it had the last three times.

Always, a quarrel after he tasted his bitter pill, never completely dissolved in the sweet coffee. Spitting it up. Half-melted powder on the surface of his cup. Always.

"Why do we have to move all the time just because he can't keep a job?" Rani said.

Hima said nothing.

"We don't move to be closer to *your* job," Rani continued.

"It's not just that," Hima said. "There's usually something about the house that bothers your dad."

"Oh, you mean the voices in the walls?" Rani asked. "Or the bugs?"

Hima turned away. She didn't say anything.

The silence was frightening. Rani couldn't stop herself from going on. She heard her own outrageous, bratty voice, but she had to keep asking.

"Why don't you leave him? Why don't you get a divorce? He's crazy, he's not even nice to you, and we're always moving!"

Hima looked back at her. To Rani's horror, there were tears streaming down her face.

"You're saying I should leave my husband? You want me to leave your father? Is that what your Western culture teaches you? To abandon someone because he's sick?"

"MUMMY, WHAT'S THE harmonium doing out in the snow?"

Hima was eating a piece of toast. Her eyes widened and she stopped chewing. She turned her head slowly, as if she were counting to herself, and looked out the window. Then she suddenly rose from the table and nearly knocked a tea tray off the kitchen counter as she darted out the back door.

It was minus ten but Hima was out in her thin, polyester nightgown, bare legs in slippers ploughing through the snow. Rani watched through the window as Hima retrieved the harmonium, brushed the snow off it and gazed at it like a mother pulling the hair out of a child's eyes to stare fondly at her face. She hugged it to her body and cradled it, her eyes shut. It seemed to Rani that she was murmuring something; she could see her lips moving.

She opened the back door and strained to listen. Her mother was saying, "No, no, Sunil," although her father was nowhere to be seen.

"THERE ARE NO BUGS in the harmonium, Sunil," Hima said to her husband that night, but Sunil showed no sign of having heard her. He was listening to something else, she knew, something playing only for him, inside his head.

The next day, Hima played her harmonium for hours, humming along in a hoarse voice. Her sons were home this week and had busied themselves doing the chores Sunil neglected. Shovel the driveway, fix leaky faucets, make sure the car was running all right. Late afternoon now. They approached the fridge but paused in front of their mother. Fingers in the pockets of their bell bottoms, waiting for Hima to look up from her harmonium.

"What's going on?" Arun asked Rani.

"Is she praying?" asked Ramesh.

"It sounds bad to my ears," Arun said.

"I know!" Rani said.

"It's like listening to an organ that's depressed," Ramesh said.

Hima paused and smiled at her children, as if they'd been saying the opposite of what they'd actually said. An idea came to her.

"One of you boys, take it with you. Your friends will like it. Indian music's all the rage."

"No thanks, Ma," Ramesh said, bending to kiss her. "We don't know how to play. You could take it to a pawn shop."

A pawn shop! Those nasty, dodgy stores crammed with garbage. Had her life come to this? She imagined her father shaking his head with disappointment.

Arun touched the wooden box with a toe. He crouched down, kissed Hima's cheek and said, "You should keep it, Ma. You're the only one who understands what to do with this thing."

AFTER HIMA HAD TO rescue the harmonium again, this time from the garbage, she picked up the phone and slowly dialled a number from the newspaper. She looked over her shoulder, but Sunil was oblivious, staring straight ahead with a glazed expression.

She placed the ad, hesitating when it came to the price.

"Are any parts broken?" asked the woman taking the call.

She couldn't say: Just my heart. I'm selling my harmonium like a woman giving a child up for adoption. It's not about money. It's about keeping it safe.

1980

THE JOB WAS OKAY. It wasn't for forever. Paid just enough so
that Rani didn't have to live with Sunil and Hima, didn't have
to leave the insanely cheap place she was basically subletting
from her roommate now. She could walk to work; the restaurant was at the corner of Saint-Hubert and Rachel. Its
linoleum-plus-red-leather decor seemed to be going from
passé to trendy, but there was a cheerful shabbiness to the
place, walls the colour of manila envelopes, menus written in
black magic marker on pieces of yellowing paper and stuck
to the wall with masking tape along with pictures of food
ripped out of magazines. The only problem was that sometimes there were no customers at all. For hours. She studied
her boss. El Gato, despite his Spanish nickname and Peruvian
accent, bore a strong resemblance to Don Vito Corleone,
especially on the occasions when he wore a fedora. Rani,
who was taking Italian that semester, secretly thought of him
as *Il* Gatto.

The little girl and her mother walked in together, both
wearing some sort of plastic outfit. Cheap, probably second-
hand, but attention-grabbing. Each in an orange raincoat that

shone like a Chinese lantern, and matching rubber boots. The mother's hair was orange too. Rani figured the mother was having fun with that; she imagined her laughing as she found the matching clothes in a *friperie* or an *aubainerie* on Mont-Royal Boulevard. But the effect was limited: the kid's hair was black, and she looked nothing like her mother.

As Rani began to walk toward them, El Gato emerged from behind the counter with a Polaroid camera. He nodded to the orange-haired woman, and then knelt before the little girl. "Wow, celebrities!" he said. "Can I take your picture, sweetheart?"

The child was drawing something on a placemat with a pen. She ignored his question. When she did speak, she said, "I'm five, almost six. My birthday's in September."

"Wow, that's so old," El Gato said. "You're almost a has-been."

A flicker of surprise in the child's eyes. Click. Rani watched as the three of them bent over the camera, waiting for the image to emerge. When the little girl's portrait was finally revealed, she quickly turned back to her drawing, as if she was disappointed that some other face hadn't shown up. El Gato stuck the photograph to the wall with masking tape, next to pictures of sundaes, smoked meat sandwiches, and Machu Picchu.

The mother ordered a sandwich, and shared it with her daughter. She and El Gato spoke together in low voices. El Gato asked Rani to bring the little girl a glass of apple juice while he hunted around by the cash register for some coloured pencils and crayons.

"Nice picture," Rani said to the child as she served her the glass. The little girl took a break from drawing and concentrated on blowing bubbles in the juice with the straw. The picture showed two tall figures and one small one. One of the taller figures had long hair; almost obscuring its body was something resembling a giant, lemon-coloured spoon. There was a box with flowers around its edges.

"Is that a really big lollipop?" Rani asked, pointing to the spoon.

"It's a guitar," the little girl said, and she strummed the lines across it with her little fingers. "La la la. See?"

Children are raving lunatics, Rani thought. She found some simple Italian words to translate her thought in her head. *I bambini sono pazzi.*

THAT EVENING, the restaurant was so dead that El Gato turned the volume up on the TV monitor and pulled up a barstool to watch a news program on an English channel. Rani cringed at the thought of Francophone patrons entering the restaurant and then quietly leaving as soon as they heard the sound of the language of imperialism. She loved her boss, but he could be so out of it, like so many men his age. Her dad's age. She looked out the window. Driving rain. Nobody would come in anyway, she supposed. She filled the napkin holders, wiped the crust off the top of the plastic ketchup dispensers and looked around for something else to do. Before the woman and her daughter had left, El Gato had had the child sign her name to her drawing: Mélanie. He'd put the drawing up next to the Polaroid. Rani straightened it now, smoothed down the scotch tape.

"She's a cute kid, eh?" said El Gato.

"Yeah. Friends of yours?"

"The mother, she's my friend Jane. I met her years ago in a French class when we were both new in the country."

El Gato disappeared into the kitchen. Rani approached the bar and looked up at the TV screen. A man on the program was complaining to a woman with permed black hair and exotic, hard-to-place features that someone called Dr. Cameron had messed up his mind. "I feel like I've been completely used. I feel like my mind has been completely invaded. I suppose if guinea pigs had feelings they'd feel like I do."

He went on to talk about the electroshock therapy and LSD that he claimed were given to him without his consent.

Sure, let's listen to a psychiatric patient. We all know how reliable they are.

She moved away from the TV and considered the pay phone next to the door. She should call her mother, ask her how she was doing. But Sunil would answer; he always did, as though expecting the call from the person who would finally recognize his greatness.

Rani's mind balked at the prospect of even a brief conversation with him. She should check on her mother; she really should. But she suddenly felt weighed down with an emotion that was equal parts guilt and dread.

MÉLANIE AND JANE came in regularly. Mélanie busied herself drawing imaginative pictures, and El Gato always taped them around her photograph on the wall.

This was a tidy enough neighbourhood, but there weren't a lot of kids around, so Mélanie got a lot of attention from El Gato and the rest of the staff. Rani was shy with children, but she did her best. Mélanie was like a mini-adult, quiet with a serious frown on her face most of the time, and Rani felt more comfortable with her than with most kids, whose exuberance usually flustered her and made her a little tired.

"Which is your favourite?" Mélanie asked Rani one day, pointing to three pictures she had drawn that afternoon.

Rani pretended to assess each picture critically. "Hmmm... I don't know. Which is yours?"

"The one with the bunnies," Mélanie answered without hesitation.

Rani searched all three pictures for rabbits, found none.

"You can't see them," Mélanie said. "They're hiding here." She tapped a point in the picture covered with squiggly brown lines.

"Oh... I see," Rani said.

"No, you can't," Mélanie said. "They're brown, and they're hiding with all the other browns. That way they're safe."

ONE MORNING, Jane and Mélanie entered the restaurant. Jane was in tears. El Gato went over to their table and signalled to Rani to get them a coffee and a glass of chocolate milk.

Rani bent under the counter to fetch a tray and as she came up she glanced over at them.

Jane was sitting with her head bent and one hand over her eyes, whispering furiously. Rani arranged the drinks on the tray and began to walk over to the table. El Gato looked over at her, shook his head and threw his arm out, palm up. Rani stopped, and then walked back to the counter to await further instructions. She looked at the untouched glass of chocolate milk. She'd read somewhere that the true colour of chocolate milk was green, that food colouring was added to make it brown. Or was that chocolate pudding? She poured the chocolate milk back into the pitcher in the fridge, and looked out the window to avoid staring at Jane and Mélanie. She wondered if Jane's hair colour came from a bottle too.

She was so bored. Her courses were over for the year, but she would be stuck here all summer to save up money. She still wanted to go on a trip somewhere. She didn't know where yet. She calculated how much money she would make that day. Flights from Montreal to Paris were cheap, but Paris itself was a nightmare, she'd heard. And she worried she might pick up the accent; she needed to sound Québécoise.

On the radio, a commentator was saying that if Québec was not ready for independence, it was a question of confidence. He predicted more confidence in the future.

After a few minutes, as Rani was beginning to daydream about boarding a plane and *then* figuring out her destination, El Gato surprised her by walking over and placing a small wad of cash in her hand. How much money was this? Had he read her mind? She stared down at the bills.

"Take her out," he said, indicating the table where Jane still sat with her daughter.

Rani gave him an alarmed look.

El Gato let out a wry, distracted chuckle. "No, I mean, the little girl, take her out for the day. To give the mother a break. It'll be okay. Erin's coming in, and it's quiet today. Here, take a cab. Buy the kid something." He took more bills from the back pocket of his black pants. He suggested the Children's Festival at Parc Jean-Drapeau, adding, "She could use some fresh air."

IN THE CAB, Rani marvelled at how calm and trusting this tiny child was. Mélanie sat staring ahead as if she were used to being whisked away from her mother and put into a cab with someone she didn't know. She was slight, even for a child her age; her features were fine and sharp, almost feline. She wore a yellow-and-white tunic. Black leggings covered her thin legs and her pink running shoes struck Rani as impossibly small.

When they got out of the cab, Mélanie reached instinctively for Rani's hand, surprising her. Rani felt like a fraud. What did she know about children? The day was still foggy, and increasingly humid. A cool breeze from the St. Lawrence River made it just bearable to walk around. They passed a few circus tents. Mélanie asked Rani what they were going to do. Didn't El Gato say they were going to get some fresh air? Rani realized that the little girl thought fresh air was some kind of treat, like ice cream on a cone, or a Slurpee. A magenta-haired clown appeared, seemingly out of the fog, and handed them a flyer.

"We could go to a kite-making workshop," Rani said, reading the flyer.

"No, I can't."

"You can't what?"

"Make kites."

"But they show you how."

"No. Even if they show me how, I won't be able to." Mélanie suddenly tried to pull her hand away, but Rani gently tightened her grip.

Rani wondered where that lack of confidence came from. Not even six years old, and so sure of her own incompetence. She didn't know how to solve this problem right now, so she suggested they walk around until they came to an ice-cream stand.

"Yes, that's a good idea because I think they also have popsicles."

"Excellent," Rani said, because she didn't really know how to talk to children.

They stood in line, listening to other people's conversations. "Why are all the signs in French?" a woman asked her friend. "Don't they understand that tourists speak English?"

"It seems like we've been waiting here forever."

"I get the feeling all these Canadians or Québécois or whatever have really been waiting forever. Do you get that too?"

"Yeah, that's exactly what this feels like. Boy is this ever going to be a let-down."

"I don't know. The ice cream will probably be like in the States."

"That's what I mean."

"You wanted exotic ice cream?"

Rani turned and looked at Mélanie, wondering how much she understood of the tourists' conversation. She found her self wondering if people would think Mélanie was her little sister. No, Mélanie didn't look Indian. But there was something about the kid's features. Somehow both unusual and familiar. And then the thought that had been unconscious rose to the surface: Mélanie's small face reminded her of her own mother's.

They ate their popsicles while watching some clowns circle them on unicycles. The clowns pointed to their own smiles and honked bicycle horns at them, but Rani followed Mélanie's lead and just slowly worked away at her treat with the same solemn expression.

"Questi pagliacci sono fastidiosi," Rani said. *These clowns are annoying.*

Mélanie nodded. She did not ask for an explanation. Rani realized they were similar: they just wanted to be left alone.

RANI WAS ON a break at the restaurant, thumbing through the pages of *Le Journal de Montréal*. Wait. Two very familiar faces. What! Mélanie's mother, standing next to Rani's idol, Serge Giglio. Her eyes scanned the caption: the woman was Jane Plant. Serge Giglio's wife! Stunned. Did El Gato know all this? The article said their "gorgeous hippie relationship" was over. It also mentioned that Mélanie had been adopted from Vietnam. Rani looked up from the newspaper at the Polaroid image, still on the wall next to a drawing of a tiger watching children in a schoolyard.

"Hey, there's Jane!" Erin, the other waitress on the afternoon shift, exclaimed, wiping her hands on a dishtowel as she read over Rani's shoulder.

"Yeah, with Serge Giglio, the guy from Sensibilité! Did you know they were together?"

Erin shrugged. Her shrug said: *Who cares about French music?*

Rani was dismayed. How to explain the music to someone like Erin? Someone, say, working at Sam the Record Man would stick it in the section called Progressive Rock. But Sensibilité didn't belong in any category. It was transcendent, sometimes soft and gentle like folk, other times dramatic and orchestral, so naked and raw, full of emotions that drew out her own.

Sometimes she would lie in bed listening to a record, imagining that Serge was singing only to her. In the state between wakefulness and sleep, she could convince herself that without meeting her, Serge Giglio knew and understood her very well. She understood him too. They had access to each other's thoughts.

Her father's face often appeared over the scenes in her dream, hovering, looking at her through binoculars. Flitting away. She'd shake herself awake. Get up and get a glass of water from the kitchen. The image never failed to alarm her; it always seemed she was channelling her father's crazy thoughts.

Rani had four shifts a week at the restaurant. She asked El Gato to increase them to six, but didn't tell him the reason, that she hoped to run into Jane and Mélanie again. Maybe this babysitting could become a regular thing. Maybe she would run into Serge at some point. Her mind began to race with excitement.

She felt a rush of jealousy for Jane, even though they'd apparently broken up. There was another wave of jealousy, for Mélanie. She, Rani, was the family Serge was supposed to have. Imagine just running into Serge. If she had run into his ex and their kid, how improbable was it that she would run into him too, sooner or later? Maybe he was lonely. Maybe he'd walk into the restaurant himself. She imagined chatting with him, casually mentioning, "I've met your little girl."

1982

MÉLANIE LOVED TO GO to the Granby Zoo, and Serge took her there often, despite the long drive, the inflated price of admission, the necessity of wearing a disguise (safari hat, black wig, glasses), and the hot hours spent under the glare of the sun. Lingering by the monkey cage, the little girl fired questions at him. She wore a backpack in the shape of a monkey.

"Can they fly?"

"No."

"Can they have babies?"

"Yes."

She was a smart little kid, much too smart for these questions. She was getting on his nerves today.

"Can they understand French?"

"Maybe a little."

"Do they speak English? Why are they in jail?"

Where was she getting these ideas? Jane? Jail. Was this about Québec? Or him? Deadbeat dad or just that he was a low-life or something. He had promised to try to get up earlier. It seemed to him that all this bad feeling had developed after their separation, rather than before it, despite the fact that he still put on a disguise and took Jane out for lunch every two weeks or so, and then to the motel, while Mélanie was at school.

As Mélanie waited for an answer, one of the monkeys contemplated her from his perch. Serge thought of the price of admission to the zoo. Eight bucks for adults, free for kids. There was a message there, one he resented.

THE DOORBELL RANG. Jane put her paintbrush down.

She opened the door to different hues of grey. A dull, hazy sky, and Serge, wan and ashen in a faded grey jacket. New streaks of silver in his mousy brown hair.

He looked completely bereft.

"We broke up," he said.

"I'm always here for you," Jane said.

"No, I mean, the band."

He was wringing his hands, as if afraid of her reaction.

He looked at her warily, and then peeked inside the house.

"She's at school," Jane said, and led him to the couch. She removed her painting smock, sat down beside him and pulled his head into her lap.

"Tell me," she said. She felt a stab of guilt. She'd thought it might happen. Maybe she'd hoped it would. More guilt: if she'd waited it out until the end of the late-night rehearsals, the fans and would-be groupies, they could have lived together in the same house. That would have been better for Mélanie.

Except her gut was telling her the last part wasn't true.

"Is this because they want you to sing in English?" Jane asked.

"They're always talking about money," Serge said. "Which means they don't want to make music anymore."

She felt him gasp and sigh and finally break down. This wasn't just about the band. She cradled his head, bent over, kissed his hair, put her hand inside his shirt and stroked his chest. Poor, broken-hearted man.

"You made a lot of beautiful music," Jane said.

"I guess we can't make any more."

"That's okay," Jane said. "You're all still friends, right?"

"Yes," Serge said, and sniffled. "Hey, do you have anything to drink?"

Jane stiffened. It was early afternoon. He probably hadn't even been awake for many hours. This would be his breakfast. She felt a wave of revulsion. She imagined Mélanie returning from school to find her father here, drunk, possibly still crying, on the sofa.

She patted his arm.

"Let's go out," she said. She looked at her watch. She'd indulge his wish for alcohol, see him safely home, and make it back in time for Mélanie's return from school. She already anticipated the relief she would feel once this afternoon was over, and she was free again.

ON THE WAY HOME from school one afternoon, there was a chill in the air and a quickly darkening sky. A cat sat under a tree and glared up at a squirrel that was screaming its head off. A sparrow chirped for a minute but eventually stopped, realizing it was alone, before flying away. A cloudless day was turning into a clear, dark-blue evening.

But in Mélanie's head, a dark and violent storm was brewing. She waited, as she always did, until the anger dissipated.

Then she calmly entered the house. The teachers at school had been gossiping about Jane today, about how she kept to herself and dressed the way someone would if they were deeply foreign and had no desire to make friends. Mélanie studied her mother. Yes. Today, for example, she was wearing a turquoise headscarf and a turquoise dress with bold yellow flowers whose material and pattern made you think of a shower curtain, and also the 1960s. A cigarette in her hand; she always smoked after visiting Serge.

Jane was frowning into the hall mirror, blowing smoke out of the corner of her mouth.

"Mum!"

Jane turned around quickly and gave her daughter a big, bright fake smile. Yellow lipstick, as well.

"You went to see him. You didn't wait for me." A statement. She couldn't bear to ask her. She didn't want to hear more made-up stories about shopping, seeing friends or looking for a job.

Jane agreed, apologized, and waited. But there was no point in saying anything else. Mélanie went up to her room, threw her backpack on the braided rug beside her bed, and lay face down on her pillow.

WHEN MÉLANIE WAS YOUNGER, her father regularly told her that he had conversations with the man in the moon, and that they both agreed that the most beautiful girl in the world lived in their house. Mélanie found the first part easier to believe. As she stared out her bedroom window, she thought that the man in the moon, with his dark shadows under sad eyes and his greenish, pock-marked face, looked quite a bit like her papa.

She'd asked her father what had happened to the rest of him. Like, where was his body?

"It exploded! His whole body exploded, Mélanie, into tiny fragments, those shiny, twinkling things you call stars. He exploded when he saw your beauty. It was just too much for him."

The way her father thought of her was very different from the kids at school, who pulled the skin at the corners of their eyes whenever she approached, as if to remind her of her difference, the difference she saw every day in the mirror at her own house. The things Mélanie's father said to her would have made her mother happy, because her mother cared a lot about being pretty.

Mélanie considered her parents dreamers. She wasn't like them, although she occasionally wondered what it might be like to live in a TV show from the re-runs channel. *The Brady Bunch*, where kids got new parents and lots of new siblings who weren't related to you. Or *The Partridge Family*, where the father was missing, but his absence, far from being shameful, was legit, as he was apparently dead and the whole family was too busy to grieve, traveling to their music gigs in a school bus.

MÉLANIE'S TEACHER had asked each student to draw a word out of a hat and write about it for homework. Mélanie's word was "femelle". If the animal is female, it is smaller and reproduces. It is small and responsible. It has a heavy weight on its shoulders, if it has shoulders.

The realization came to her that afternoon: Her real mother had abandoned her. But why? Was there something wrong with her real mother's shoulders? Or was there something wrong with *her*?

THE NEXT MORNING, a Saturday, bright sunshine poured through Mélanie's window, waking her up. She came downstairs as Jane's hippie door-chimes tinkled and the backyard patio door opened.

Mélanie followed her outside.

Jane was already on her back on a lounge chair in the backyard, opening a magazine.

Mélanie crept next to her and whispered, "Can I feed the birds, mama?"

She'd startled her. For a second, Jane didn't say anything. Her lips went inside her mouth and her whole jaw seemed to change shape. Was she finally going to lose it and swear at her in that odd half-British, half-Québécoise way of hers, as she did on the phone with her father? *Bleeding hell, hostie, sod off, won't you?* But all she said was, "Sure," as she rose from her chair and went inside to the kitchen. Mélanie went to check the radish plants she had planted back in June, in the garden patch behind the house. The leaves were long and full, but when she tugged at the stems she saw that the radishes themselves were still puny. She pulled one, studied it for a moment and then dropped it on the ground. Jane re-emerged with a slice of bread.

Mélanie tore the bread into four pieces and threw them up in the air, watching them fall again. Jane lifted her sunglasses and narrowed her eyes at her daughter as she blew out smoke. Without her sunglasses, there was no doubt about her bad mood. Mélanie guessed the reasons: her resentment, the fact that Mélanie wasn't even her real child, her real burden. Mélanie knew—and this wasn't a guess—something else Jane was thinking: She was wondering why Mélanie did this, why she behaved like a four-year-old.

But how was she supposed to know she was turning eight if her parents almost always forgot her birthday?

Let her wonder. Let her realize it was her daughter's birthday today.

Even if it might be a fake date.

You're not going to ignore me. I'm somebody. Tell Papa.

The last time he was here, he'd handed her a thick transparent plastic bag filled with clear water, sunshine, and one shimmering goldfish. She'd asked where the goldfish had come from originally, although she knew. He hadn't answered her, because Jane had pulled him into one of their arguments that always seemed to be about the thing they were actually talking about as well as the other things they would never talk about when she was in the room. "No aquarium, no goldfish bowl even. Just a bag. It's going to live in a bag, is it?"

When Mélanie got tired of holding onto the bag, she went to the bathroom and held it open upside down over the toilet bowl. The contents slid out and landed with a splash. She wished the fish luck finding its family before flushing it away.

"Mélanie, you have to tear the pieces into little crumbs," Jane said now. Her voice was muffled, irritated, but too sleepy to make itself clearer.

Mélanie picked up one of the quarters and tore it into four more pieces.

"This small?"

"Smaller. Make them tiny."

Mélanie bent down and looked for the pieces of bread in the grass. She stood in the garden, tearing the breadcrumbs and asking "like this?" as the sky darkened and Jane fell asleep, oblivious to her daughter's rage, nodding off under her sunglasses, magazine on the grass beside her.

7. Chercher un ami
(Looking for a Friend)

1983

"HELLO, RANI, are you busy?" said Hima.

"No, actually, I was just going to call you."

"Why were you going to call me?" Hima said.

Rani knew that of Hima's three children, she was the one who called the most, though it was by no means often.

"To say hello," said Rani.

"That's nice," Hima said. But it was clear she didn't believe her. "So what is new?"

"Uh, well, my classes are over," Rani said.

She'd have to tell her.

In a minute.

"How about you?" she asked instead. "Have you finished teaching yet this session?"

"Yes, just exams to mark now," said Hima. "So, finishing second-year university, is it? Time is going so fast. Your classes are over? You'll come home now?"

"Why would I come home now?"

Rani braced herself for an argument. She put the phone down while Hima went on about how she couldn't understand why an unmarried girl would want to live separately from her parents. She poured herself a glass of water, looked in the mirror, and then picked the phone up again. When she returned, Hima had finished ranting, had not noticed her absence, and was now asking her a question.

"Rani, can you just promise me one thing?"

Rani hesitated. She remembered her airline ticket, with both delight and trepidation. She would have to tell her some time.

"Rani, are you there? Can you just promise me one thing?"

"Depends."

"I want to invite you and Arun and his girlfriend and Ramesh and Ramesh's girlfriend here for your dad's birthday. Will you come? Do you have a boyfriend we should invite?"

"Oh. No. Sorry, I can't."

"Why not?"

"I'm going to Europe."

"What! What are you talking about now?"

"I have my ticket, Mum. I'm leaving in ten days."

"When were you going to tell me this? Is this something you've known for a while?"

"I was going to tell you today, actually. But...I've been saving up the money for a while."

"Yes, this restaurant job. Like we raised our children to be servants. What are you going to do in Europe? Are you going alone?"

"Just, I don't know, walk around. Yes, I'm going alone."

"That doesn't sound safe. Walk around where?"

"The streets…"

"Just walk around the streets? Like what, a streetwalker?"

"Excuse me?"

"Or do you have a boyfriend? Are you going with a boyfriend? You can tell me."

"I don't have a boyfriend, no."

"Don't you think you should be thinking of settling down now? You are getting a bit old. You're going to be left on the shelf."

"I…what? I'm turning twenty-one this summer."

"Do you want me to help you find a match?"

Oh, for God's sake.

"No, I'm not interested," Rani said, "And anyway, from what you've told me, an Indian man would not want a headstrong young woman like me, one who insists on waiting tables just to live away from her family."

Hima was silent. Rani regretted her tone.

"Look, I'm sorry," Rani said. "Don't worry, I'm only going away for a few months. Plenty of time to marry me off."

"Such a comedian," Hima said. She added—perhaps to Sunil, listening in?—"She thinks everything is so easy. Let her find out!"

RANI HAD A SEATMATE, an attractive older guy. At least thirty. Curly hair and olive skin. He was asleep, despite the noise: lots of babies on this flight, a chorus of wails, subsiding only to rise again every few minutes. Also, a woman wearing a bra and a pair of shorts, who asked the flight attendant for a blanket. The flight attendant said no. Rani looked at her watch. She unbuckled her seatbelt and pulled her sweater over her head. Underneath, she was wearing a t-shirt proclaiming the independence of the République du Québec.

As if on cue, the curly-haired man sitting next to her began to blink awake. His eyes fully open, he turned and read these words aloud. Then he asked her why she was going to Brussels.

Alone, in the air, she found she had a flair for conversation. She batted the question away, since there was no particular reason, besides having to get away. She made him talk about himself. He was a physician with the Red Cross, on his way to a conference. Hima and Sunil would love it if she got engaged to a doctor, she thought. The mere idea of that kind of security made the air feel stifling. She couldn't wait to get off the plane and begin wandering.

AT THE DOOR to the Musical Instruments Museum she felt someone standing next to her as she read the sign, which was in Flemish, English, and French.

"Shit," he said. "Closed Sundays, huh?" But for Rani, this was a relief. No intention of paying twenty-six Belgian francs when she could spend it on food. She turned to him and smiled. It was a dull, drizzly day. They walked on, more or less together, but in silence.

"Are you American?" she said after a moment, and he said he was.

"Are *you* American?" he asked after a moment.

"No, I'm from Montreal," she said.

"Canadian," he said.

"Maybe. Maybe I'm Québécoise."

He laughed, a short snort.

"No, baby, you ain't French," he said, and his laugh was so infectious that Rani broke down and snorted along with him, even as a French word popped into her mind: la complicité. It was like they already knew each other. They walked on.

"Are you Indian?"

"Ah, I don't know about that."

"Okay, well I do. You're an Indian girl, all right?"

"Fine," she said.

They smiled at each other.

"Where are you going? You off to see the Manneken Pis now?"

"Yeah, I don't know."

"Yeah, me neither. I don't know where you're going either."

"Maybe we should walk around together," Rani said, her face warming as the words came out of her mouth.

"Aren't we already doing that?" he said, laughing. "Sure, we could, we could. Wouldn't want you to get lost all by yourself."

"Great. My sense of direction is pretty lousy," Rani said.

"Oh really?" He turned and looked at her. He looked up and down her body. Rani wondered if he liked her clothes—a navy rain jacket, unzipped and open, over a black turtleneck and khaki trousers. It was summer, but in northern Europe you had to dress for fall. He was a big guy, in a t-shirt and cotton pants. Probably didn't feel the cold. His arms would be warm around her.

"There's a trick, you know," he said after a while. "You have to look at things. If you're the kind of person who gets lost a lot, it's that you're not looking. You spendin' too much time in your head."

Rani nodded, feeling exposed.

"Like you see this house? Blue walls, white shutters. Remember that. That's your first landmark. And now, this place. It's like a school or something, and here, this church coming up right across the street. Remember, blue house, white shutters, then the school, then the church across the street."

"Sure, okay," Rani said.

They walked on a bit in companionable silence. They passed other pedestrians, tall, older, white-haired white people in long coats. These ones were real Belgians, Rani felt. She felt him looking at her again. She realized that she'd been smiling all this time. His look. He was considering something.

"Okay, now I gotta get back," he said.

"What?"

"I was just on a break, gotta get back now."

"A break from what?"

He shrugged his big football-player shoulders, turned abruptly and ran off.

Rani stared after him. She wanted to call him, but realized they hadn't exchanged names.

ON THE TRAIN from Brussels to Amsterdam, Rani shared a wagon with a group of travellers her age, all girls. Two from Denmark, one from Australia. All three of them said they were on the road after a heartbreak. The Danish girls were having lots of flings. They wore yellow t-shirts and beige harem pants as if to accentuate their blondness. The Australian girl said that she was trying to have flings as well, but she wasn't able to have sex unless she was drunk.

"Yes, and I'm quite hungover now," she said, and the Danish girls giggled. "But it's nothing compared to my backache."

Rani felt awed by the girl's candour. All the way from Australia. This distance, travelled alone, seemed to give her a special kind of strength and self-assurance. Rani studied her. She had short, brown hair and a fresh, apple-like face. And a very large bust.

"Oh, these," she said, stunning Rani as she caught her eyes. *She saw me looking at her boobs. Like a man.* She found she couldn't speak.

But the Australian girl didn't care.

"Yeah, these don't help my back," she said cheerfully. "And it's why I have to take trains."

"What?" said one of the Danish girls. "Why trains?"

"On buses, you know how you go over a bump and your breasts go *bang, bang, bang*."

The Danish girls agreed, tittering.

"Do you take buses?" the Australian girl asked Rani, spacing the words out as if, Rani suddenly realized, she had doubts about her grasp of English.

"Yeah, I don't have that problem, though," Rani said. "My breasts just kind of go blip, blip, blip."

The three girls stared at Rani in surprise. She shrugged, looking down at her chest, which made them laugh. Rani joined in, suddenly tickled by what she'd said, and the laughter surged again, rolled, surged, and they were transported by the wave, carried all the way to Amsterdam.

Far away from home, Rani thought. Suddenly normal. Friends. Suddenly. Laughing. Laughing like teenage girls.

WHEN THE TRAIN reached Amsterdam, the Danish girls remained in their seats. They were continuing on to Paris. Rani found herself following the Australian girl, whose name

143 //

was Donna, upstairs from the platform. Rani had been telling her about her baffling encounter with Football Shoulders.

"So here's something I've found useful," Donna said, but she was out of breath as they climbed the stairs, so Rani had to wait in suspense. Were there tricks?

But Donna was pushing open the door to a room marked Baggage Office.

"You leave your bag here, see, and then you don't have to be hauling it about all over town as you look for a place to stay."

So no tips about what made that stranger run away like that. She helped her new friend heave her backpack onto the counter and then swung her own down. The middle-aged and slightly peeved-looking clerk handed them tokens.

They walked out of the train station into a mild, overcast afternoon. They walked for miles, stopping in cheap hotels, of which there seemed to be dozens, inquiring about the price of a bed. The city did not smell of marijuana smoke, as Rani had expected, and there were definitely fewer tulips too, but it did look like Amsterdam—the streets a series of circles surrounding dams, crowded with cyclists. They agreed on a hotel, finally, and made a plan to part ways for the afternoon and meet up later. Donna was going to rest for a while before taking a cab back to the station to get her bag. Rani said she wanted to wander a bit more to take advantage of a day in northern Europe when it was not actually raining.

"The thing is," said Donna out of the blue. "You don't want sex. You want love. People can tell. It can scare a bloke away."

A jolt of hot anger. And fierce embarrassment. She tried to remember if Football Shoulders had looked scared.

Donna's round, smug face, suddenly hateful.

Before Rani left the hotel, she quietly cancelled her reservation.

SINCE SHE HAD ditched Donna she came up with a new plan. She'd go to the Keukenhof gardens and look at tulips. But then she changed her mind, as she realized that looking at tulips was just something she was expected to do, not something she would actually enjoy. She could go to a café and smoke some pot, talk to some locals or some other young backpackers like herself. But no, she had had enough of socializing for the moment. Maybe tomorrow. She found she enjoyed this very much, making plans and cancelling them as she pleased. And her mother ready to marry her off. She didn't need anyone. Not even friends. Not worth it, if they were going to be like Donna. Being invisible was better. She wandered until she found herself at the Van Gogh Museum. She paid the entrance fee and spent many minutes gazing at melancholy self-portraits.

An older American woman with sparse hair ran through the room, shouting, "This is the work of a madman."

And out the door again. A guard came in and looked at Rani, who pointed toward the exit.

IT WAS APPROACHING dusk in Amsterdam. Rani's second day here, and her twenty-first birthday. She looked around at the young people standing about in small groups. Nobody here knew that it was her birthday. She would have one drink, alone, to celebrate. Congratulations were in order, she decided. Money was tight, but here she was. She'd saved every penny she could spare from her restaurant wages and she'd made it, finally.

The evening promised to be warm and pleasant. She recognized a song by Echo and the Bunnymen and went into the bar where it was playing. She sat down on a stool directly in front of the entrance, and began a postcard to El Gato. At the far end, around the corner of the L-shaped bar, an old man was shouting and gesticulating. He wanted something from the bartender but was failing to make himself understood because he was speaking Italian. The man was hairy, with fierce dark eyes. He reminded Rani of her father, because beyond the physical resemblance, he was speaking Italian to someone who clearly understood only Dutch and English: he was being irrational. At one point, the man shouted, "Ecco!" and the bartender answered, "Right, and the Bunnymen!" as he rolled up a tea towel and began rubbing it around inside a glass. The bartender glanced at Rani and rolled his eyes.

"I can speak a little Italian," Rani said.

"That's great," he said, his face impassive. "I could use a translator here."

Rani slid off the stool and went to stand directly behind the oblivious, wild-eyed customer. But as she listened carefully, she realized he wasn't making any sense. She understood his words, but the sentences didn't follow each other. He was just ranting. Panic thrummed in her chest.

"Hey, I'm sorry," Rani said. "I can't understand him."

She felt the bartender give her a doubtful look. *I knew you weren't Italian.*

She hastily paid her bill. There was a park next to the hostel where she was staying; she'd finish her postcard there.

The park was in a square surrounded by four buildings, each taller than the others in the neighbourhood. It was like being in a protected, enclosed courtyard. Tulips grew neatly in rectangular boxes. Two silent old men in flat caps faced each other across a chess table made out of concrete. A nursing mother adjusted a blue scarf over her baby's head and called out encouragement to a child of about four, who remained frozen at the top of a slide.

A dark-skinned teenager played catch with someone who looked like a younger version of himself. The teenager spoke Arabic, and the boy answered him in a mixture of Arabic, Dutch and English. As Rani finished her postcard and rose from her bench, the boy approached her and spoke to her in English. He asked if he could help her with anything.

She laughed. How was it so obvious that she was a tourist, even to a young boy? Was it the postcard? Or something about her clothes? Or her skin, brown like his. She realized the boy was probably hoping she spoke Arabic, that she was a potential friend in this cold country.

The teenager walked up, grinning. "Brother," he said, pointing to the younger boy.

The younger brother explained that they lived by themselves here in Amsterdam, that he was ten and his brother seventeen, and that their parents were in Morocco. She thought of asking why, but it occurred to her that the younger one probably didn't quite know, and the older one didn't speak enough English to explain.

"Mohammed," the teenager said, pointing to himself. He pointed to his brother, who then took over again. He told her that his name was Khalid, and that, anyway, they were wondering if she wanted to have supper with them.

She laughed. "Really?"

"Yes. We will make tagine."

"You're inviting me to your apartment."

"Yes." This time it was Mohammed who answered.

It wasn't something she normally did, accept dinner invitations from strangers. But then, when was she ever invited to dinner by strangers? Yes, of course her parents had warned her about such things, but here everyone was a stranger, no one more than herself. And her father had even once mentioned that strangers—Muslims—had saved his life, back in India. And the two boys were young, skinny creatures, two kids on their own with huge, dark eyes. A memory came to her, something that little Mélanie had said to her at El Gato's. Her picture of the bunnies. Browns with other browns, staying safe.

The apartment was shabby and sparsely furnished, but clean. Mohammed went to the fridge and took out the tagine. The chicken and vegetable stew was carefully arranged on a metal platter, but it was also a little burned. Khalid recited the names of the spices: ginger, turmeric, cumin, cinnamon, and saffron.

AFTERWARDS, MOHAMMED SERVED hot mint tea sweetened with sugar cubes.

"It tastes like liquid candy," she told them, and laughed.

Mohammed frowned, as if she had offended him. The two of them had hardly spoken during the meal. The language barrier made conversation awkward, despite their eager young translator.

But no, it wasn't about the tea. Mohammed turned to Khalid and barked something at him in Arabic.

Khalid's reaction made it clear what had been said. "You! Why are you still here?" The boy wiped his mouth with a napkin and then, without looking at either of them, got up and went out the door. They listened to him run down the hallway, down some stairs. They heard the front door open and slam shut.

It had never occurred to her when she accepted the boys' invitation that after dinner she would be told that she now had a debt to pay, that the younger boy would leave and the older one would shout at her to lie down. Everything had suddenly changed and she was no longer herself, no longer a person, but a dog, something to be ordered about and threatened.

She said "no" and also "sorry." She wasn't sure what this was. Rape was hate and violence. Not this lost, uncomprehending boy, confused by his own raging hormones, the sexual repression of his home mixed up in the sexual messages of this new country. He saw sex all around him and didn't know how to get it. This was a misunderstanding.

She apologized again and headed for the door. Her sense of what was going on skipped the next few moments, only revealed a knife pointed at her throat, a feeling of humiliation and fear, in that order, and of refusing to accept that this would happen to her. There was no way that he would penetrate her. She would not let that happen. She tried to wrest the knife from him. When he grabbed her hands, the blade tearing her skin, an idea came to her. She offered him an alternative, like a prostitute cutting a deal with a john.

Afterwards he seemed calm and spent, but there was still a shard of violence left in him, in his words. He told her in a quiet voice that he wanted to kill *himself* now. She remembered a word that she'd heard somewhere, on the TV news maybe, or in the stories she half-understood that her parents told about India and Pakistan, a word she knew would calm him down. She said, "Think of Allah."

He frowned and then shot her a suspicious look. He pointed the blade at his own throat again. She shook her head.

"You go home now," he said.

But he didn't mean that she was free yet. He would take her back to the hostel.

How gallant, she thought, his bitter taste still in her mouth, sick laughter bubbling up in her gut.

IT WAS DARK outside now. She wondered where Khalid had gone. Were they even really brothers? Mohammed had her sit in front of him on the bicycle seat. He gripped her wrists and held them in his own right hand; in the same hand he held a knife. It would not have been obvious to anyone on the street that she was a captive. There were different kinds of cold running up and down her skin. Fear hadn't completely left her yet, but on the other hand, she was no longer locked in that stuffy apartment, and the night's cold fresh breeze felt wonderful. *Happy birthday! You're alive!* His hand was tight on her wrists, and the knife cut into her skin. She jumped off the bike at the hostel and the sudden movement made the blade slash her hands more deeply. He yelled at her not to go to the police, and she shouted back in a friendly voice. "I won't! I promise!" She walked inside the hostel and up to the reception desk, and asked for the same private room she'd had the night before. The middle-aged woman behind the desk was British. She told Rani with bored, half-felt regret that she hadn't actually reserved a room for that night, that there were no private rooms left, that in fact, there were no beds left at all, not even in the men's and women's dorms. Then, as her eyes fell on Rani's right hand, which was badly cut and bleeding, her expression changed and she jumped out of her chair.

"What happened to you?" she asked, her voice rising as she came toward her.

Rani backed away, afraid the woman was about to kick her out, making her mind up even as she asked the question that Rani was *trouble*. And even if it were all right to say what had happened, would she be believed? The woman shocked her by roughly grabbing her arm and then again by quickly bandaging her hand with a towel that had been draped on her chair. She insisted on an answer to her question.

"I was attacked," she said.

"And you struggled."

She looked away. What was the right answer to that? Where else could she go now?

"It's all right," the woman said. "There's a bed in the office. You can sleep there."

Rani thanked her, went into the bathroom and washed her face with scalding hot water and pink liquid soap. She rinsed her mouth, almost vomiting as she spat into the sink. The British woman was waiting for her with a towel as she came out. She made Rani tell her story. As soon as she finished, she regretted it, saw no point, waited grimly for her to urge her to go to the police. To her surprise, the woman only agreed that there was no point, that she would never be believed, and that it was not worth the bother.

Rani lay on the narrow cot that night trying to stop the swirl of words in her head.

Nobody will believe you. You spendin' too much time in your head. You have to look at things. Not a good idea for a young woman to be travelling alone. Just walk around the streets, like a streetwalker? You are getting a bit old. You're going to get left on the shelf.

In a state between wakefulness and sleep she thought she saw a man hovering over her with a knife. She blinked herself awake. Safe again, and very lucky.

The backpacking trip would continue. No, not afraid, just more cautious.

AND THEN SHE met an Irish boy on a ferry between Brindisi and Piraeus. Rob was thin, pale and quiet. He didn't ask her where she was from, or where she was really from.

Instead:

"What happened to your hand?"

His voice was gentle, his concern real. She found herself suddenly opening, telling him the whole thing. She knew immediately that he would believe her, and wouldn't tell her off for being careless or naïve. There was something about him that was unguarded too, and which naturally invited candour.

"Does it hurt?"

Also, he did not seem to have a threatening bone in his body.

He reached out for her hand, unravelled the bandage. He took a plastic bottle of antiseptic lotion and some cotton balls from the outside pocket of his knapsack and busied himself with cleaning the wound.

"Well, this is nothing compared to what you just went through, but I got mugged this morning just before boarding."

"Really? By whom?"

"By whom? A couple of Italians. They didn't tell me their names."

"Oh, I mean—what did they take?"

"They took my sleeping bag."

"Why did they take your sleeping bag?"

"I don't know. Fancied it more than me, I suppose."

A sudden blush.

"Sorry, that was pretty idiotic—"

For some reason they were both laughing now.

"Did you reserve a berth?" Rani asked.

She knew it was unlikely. Backpackers slept outside on the deck. Because it was free, and, also, the freest thing you could do.

No, he planned to spend the night curled up on the deck without a sleeping bag, he said, and then his eyes widened as she insisted that he share hers. There was a lack of self-confidence that showed in his eyes and in his shy, grateful nod, which Rani understood as a need for love. A lack of confidence but an abundance of trust. And within this trust was the safety she had been searching for. So here, in the middle of the Mediterranean, is where it had been waiting. Love.

RANI FELT HER life was beginning to take shape, beginning with a new story in which she was part of a couple: two skinny stowaways, Rob and Rani, sharing a sleeping bag. Rob and Rani found a pair of scissors and cut each other's hair very short. They got sunstroke. They began to run out of money. They hardly ever ate anything at all. They drank the tap water in the WCs. Time was just one huge expanse of every shade of blue, the smell of salt, the shrieking of seagulls.

In August, Rob went home to Ireland, and brought Rani with him. They stayed with his parents, who were retired. He went out to work at a store during the day. She looked out the window of their red brick house at all the other red brick houses, just sat there and waited for him. It rained all day, and that was her excuse for never going outside. She wore a sweatshirt, jogging pants and wool socks and kept a blanket over her knees like an old person. She sat in the living room with his parents and watched Irish television shows, and then she helped his mother prepare the evening meal.

In late August, when Rani went home to finish university, she insisted that Rob follow her. She insisted that they get married so that they could live in the same country together. They would have children, at her insistence, to help pin them down further, to make the marriage stick, so that there was no time or space to escape, so that there were no unfilled cracks through which one could fall.

8. Partita: Deux coeurs et cinq rivières (Two Hearts and Five Rivers)

1945

SUNIL EXPLAINED to his math teacher that he'd missed the first week of classes because he hadn't been able to come up with his registration fees on time. The teacher suggested he study with Hima, one of only two girls in the class, and the top student.

As the two men discussed her, Hima picked her books up from her desk and headed out of the room without a word. She had a small face, and tiny, delicate features, but her expression was loud and frank with irritation. Sunil managed to catch her eye before she left and to look at her with similar frankness. She responded with a shrug, but also a slight nod. She had a soft, pillowy chest, slender arms, and strong hips and thighs that were outlined through her salwar kameez. Her long braid swung from side to side as she walked out the door. He found himself following her down the hall, drawn to the heavy chunk-chunk of her bangles, thick and gold.

Sunil thought of his sister Rani, whose bangles were thin, glass, clicking things. The name Hima, he mused, was short for Himalayas. He felt his courage dwindle. Hima turned at the door to her dorm room—a private one she shared with another female student—and asked him to hurry up.

After the tutoring, they talked. That is, *he* talked, mostly. Nevertheless, it was clear—no surprise here: her family had means. There were almost a million people in Lahore, but fate would have it that two of Sunil's brothers worked as assistants for Hima's father, a stationmaster. *Means.* He thought about the words his brothers used, what they meant. This father had sent his daughters to college so that they would marry well. Hima was the eldest. She was also the only one interested in pursuing her studies. One of her younger sisters was asthmatic; Hima used the word "sickly." The other was considered the beauty and had already been found a match, a confident, promising, if slightly dodgy young businessman. The family, he gleaned, was looking for a match for Hima to get her marriage out of the way.

BUT THEY WEREN'T looking very hard. Hima knew that someone like Sunil would never be considered a serious contender; it simply wouldn't occur to anyone. Though Sunil was self-confident, he wore the same clothes every day. He was gangly and pale, with straight, shiny black hair, large, almost bulging eyes, bushy eyebrows, long, thick eyelashes. There were dark, purplish circles under his eyes, and the area around his mouth was shadowed with stubborn, grainy traces of black stubble. His nose was large and hooked. He had a loud, deep voice and a habit of speaking too slowly, which made Hima impatient.

After a few weeks, her tutoring was no longer needed, but he would still appear next to her as she crossed the campus gardens, and they would walk together.

"What do you want?" she asked him. Part of her wished to intimidate him, push him away. But another part, one she was slightly ashamed of, was hoping he would be up to the challenge that she knew she represented. It wasn't just her beauty. It was everything: her self-assurance, her daunting name, her father's status, her tennis-playing brothers, the bright buzzing gardens that she seemed to carry with her, with their parrots and hummingbirds, mango groves and peelu trees, the skinny servants bowing as they walked backwards away from her. She knew he could see all these things.

Sunil had a rival, another young man on campus who greeted her every day and told others of his interest so that the rumours gradually filtered back to her. A dashing man, his family large Rajasthani landowners. There wasn't much to know about them, Hima reflected. At one point they had been princes. Of course, it would be so easy, she thought, to go on being a rich girl. The mathematician in her was dismayed by this idea. She wanted her life to be complicated and surprising.

Yet in the end, it was the simplicity of Sunil's approach that won her over. Everything he said was straightforward, though slow as syrup.

"I was wondering," he finally said to her in English, "if Madam would like to have lunch with me."

All the students spoke to each other in Hindustani mixed with some English. Sunil's English was less polished than hers and the other students'. His pronunciation seemed dirty and of lesser quality somehow, like the fabric of his kurta, and it marked him as poor. She knew, from his last name, that he was Hindu and of the same caste, Kshatriya. But it was clear that they lived different lives. She felt she could imagine his house, the sort she had seen while out driving with her father. Women with tiny figures and thin saris fetching water from the well and carrying it inside in pots on their heads. She doubted that Sunil had ever been to a restaurant, and wondered what this invitation was, exactly.

It turned out that what he meant by lunch was a picnic in a coconut grove. He so obviously lacked guile: he produced a large wicker basket filled with fruit, cashews and baked parathas filled with cauliflower and onions, wrapped in tea towels. He said he had made the parathas himself. The picnic basket seemed to symbolize the dogged earnestness of his pursuit.

The backs of their hands brushed together as they both reached for a piece of orange. Sunil withdrew his hand and motioned for her to take it.

"Go ahead," he urged. "*Meri rani.*" My princess.

This comment sparked something in her, some permission to be audacious. The awkwardness between them broke and they began wrestling each other for the contents of the basket, tugging food out of each other's hands.

Later, as they walked back through the forest, she allowed him a full fifteen minutes of surreptitious hand-holding. Darts of heat came from those fingers in hers, piercing through and spreading inside her, all over, head, heart, loins, everything throbbing. Words whisper-rang through her head: *surreptitious, shame, brazen.*

During the months that followed, they arranged to meet for walks so that they no longer had to agonize over whether they would run into each other. Soon there were kisses. It stopped there, but these kisses felt shockingly intimate to Hima, and they left a lingering, sharp heat that confused her and made her want more. They were breaking a myriad of taboos as they did this, as they fell in love.

1946

PROVINCIAL ELECTIONS HAD taken place in January. The Indian National Congress swept the non-Muslim seats, and the Muslim League won the great majority of the Muslim ones. The country was effectively divided, now made up of two antagonistic sides. One side wanted unity, and the other demanded a new state, Pakistan, where Muslims would not be dominated by Hindus. A political crisis was brewing, one Hima knew worried Sunil more than it did her. One day he told her that he would be going home for the weekend and didn't know if they would see each other again. He asked her a question with his eyes. She frowned and shook her head. As he left her room and she closed the door, she shook her head again. Then she wondered what his question had been.

Nothing happened that weekend. Sunil reappeared in class on Monday, a little sheepish. But he had awakened something in her that she couldn't turn off. She found herself glancing across the room at him during lectures.

A YEAR OF CLASSES, a mix of hopeful and threatening political speeches, and Sunil's increasingly insistent kisses. To Hima,

India seemed to be getting louder. It was expanding with self-awareness, but it was clear that there would be trouble too, and that afterwards it would shrink again. The sky was white, and it was too hot. There was shouting in the streets most of the time, and noise like thunder, but this was in the distance. Her father produced a submachine gun and had all of his children take turns drilling bullet holes into a section of the wall that surrounded their swimming pool. The higher wall around their house was topped with pieces of jagged glass, threaded with electric wires, but even that wasn't enough, Hima realized. Soon enough, they would have to leave Lahore for the new India.

SUNIL KNEW THAT Hima blamed the Muslims. She read the Hindu papers. Sunil read all the papers, listened to all the conversations that took place around him, tried to dig out the core of the truth, the things all parties agreed on. It was a habit he'd taken up, whenever his version of reality seemed to collide with that of the people around him. He could be sure of some things that had happened to his country, what the British had done, although they themselves had different words for *plunder*, *massacre*, *subjugation*, and *division*. All his countrymen seemed to agree on these points, yet the divisions were holding. Sunil understood his Muslim class-mates and their fear of what would happen if they found themselves under Hindus, people like himself; one day he'd joined a group as they sat around a radio on the college cam-pus, listening to the buzzing voice of Muhammad Ali Jinnah. He found it strange, looking around himself at that moment, that he was suddenly their only Hindu friend, that other Hindus could not see why Jinnah rejected Gandhi and Nehru's plan for a united, independent India, how they scoffed when Jinnah said it would put his people at a disadvantage. He didn't agree, exactly, but he could *see*. He was sure Gandhi could see this too. They had this in common, he felt, this helpless *seeing*. People weren't communicating properly. He tried to tell Hima, who loved mathematics, that it was about numbers; you could not blame the Muslims for their fear of being outnumbered and perhaps annihilated; but Hima's head, like so many others, was clouded, filled with her bias, the simplistic prejudices she got from listening only to one side. For her, the world was divided into neat, warring halves, the good, honest people on one side and the hateful, duplicitous thugs on the other.

THE NEWSPAPER HEADLINES shouted, and the radio too. Jinnah called for a Direct Action Day to take place, a huge mass rally and general strike. The Hindus said they would not close their shops on that day. Sunil knew that his people— even he had started to think in these terms—would always insist that their brand of nationalism was not separatist.

Sunil thought that both sides seemed to do everything possible to help the British prove to the world that India was backward, doomed to chaos. Although when he read the planned itinerary for the Direct Action Day in the Muslim *Star of India,* he was impressed with the care with which this *hartal* was organized. The notice cited divine inspiration from the Quran, emphasized the coincidence of Direct Action Day with the holy month of Ramzaan, and claimed that the upcoming protests were an allegory of the prophet's battle against heathenism and the subsequent conquest of Mecca. Sunil imagined explaining to Hima that he admired the elegance of these plans, their poetry and spiritual commitment. Yes, they wanted to break up his country, but they were not the mindless goons she and all his fellow Hindus said they were. And anyway—there was a lack of logic here too that made Sunil's head ache—why fight for a united country if you thought your brothers were all goons?

You believe they are goons because you stay barricaded inside your house, only aware of one side of the story! The version Hima would know: truckloads of Muslim men attacking the shops that had stayed open, with brickbats and bottles. Of course, if you listened to Muslims, the Hindus were lying in wait for those attending the rally, similarly armed.

THE RADIO REPORTED hundreds of people killed, thousands suddenly homeless. Words became fire, and the Bengali riots spread all the way west to Punjab. Sunil and Hima were both genuinely shocked that it could happen here, where there were so many Sikhs. It seemed so senseless, so random, that it was suddenly the Muslims against the Hindus *and* the Sikhs. Sunil shook his head. Former friends slashing each other, cutting each other into pieces. Unbelievable now, their province cut in half, Punjabis like them fleeing in either direction, to their respective sections of the province. No, not just *like* them. Suddenly they *were* them. Did Hima feel any of this? Or was she cut off from it all, the way rich people somehow still managed to be?

1947

WHEN CLASSES ENDED for the summer, the students had a choice: take their final exams in July and get them over with, or do them later in the new India. Hima chose to write them early. But Sunil said he wanted to be sure to have the best marks. He told her it had to do with his "destiny," and ignored her when she burst out laughing.

He returned to his village, Mandi Bahauddin, a hundred and twenty miles away—to study, but also to prepare to make the journey east to the new India. Hima wondered when they would see each other again. When people asked Hima why she seemed a thousand miles away, she would just nod, yes, a hundred and twenty might as well be a thousand. She felt numb, and nothing more, as she stood on her balcony, heard the sounds of bullets and screams, smelled smoke and saw flames in the distance. It was coming closer, but she knew her father would wrap them tightly, whisk them to safety. At home, she sat with her harmonium and played, singing along but without words, falling into a daring dream, imagining that the music made her desire audible to her lover, imagining he could hear her.

ALL AROUND SUNIL, people were arguing about what had led to this. Everyone agreed that the British had deliberately let them down by failing to intervene when the riots began. But beyond that, there was the disagreement and bad feelings that had led to the riots in the first place. Sunil walked by a mango juice stand where a group of people were having a loud conversation. They were describing how a gang of Hindus had started the riots, with a massacre of Bengali Muslims.

"My nephew was there," said a man with wild eyes. "The people had no chance. So surprised and defenceless. Those Hindu bastards ran after them, used whatever they could find to throw at them, bricks, glass bottles. And as soon as they managed to hit someone and make him fall to the ground, they ran over and stomped on him and tore his body apart. They behaved like packs of lions, those *kafirs*."

Sunil thought that what the men in the street were saying could be true. It also occurred to him that they might want to kill him, so he gave them a wide berth, retreating to the opposite side of the street as he walked along.

Yet when the riots started in his own neighbourhood in Mandi Bahauddin, it was his family's Muslim neighbours, the Hassans, who hid them for two days. A family of seven taking in a family of nine. Their hosts lay mats down on the floor for the children, gave Sunil's parents their bed, and lay down on the floor with the others. They thinned the yellow mung dal with water, made it feed sixteen people.

When twitchy, sharp-faced young men appeared at the door, scanning the faces in the apartment, the Hassans claimed the extra people were relatives.

"They're my wife's sister's family."

"They're visiting from Karachi."

"Don't worry. These aren't Hindus."

"Have a good night."

The father and the oldest son were the ones who spoke, and they both had teeth missing. They joked later that this must have distracted the rioters from the terror in their eyes. Sunil lay listening to the family's conversation, awed at how their fearful silence had slipped into hilarity.

But then at this same house two nights later, he was awakened by rioters banging on the doors, shouting "Allahu Akbar, we will not..." Sunil couldn't make out the rest. He opened his eyes and at first thought that he was alone. Then he distinguished the shapes of two members of the Hassan family. They nodded at the window. He crawled to it and then slid out, as silent and agile as a cat. As his feet dropped onto the ground, a short, skinny boy he didn't know beckoned to him, whispering that he was a friend of his brothers, naming them all when Sunil hesitated. Where *were* these brothers? Why had they left him behind? The next thing he knew, he was in a truck rattling down the road. The driver and the skinny boy left him in the next village and told him where to wait and get his next ride.

HE LEARNED FROM this driver, a man who knew his father, that his family was safe, that they had left earlier in the night and were driving somewhere ahead of them in the convoy. He said they had tried to wake him up but then decided it was too much trouble because he had been raving in his sleep. *Raving.* So maybe he had been talking in his sleep. Was this a reason to abandon a member of their family? And which of his brothers had convinced the others not to wait for him? Maybe there wasn't enough room in the truck. They had to leave one behind, so the dreaming laggard drew the short straw.

It was *all right* to be mad right now, the driver's sympathetic eyes were saying. It was clear he thought Sunil had seen something terrible. He told him he regretted very much that he had to pick up his own relatives in the next village and that there would be no room for Sunil.

"I am so sorry, son. Walk with the others. Only twenty, thirty miles left now."

AS SUNIL TRUDGED along he wondered when he would eat again. Would he end up going without food as long as Gandhi? He marvelled at how good water could taste; he'd been given some first by a Sikh man and then a Muslim woman.

A farmer driving by slowly in a truck full of goats beckoned to him to jump on.

Why were people being so kind to him in the midst of all this murder?

"Why me?" he asked the driver.

"Because you're alone," the driver shouted back.

Sunil thought of what Gandhi must be feeling now, how he had wished to keep the country together. Gandhi had walked too. He had rested in a Muslim house, a Hindu one, and then a Sikh one. Sunil had gone to see him speak once, dressed like him in a long white tunic and loose matching pants. Gandhi insisted on speaking Hindustani, saying this mix of Hindi and Urdu had to replace English as the national language.

"Have love for your own language," he said.

Sunil had looked into his eyes; he felt Gandhi hold his gaze for a long time, as if he recognized him.

Some people spread thorns and bones on the path Gandhi walked, because he was barefoot, practically naked, one arm around one girl, another arm on another girl. This style of his, and the way he spoke, could never appeal to Muslims, Sunil reflected. Nor to Hima, who listened to nasty rumours.

"Do you know what I've heard about your hero, your Gandhiji?" she had goaded him in English. "He beats his wife!"

Hima had strong opinions about everything, and they were often opposite to his. When she spoke in her careless, certain way, he became angry and also aroused, which shamed him and then angered him more, and the memory of this now intensified his longing to see her.

He wasn't worried about her. Her father's position, the family's wealth and status meant there was no need. She would be safe, on her way to the New India in a private railway carriage. He shook his head now as he recalled her saying that she thought Lord Mountbatten was charming and handsome. Sunil thought he was an arse, a film-star arse. He remembered a newsreel he had seen. With chaos spreading, Lord Mountbatten had been appointed to get Britain out. The ridiculous uniform, the pith helmet, the Rolex watch, the kind whose date changed automatically at midnight. Mountbatten never appeared alone, always with horses and trumpets. He went on tiger hunts.

As Sunil continued his quarrel with Hima in his head, dust and saliva collected on the roof of his mouth, behind his front teeth. He spat on the street, imagined her disdain, but continued to turn his observations into words, into arguments.

A SMELL OF burning wood and kerosene. From the truck Sunil saw families making slow progress on the side of the road with their belongings and their babies, such paper-thin bodies, grim, desperate faces, none speaking, as if they were too exhausted or consumed by fear. That heavy, acrid smell, the smoke in the distance, where houses like his own were burning. Suddenly, within view: corpses with staring eyes, splayed in the street. Sikh men unwrapping their turbans and covering their own faces with the cloth as they picked up bodies or added straw to the flames on makeshift pyres. Sunil looked away. A breeze lifted a layer of ashes from the ground and threw it against his face, burning his nostrils. He closed his eyes.

On the outskirts of Lahore, he spotted a couple of women about a hundred yards off the road selling water and lemons, asked the driver to wait, and jumped off the truck. As he was about to stuff the lemons in his pockets he felt something poke him in the back.

"Turn around."

He did as he was told, slowly, and the sharp poke in his back softly twisted and then withdrew. Had it been his imagination?

Two men, one middle-aged, the other young, with dirt-streaked faces and bloodstains on their white shirts. Likely hot and thirsty like him. He considered offering them water.

The sight of the rifle registered. He tried to push it out of his mind. It would not move. He finally connected it to the sensation he had just felt in his back. He found he could not say a word.

This is how he would die. With lemons in his hands.

"Looks like a Hindu," the younger one said.

"What's your name?" the older one demanded.

"Roshan," said Sunil. "Sunil Raj Roshan."

"Kill the kafir," the younger one said.

The older one gave Sunil a frank look of surprise. He put his hand on the younger one's arm. "No," he said. "He told the truth. Let him go."

Sunil stood staring at them, clutching his lemons. Like a rabbit, he stayed frozen until they barked at him again. Then he sprang off, kept running all the way back to the truck.

HIMA LIKED TO call her father by his title: Chief Engineer of the Northwest Railroad Service. He was temporarily reassigned to a new post, and now she called him "Officer, Sir." As Transfer Officer, he was in charge of getting his staff and their families to Delhi. His own family went first. They travelled to Delhi with their servants in a bogie, a luxurious, private train carriage. Hima found the journey enjoyable, a welcome distraction and relief from her confusing feelings for Sunil. She felt like a child again. She and her brothers and sisters had pillow fights, sang songs, played music together. To their delight, there was a tea cart with desserts in the little wagon, even a toilet with a washbasin. Heavy brown curtains covered the windows, but they peeked out from time to time and watched the monsoon rain beating against the panes; they imagined they were travelling through a waterfall. The rain had begun too late, after they'd stopped at the last station and received the wire about their house being set alight. *What is done is done.* When they'd left, they hadn't had the time to take all their belongings from the house but they did have their clothes, kitchen things, books and musical instruments. Hima wondered if she would remember the house, later, what memories she could keep now that their photograph albums had burned with it.

When they arrived in Delhi, they saw a group of Muslim women, their heads draped in grey fabric, boarding a train in the opposite direction.

IN THE SITTING room of her family's new home, Hima tried to read Nehru's speech, as reprinted in the *Times of India*, thinking that somewhere Sunil was reading it with the fervent enthusiasm and seriousness she never seemed to feel about these matters. She imagined him immersed in the text, herself somehow *outside*. Her mind wandered further; her head filled with Sunil's face, his lips and hands. Whenever this restless longing returned, she felt sick and ashamed at how her body seemed to burn. And the maddening, hot, moist festering. So unclean. She examined her harmonium and then put it back in its case. Afraid of what sounds might emerge if she began to play it now.

The next morning, after everyone else had gone out, Hima and her two sisters left the house together and walked the short distance to Connaught Place. They entered the office of the *Times of India* and stood in line with the other people who were there to place a free Missing Persons ad. It was a warm day in early September, and two ceiling fans whirred noisily above their heads. There were about thirty other people in line, most of whom looked completely distraught. An old man wore one chappal; his other foot was bare. A middle-aged woman in a thin white sari kept letting people ahead of her in line, as though she realized there was no hope. She spoke aloud every few minutes, to no one in particular, explained she'd already lost everyone.

Hima knew she and her sisters looked as if they didn't belong: teenage girls, their beauty in full bloom, in freshly pressed, floral-patterned salwar kameez. Flies buzzed around some of the people in the line, but left the sisters alone.

When it was Hima's turn, she recited the message she had finally decided on while standing in line: *Rani wants to know the whereabouts of her brother Sunil.* She knew that Sunil would understand that the ad could not have been placed by his sister.

Connaught Place consisted of off-white buildings of one to three storeys, stores, offices, and restaurants arranged in concentric circles. The girls walked in the middle of the wide street, ignoring the catcalls of the cyclists riding slowly in a group all around them. About half of the men in the group were Sikhs. Hima shivered, remembering stories of how their turbans had made them easy targets in Lahore, where they were thought to be on the Hindu side. She wondered why the Jains and Christians were exempt from the violence most of the time. The rules for killing people were random, mad, and useless. Here on the Hindu side, Pathans in the Indian Army were charged with shooting on sight anyone suspected of looting. She'd heard shots at night. Someone was not respecting the curfew, she told herself, and this is what happened if you broke the rules. She liked things to make sense, and this was why she preferred mathematics to history. They were safe now, always had been. Sunil and his family would not have it so easy.

She tried to feel more fear.

Her impatience to hear from Sunil was already driving her mad, although it had only been a few minutes since she had sent the message. The air smelled of smoke, but it was just the cow-dung patties that were always being burned by the poorest wretches to cook outside. She heard the voice of Miss Candace, her sixth-form teacher: *poor wretches.* It was not that stench she had smelled in Lahore, that she had connected to the stories of babies split in two, then roasted on a spit. A rickshaw driver slowed his horse and joined the chorus, calling to the girls. He called them *ranis*, princesses. The three sisters looked at each other and burst out laughing. They walked the rest of the way home arm in arm despite the heat of the day, leaning on each other giggling, covering their mouths with their pretty hands.

IN A CROWDED apartment a mile east of Connaught Place, Sunil's brothers were telling him what they would do about this rich girl he was obsessed with: spoil her and then blackmail her parents. They would not help him. If they did, they said, he would soon be asking them to help him buy jewels and gold-embroidered silks for this princess.

"She'll be one of these chiffon ladies, wanting saris with patterns like the ones in British bathrooms and kitchens. One of those idiotic rich girls, wanting idiotic things."

They spoke this way because they understood how hypersensitive he was, how easy it was to make him miserable. They delighted in tormenting him, found it hilarious to see him react to their words: "*Haye mere rabba*, oh my god. Such a weakling!"

Indeed, when Sunil called Hima *Rani*—which also happened to be his sister's name—it was to tease her about how she exuded wealth and privilege. He always enjoyed her reaction. It seemed to make her frisky.

The trouble was, he had spoken to her in his sleep. He had been exhausted, still recuperating from the journey to Delhi. He woke to find his brothers surrounding his bed, demanding to know what was going on between him and their sister. They chanted *Bahen Chod*. Sister-fucker.

They laughed when he told them the truth. But they knew Sunil had never had sex, which made the story incomprehensible to them.

By "spoil" they did not mean indulge her every wish: they meant deflower her and potentially ruin her chances of getting married. They laughed and used crude gestures to make the message clear. Without a word, Sunil made himself a cup of tea and went to sit outside on the curb. He sighed. How had he failed to realize that his family had no understanding of pure emotion, that they could be this self-interested, cynical and conniving? He thought of his older brothers' faces. Something about their sharp noses and jaws made them resemble the rats he had seen his whole life, sitting twitching or scurrying past him in markets, toilets, even in plain view on the steps of temples.

He heard someone whistling a tune. A car parked across the street moved away, and it was like a curtain parting to reveal the whistler: his youngest brother, Krishen, squatting on the ground as he replaced a chain on a girl's bicycle. He watched as his brother stopped whistling and working to compliment the girl on her strong calves. Krishen was sixteen, with the soft, feminine eyes and strong jaw of a movie star. It was rumoured that he had impregnated a girl back in their village. Days before they left, a woman had appeared at the door, screaming that she wanted Krishen out of the neighbourhood before the rumours spread to the man her daughter was engaged to. Sunil had watched, appalled, as Krishen had given her a sweet smile while his three other brothers yelled at her to get out. There was no money in that family.

He noticed a copy of the *Times of India* on the ground and picked it up. He blew on the top of his cup of tea and turned the pages slowly, past the news from the war trials in Europe, the opinion piece about the place of English in the new India, the obituaries, the full-page ad for Omega watches.

There was an ad for the contest he intended to enter, for the Commonwealth Scholarship. He remembered how Hima had laughed when he'd brought that up.

"You, out of how many million students, will win that, will you?" Hima had said. "And Canada? What is this nonsense?"

For most Indians, the dream was to study at the University of London. But Sunil told her that his heart was set on McGill University, in Montreal.

He said he loved snow, loved hiking with his brother Krishen every December up in Kashmir, though not because he particularly enjoyed hiking. He wasn't sporty. He just liked to be surrounded by this cold, wet, sugary stuff. Krishen was very enthusiastic about Sunil's dream. "Sunil Bahji, if you go settle there, you will send for me, won't you?"

He had watched her, waiting, confident there was interest there. He knew she understood what his eyes were saying. They could get married; it didn't matter what people thought. They could run away. He had been shy with triumph, watching this realization settle on her face.

He smiled now, remembering. He turned to the Missing Persons ads and quickly scanned the page, his body bracing for disappointment. His eyes alighted on his name.

Come find me.

HIMA WAS IN a wicker chair in the upstairs sitting room reading the newspaper when she felt the urge to play some music. She was itching to fill the quiet with anything, a raga, a popular song, a love song, why not? She was feeling bold and agitated.

Her younger brothers and sisters were lying about on cushions and on the yellow settee, reading and doing crossword puzzles. The overhead fan whirred above them, and a fly buzzed around the room in wide circles. She went over and sat on the floor behind her harmonium. Her younger brothers looked at each other and nodded. They moved toward the tabla and the sitar. Below them, in the kitchen, a servant began banging on the floor; he had started grinding spices and the sound reverberated through the house. Hima and her brothers waited, but when he stopped, another noise took over. Someone was knocking on the door. Hima heard her name being called. She got up and followed the sound of her name, passing a hand through her younger brothers' hair as she walked toward the stairs. Her bangles jangled as she moved.

From the landing above, she could see her parents at the door talking to someone.

She inhaled sharply. Her chest and belly ached. She didn't dare to believe it was him. Yet there he was, gaunter than ever, but clean-shaven and in pressed clothes. Her father led the way upstairs and the four of them stood on the balcony to the right of the sitting room. And here was another surprise: after they walked upstairs, her father gestured to his wife that they should be left alone to talk. Hima watched, open-mouthed, as her parents simply left them there on the balcony.

She marvelled at her father's leniency. Ah, of course it had to do with Sadhana's "marriage offer" from a rich businessman; they were getting nervous about being able to marry the older sister off so that that deal could go through. But they would expect Sunil to have job prospects.

As soon as they were alone, Sunil reached for her hand— and then broached this subject himself. He was confident; it was a simple matter. They just had to prove to her parents that they were ready to start a life together.

Of course, he said, he would train to be an engineer. Hima would begin her Master's degree in a few months and Sunil would have to enrol somewhere.

It meant it would be years before they could marry.

She had stood on this same balcony in the moonlight a few nights ago and seen a man being gunned down by two Pathan guards. A looter, a Muslim most likely. Some people were so greedy, they refused to pay for things. She would tell Sunil this story another time, she thought, and he would argue with her about what she had actually seen. She felt him staring at her now. She turned from looking at the street below, focused on his face. She let her hand drop out of his. Suddenly, all her feelings turned into their opposites.

What have I gotten myself into?

Sunil reached for both of her hands now, brought them to his mouth and kissed them. She took in his familiar smell, his straight shiny hair, his huge eyes and long lashes. He stared at her, and she stared back, but it felt to her as if she did this because it would have been awkward and impolite not to meet his eyes. What was wrong with her? She had missed how his eyes bore into hers. And now she felt the return of the slight annoyance he had always provoked in her when they were together. It was too much, this silly staring. Yet she didn't look away, and neither spoke. Hima scolded herself. *I did the right thing, and he is here. Why don't I feel safe?* This last thought startled her as it came.

1948

THE NEWS WAS A BLOW. Of course, it was to her as well. Gandhi was dead. Killed by a Hindu nationalist apparently upset that the Mahatma had expressed tolerance for his Muslim brothers. But what was this Sunil was telling her now?

"What do you mean, a personal threat against you?"

Sunil looked a bit embarrassed. He avoided the question, returned to his favourite subject: how narrowly his family had escaped. So amazing that they had come through all the carnage, had been able to flee by car—or on his case, by car and on foot—and avoid the horrific attacks on the trains. Not *reserved* trains. Hima caught his reproach: not like her father's. The other ones. Other people had not been so lucky. He began a familiar refrain, how he had not believed, until he saw the pictures in the newspapers, that this could happen. A train crammed with hopeful, smiling refugees, a dozen at the base and sides of the locomotive, hundreds riding the roofs of the wagons. Arriving silent, blood oozing from the undercarriage. More efficient than the Germans, their people proved to be, in their killing sprees. For they were all their people, Sunil insisted. That the country would actually fall for this, the imperial ruse of divide and rule!

"What a great nation we could have been. How much energy, money, and men lost on border skirmishes and fake political agendas. We all got along. Two extreme groups broke our country. What does that mean, that they succeeded?"

Hima sighed. Why could he not let this go? And what could she say, when Sunil started making speeches like this, as if there were a crowd listening to him? What was there to discuss? What was the point? She had seen the newspapers too. A million people killed in riots in only two months. Bodies lying in the streets, in open gutters. Vultures gathering on corrugated tin roofs, biding their time. When she looked at the photographs, she could almost smell the wood and kerosene—and death—of the cremations on makeshift pyres. But this was in the past, and not what they should be talking about now. It was not as if other countries were perfect. There had been mass murders everywhere.

"It makes me so sick, Hima. And this latest thing...It is telling me to leave."

"It is telling you—what?"

"It is not safe for people with my views to stay in this country."

But who is listening to you besides me?

"All right. You are set on going abroad. But what does this mean for us? Look, Sunil, do you still want to get married or what?"

These questions flowing from her mouth, despite all her misgivings. The urgency seemed to be coming from her body;

she was on fire again. How strange, how these shameful feelings came and went. And the shame about the shame. She felt she was going mad. She could not wait much longer, it seemed to her, to be married.

1949

IT WAS A SWEET, hot October day, all blue sky and soft white clouds. Hima took a break from working on her Master's thesis to drink a cup of tea in the gardens at St. Stephen's College. Suddenly, she spotted Sunil. A stirring breeze, a shift, and the clouds began rolling across the sky. She put down her cup and wondered if she had time to run back into the mathematics building. But no, he was waving to her now.

It embarrassed her when he came to see her here, his clothes in tatters, his bare, hairy legs in cheap chappals. He made the trek all the way from Roorkee, skipping his classes. The engineering college gave him a small stipend, and it seemed he spent it all on these trips to see her, rather than, say, a pair of shoes.

She was always careful not to hurt his feelings whenever she slipped a one-hundred-rupee note in his pocket. They both pretended that she wasn't actually doing this. She worried that her father knew that she was giving away the pocket money he gave her. He always seemed to know everything, had asked her if she was in love even before Partition, when she had just met Sunil and he had found her wandering dreamy-eyed in the orange grove inside the front gates of their property. When he'd asked her, she found she could not lie to him. At the time she said yes. Now she and Sunil had kissed so many times, she felt tainted. Not in love. Tainted. She tried not to think of the other boys in her class at this private college who were better dressed, less nervous and desperate. She knew they were interested in her. But she had been giving kisses and rupees to Sunil since she was seventeen. You make your bed, she heard her sixth-form teacher say.

"Hima," Sunil said, panting a little as he caught up with her. "My brothers have been to see your father."

"Ssh," Hima said, looking around. She patted his arm. "It's all right. I know. Don't worry."

Her brother Ashok had told her what Sunil's brothers had said. "He is a weakling, he'll not make a good husband. Don't let her marry him." But sibling rivalry struck her as more or less normal. In her own family, despite their wealth, it was survival of the fittest. Her mother had had twelve children but Hima had been the first in her family to live longer than ten years. The six siblings that followed her ranged from a bit round to a bit sickly. Would she have children someday? She forced her thoughts back to the man with the imploring eyes. With this fellow? She felt very far away from him, somehow.

"They are trying to ruin things for me," Sunil said.

"Ruin things for *you*? Isn't it more like they are trying to ruin things for *us*?" Hima said this because she felt she had to say something, but as soon as the words were out of her mouth, she realized her heart really was not in this anymore. She wondered if he noticed. No. There was something else, she saw now, that he was dying to tell her.

"We can get away," Sunil said, still panting a little. "Two of my professors have written very kind reference letters for my application. Everything is falling into place. We can go to Canada."

This Commonwealth Scholarship business again. All of Sunil's professors thought he was brilliant. But these leaps in logic! Ten Indian students would be chosen. The country's population had reached 390 million that year. He really did believe he was special. Yes, okay, he *was* special.

"I brought you some cashews," Sunil said.

Of course you did! Is that what you spend those rupees on?

"I know you like nuts," he said, as he took a crumpled bag out of his pocket and began pouring cashews into her hand.

"Yes," Hima said. She couldn't find any other words that she could actually say. She looked at her hand as it filled with cashews.

It was a hot day, and she wasn't very hungry.

She suggested they walk around the campus, as she always did. When they were moving around, there was less of a chance that other students would recognize her, and notice him.

1950

HIMA WAS READING a book on the steps outside her family's house, dressed in a deep yellow salwar kameez that matched her heavy gold bangles, and a rather dainty pair of brown leather shoes. Sunil wondered if he should have hailed a rickshaw on the way here from the train station. She wouldn't want to walk a mile and a half in those shoes. But as soon as she noticed him, she rose, turned and shouted something at a servant, and by the time she met him at the gate, a rickshaw was visible in the distance.

There was little space between them, and out of habit, he leaned over and tried to kiss her, but she pulled her chunni over her face, laughing.

In truth, he was quite nervous. Hima's father had given them his blessing to go forward, though he also said he "wasn't going to make a big splash of things," which his family had taken to mean that any dowry offered would be modest. Hima told Sunil she would be needing a ring, and he'd played along, saying of course he'd buy her one, agreeing to this little trip to the bazaar—but his brothers refused

to even lend him the money for such a gift. She would realize, at some point, that he couldn't afford to buy her
anything.

When they arrived, Sunil followed as Hima led the way
through the labyrinth of little shops and stands, the racks of
sarees, the tables piled with clocks and gramophone players,
the mounds of turmeric and vermilion. It was clear she knew
where the jewellery shops were; moreover, she knew the jeweller whom they were facing now, who had risen from a short
wooden stool to greet her.

A row of gems shimmered, like a strip of night sky.

"Which one do you like?" Hima said.

Sunil shrugged, helpless.

Hima picked up a ring and put it down. Then she picked
up another and slid it onto her fourth finger. She gave him a
questioning look and he shrugged again.

"This one," the jeweller answered for him. He began to
describe it, as if they were both blind. "This prong set here at
the centre holds a heart-shaped ruby. It is really very bold
and captivating. This V stripe here is lined with little glass
diamonds. The ring itself is silver, very shiny."

Sunil turned to Hima. He knew he was expected to keep
this conversation going.

"What are glass diamonds?" he said.

"They're fakes," Hima said. "But the ruby is real."

"It's very nice," Sunil said. He had no money, but he felt
happier knowing that Hima was not beyond settling for a
shabbier sort of ring.

"It *is* lovely. Nothing shabby about it," Hima said, as if reading his mind.

Then, a series of surprises: he heard her ask the jeweller the price of the ring, bargain him down, settle on a price— and, here, now, what was this, an envelope was being pressed into his hands?

Riding back to Hima's house, he picked her hand up off her lap and kissed it. She was more yielding now, let him kiss each finger, take his time. That they were in public seemed to bother her less, as if the ring was a reason to be less circumspect.

He asked her the question he'd been avoiding, about the envelope she'd passed to him in the market.

"It's part of the dowry," Hima said. "You can keep the change, and buy yourself a new kurta."

Sunil understood. The dowry would be given to Hima to manage. Hima's father did not trust Sunil's family. They probably seemed very nasty and poor to him. He didn't have to be told. That was fine with him. They *were* nasty and poor. To hell with his family. He was going to be royalty now. He had his princess; he was on his way to fulfilling his destiny.

1951

IT WAS TWILIGHT, weeks after Diwali, and there were tea lights on top of the wall around her parents' new house. Hima sat on a stool on the terraced roof in her beaded red-chiffon sari, lulled by the sounds of her two aunties' voices singing as they drew on her hands with henna. Life was going to be very different soon; this thought repeated itself like a mantra, and she felt shivers of excitement, trepidation, and also the sense that she had won something—the right to pick her own husband, silly as that sounded, even to herself. Suddenly there were male voices competing with her aunties, and the bright loud noise of percussion instruments and horns. Sunil's family had arrived. She smiled as she saw him arrive on a white horse, dressed in the new white khurta and pyjamas they had bought with her dowry money, a turban with a peacock feather and a curtain of beads in front of his face. Of course, she understood that tradition dictated that he was not supposed to have seen his bride before today. But what were they thinking, putting him on a horse and half-blinding him!

"Go on now," her aunts told her. "Go down to him. Time to get married."

She took her time, stepping carefully so as not to tread on the gold embroidered hem of her sari. She arrived in the courtyard as he disembarked from the horse. They were both given garlands of flowers and they placed these around each other's necks, smiling broadly now like children.

They were to be married right there in her parents' garden that cool evening in December. There were two hundred guests, half from Sunil's family. As Hima sat on the dais, her head covered by her veil, she listened to her father negotiate with the pundit to shorten the ceremony, to go easy on the mantras, have them walk around the fire four times rather than seven. Hima knew that her father was not religious but suspected something else was at play: he was not enthralled with Sunil, and especially not with his family, whom he put up in servants' quarters for the night; the servants themselves were sent to a hotel. As she sat waiting, she considered her dowry, which he had given to her directly, in cash—with which she'd bought her red-chiffon sari and gold jewellery and Sunil's new clothes—and in stocks: Tata Steel, associated cement shares, mining companies, the cheque and the certificates clearly in her name. Her sisters and brothers milled about, close enough that she could hear their conversation as she sat there in silence, waiting for the ceremony to begin. They were having a discussion, but it seemed they all agreed with each other; to Hima it seemed she was listening to one voice, rather than six.

"When you have a Western marriage like Hima and Sunil, you are basically crazy in love, on top of the world, and you have nowhere to go in your life but down, because that's what happens as reality sets in. With our traditions, there is no romance until afterwards, as you learn to find things to love about each other. The work pays off in the end. And who knows us best, after all? Our parents, of course."

Her feelings, as she listened, kept shifting between rebellious joy and irritation. And always, beneath everything: the clawing. Fear.

When the ceremony finally began, time seemed to speed up; it seemed to end only seconds later. After they had tossed their herbs in the fire, chanted Sanskrit words they didn't understand and once more placed garlands around each other's necks, Hima thought mischievously of kissing Sunil's lips, right in front of everyone. You want a Western wedding? You can have one. But as she brought her face close to her bridegroom's her siblings suddenly mounted the dais, nudging them apart and aside as they began clearing a space for their instruments. The religious hocus pocus over with, the entertainment would now begin. The guests applauded in anticipation. Hima and Sunil took the hint; Sunil took her hand and helped her down.

1952

HIMA SIPPED HER mango lassi as she walked around the kitchen with her watering can. The ceiling fan made the plants' leaves dance about. So much beauty. Such joy. She and Sunil were both relaxed from their lovemaking that morning, but Sunil was never *completely* relaxed; he was itching to go outside. The apartment here in Delhi was much larger than the one he'd had as an intern at Bhakra Dam, but he claimed it felt stuffy to him. Open space was what he craved now, he was saying, even if it was just a little walk in the courtyard.

She'd asked him to fix a link in her pearl necklace, but he confessed he didn't know how to use a pair of pliers. He sat there with the pliers sitting on his nose, saying "Ow!" from time to time. Goof. She told him it was all right—she didn't know how to cook—and they laughed. They had known each other seven years but living together still brought plenty of surprises, as if their marriage had been normal: arranged, between strangers.

"Come on, don't be a sloth. Let's go out for a walk."

"A sloth! Sunil, I have all these plants to water, and the monsoon is coming."

"What kind of sentence is that? Why would you water the plants if a monsoon was coming?"

"It's going to rain inside, is it Sunil?"

"On the radio they were talking about next month. The rains are coming in June, Hima. Not this morning."

"Are they?"

"Yes." Sunil said.

Hima could see that Sunil was pleased to be right. He was usually the absent-minded one, getting such things wrong.

"Can't you understand Hindi radio programs properly?" he said. "Or does the princess only understand the Queen's English?"

She laughed and swatted him with a tea towel. He grabbed her around the waist and pulled her to him. This freedom with each other's bodies still felt new and exhilarating. She could barely believe it. So little shyness, and almost no shame.

Yes, it was still only May. Of course, Sunil was right about the rains. What was happening to her memory?

"I've been feeling so absent-minded. I'm turning into you."

"Ah, you must be pregnant."

They both beamed, proud this was a possibility. They were waiting for the test results. Eleven more days, and they'd know.

"I want a boy," Hima said. "I want to have the first son, before my sister."

"Then let's make one," Sunil said. "One with your wavy hair, my eyes. Not your slothfulness."

"Not your nose, please, God," Hima said. "Anyway, I thought you said you are sure I'm pregnant."

"Okay, let's make another one."

"I thought you wanted to go outside."

"Ah, you are clever. Your brain is waking up. That is why I married you, for your brains."

SUNIL STOOD ALONE with a cup of tea and observed the dam that stretched across the 1700-foot canyon on the Sutlej River. The promise was great, the promise of the greatness of the new India, a new giant structure that would prevent floods and carry water and electricity to the fertile fields of Punjab. But what if, instead, the massive water pressure broke the dam, and instead of suppressing floods brought devastation? What if someone on the team were to err in their calculations of internal erosion?

His professors would not like to hear of these thoughts. But he couldn't stop them. A crack opening up in the dam. A rift could become a canyon. A local surface depression, an unstoppable burst of water, a roar like thunder, the force of a ruptured dam uprooting trees, obliterating villages.

If he shared his fears, he would be told he was irrational. But what was rational about this country?

Back in his office he worked for hours on the sketched flow nets, estimating the rate of seepage, the rate of water flowing through the soil.

At sunset he reread his notes.

No water had been observed before this year's monsoon, but since then water levels had risen with the upstream and downstream levels. The installation of cross-arms was continuing. How much pressure could the dam hold without cracking? If there was a crack, how to fix it? Was there any back-up, if it rained again? They'd asked him if it could be possible to go with cheaper material! Damned country. Destructive forces able to wreak havoc if you underestimated their strength. Water, so powerful, destructive, and elusive, always found a way through.

"Talking to yourself, mate?"

Cheeky fellow.

"What is it?"

"A letter," the young Brit said, handing it over.

From the Commonwealth Scholarships Committee. Sunil tore open the envelope, read the first line and quickly sat down as an earthquake passed through his heart.

He had passed the first round.

"And you had a phone call from your wife. The message is 'Confirmed. Expecting, due November.'"

Sunil found he could not speak; nor could he pull his gaze away from the letter. He so wanted to go on to the next round. His father-in-law's disapproving face intruded on his thoughts. Hima's father wanted him to stay here where he could keep an eye on him. Why did he want to keep an eye on him? Sunil's heart sank as he realized that his father-in-law would never support his going on to the next round of the contest now that Hima's pregnancy had been confirmed. Well, he would have to keep quiet about it, then.

"Congratulations, mate!"

Sunil finally folded the letter and looked up, into the light blue eyes of the chief engineer's son. He would have to get used to eerie eyes like these, if he did get through the next round and end up sailing across the world. But hold on, why did the young Brit offer congratulations? What did he know?

"IT SEEMS INCREDIBLE that we'll be parents in less than a month," Hima said. They were in their Delhi apartment, packing a bag for a visit to her own parents' house in Lucknow.

Sunil handed her the tiny sweater and pair of booties she'd knit.

"You might end up having the baby while you're there," he said.

"Yes, who knows?" said Hima, tucking the clothes in a corner of her suitcase. She had gained twenty-five pounds and felt swollen and achy, but not quite ready to give birth. She looked around the apartment. The space they had for the baby's things here was only about eight foot square, and presently contained a few mismatched chairs and a filing cabinet.

Sunil's brow was furrowed.

"Don't worry," Hima said. "He'll come out when he's ready."

Sunil gave her a faint smile.

"I CANNOT TELL YOU where the postmaster lives. And with respect, sir, even if I did, do you think he is just going to open the door to you?"

The rickshaw driver seemed to enjoy the sound of his own voice. Repeating himself over and over again as he drove around the same square mile in the city of Agra, Sunil's fare increasing by the minute. It suddenly came to Sunil, how to unlock this particular door. He leaned forward and slipped the man a wad of bills.

"Very good, sir," the driver said, and finally shut up before turning the corner into a leafy neighbourhood.

As he helped Sunil unload his suitcase, he called to the gardener, whom he seemed to know. The gardener went inside and a few minutes later, a tall grizzled man came and stood on the verandah, shielding his eyes from the sun.

"Please sir," said Sunil, standing on the pavement between his suitcases. "There is something waiting for me at the post office, and I need to pick it up today."

"Someone will be there tomorrow," the man said in a dry, sensible voice. But he lingered, his curiosity obviously piqued.

"Of course, sir. But I need it today. It's my passport. I've managed to get a train ticket to Bombay today, and a boarding pass on a ship that is leaving for Canada on Tuesday. But these things are useless unless I have my passport."

"Canada? What is in Canada?"

"My life, sir. My life is waiting for me in Canada."

He felt the postmaster examine him. His thinness, his simple, sweat-stained clothing, his suitcases. He knew the man could see his desperation. Could he also see his brilliance, his potential for greatness?

"I have one chance, sir. Please help me. I am quite sure that someday you will understand that you have done a great thing."

IT COULDN'T BE right, what her father was saying to her. Sunil would never leave for Canada without saying goodbye. Surely he was still at work on the Bhakra Dam, he would not throw that chance away. He'd gotten the internship through a friend of her father's. After he completed the training, a good career in India was assured.

He had said he would go ahead to the next round, but no, of course he wouldn't leave her. She hadn't really believed he'd win. The odds were against this.

But he'd succeeded, against these odds—ten winners in all of India.

Still, he'd told her he agreed with her father, that he would not accept the offer, not go abroad, no, of course he would stay here. But her father was saying he had changed his mind, and decided to accept the scholarship. He'd boarded the ship.

But how could this be when her father had assured her that Sunil would do the right thing, stay with her, stay in India, where his prospects were more certain, where her father's connections would always result in good, stable employment?

"He doesn't even have his passport!" she said.

"He went to the post office and picked it up two days ago, before he boarded the train for Bombay."

"But that was a Sunday!" Hima said. She would not believe this.

"Hima, what do you want me to tell you? He convinced them to open."

He *could* be very convincing. But this couldn't be right, she heard herself screaming, he would not do this to her, he would not just sneak away, not now, when she was eight months pregnant! She felt cramps in her abdomen as it seemed to harden and grow as heavy as stone. She threw her arms around her father, leaned into him as the pains grew sharper.

"Make him come back, oh please make him come back!"

DISQUE 2

Face C

1. Shakti: Sonate en quatre mouvements (Sonata in Four Movements)

i. Se retrouver (Finding Yourself/Meeting Again)

1995
September

RANI WAS ON the phone with Ginette, a college admissions officer, when an argument outside her door began to drown out the conversation. She excused herself, asked Ginette to hold for a second.

"It's a myth," a young woman was insisting. "It's a story we tell ourselves because—"

"The fact is," a male voice interrupted her, "African slaves risked their lives to escape to Canada."

"Yeah, okay, that part's true, but..."

Rani got up to close the door, and the young woman quickly apologized for disturbing her. Then she turned back to the young man and told him to let her finish her sentence. There was something impressive in the girl's insistence on getting her message across. Instead of closing the door, Rani waited, curious to hear what was coming next.

"The British didn't outlaw slavery out of the *goodness of their hearts*! They needed soldiers to fight against the Americans. There was a war going on!"

"Oh, come on, I've never heard that."

"You have to *read*," the girl said. "And so, yeah, anyway, what better people to fight the Americans than angry ex-slaves?"

Rani closed the door. She finished her phone conversation, and then found herself wondering about this girl who seemed so passionate and intelligent. It was the lazier, unexceptional students she tended to meet in her job.

THE SAME TWO STUDENTS beside her, walking down the hallway, as she made her way to a meeting. The boy racing ahead of the girl. They looked like brother and sister; both had the same medium-brown complexion, with thick, black hair. The girl's hair was very long. Her features more East Asian, Rani decided. She was walking quickly to catch up to the boy, a bent soft drink can in her hand.

"I can't believe you drink this stuff. Coke: the drink of imperialism. And you just throw your can on the ground like that. What a douchebag."

"Yeah right," said the boy, laughing. "I threw it in the dumpster outside. What are you doing crawling around in the dumpster? What the fuck is wrong with you?"

"You missed!"

"I did not miss. Get the fuck away from me!"

Rani watched as the boy trotted down the hall, and the girl, after swearing under her breath for a few seconds, ran after him. As she caught up to him it seemed to Rani that she had misinterpreted the situation, that they had just been messing around, joking. The boy took the can from the girl's hands and put his arm around her waist.

IT WAS JUST ONE narrow three-storey building, this college campus, without gym facilities, and from the outside it resembled an old-fashioned hotel more than any kind of school. All the classrooms and offices were much smaller than what you would normally find in a college. Her own office was cramped, but she liked it, found it cozy. The other unusual thing was that it was an English-language college on the east—French—side of boulevard Saint-Laurent. Many of the students spoke a third language at home, which endeared them to Rani. She looked out her office window at the Québec flags and *Oui* signs across the street. The same ones that had been around when she herself had been a cégep student. Some of her colleagues probably hated the sight of them. Not Ginette, probably. But all the Anglo ones.

To Rani, it made sense to break away from Canada, to resist the encroachment of English—the language of imperialism. She thought of her dad, quoting Gandhi. Something they'd agree on, she supposed. Ginette had once said to Rani, à propos of nothing, "You must be Indian. You have something of the Mahatma in your eyes." Rani rushed to explain that she had been born right here, and then thought, well, the remark was a little silly, qualified as a kind of prejudice, but it wasn't *hateful*. She wondered if, for Ginette, Mahatma Gandhi was a hero.

Rani suspected that she herself was a bit prejudiced against les *Anglais*. She wondered again about the girl in the hallway. She and her friend had looked, what—Asian, or, no, maybe Latino. First Nations? There was a flavour of another language, maybe just French, on the tips of the girl's *t*'s.

RANI PUT HER bag down as the kids ran to her, hugging her around the waist. Kira was screaming something, but the sound was muffled because she was screaming into her stomach. Rani gently took Kira by the shoulders and stepped back, looking down into her face.

"What?"

"It's my day to pick what we'll have for dinner."

"But Mama," said Rita, "She wants macaroni and cheese with grapes!"

"Why not?" said Rani. She was tired.

"That's what Daddy said," said Kira.

"You're all crazy!" Rita said, and ran off, stomping her feet.

Rani picked Kira up and walked into the kitchen. Kira jumped out of her arms and began spinning in circles in the hallway. She was wearing a purple bathing suit and bunny slippers.

"How was work?" said Rob.

"Boring," said Rani. "What's an e-mail address?"

"You know, like 'Rob at AOL dot-C-A.'"

"What?"

"Why? Why are you asking?"

"Oh, someone at the meeting said we all have to get one."

"We have them up at the hospital," Rob said, handing her a cheese grater. "It's so you can write a message to someone instead of ringing them."

"Why would you do that?"

"I don't know. What else did you talk about?"

"Oh, it never has that much to do with me. I was sitting next to the French teachers, and they were all whispering about the referendum."

"Not long now."

"Yeah, the French teachers are like, This is our chance, to have a new, free country where our language can finally thrive. Meanwhile, all the English teachers are freaked out at the idea of becoming a minority."

"It's like that at the hospital too," Rob said. "I don't get involved."

Rani knew the subject meant little to him; he was not even a Canadian citizen. When he drank a bit, he would sometimes talk about going back to Ireland. There was no reason not to. The economy was picking up there. But they had jobs here, Rani would remind him, and their rent was cheap.

She didn't talk about her attachment to Québec, even made her voice sound slightly sarcastic when she quoted her Francophone colleagues. It wasn't something she could understand herself, let alone explain to him. *Un jour.* Someday Québec would be recognized as the special place it was. She felt a sentimental thrill as she gave her imagination free rein. That day would be bathed in golden light. She suddenly thought of the fresh mornings she often jogged through, the exhilarating feeling of escaping her family as they slept. On one horizon a full moon lingered, and on the other the sun was pushing its way up.

AFTER PUTTING THE KIDS to bed that evening, Rani and Rob decided to tackle the huge pile of newspapers and magazines that was growing in their storeroom. But half an hour later, they were sitting on the floor, reading. Rani wasn't surprised. They were both too tired to do any serious sorting out. Maybe when the kids were a bit older. This was really just an excuse to catch up on old news. Rob read aloud headlines from the end of June, just before Canada Day, which was really moving day in Québec—that summer there had been seven vans double-parked on their block alone. They had all three newspapers from that weekend. *Le Devoir* and *La Presse* had ignored the official holiday and instead featured articles about rentals and real estate. The English newspaper, the *Montreal Gazette*, meanwhile expounded on "What It Means to Be Canadian."

"What *is* this question?" Rob said.

Rani seconded his scoffing with a little murmur. She imagined what Jean-Claude, one of the teachers at work, might have to say about July first. "If the United States annexed English Canada, would you be celebrating the Fourth of July?"

"You know what I think is overrated?" Rob said.

"What?"

"Immigration."

Rani wondered if he could see her back go up. Where was this Irishman going with this?

"It's a terrible idea," he said.

"Okay…?"

"You spend your childhood and teenage years learning how to live in your environment, and then you upsticks yourself out of that place, go to another place where you have to learn all these new rules, when your prime learning years are over…"

"Oh. *That's* what you mean. Is that immigration or emigration?"

Rob frowned and rolled his arms as he thought about this. Rani knew that his work as an anesthesiologist meant he spent his days bent over childrens' bodies with needles. The arm-rolling was to relax the tension in his body. It also served to mimic flying.

"I think emigration is flying away. Immigration is flying in and landing."

"And how has that been for you?"

They rarely talked about Rob's culture shock. He'd had to get used to the money, which he found too light and flimsy, and also to kissing women on the cheeks. When he first arrived and they encountered a female bus driver, he had turned to Rani and asked, "Do I have to kiss her as well?" He would probably continue to speak the same little bit of French he'd learned for the rest of his life, maybe with a new Québécois expression or two thrown in the mix.

Rob's furrowed brow resembled little Kira's when she struggled to express something after wandering into a conversation that was over her head.

"It's not as easy as you might think. But I can't explain it."

"Are you unhappy?"

"No. Just always a wee bit uncomfortable. Like I'm sitting in a plane and can't adjust the seat properly."

"In a plane."

"Yeah, a plane."

"So you're going somewhere."

"I don't know. No."

"A plane. That's pretty cramped. Are you feeling…crowded?"

"Never mind," Rob said, shaking his head. "Obviously it's not a big deal. It's not the biggest culture shock. Everyone here seems to think they're Irish."

Rani knew he was thinking of St. Patrick's Day, of all the drunken proclamations of Irish ancestry he had heard in various pubs on Stanley and Crescent Streets.

"Well, all the *white* people do," said Rani.

She knew she wasn't making him feel more comfortable, but *he* was making her feel something even more frustrating, something she could not articulate. What exactly had he had to get used to? She thought of her parents, how lonely and bewildered they must have been when they arrived. Their Indian accents, unlike Rob's Irish one, indicated that they spoke more than one language, and yet Rob's accent increased his social status while theirs marked them as less competent. And on top of everything else, they had never been accepted as Canadian, not even by their own children, she thought with regret. Not that their own children could ever feel Canadian. *Where are you from? No, I mean, really. Where are you really from?* She thought of the time she and Rob crossed the border into the United States and how, while she was being grilled about her life and her ancestry, he'd sat there in the passenger seat, holding his Irish passport in his lap, waiting to be asked a question. When the American customs officer was finished with Rani he just looked over at Rob, nodded and gave him a little wave. Rob had cleared his throat and said, "Hello." Well, at least he knew to be embarrassed.

"I've never been comfortable, in the way you mean," Rani finally said to her husband. "But I think there are worse things."

ii. Enfants sans nom (Nameless Children)

THIS TIME, if the guidance counsellor asked Mélanie about her childhood, she knew what she'd say; it came to her suddenly: she'd been angry most of the time. The most vivid pictures her brain kept from the past were of herself outside a room, looking in, completely livid.

Would it be exactly the same questions again, the ones they'd asked at the two French-language cégeps? Two years ago, and then again, almost a year later, before finally ending up here. Starting and quitting school for three years now.

She hated this, but she was resigned. She'd have to talk to the guidance counsellor if she wanted to get back the student fees she'd already paid for the fall session. She figured she was an expert on how this worked: she'd have to defend her decision, which meant she'd have to talk about herself. It was almost impossible to do this while depressed, and it wasn't going to be much easier in her current state of agitation.

The name-plaque on the office door read "Ms. Rani Roshan." Mélanie rehearsed what she would have to say in order to get her course refund. Why did she always have to explain and justify every fucking thing? "I have to get away," is all she really wanted to say. She hoped it wouldn't take too long.

THIS WAS THE GIRL who had been arguing with her boyfriend in the hallway. Rani felt stunned as she said her name. As this was an *Asian* Mélanie Giglio, there could be no doubt who she was. But why would Serge Giglio send his daughter to an English cégep?

This taller, womanly version of the little girl she had met years ago blurted out that her marks looked like they were going to be pretty high. But she wanted to withdraw.

"Oh!" Rani said.

So much to process. She told herself to remain professional. After a pause, she asked, "How high?"

"They're always in the nineties," Mélanie said with a slight shrug, as if this were something she had no control over, like her body temperature.

Students didn't usually drop by like this. Normally the college administrators flagged the ones whose attendance was dropping, or who were failing, and insisted they meet with her. These were the students who were normally in danger of dropping out. Despite her job description as a kind of career counsellor, Rani's main job was keeping kids in school.

"You know," Rani said, clearing her throat as she recovered from her surprise, "You could get any number of scholarships with those marks. I'm going to give you some materials to read, and ask you to come back when you're sure you've considered all your options."

Mélanie explained that she had gaps in her school records because she had taken some time off; she hadn't come here straight from high school. She wasn't going to get a scholarship.

She asked for a course withdrawal form. Rani stared at her for a moment. Then she rummaged around in her desk, and announced that she seemed to be out of forms, that she would have some tomorrow. Mélanie seemed to be about to say something, and Rani interrupted her.

"You'll get your refund, if that's what you're worried about."

"Fine," she said. "I'll come by tomorrow." And she left.

Of course she took some time off, Rani thought. *She's an artist. Like her father.* She remembered Serge's face, contorted with emotion as he sang. Mélanie's expressive drawings covering El Gato's wall. Back then Rani had occasionally taken one home and put it on her fridge, thrilled to possess something with a connection to the lead singer of Sensibilité. She tried to remember the drawings now. She wondered if Mélanie's artwork had shown promise, if it had been in any way more complicated or compelling than the cheerfully chaotic pictures her own little daughters produced these days.

ANOTHER FIGHT WITH Pepe. A wave of nausea, the sick feeling of all their arguments. They always felt so one-sided, which made her feel even lonelier than before she met him. Nothing affected him, not even her raw anger. This most recent fight was about China's one-child policy. When he'd said she shouldn't take it *personally*, that was the last straw.

Only her first boyfriend. But impossible to imagine others. A waste of time. Maybe she would miss having sex with him. She would. She'd be back, and he knew it. In the beginning, it was different; he'd been the one who was so pushy about sex. All the time she'd wasted waiting at the medical clinic! Having to tell the doctor she was a virgin, having to justify her birth-control choices, being examined, splayed out like a turtle on its back, poked and prodded and made to bleed. She still felt raw from it all, from everything. One of the irritating things about Pepe was his own cavalier attitude about these details. Maybe all boys were like that. They didn't have to worry about the consequences. *What consequences?* he'd argued sleepily. *You'd just abort it.* There was a connection here, between this and all the other things that made her mad. She felt afflicted with something between a twitch and a mad itch.

What if she *had* gotten pregnant and *hadn't* aborted "it"? Who would this child have been? Pepe knew exactly what village his parents and grandparents had been from in Mexico, and he spoke Spanish as well as if he'd grown up there. All his friends, from Mexico, Guatemala, El Salvador, and Honduras, the pride they all had in their respective origins, and their language, the way they only sometimes remembered to stop and translate for her.

People occasionally said she and Pepe looked like brother and sister, despite what *he* called her—*ojos chinos*. It sounded less harsh in Spanish. Pepe laughing, telling her how when people talked about getting high, they said they got *ojos de chinos*. Everything was a big joke for Pepe, and occasionally it comforted her, calmed her down. But no, he was like everyone else; he just didn't get her.

Mélanie had been told many things about herself by complete strangers, teachers, even Pepe's parents. That she must have been one of the first little girls adopted from China; that she would normally have been aborted or killed in infancy. If she seemed taciturn, uninterested in dairy products, good at school, well, that is what Chinese people were like. This despite the fact that she always gave the same truthful, if mechanical, answer about having been adopted from Vietnam when asked *what kind of Asian* she was.

Just because people asked questions didn't mean they were necessarily curious. Some people just liked to hear themselves ask questions.

In an Introduction to Anthropology class, Mélanie had learned that she did not have slightly slanted eyes, but small epicanthic folds. That the facts of her parentage could not make her a "half" anything, as the concept of human races was a fallacy. But she was ready to quit her studies, because it didn't make any difference if she knew things. It would always be the other people, the ones who never read, who were the problem.

MÉLANIE UNLOCKED the front door and switched on the hall-way lights. No Serge, but he had left behind his smell of stale cigarettes. She tried to remember the last time she had seen him. He could be in California, or out on a bender, or even with her mother, maybe in a motel room. Mélanie wondered about them but was pretty sure they didn't wonder about her. She didn't owe them anything.

When her dad was home, it was hard to get a decent night's sleep because he'd be jamming with other old people until eight in the morning. When she came downstairs and began preparing coffee, they would just be winding down, their instruments taking up the whole living room.

One day, Marc, an ex-bandmate of Serge's, asked Serge to introduce him to his latest conquest. Serge must have told him in a soft whisper who she was. Marc laughed and said he remembered now, added something about baby broccoli actually belonging to the cauliflower family. Did she imagine it, or did her father laugh at that? Enraged, she'd stormed out, slamming the door as she left. There was a kind of residual rage from that afternoon that still burned inside her, a hot ache in the hollow beneath her ribs.

When she said *my mother, my father* now, the words felt like masks that didn't fit her parents' faces anymore. She was so sick of pretending that they did, that nothing was wrong, how marvellous, the emperor's new clothes.

It was all such bullshit. She remembered her father pointing out a Québec government slogan to her; it was on a sign on the side of a bus, a picture of a little brown boy, somehow not *too* brown, smiling, the words across his curls that her father read to her: *La peau basanée, le coeur québécois.*

Yeah, right.

Some of her father's friends played music they called "traditionnelle," which harkened back to where they really hoped to go, a white, French, past. They sang about being colonized by the British as if the fur hats they wore in their videos were not obvious symbols of their own colonialist history.

The way her parents' eyes slid away when she asked about her own past made her feel like the loneliest person in the world.

At the library she spent hours searching for names of agencies and orphanages, hours searching and finding exactly nothing. In the process, she kept getting waylaid by articles about the war—the one the Vietnamese, she read, called the "American War." The more she learned, the more incensed she became. She asked herself the questions that she often used to torture herself: Had her real mother been raped by an American soldier? Was it the lightness of Mélanie's eyes and the texture of her hair that had made her unlovable—had she reminded her mother of her attacker?

How did her real name, Thuy Thi Diep, sound in her real mother's voice? Her mother had given her a name, a name Mélanie did not even know how to pronounce.

IT'S ALL SHIT. *Everything. All shit.* She filled a white plastic ice tray with water and slid it into the freezer. She took out another tray. The ice wasn't completely formed. Only a few minutes had passed since she'd replaced the water when she'd poured her last drink. She impatiently shook out these half-formed cubes into a jug of vodka and orange juice, shouting a slurred "all shit, all shit," splashing juice on the floor as the cubes plopped into the jug.

Through the fog in her head, a dim awareness of night falling. Her own voice, still muttering to herself. The door clicking open. Serge pausing in the hallway before approaching her. His trepidation as he stood behind her. Her fingers yielding as he gently peeled them off her glass.

She began to swear a little louder.

Serge sat on the floor at her feet and motioned to her to go on.

When she had run out of these words, she looked down at him, pointed into his face and said, "You have an alcohol problem."

"Yeah, probably."

"No, I mean, there is too much alcohol in your house. It was way too easy for me to get this drunk, *hostie*."

"Yeah. I don't know. I try not to drink at home. I mostly go out..."

"You go out and leave me alone with all this alcohol in the house."

"I'm so sor—"

"I'm so lucky," Mélanie said.

His frown said, "I don't follow you." They sat in silence.

"Something bothering you?" he said.

It came to her, what she needed to say.

"I'm so lucky they rescued me, and all the little babies!"

She heard how clear she sounded now.

She caught the expression on his face. He hadn't seen this coming.

"What are you saying?"

"You want to know what is bothering me? Do you even know how I came to be here?"

He looked at her blankly, so she went on. As she explained, she enjoyed the anger and energy in her own voice.

"So noble! 'Rescuing' little babies from the country they helped to tear apart. When Saigon fell, they fled—but oh first, look, the great rescue! Taking babies from orphanages that never actually were attacked by the North Vietnamese, that never actually were under threat. Oh, how lucky I was to be a pawn in a bloody propaganda war.

"You know what they called us? *Children of the dust!* We were pawns, just like all the Vietnamese! Our lives, who we were, meant shit in that war. They weren't there to help us. And here I am on the fucking other side of the world, in this freezing-cold country, with you, no idea who I am. How lucky! Lucky me!"

Serge seemed too shocked to speak. She watched him as he got up, filled a glass with water and put it into her hands. Disappeared upstairs. Back with—what was this? Aspirin!

"I don't have a headache. That's not my problem. Have you even been listening?"

"Look, you *will* have a headache," Serge said. "And I want you to know something."

"What?" She was crying now.

"This is really going to break your mother's heart."

"Right."

He held out the bottle of aspirin. *Oh, just go away.* She took two pills and swallowed them. Serge went to the cupboard, pulled all the liquor bottles from the shelves and emptied them into the kitchen sink. She rolled her eyes and clapped. He took a bow. When he straightened again, his expression said, "Okay?"

"It doesn't mean anything. You go out to drink. You just said so."

"This is about taking care of you."

"Right. You really excel at that, Serge."

She caught his pleading look. She didn't owe him anything. She'd sleep this off, and disappear in the morning.

iii. Le miroir (The Mirror)

October

JEAN-CLAUDE WAS ASKING Rani a favour when she spotted Branka coming through the door of the staff room. Pronouncing the words blithely as if he didn't realize how loaded they were, here in this English cégep. Rani had seen him having this conversation with other people, always ending with his big charming smile, and: "Why not?"

He taught artsy French courses: chansonniers québécois, cinéma d'auteur français et québécois. At least half of the kids here were Greek or Italian-Canadian, trilingual like Serge Giglio. But unlike Rani's idol, they tended to side with the *Non.*

All month, Jean-Claude was asking everyone, students and staff alike, to at least consider voting *Oui.*

Today he had brought a box of pastries, taken them out and laid them on the table.

Branka, who taught Physics, was the first to answer him.

"Oh come on! Look at what happened to my country—

(By which she meant Yugoslavia.)

"—and look at what happened to Rani's!"

(By which she meant India, in 1947.)

Rani didn't mind this so much, coming from her. A refugee from Bosnia could not be expected to—

"One day everyone's getting along. Then someone lights a fire. It spreads. You have no idea," Branka continued. She gestured toward Rani. "She knows."

"You know," Rani said, addressing Jean-Claude. "I would have liked to be on your side. I'd have loved to go to French school, but they didn't use to let in unbaptized children. But anyway, I never actually said I *wasn't* on your side."

"So you support the *Oui*?" Jean-Claude said. He licked cream off his grey moustache.

Rani waited until Branka had retrieved her lunch from the fridge and left the room.

"Why not?" she said.

IT WAS RAINING HARD as Rani left her office, so when she saw the bus pull up, at the last moment she decided to leave her bicycle at work. As she ran to catch the bus, she noticed Mélanie boarding. She'd wondered what had happened to her. It had been two weeks since the girl had been in her office. So, she hadn't disappeared; she'd just decided not to quit school. Good.

Rani paid her fare, nodded to Mélanie, and sat down alone near the front. The young woman didn't give her any sign that she wanted her company, and she decided not to push it.

Rani watched the giant windshield wipers as the bus drove down Sherbrooke and made a wide turn up Saint-Denis— past a theatre, cafés, a theatre school, bookshops, boutiques, apartment buildings—continued several more blocks, and then slid to a bumpy stop. A couple of passengers got off. The next stop would be hers. She quickly glanced back to make sure that Mélanie was still there. Memories came flooding back of the trusting child from the diner, the long afternoon at Parc Jean-Drapeau. She began a little daydream in which she stayed on the bus until Mélanie got off, followed her home, stood on the sidewalk outside Serge Giglio's house, tried to catch a glimpse of the two of them in the window. The heavy, rhythmic clicking of the windshield wipers and the quieter whoosh of the bus rolling through the wet streets lulled her into a dream. Would Serge neurotically peek out of curtains, open the front door and quickly usher Mélanie into the house? No, that would be *her* dad.

Suddenly, as if she had summoned him, a man with a strong resemblance to her own father strode over to her from the back of the bus. He was like a different *version* of Sunil, Rani thought, bearded and turbaned, older, taller and zippier. His clothes were soaking wet, his skin the colour of a faded wicker doormat. His face was so much like Sunil's, the same dark circles under his eyes, eyes that were wide and bright with fright.

Holding the overhanging supports with both hands and facing her with a panicked expression, he asked her a question in Punjabi.

She stared back, feeling useless.

He repeated his words, and indicated the dark, rainy street outside with his chin.

Of course, he would ask *her* for help. She had her dad's face too, a typical Punjabi face: heavy eyebrows; large eyes, nose, and mouth, the same tawny skin. Of course this old Sikh would assume she could help him. Any reasonable person would expect her to. And she did vaguely understand his words, could guess half or so of the information he needed, but had no words of her own to help him with. Some useless Italian words formed in her mind, then turned into French, and finally into English: "I'm sorry, I don't speak your language."

The Sikh fixed his pleading eyes upon hers. He uttered a phrase she recognized from her parents' conversations. She felt pretty sure it meant "What the hell?" He stood hovering over her, trembling.

Finally, he stopped speaking and sat down across from her. There was a silence in the bus that hadn't been there before. Everyone was breathing it in. The windshield wipers beat on. Each passenger, she imagined, was working on a theory about what was going on.

The bus came to her stop. She rose from her seat and, avoiding the man's eyes, made her way to the side door. Just before she stepped down, she turned her head and caught the questioning look Mélanie was sending her way.

HOW ODD THAT the girl reappeared in her life just when her own teenage obsession with her former idol had recently resurfaced. Just a few weeks before, Rani and Rob had been clearing out some junk drawers. They had both agreed to cull their collections of cassette tapes to free another drawer. Rob picked up a Sensibilité cassette Rani had dubbed from an LP and started reading the sleeve.

He popped the tape in the cassette player and stood frowning, listening to the lyrics.

Encore une fois je nais
l'évolution inusitée
d'une erreur contraceptive

"What is that supposed to mean?" Rob asked. "Being reborn?"

"Yeah, I guess they were into reincarnation," Rani said.

"Huh?"

"You know, it was the seventies. They had all this Hindu iconography on their album covers. I'd show you but I just have these cassette tapes now." She'd sold her records and thrown out her turntable after being laughed out of a store for inquiring about new needles.

Rob's face was thoughtful as he listened to another song. Rani remembered how her weird younger self would fantasize that the lyrics were for her, that Serge Giglio knew all about her—"l'Hindoue"— his most devoted fan.

"That's a whole lot of synth," Rob said.

"Well, yeah. Like I said, it was the seventies."

She wanted to change the subject before she blurted out anything too crazy. She looked through a pile of Rob's music and found four Genesis tapes. Rob said that he had been a big fan of the group as a teenager, but couldn't seem to hear the music the same way anymore.

"It's like the lyrics made sense when I was young, but just don't anymore," Rob said.

"Yeah, like some truth you lost," Rani said, nodding.

A flash of her mother running outside in a nightgown on a winter day. She tried to push her memory further, but it just settled on a wide expanse of snow, covering the backyard like a blanket.

IT WAS MOSTLY OKAY, staying with Pepe's family. They lived only a few blocks away from Serge's house, but in a modest, barely decorated apartment. This family was like the opposite of Mélanie's. Nobody was all that interested in art or politics. Pepe said that all anyone in his family cared about was soccer and calisthenics.

"What are calisthenics again?" Mélanie asked.

Pepe's father, a compact, muscular man, promised to show her.

"First, sit down with me," he said in his raspy voice, beckoning to her. "Get your boyfriend too."

They sat on either side of him and he hugged them close. Then he lifted Mélanie's hair out of her eyes and snickered.

"What?" Mélanie felt her back going up.

"It's just that—" and then he turned and said something in Spanish to his son.

"That is so rude!" Pepe said.

"What?" said Mélanie. But she didn't want to know.

"He says you look like my sister."

Oh, that.

"No kidding," Mélanie said, but she felt happy

"He says, so, how can I—you know...?"

Pepe's father gave a wheezy laugh and got up. Pepe and Mélanie both kicked him in the seat of his pants, lazy soft kicks with their stockinged feet.

Pepe reached for Mélanie's hand and they kissed. But then a moment later they were fighting again.

"Can you stop talking about these friends of yours who love my dad's music?"

"What's wrong with that?"

"I'm here because I'm not talking to my dad, remember?"

From the kitchen, Pepe's brother Miguel called out a sentence that ended with the word "refugiada." This was followed by a rebuke from his grandmother.

"Look," Pepe said, ignoring them. "They're on their way. They're bringing some pot. They're going to be *so* pleased just to meet you."

"You're not smoking marijuana in this house," Pepe's mother called, also from the kitchen. His grandmother repeated these words in Spanish.

"I'm going out," Mélanie said. "Can you imagine how disappointed they'd be if they saw my face?"

"Aw, baby."

A long look of something like mocking, fake pity before he wrapped her in his arms.

"Mélanie, you have, like, a sister, for Miguelito?" Pepe's dad asked from the floor, where he was now doing sit-ups.

"Pa," Pepe said. He held up his hand.

"Oh right," Pepe's father said, half-exhaling, half-giggling as he brought his trunk up to his knees, "Pepe told me about your country's one-child policy!"

Mélanie felt stunned. She wriggled out of Pepe's arms and stared at him.

So he'd actually told his family about that fight. She felt exposed and betrayed. Even more enraging was her own jealousy. She had no idea how that felt, to be part of a close family.

Pepe was laughing along with his father now.

Hilarious.

MÉLANIE WAS COLD. She was waiting at the bike stand outside the cégep for Pepe to arrive with a wool sweater she'd left behind when she stormed out of his house. When she'd called him from the phone booth she said she was never coming back, but they both knew she had nowhere else to stay—as well as what leaving behind not only the sweater but several other items of clothing really meant. He had this cheerful indifference about their situation that enraged her. His whole family seemed to look upon her with detached amusement. They all had each other, they were happy, she made no difference.

Almost nowhere else to go. She could stay at her mother's. But that would mean living in the suburbs, far from the college. It didn't matter. She was going to quit school anyway. She just hadn't gotten around to it. But she didn't want to be around Jane as she tried to figure out where she was going. Never any help, always absorbed in her own weird, mysterious problems. *Finding herself.* Mélanie was going to find her real mother, her real people. She had a gut feeling that they would be more sensible. Everyone here was so irritating.

Ten minutes late. She scanned the street. No bicycles. He usually came to school by bike unless it was raining, but maybe he'd taken the bus. The weather was calm but there was a new bite in the air.

In the place where she belonged, on the other side of the world, it was always warm. She looked at the brochure she'd picked up at the travel agency. In Vietnam, there were just different kinds of warmth—sunny, pleasant, hot and humid— and many hues of green.

She looked up as a woman walked up to a bicycle, patted the seat and then began to walk away. Their eyes met, and the woman smiled at her. A brown woman in a blue coat. Oh, her.

"Just checking on my bike," Ms. Roshan said. "I left it here and took the bus home last Friday because it was pouring."

Mélanie remembered the man on the bus talking to her in some Indian language. What had that been about? Awkward.

"Oh—hi, Ms. Roshan."

"Call me Rani."

Mélanie saw the guidance counsellor's eyes drop to the brochure in her hand. She held it up.

"Vietnam," Rani said.

"Yeah," Mélanie said, shrugging.

"Ever been?"

"No," said Mélanie. "Have *you* ever been to Asia?"

"Yes," said Ms. Roshan. "When I was a kid I went to India with my dad. All I really learned on that trip was that I wasn't really Indian."

Mélanie was surprised by this sudden burst of honesty. There was warmth in her dark brown eyes. Her skin a warm brown too.

"Anyway," said the guidance counsellor. "if you ever feel like talking about this stuff, you know where to find me."

Ms. Roshan followed this with a little laugh, at nothing, a nervous wave as she went into the building. Mélanie stood with her arms by her side watching her. The lady was so awkward.

And yet—Mélanie felt a bit of relief, a sudden softening around her shoulder blades as some of the weight she always carried around with her seemed to shift.

iv. Ciel indigo (Indigo Sky)

RANI WAS DIPPING her rubber stamp in blue ink when she noticed Mélanie standing outside her office again. She was dressed in khaki trousers and a black sweater. "I know what you're going to ask me."

Rani's thoughts raced. What could she be talking about? Some kind of telepathic connection?

"I know I'm supposed to have, like, a career in mind to discuss with you, what I'm going to do after this." She played with the doorknob as she spoke. "But actually, I just want to quit school. I want to just...go away."

She looked down at her blue Keds, a sheet of black hair falling over her face, hands in the pockets of her pants. When she looked up again, she finally met Rani's eyes. Like all these kids, boys and girls, Mélanie was troubled, self-absorbed, and yet healthily unaware of her stunning beauty.

"Have a seat," Rani said. She pulled out her file and began turning the pages carefully with her fingertips to avoid smudging them with the ink she always managed to get on the heel of her hand. At some point Mélanie had changed from Pure and Applied Sciences to Social Sciences, the program many college students chose when they had no idea where they were going. Her marks, as she had said, were all in the nineties.

"Surprised?" Mélanie asked.

You have no idea.

"It's just that you're such a high achiever."

"Oh, that must be because I'm Chinese," Mélanie said.

Where did this come from? Was that sarcasm in her voice?

"I thought you were…" Rani said. "You're Serge Giglio's daughter, aren't you?"

She couldn't meet Mélanie's eyes as she said his name. Her star-struck past had to be somewhere on her face.

"I'm Vietnamese," Mélanie said. Oblivious to Rani's embarrassment, apparently used to this sort of comment, a bit irritated all the same. "I'm not like them. They're *creative*, my parents. Anyway, they're not my real parents. I guess that's sort of obvious."

There was so much hurt in those frank words, in her posture and in her frown. Her long black hair like rain.

Rani remembered a drawing she had brought home from the restaurant: a normal family scene on the ground, the typical artwork of a five-year-old—everybody tiny, potato-shaped, with bird feet. But in the sky: big orange cats, clowns with balloons, striped birds, all as big as the clouds. And in mid-air: a lollipop that was really a guitar, a little brown square that was *une boite à surprises*, according to little Mélanie, who'd spoken to her in a mixture of English and French.

Rani asked her now how she'd ended up at an English college. "Isn't your father this big Québécois nationalist?"

"Well, he did send me to French school. It wasn't the greatest experience. I was the only Asian kid, and people couldn't get past that. Everything about me, that I didn't like milk, or whatever, was always: *elle est chinoise*."

"So you figured things would be better at an English college?"

Rani thought Serge would have something to say about that. Her own awful experiences at English school seemed to echo what her father said about the British: there was something particularly viciously colonialist about them. She pushed the thought away.

Mélanie hadn't answered. Head down, studying her Keds through her black bangs.

"How's your dad these days?" Rani said after a while. "What's he up to?"

What she'd really wanted to ask Mélanie all along. "*What's he up to?*" Cringing at the false casualness in her own voice. The girl took a moment before answering.

"He's pretty pissed off at me for being here," Mélanie said. "I think he was hoping I would be writing French poetry for a living."

"For a living!" Rani said, with a nervous laugh. But if Serge Giglio was your father, maybe that could work.

Silence. As Rani waited for Mélanie to continue, she looked through the girl's file. Busied herself with her blue stamp pad, marking the date of Mélanie's visit on a form. She considered telling Mélanie, "I knew you when you were a little girl. I used to keep your drawings on my fridge," but she hesitated and the moment passed. She'd been caught off guard, and quickly decided not to reveal anything about their shared past; her instinct was that it wouldn't be professional. Above all, she had to gain Mélanie's trust: she could imagine her eyes widening with outrage if she knew that when Rani looked at her, the memory of a child's face sometimes floated there.

"I can't go to school anymore," Mélanie said. "I want to go to Vietnam."

"To look for your parents?" Rani said.

"My mother. For all I know, my dad's some American vet."

Rani thought this seemed plausible. Mélanie's eyes were a very light golden brown, and something about her features and her hair—which, Rani noticed now, was still straight but slightly rough-looking, like thick black twine—made it impossible to say what her parentage was. She didn't have the kind of beauty that you could label. Kind of like Hima, or Rani's own two little girls, for that matter.

But in Mélanie's case, Rani reflected, not knowing anything about your father, whether he had been your mother's lover or her rapist, would be an awful question to live with.

As if reading her mind, Mélanie said, "You can't imagine what it's like. *Nobody* understands. Your whole life *you* get to say, 'Oh, I'm a dreamer like my mother,' or 'I have my dad's big nose and his love of baseball,' or 'I'm gonna be fat like all the women on my mum's side of the family.'"

She said she had tried to find her birth mother, but didn't have much to go on; certain details remained vague, as if someone was trying to hide the truth from her.

Rani felt slightly alarmed. Did Mélanie really suspect a conspiracy on the part of her parents?

"You know, it could be that someone is trying to save you from being hurt," she said, and she thought, but did not say, that Serge and Jane might not want her to know that she had been sold, or that her mother had been brutally killed.

"I *have* to go to Vietnam," Mélanie said, in a voice that suggested she had just thought of something that sealed the decision.

"Have you discussed this with your parents?"

"My father thinks I'm breaking my mother's heart," Mélanie said. "I'm not sure he cares beyond that. My father…" She shook her head, rolled her eyes. "*On veut un pays! Le Québec, un pays!*" She pumped her fist in the air, mimed strumming a guitar, and then pausing to smoke.

Rani marvelled at how differently she'd felt, how attracted she had been to all that at Mélanie's age. She felt nostalgic for the idealism of that time. How contagious Serge's passion had been, even to someone like Rani, peeking through the door. Maybe being the kid bullied by all the Anglo kids just made you naturally sympathetic to the Franco cause. She gazed sympathetically at the girl sitting across from her. Serge was just her father, the same archetypal figure that so many kids rolled their eyes at, at this age.

"Meanwhile, my mom keeps saying she's leaving for England, going back to where *she* came from. I don't look like them, don't feel like them, don't know who I am and I'm not sure where I'm going, but…"

As Rani listened, she couldn't think of a thing to say. Mélanie's words were simple and poignant; she would be furious if she knew how much she sounded like a hippie herself. By the end of her rant the anger seemed to have blown out of her and she just looked utterly dejected. Rani wondered what she could offer her.

"Look, I understand, I really do. But frankly, you're such a shoe-in for a scholarship, Mélanie, that it would seem a waste to—"

"But here's the thing. I've already dropped out a couple of times. I'm twenty. No, wait, I just turned twenty-one!"

Rani remembered, "I'm five, but I'm almost six." And also, "I can't. I won't be able to." She wanted to hug her. She wished, at the very least, she could share those memories with her.

No. She had to keep her professional distance. Anyway, she had to agree that a record of dropping out of school more than once would not help Mélanie get a scholarship.

She gave her the course refund form. Mélanie thanked her and left.

SATURDAY MORNING. Quiet in the house. Pepe's family gone to watch Miguel play soccer somewhere, or maybe they were doing their morning calisthenics in a park.

She pulled off the covers, which smelled of the Mexican soap the whole family used, and pushed herself up. Pulled on her jogging pants, her bra and sweatshirt, her socks, laced her shoes, all the while in stubborn conversation with her other self, the one who wanted to return to bed. Those heavy feelings always threatening to overwhelm her. This was what she had to do, run outside, run away from herself.

This mid-October morning seemed infinitely colder and darker than it had been only two days earlier, the last time she'd left the house this early. Her thighs ached and her neck was stiff, but it was always a bit like this at first. In a few minutes those tight spots would *unroll*. Something in the backs of her legs was already coming unlocked.

Jumping across the cracks in the sidewalk now, leaping over piles of wet orange leaves. The waking sun beginning to illuminate the trees, the light on everything, everywhere now. Low-rise buildings and vast, empty parking lots. Flat and desolate. The moon. Suddenly wanting to tell Rani Roshan: *When I was little, I thought if I dug through the back garden I'd end up in China.*

A bus approaching. She felt in the pocket of her jogging pants for her bus pass. She'd ride awhile, maybe go running on Mont Royal.

AS RANI WAS lacing up her shoes, her little girls suddenly appeared in the vestibule, rubbing their eyes and yawning. They asked her where she was going.

"Just out for a run."

"What do you mean?" asked Rita.

Too early for conversation. *Go away.*

"Why do you do that?" said Kira.

A fair question.

"Go back to bed," she said.

"Why can't we come?"

"Rob, honey!"

The dear man swooped in, and scooped the girls up with a swift but inelegant movement. "Let your mother be."

"Daddy, you're a dinosaur," Kira said.

As soon as she stepped outside, the bracing cold startled her awake. She gasped. Scarcely a moment later her breathing fell into rhythm with the tapping of her sneakers on the sidewalk. Looking for that extraordinary moon. Finding it. She turned a corner, for no reason at all. Always on the move. Something restless in her. *I'm just like my dad. No.*

Jack-o'-lanterns, a witch, a skeleton. Nothing on her own family's door yet. *Are we late or are they early?* What would the normal time be?

A bus rolling up. A sudden urge to leave the neighbourhood.

She fished in her sweatpants. Keys, tissues, bus pass.

She rode the bus to Mont Royal, got off at Beaver Lake.

NO, COULDN'T be her. But it was.

What did it mean?

Coincidences don't mean anything.

A memory of her mother arguing with Sunil: "You make up these links. You notice all these coincidences. You don't notice the perfectly ordinary things."

Rusty leaves, mud. Dogs greeting each other, the sniffing, the short, matter-of-fact barks. The crunch of the gravel. The weak light, as the sun persisted in its slow climb over the horizon.

Too hard not to say anything.

"Mélanie!"

"Oh, hi!"

The girl slowed down. She actually smiled.

"Come here often?" Rani said.

Stupid. She bit her lip.

But Mélanie was smiling.

"No," Mélanie said. "It's pretty nice here, though."

A swivel of her head, taking in the autumn colours.

"Do you want to run around the lake together?" Rani said.

"Sure."

A companionable silence.

"Do you run every day?" Rani said after a while.

"No," said Mélanie. "But I have to run fairly often because if I don't…"

She seemed to stall there.

"Do you run for the happy hormones?" Rani said.

Goof.

But Mélanie didn't seem to mind. She nodded. She was smiling again.

"That's why *I* run," Rani said quickly. Panting. Trying to keep up. Mélanie was younger, faster.

But they ran several circles around the lake.

2. Chimérique (Quixotic)

October 30–31, 1995

TODAY WAS THE DAY. Sunshine poured through all the windows. Serge picked up the phone.

"You said to call when I woke up," Serge said. "I'm up."

"The *Oui* is going to win. It's been leading in the polls. We're going to have our country, Serge."

Serge's eyes filled with tears as he remembered René's speech, the last time, when they lost. The emotion was too much.

Yvon was *un bon buddy*. He understood. He gave him time to find his words.

"Do you think? Is it going to happen this time?" He didn't know how to control his anxiety. "I have a bad feeling."

"I'll come into town and meet you at La Muse," Yvon said. "We'll have something to celebrate."

Serge took a shower and got dressed. As he was walking outside, the light was already draining from the sky. It was just autumn. No reason to take that as some kind of sign. He felt almost ill with nervousness. He'd have a drink first and then he'd go vote.

One, quickly, and then he'd go. Oof, that drink went straight to his head. Maybe Jane was right. *Someday, your liver won't function anymore.* He'd stay a bit longer until he felt a bit less woozy.

Yvon arrived. Serge stood up and they hugged.

"It's going to be beautiful," Yvon said. The mood in the bar was electric.

An earnest Anglophone patron sent them drinks, saying he was a huge fan, and that he knew people in Toronto who loved Sensibilité. This made Serge and Yvon crack up. Serge looked around. He had to go vote for his country now, but they were hemmed in, he couldn't get up, there was a small crowd of fans surrounding their table, hanging onto their words.

"We Québécois," Serge said, gesturing with an unlit cigarette. "We're like the inhabitants in Parc Safari. People come to watch us—"

"And pay us, feed us, say we can preserve our language, our special culture," said Yvon, pretending to write on the tablecloth.

"But we're dreaming to escape," said Serge. "Can we? D'you think?"

He looked around the restaurant, wondering which patrons would vote *Oui*, which *Non*. Surely everyone here would vote *Oui*. Voting *Non*—why would you do that? Someone turned up the volume on the TV above the bar. Bernard Derome was announcing that the polls had just closed.

Wait. What time was it?

"Shit, the polls are closed! Did you vote?"

"Yeah, of course, in Lachute, before I came to meet you."

Serge closed his eyes, put his hands on his head, slowly stood up, let out a groan, let himself fall back in his chair again. "It's so hard to know what time it is these days, it's always so dark, *hostie*."

"Yeah, the end of October, not the, um, brightest…"

Serge shuddered. The referendum result would be announced tonight, or latest tomorrow, Halloween. To say he had a bad feeling about it would be a gross understatement. That flesh-eating thing that happened to Lucien Bouchard, well, that had haunted him, worst omen ever. Bouchard ending up losing a leg, just unbelievable! Why was the universe doing this? He hadn't meditated for a while; he had to start again. He imagined bad news late tonight, another binge of drinking just to cope, and then, tomorrow, happy, oblivious kids in their freaky costumes ringing his doorbell, leaving after a few seconds, let down and pissed off. He would feel guilty forever for not having gotten up off his ass to go vote today.

"I need to get out of here," Serge said.

"You don't want to watch the results?"

But actually, when Serge looked up, the only people left were restaurant staff; he and Yvon were the last customers. His fans had gone somewhere else, somewhere with a bigger screen. Their actual departure, and time itself, had disappeared from his view in this boozy fog. Serge caught the resentful look one of the younger waiters was sending his way. That one was always waiting to close and go home at the end of the night.

"I have a bad feeling," Serge said. "What happened?"

"It's okay," Yvon said. But he looked miserable.

What did that mean?

"What time do you get up in the morning?" he asked Yvon.

"I dunno," Yvon said. "Before noon, for sure."

"I'm gonna start doing that," Serge said, and he stared into space, imagining a better future. His problem, he admitted to himself, was his own personal lack of independence. He was dependent on alcohol. And now that he had admitted it, he would do something about it. It was easy enough. It was about not doing. Not drinking. No effort required. He winced. He knew Jane and Mélanie found him lazy. He would go home and clean up his house. That would be a start.

RANI STEPPED BETWEEN the carved pumpkins on her doorstep and opened the front door. She had just come home from casting her ballot.

She was thinking of the first referendum, in 1980, that spring day with the mild breezes, when she was still too young to vote but would have liked to. In 1980, if she had been old enough, she would have done it for her teenage idols, the members of Sensibilité. She wouldn't have wanted to stand in the way of their dreams. She thought of Serge Giglio's face, its pale agony as he sang, how dispirited the band must have been by the defeat. In the intervening years between referendums, even Rani's hero worship had been buried, all the pop music from her youth drowned out by the kids' preferences: Sharon, Lois & Bram, Fred Penner, Raffi, Passe-Partout, Carmen Campagne, and Annie Brocoli. Sometimes Rob would put on some U2, and the two of them would feel as if they were breaking some school rule.

But recently, Rani had woken up realizing she had been dreaming in French again. The refrain of one of Sensibilité's hits, "Chimérique," Rani recalled now, insisted on dreaming in French. "Tout ce que je te demande, s'il te plait, c'est que tu rêves, rêves, rêves—juste un peu en français."

Rob was tiptoeing out of the girls' room, carefully closing their door. He was the kind of Irish guy who could profess to see reasons to vote for the *Oui,* but lived the life of an Anglo-Montrealer, confining his forays into the French language to short exchanges at grocery stores or cafés. ("Ça va. Merci. C'est tout, oui. Non, merci.") He administered needles at work, where the staff were mainly Anglophone anyway; he claimed he didn't talk to the kids, only smiled at them or made goofy faces. He didn't share Rani's interest in Francophone culture, but on the other hand, didn't find it baffling or eccentric. She suspected he was tired of ethnic conflict; she remembered that at his parents' house, he said nothing whatsoever whenever his father ranted about the British. All he would say about the referendum was that he wasn't a Canadian citizen, and that it was none of his business. Sometimes he would say, "I'm Irish. Of course I sympathize with the struggle." But was that sarcasm? As with Mélanie, Rani wasn't always sure how to take his words.

WEEKS OF THEM ecstatically waving flags and chanting, reaching out just to touch Bouchard's clothing as he hobbled by on one leg. They had such faith in their messiah. And now those same people sad and broken-hearted again, as the *Non* squeaked out another victory. Premier Parizeau on the stage, possibly drunk, ending the night on a sour note, blaming the defeat on "money and the ethnic vote."

The camera panned the crowd, landed on the faces of two young Black people, who blinked in surprise and then looked around themselves anxiously.

Hima got up and turned off the TV.

"Good for him," she said bitterly. "He took off his mask."

Sunil looked up at her from the couch. Ramesh shared this view, that nationalism was always against someone. The ethnic communities would be the scapegoats.

"No surprise here," his son would probably say. He was already planning to move to Toronto. For Arun, it was more complicated, because his wife, Geneviève, was attached to Québec. Rani would stay, Sunil thought. She was attached to Québec too, wanted her kids to be as bilingual as Krishen's. A couple of them had left for Ontario too, though, he remembered. He recalled hearing that they didn't speak French anymore. He remembered the crowds roaring as Gandhi said, "Have love for your language."

"So now what?" said Hima. "Wait for these people to burn down our houses?"

Sunil saw her expression change. She looked worried about what he might be imagining. But the memories were as vague as dreams now. It was almost half a century ago. Some trauma had finally left him, and most of the rest was under control. There were times he hated his pills, the dull, quiet feeling they gave him. But he was getting older now and he had to admit that what he valued above all was the peace of mind they gave him. And Hima. As long as he took them every day.

"Don't worry," he said. "I don't think there will be riots. People here are too comfortable for that."

Comfortable. He felt a pang of guilt as he surveyed the half-unpacked boxes cluttering the living room. For Hima's sake, he could allow himself no more lapses. Keep his ship on course as they navigated a choppy sea. No. Small boat afloat.

No. Raft steady. A raft steady as they navigated a choppy sea. A few pills a day was not the greatest sacrifice to keep his little raft from going under.

THE NEXT MORNING Jane called Serge, to offer her condolences, but she got his answering machine. In the afternoon, he showed up at her door, looking devastated. She led him to her bedroom and once more he cried in her arms. She badly wanted to ask how Mélanie was doing but he was too sad to speak. He didn't ask for a drink. She stroked his hair, and when he was finished crying, he went home.

CATHERINE, A STUDENT Rani had counselled, offered to spend time with Rani's kids on Halloween. The kids themselves didn't mind going trick-or-treating with a stranger, although Rita's preference would have been to go alone. She was six; Kira was four.

Catherine came up the steps in a blue cloak and a black pageboy wig, her skin covered in white powder.

"Great costume," said Rani.

"You're beautiful," Rita said, in awe.

"Thank you," said Catherine.

"You're Snow White," said Kira, "Right?"

"Yes, that's right," said Catherine. "And you, you're a ... a little bear cub, right?"

"No," said Kira. "It's just a costume."

"She would have dressed up as Snow White for Halloween too but she's not white enough," Rita told Catherine.

When Catherine left with the children, Rob and Rani settled down under a blanket on the couch to watch the TV news and eat candy. The news was all about the defeat of the referendum; they were interviewing Anglophones about whether a *Yes* victory would have meant joining an exodus from the province. They switched to the French channel. Jacques Parizeau was being interviewed about the date of the next referendum.

"Plus ça change," Rani said aloud.

"I'm not moving," Rob said.

The doorbell rang.

"Not moving," Rob said again.

Rani stepped out of the blanket and answered the door.

"Halloween!"

When they'd moved into this apartment seven years ago, Rani had explained to Rob that this is what Francophone kids said. In about half of the neighbourhoods where Rani had lived, where there were more Anglophones, they said, "Trick or Treat!"

"Bonjour, toi. Bonjour le...le...lion, c'est ça?"

"Non, c'est juste un costume."

"Is it me," Rob asked her as she flopped back down on the couch, "or are kids less playful than they used to be?"

A commercial came on, advertising a shiny car that accelerated around the edge of a cliff for no reason that Rani could see. "Plus ça change," she said again.

Her eyes fell upon the phone on the coffee table. She remembered, with a shiver, typing in Mélanie's phone number and address on a form that day, then copying it down on a piece of paper and stuffing it in her purse. She thought of a pretext. She remembered that she had some information about a course transfer that Mélanie had asked about. She couldn't sit still on the sofa anymore. She wondered if it was an effect of the sugar she had been eating all evening.

She got up and dialled the number. The blue ink was a little smudged, and she almost hoped she was misreading it. The voice on the answering machine was Mélanie's. Serge was not mentioned in the outgoing message. She didn't leave a message.

Rob looked at her curiously from the sofa. He patted the empty space next to him. She apologized and told him she was coming.

Then the phone rang, startling her.

"Hi, what's going on?" It was Mélanie, speaking as if to one of her buddies.

"Not much," Rani said, as if she *was* one of her buddies. She said some of the words that she had chickened out of saying to the answering machine. "Hey, you should come by and see me some time."

"Yeah, I'll come by, but I don't know if I'm going to hang around school much longer."

Mélanie had changed her mind several times over the past few weeks. Quitting, staying, leaving; she would announce her plans with complete certainty, then cancel them the following day. The only new thing was this phone call, which Rani felt drew them closer.

"Something happen?" Rani asked.

"No, no."

Mélanie's voice was friendly and cheerful but she did not seem to have anything to say. Oh! She must have that new thing on her phone that let you see who was calling, Rani thought, with sudden embarrassment. It would make sense for a famous rock star family to have that. She couldn't talk about her pretext for calling; she could barely think.

"So I guess I'll see you tomorrow," Rani finally said. "Or not."

"Yup."

"How is everything?" she added quickly.

"Oh, fine. I just came home to pick up some clothes from my dad's house. I'm staying with a friend."

"How is that going?"

"Oh, not great."

"Oh. How's your dad?"

"Haven't seen him."

"Oh," Rani said. *He must be shattered by what happened last night.* "Well, don't hesitate to ask if you need anything."

"Cool, maybe I'll take you up on that someday. Thanks."

3. Courir ensemble (Running Together)

November

RANI SCANNED the pictures and articles Mélanie had brought to her office. A man carried his wife. A child followed them, carrying a doll in an English bonnet.

Over fifteen million people were forced to leave—by train, in bullock carts and on foot—but did so with smiles on their faces because they were told they were going home, to Pakistan, to the new India. Thin, wrapped from head to toe in white fabric, carrying cloth bundles on their heads, family members in their arms. An elderly couple sat by the roadside with their grandchildren, having missed the caravan because of the old man's exhaustion. The man was a bearded bag of bones, leaning on a bedroll on the ground, staring into the distance with his mouth half open, as if he thought he could summon death by imitating it.

Rani looked up at Mélanie. She hadn't officially quit school, but it didn't seem as though she was attending many classes these days. She spent a lot of time at the municipal library, having discovered the microfiche room. She'd also taken to coming to Rani's office with photocopies of newspaper clippings. All of this had started when Mélanie had complained that she didn't know how to pronounce her real name, and had no idea what it meant. Rani told her that as a child she always insisted she couldn't be Indian, because she was born in Canada.

"Everything we learn in school," Mélanie said now, "is about white people."

"True," Rani said. She had never thought of education the way Mélanie did. She'd thought of it as a means to an end, a way to get a job.

"But we're grown up now," Mélanie said. "There's no excuse anymore."

She had challenged Rani to tell her about her heritage. She could barely hide her disbelief—or was it disgust?—at how little Rani knew.

"What does your name mean?" Mélanie asked.

"I don't know," Rani said. "I was named after an aunt."

"Which aunt?"

"Aunt Rani!" she said, laughing.

Mélanie glared at her. She was so fierce! It was pretty clear that Mélanie was frustrated with her search for own personal history, and wanted to put her energy into someone else's. She was on some sort of political crusade that completely sidestepped what had just happened in this province. Also, the days had recently begun to shorten dramatically, and

Mélanie had been in a dark mood, complaining that school was so boring she wanted to put a bullet in her head. Rani had suggested getting a sunlamp to ward off the winter blues, and Mélanie had made a face that said, "And how would that make school less boring?"

But they arranged to meet that afternoon, at the bike stand, for a run.

A STORY RANI told Mélanie: When she and her husband Rob got married, the clerk at city hall said that according to Rani's birth certificate, her name was "Noname." He pronounced it *No-namé.* He'd held the paper out to her so that she could see for herself. He advised her to see a lawyer to get her name officially changed.

"Your parents forgot to name you?" Mélanie said.

"I think they just forgot to do it officially," Rani said. She hadn't really wanted this to be about her parents.

So anyway, they'd thanked the clerk. As they left the office, Rob pointed out that this was her chance to have any name she desired. She asked him what he would have liked her to be called. He said, "Maybe Rodney? Or Roger?"

Because, Rani explained, when they'd met, he'd thought her name was "Ronnie" and asked her if she was supposed to be a boy.

She was laughing as she said this, but Mélanie didn't join in.

"So, I told him about being named after my aunt," Rani said. "What I remembered hearing. It amounts to this: she helped my parents find each other after Partition. Or no, it was just her *name* that helped."

She repeated the story she'd been told, the same version she'd told Rob. An ad in the newspaper, when her mother was looking for her dad. Her mother had claimed to be Aunt Rani. Her dad had figured out who was really looking for him, and gone to her house.

"I told Rob at the time that my father waited behind a tree until she came out," Rani said, "But maybe I made that up. Rob told me that hiding behind trees sounded about right. He said it was very common in Indian movies."

She laughed again.

But Mélanie was frowning.

"Your husband's Indian? And he didn't recognize your name?"

"No, he's Irish."

"He goes to Indian movies?"

"I... don't know."

"Do you go to Indian movies?"

"What?" Rani said. "No."

Dusk was falling. Streetlamps blinking on. They'd stopped to wait for a light to change at an intersection.

"So anyway, I was given the name Rani because my aunt—or just her name—played a role in my parents' love affair," Rani said.

The light turned green and they ran across the street.

"Your parents had a love affair?" Mélanie said, but she was passing her now.

"Okay," Rani called out, "You'd rather hear their story? Here's what I remember."

Mélanie slowed a bit. She almost smiled.

"So there was that war, right?" Rani said. "People got separated. When my mother wrote her missing person's ad, she had to use my aunt's name because she couldn't very well write her own. Their romance was taboo, you know, there was no dating in India, only arranged marriages. But my father knew his sister wasn't looking for him, so he understood the message had to be from my mother and—"

"Weird, though," Mélanie said, cutting her off, "that there was a war even though Gandhi preached non-violence."

This was a statement, but Rani understood she was supposed to have an opinion about it. She heard the challenge in Mélanie's voice. She spoke with sarcastic innocence, and Rani felt chastened. Mélanie ran ahead again. She shouted over her shoulder:

"You know what Gandhi said about British civilization?"

"That he thought it would be a good idea," Rani said with a relieved smile, feeling like a student who finally got an answer right. As if in acknowledgement, Mélanie slowed her pace.

RANI FELT EXHILARATED by each visit from Mélanie, each run. Toward the end she would get very tired. And then she looked forward to the next.

MÉLANIE ARRIVED IN Rani's office with a file folder. She plopped it down on her desk and waited. Rani peeked inside. Mélanie was looking at her expectantly, like a cat who'd just dropped a dead mouse on her doorstep. Rani opened the folder. There were various historical articles. The first was a paper by an Indian doctoral student.

"That one explains how the railroad was paid for with Indian taxes but was really meant for the British," Mélanie said. She crossed the room and began reading over Rani's shoulder.

"For the continued looting of Indian goods," Mélanie read aloud over her shoulder, with something like angry glee.

And she continued: there was a bit about how the British ruined the Indian textile industry by cutting off the thumbs of Bengali weavers. And the brutal suppression of riots, Churchill's deliberate starvation of peasants.

Mélanie was so excited, Rani thought. No wonder she couldn't sit still through her classes. It was as if her brain was burning. Too bad she couldn't make a living standing on a soapbox, ranting like this.

Rani yawned.

"What?" Mélanie said, glowering.

"I've heard some of this before," she said.

"And?"

"Well, just that nothing's black and white. You know, Indira Gandhi was pretty repressive. She was as harsh as the British ever were, to the Sikhs. Before she died, though, she said something that I really agreed with—that there wasn't a lot that was really black and white, that more and more she was starting to realize that the truth was grey."

Rani read the message on Mélanie's face, her quiet, cat-like eyes: *Great. Thanks for the empty cliché.* And something else. Pity? Did her words remind Mélanie of Serge's songs? Did she find those songs silly? Rani felt an urge to defend them. If they ever came up, she would be ready to. But Mélanie was flipping through her articles again. She showed Rani a grainy photograph of a half-naked corpse.

Mélanie said, "The British created a mess. On purpose. And then they withdrew. I feel like—I feel like I can hear them laughing! People who'd been living together in harmony joined gangs, suddenly did the most horrible things to each other. Set fires. Raped and killed women, cut out their wombs."

"This reminds me of—"

Mélanie's eyes said, *Of course.*

"—Vietnam," Rani finished. "That must have occurred to you."

"Right," Mélanie said. A new, chilly tone. "I'm *so* lucky."

"What?"

"That's what people have always told me. I'm so lucky to have been rescued."

Mélanie got her binder out of her bag and flipped it open. She removed a loose-leaf page and handed it to Rani. The page had a small newspaper clipping glued to its centre, with notes underneath and on the margins in both pencil and blue ink, featuring plus signs, equal signs, and a great number of exclamation marks. Rani felt dismayed. *She's more like my father than hers.* She was beginning to feel irritated, but it was too late to end this conversation. Maybe she was responsible; maybe her interest in the girl had somehow brought this on. Mélanie began to say something, but Rani held up her hand.

"Look, I can't read and listen at the same time," she snapped.

Mélanie went silent. The article said that Operation Babylift in 1975 was authorized by President Gerald Ford shortly before the fall of Saigon. The first group of war orphans were flown from Tan Son Nhut Airport on a U.S. Military C-5A Galaxy cargo plane. They were followed by about 2,500 other children, many of them Eurasian. In blue ink, more facts were scrawled: Mélanie was seven months old when she was put on the final flight on April 25th, just three days before the complete evacuation of American personnel in Vietnam, and the effective end of the war. She ended up being adopted by Serge and Jane, who named her Mélanie, but called her Tweetie. The nickname was underlined three times.

When Rani looked up from the paper, Mélanie said, "I'm at a dead end, and it really sucks. But I do know one thing. Operation Babylift was a propaganda mission. It wasn't true, what the Americans were saying to justify it. The Saigon orphanage where they got me from was never going to be attacked by the Communists."

Rani thought about what she was implying. It was all about the Americans withdrawing with some semblance of honour. Orphans like Mélanie helped the Americans save face.

It occurred to Rani that Mélanie was as outraged about the Vietnam war as young people had been in the sixties when it was still happening; that fire was still blazing inside her. It must strike her father, Rani thought, how much more she cared about this than anything that had happened in Québec.

"If I'd been left in Vietnam"—Mélanie was practically shouting now, as if Rani had objected—"I wouldn't have grown up hating how I look. And I'd know how to pronounce my own name."

December

AUTUMN PASSED QUICKLY, but winter took its time. The third week of December was unseasonably mild. Squirrels jumped heavily between branches, overweight from the extended gathering season; birds sang, people walked around in the kind of light sweaters you might wear at that time of year in, say, South Carolina. Rani had just finished work. It was about five thirty, and already dark. She walked along René-Lévesque and then down to the Lucien-L'Allier metro station. The metro seemed stuffier and more overheated than usual this evening, and each time it stopped, it became more crowded with shoppers and their packages, the air denser with their sweat and perfume. On a whim, Rani got off a few stops later at Champ-de-Mars. Nobody was waiting for her at home: Rob and the girls were in Ireland. She felt lonely and free, and this felt pleasantly nostalgic. The escalator carried her up to street level, and the crowd behind her pushed her out the doors of the station onto the sidewalk. Unsure where to go now, she paused in the middle of the sidewalk, breathing in the cooler air and its mineral smell. She looked toward the glass-covered pedestrian tunnel that would take her to Old Montreal, with all its architectural remnants of New France. She took a wandering, diagonal route, back west on Viger and then up Saint-Laurent to Chinatown where a smaller, older group of tourists, dressed in parkas, waited at the elaborate red-and-gold archway. Maybe, she thought, she should have backpacked in Asia.

Rani continued past the group, through the gate, down the pedestrian walkway, past grocery stores selling dried mushrooms and seafood, gift-shop windows displaying cheap tea sets and paper lanterns. A fragrant odour of ginger-flavoured broth enveloped her, and seconds later she was inside a Vietnamese restaurant, as if the aroma had pulled her in. The place was bright, nearly empty, the floors slippery, apparently recently washed but already covered in boot grime. She ate Tonkinese soup while watching the other patrons. She thought of Mélanie again. She imagined the young woman eating alone.

Rani would have gone with Rob and the girls to Ireland, but as her brothers were both staying with their wives' families, she felt she needed to keep her parents company on Christmas Day. They always said the day meant nothing to them, but she hated to think of them alone in their house, watching TV specials about family suppers, eating leftovers because they both had a habit of cooking too much for the two of them. When she told them she would come over alone on the twenty-fifth, they didn't say much, but she thought they sounded worried. Were Rob and Rani not getting along? Was money tight? She heard these questions in the way they breathed on the phone. Her mom was talking to her from the kitchen while her father was clearly on an extension, breathing heavily but not speaking, as if trying to spy on the conversation.

Rani hoped Rob's parents didn't feel snubbed by her this Christmas. She had enjoyed visiting them in Cork the year before, but always found she was apologizing for herself, for the long black hairs she left in the bathroom, for cutting her food with the wrong hand, for the fact that the girls' eyes were dark brown like her own, and not blue like their father's. When the basket of white baguette was being passed around the table, some surprising words had left her mouth: "Thank you, but I never eat white bread. I guess it's an Indian thing."

Rob had passed her the basket of brown soda bread, frowning.

"Sorry, I don't know why I said that," she'd added, taking a piece. "It's not even true."

"Why do you keep doing that?" Rob had whispered to her. It wasn't an unkind whisper, but there was some exasperation in it. His parents paused, looked up at both of them, and then resumed eating.

Rani was relieved they hadn't said anything.

"Sorry," she'd said again. "I'm just naturally awkward."

She'd wondered if this was something she got from her father. She'd taken a sip of water, and winced. Ever since she had come across Rob's mother washing the glasses with vinegar, the water tasted sour to her.

She'd asked Rob later if he tasted it, but he said no.

She smiled as she imagined telling Mélanie this story. She looked at the remaining noodles in her bowl and focused on folding them around her chopsticks. Her technique could use some work. She glanced up: no, nobody was watching.

She finished her soup, paid her bill and threw on her coat. She went back into the metro station. A train was waiting. She entered a crowded car and stood near the doors, but wondered if she should get out of the way. Only four stops. When the train came to a halt at the next station, she turned to look at the other passengers in case she had to make room for someone leaving the train. As she did, a seated woman with thinning hair and thick glasses leaned forward and gazed into her eyes. She said something to her that she couldn't hear.

"Pardon?"

"I said: Why do you think you're inferior?"

"What?"

"Why do you think you're inferior? Is it because you're Indian?"

Rani looked around at the other passengers. They showed no signs of understanding this, or any English conversation. The woman continued to stare at her, waiting for an answer.

Rani turned around, and counted the stops. Three.

Was the woman going to keep talking? Rani's gut filled with dread. She felt exposed, and also, crazy to feel exposed. Nobody cared.

Rani got off at Laurier, walked the three blocks to her street, which was still and dark. Her gait was stiff. Somehow frozen despite the mild temperature. She felt completely rattled. She tried to distract herself with thoughts of the weather. Colder temperatures were coming; by the time her family came back, she hoped, the streets would be bright and twinkling with snow. She unlocked her door and collected the mail that had come through the slot: two tickets and an invitation to something called a real-estate show. A grey-haired man in a grey overcoat and black scarf approached, walked up the steps to his own apartment and glanced at her before putting his key in his own front door. How did she look to him? Did she always do this—wonder, deep down, if she seemed somehow *less* than other people?

CLASSES HAD ENDED for the semester. Only Rani, the janitors, Ginette from Admissions, and her staff had any reason to come in. It was a good time to catch up on paperwork, but her days matched the colourless winter sky.

And then, delight: Mélanie dropped by.

"What are you doing here?"

"Don't know. Just saying hi. I was in the neighbourhood. I'm looking for a room to rent."

"I'm so pleased to see you," Rani said. "So pleased you haven't disappeared."

She got up from behind her desk and gave her a hug. She felt Mélanie's surprise, the stiffness through her body, and then something loosening, letting go, and relaxing. The girl was lonely, she thought. She imagined Mélanie walking around by herself in the hallway.

"How are things? Don't you have anyone to stay with during the break?"

"It's nice of you to ask. But I'm an adult."

Rani knew better than to contradict a twenty-one-year-old about that, and she backed off.

"So I guess you aren't thinking of going to Vietnam anymore?"

"I have to save up the money. Which is impossible because I have to pay rent."

There it was. The anger in her voice. But she still stood there awkwardly, as if awaiting instructions.

"If ever you need a free place to stay..." Rani said. She let her voice trail off. She let the sentence hang there. She was embarrassed to have blurted the words out, and guilty—she should have at least checked with Rob first—but also relieved that Mélanie didn't seem to find the invitation strange.

WHEN ROB CALLED from Ireland, Rani asked him how he would feel about another girl in the house.

"That would be a lot of girls," Rob said.

"I'm cold!" she heard Rita shout in the background, "Why won't Grandpa and Grandma put the heating on?"

"Why is she cold?" Rani asked. She missed her kids, but admitted to herself that she enjoyed them being someone else's problem.

"So this student," Rob said, sighing. He sounded very tired. "Would she be paying rent? Hold on, Kira wants a word with you."

"Mummy, tell Rita she's not allowed to hog the Hobnobs," Kira said breathlessly into the phone. She sounded a little stuffed up.

"Sure, okay," Rani said, unsure what Hobnobs were. "Did Santa bring you those for a sort of pre-Christmas present?"

"Yes, we got a pack each," Kira said.

"That's why I don't have to share mine!" Rita screamed into the phone.

Muffled voices, some shushing.

"Sorry," Rob said after a moment. "You were saying?"

"I don't think she'll be paying rent, no."

"Can she help with the girls, then?" Rob asked. "Does she like kids?"

"Everybody likes kids," Rani heard Kira call out confidently in the background. "My teacher says we are *comme des fleurs*. Which student is it? Is it Snow White?"

"She's Serge Giglio's daughter," Rani said. She couldn't help blurt it out. It meant nothing to anyone in her family, she thought, but she had to tell somebody.

"Uh-oh…celebrity families," Rob said right away, surprising her. She must have mentioned the girl before.

"She probably has drug problems," Rob said. "*Lots* of drug problems."

Rani's rush of guilt flipped over, turned into impatience. She loved Rob's sense of humour, but not when she wanted a straight answer. He hadn't said yes. Well, too bad. He hadn't said no, either.

She heard Rita and Kira ask what drug problems were.

"Merry Christmas, everyone!" she called out loud enough for all the people clustered around the phone in Cork. She imagined the wet cold, the grey skies.

Part of her couldn't wait to cuddle her daughters, warm them in her arms. Another part thoroughly enjoyed the uninterrupted sleep she was getting, the lack of fuss around suppertime, and, most of all: the ultimate guilty pleasure of digging out her old Sensibilité cassettes, returning to the fantasies of her unencumbered, if lonelier youth.

RANI CONTINUED TO GO to the office that week. Classes would not start again for a whole month, and she had no appointments, but she took advantage of the quiet to catch up on her files.

There was a folded piece of paper Scotch-taped to her door when she arrived to work on Tuesday: "Hi, hope you are well. I just wanted to let you know that you don't have to worry about me. I'm managing to keep out of trouble. I'm in the library most of the time."

Rani was pleased. All of these kids were self-absorbed and self-important, and many loved the personal attention she gave them. But Mélanie was an intelligent girl, and she had correctly picked up that she wasn't just another student to Rani. It must have been something about the patience with which Rani listened to her. She congratulated herself now for this. She liked Mélanie. Her interest was genuine.

Four days before Christmas there was a tell-tale puddle of dirty water outside Rani's office door: melted snow from a pair of boots. Hanging from the doorknob was a plastic bag. Rani opened the door and looked inside the bag: a note from Mélanie, and more bags, a cellophane baggie of shortbread cookies in the shape of Christmas trees.

The next morning, Rani was stamping forms and putting them in her filing cabinet when she felt someone watching her. She turned to see Mélanie in the doorway. Now this was a little creepy. It was only seven thirty. She usually had this half hour to herself, even during the regular semester. With her toe, Mélanie dragged something from outside the door into the office. A large black knapsack.

"I had one like that," Rani said with a smile. "Lugged it around Europe. When I was your age. Are you going somewhere?"

"I wish."

Rani nodded. A ticket to Vietnam would be what, three months' rent?

A silence.

"It's not really working out with my roommates," Mélanie said.

"I told you, it's fine."

"SO, THIS IS the living room, obviously. And here, to the right, there are three bedrooms," Rani said. They continued down the hall, where the apartment opened up to a sunny kitchen. "Kitchen." Beyond the kitchen, she opened the door of the storage room, which was spacious but decrepit.

"Bicycles," Rani said, pointing. "Guitar." Rob's guitar sat on a toboggan, which lay diagonally across the middle of the floor. Rani hung the guitar up on a hook by the straps, then picked the toboggan up off the floor as well and stood it against the wall. She felt Mélanie staring at her intently as she did so. She turned and told her that she could park her bicycle in the space she had freed up next to the girls' bikes, if she needed to. At first, Mélanie didn't speak. Then she cleared her throat and said, "It's a little cold to bike, isn't it?" and hugged herself.

"Okay, there's a space for your toboggan then," Rani said. She was nervous, trying to make jokes the way Rob would, if he were here. She took Mélanie's silence to mean she was saying weird things, and resolved to be quiet, to not frighten the girl away.

To the right of the kitchen, the apartment kept on going. Just past a cozy alcove with a loveseat and a child's hammock, there was the bathroom, and finally Rob and Rani's bedroom.

"You do have a lot of guest rooms," Mélanie said.

"Well, two. Well, one is in case there's another kid someday."

"Your husband's hoping for a son," Mélanie guessed.

Rani thought this could be true. She was impressed by the girl's perceptiveness, but also a bit unsettled by it.

That night, Mélanie sat on the sofa in a tight long-sleeved t-shirt and pyjama bottoms, reading. Rani had asked her how she would spend Christmas Day. All she could get out of her was that she would avoid her father.

"What was it like, at home, before?"

Mélanie looked up.

"With your dad." Serge's smile flashed in her memory. Her face felt warm.

"Oh, well, I didn't live with him for that long. My mother had been talking about going to England since I was about eighteen, so I said, 'Just go!' And I thought it would make sense to leave the suburbs and move in with my dad because he lived closer to school."

"Has she left?"

"No, she has to sell her house. But she's going soon."

"And then you didn't stay with your dad because..."

"Oh, he has this lifestyle, he's like the worst of a young guy and an old guy. Sometimes he's a neat freak, and nags you about keeping the house clean. But other times he drinks, and leaves beer bottles all over the place. He stays up late. Once in a while his friends come over and jam, and that is just the worst. I don't really like that kind of music, so..."

"Not at all, eh?" Rani said, her face impassive. The memory of the music, of Serge's smile.

"No. Not my thing. Sometimes friends would ask to come over, and it was obvious that it was about meeting my dad, not because they really wanted to hang out with me."

Hurt shone in her eyes. "And some of *his* friends were kind of creepy," Mélanie continued. "I'd get up to go to the bathroom and they'd be like, *looking* at me. I think my mother left because of all the people that used to hang around. I guess it was probably worse back then, when I was little. There were always people around. Lots of girls. My mother decided she'd had enough. It wasn't a good environment to bring up a kid. It wasn't because they'd had a fight or anything. They just couldn't live together."

"MA, YOU DON'T have any photographs at all, from before Partition?"

Hima shrugged, stirred the milk in her tea, rested the spoon on the saucer, and ran her fingers tiredly through her thick, short hair. They were sitting across a table from each other in the duplex Sunil and Hima had moved to in Côte-des-Neiges. Which kitchen was this now, Rani wondered, their thirtieth? How many kitchens, how many homes had Sunil and Hima lived in?

"We always leave something behind in a move," Hima said.

A recent conversation with Mélanie popped into Rani's thoughts.

"That's funny. One of the students I counsel was just saying that. Something she learned in her anthropology class. People move but they always leave stuff behind."

She felt compelled to go on. How the student was Serge Giglio's daughter. Unusually bright and curious. And so complicated, dark and intriguing. Her cheeks felt warm as she spoke.

Hima didn't look very interested. Rani stopped talking and looked around the kitchen instead.

So many moves. The cupboards were full of various sets of china, all incomplete, some chipped and missing pieces. Rani knew her parents didn't care about these things, felt only burdened by the material detritus of their lives.

Apart from four Christmas cards on the windowsill, there were few signs that it was Christmas Day. No strings of festive lights on this building or others on the block. Their neighbours, according to Hima, were all different kinds of Jews: the old-fashioned kind with the fur hats, the ordinary, modern kind, and some from Morocco who spoke French.

"Those ones that speak French, they're just like Arabs. Indistinguishable!" Hima marvelled. "I don't know how they voted in the referendum. Can't take anything for granted."

That's true, Rani thought. *How do you know I'm not an indépendantiste?*

Some apartments were rented out to students from the nearby Université de Montréal, but these young people had gone home to see their families, leaving the street in relative darkness. It was late afternoon; dusk had fallen. It was pretty clear that this day meant nothing to her parents, especially without their grandkids. The artificial tree stayed in its box. Sunil was in the bedroom taking a nap.

From the window above the kitchen sink the view was of snowdrifts, snow on the roof of the garage, in the bare trees, covering the neat square of lawn in the backyard. But it was mild, it had rained that morning, and the snow looked sad, like melted ice cream. A picture suddenly filled her mind, a clear, black-and-white image of a harmonium half-buried in snow. Some trouble. And then she remembered something else, a conversation she'd overheard, friendly haggling with a visitor, an exchange.

"Wait, didn't you sell the harmonium?" Rani said.

"Yes, okay, but when did you ever see me playing it?"

Rani felt a pang for her mother. Who would she have played it with, here in this cold country? As a child Rani had just seen its strangeness, but what came back to her now was its beauty: a box made of smooth mahogany with ornate metal knobs, a curling vine of Hindi script carved into the lid. Her mother playing it, sitting all alone in the middle of the living room floor. It must have been a long time ago.

These thoughts followed by blurry imaginings, like old film footage: Hima young, dressed in thin, brightly coloured silk, playing music and laughing with her brothers and sisters on a sunny verandah—suddenly frozen, immobile, like a doll, swiftly wrenched off the floor by a pair of hands around her ankles, uprooted, placed on a boat to join Sunil on the other side of the world.

Her mother had tried to interest her in learning to play the instrument when she was about eight. But she hadn't liked the sound that came out of it, had seen it as a weird contraption, too heavy to hold in her arms, making an alien noise.

"Do you remember who you sold the harmonium to?"

Hima shook her head. "Some hippies," she said, and shrugged.

"But the pictures," Rani said, already regretting it. *I'm just salt in her wound, always.*

"How would I know my father had hidden our pictures in the case? I only found out from you. Maybe you don't remember. My family was more concerned about the other things that survived the fire, the various deeds and envelopes of cash stashed in other secret places. You were the one my sister told about the pictures, and only when you went to India."

"So you really don't remember who you sold the harmonium to, huh?" Rani said after a while.

Hima shook her head. She was looking at her hands. After a moment, she got up and went to her sewing room.

"Come, look, Rani," she said, a new brightness in her voice.

Hima smoothed out the wrinkles on a long piece of orange-and-white fabric.

"It's nice," Rani said. She wondered if her mother was going to try to get her to try it on. Once in a while, Hima would request that she do this, put a sari on. The material was always gorgeous, but draping herself in it felt too weird.

"Special occasion?" Rani asked, without much hope.

Yes, actually. Hima explained that her brother Ashok had invited her to his son's wedding in India. He had invited her at the last minute, because she usually said no to these things. But this time the occasion fell at a convenient time: she'd finally retired that year. She was leaving in a week. Her sister had sent her this sari, to coax her to come.

"Is Dad going with you?"

"No," Hima said.

Rani glanced in the direction of the room where Sunil was napping. He had just had an operation to have some varicose veins removed from his left leg. Hima said he had asked her not to go to India, but she'd held her ground. He was doing okay, recovering well. Uncle Krishen had offered to stay over if he needed help, but Sunil refused his help, telling Hima it was about "appearances."

Rani wondered if her mother wanted Sunil to accompany her. After all, appearances meant a lot to Hima too. Rani was grateful her in-laws were Irish. She imagined rubbery, reptilian tentacles hugging her from behind; that is what marrying into an Indian family would have felt like. Rob's parents didn't seem to care what she did, whether she showed up with Rob at Christmas, for example.

"Would you take him?" Hima said, surprising her.

"What?"

"Would you take your father? He'd go to you."

As if he were a dog.

"I don't know. We have a student staying with us."

"Oh, you already have one refugee at your asylum? Is that this girl you're in love with?"

"I'll talk to Rob," Rani said, determined not to let this get under her skin.

"Promise," Hima said, with a satisfied smile.

SUNIL AND HIMA had not come to Canada as refugees—they considered themselves professionals, and also "pioneers" in the Indian community, a whole other category; they even had a plaque on their living room wall that announced they were the first Indians to immigrate to Québec.

Of course, they had no appetite for another Partition. Rani thought about the fire that Hima referred to sometimes, this fire that had consumed the past. Only recently had she realized that her mother wasn't talking about a house fire, an accident, but that her parents had actually lived through a war. Only recently had it dawned on her that her parents had had an incredible life.

4. Un jour, un voyage
(One Day, a Journey—reprise)

1970

HIMA REREAD the letter one more time.

December 1, 1970

My dearest Sadhana,

Thank you so much for your letter. It gladdens my heart
to know that you are all healthy and happy. You must be
very proud of Virendra and Sushiri, coming along so well,
top of their class, both of them! And Devdas's business continuing to prosper. This is such wonderful news.

Here in Canada things are good but I am quite busy. I
am teaching full time and also hard at work on my Ph.D.
We are in a new house which is very nice and all the ame-
nities are nearby. Arun and Ramesh are pursuing their
studies at good schools. I think it won't be long before

they are married, but it will be their choice. Rani is at a new elementary school. It is a modern building and seems cheerful and bright.

Little sister, I don't know if you keep up with what is going on in North America, but I must tell you frankly that I am rather worried about the society in which we are bringing up our daughter. On one hand, a woman can reach a decent position when jobs are available, like me, I was able to get a university teaching job with just a Master's although now they want me to get my Ph.D.

But on the other hand, this woman's liberation movement and sexual revolution is going very far. Sunil and I worry that Rani will face some peer pressure and will not make a suitable bride when it is time for her to get married.

Frankly we are wondering if you would find it in your heart to adopt her. We think that India would be a better place for her to grow up. Once she has finished her studies and can be married, she will have no shortage of suitors, I think, since the possibility of emigrating to Canada would be a valuable dowry present in itself.

Please let me know what you think. We can speak on the phone if you like. Let me know what time you and Devdas go to bed so I do not call at an inconvenient time.

Your loving sister,
Hima

Hima heard the phone ring downstairs, and Sunil's voice as he answered it. She stood at the top of the stairs and listened. Sunil was speaking in a mix of Hindi and English. He was asking how something had happened. Now he was saying that, yes, Hima was home. Fear chased her down the stairs. She took the receiver from his hands, already heartsick.

"Sadhana, it's you? I was just about send you a letter! What's happened?"

PS Dear Sadhana, I am still reeling from the devastating news of our mother's death. It is tearing me apart but I cannot leave my job right now.

Sobbing, she folded up the letter and put it in an envelope. Besides being upset, she was exhausted and scattered, so much swirling around in her head at the same time: grief, guilt, work, her doctoral thesis, Rani's upbringing, Sunil's intermittent unravelling. When was she even going to get ten minutes to walk to the corner store and buy stamps? Even this suddenly seemed an insurmountable problem. She ordered herself to calm down. She sat on her bed, closed her eyes and said, "Om."

An idea came to her.

She would have Sunil deliver it personally.

On the back of the envelope she wrote:

PPS I am sending Sunil in my stead. He will bring Rani. That way you can see how you get along.

HIMA HAD BEEN urging Sunil to go back to India anyway, and make up with his brothers. He was driving her crazy, writing bitter letters to them at night, running out of space and fitting in extra words around the margins of the thin blue airmail letters, reading aloud as he went along, these foolish letters she would pretend to mail, but toss in the garbage on her way to work.

So it was settled. It would be Sunil who would go back to India to offer his condolences, and he would bring Rani with him. Hima told Rani that she would be representing her and that she had to be on her best behaviour.

Sunil was still unemployed or "between contracts," as they told everyone, and Hima had to prepare her students for their exams. She had to be the best employee imaginable, she told herself, now that it was clear who the breadwinner in the family would always be. And since she was Hima Roshan, and not, say, Rusty Armstrong, she had to prove to everyone that, no, she did not need a break just because her mother had died. She would not cry, she would not become overcome with grief and stress. Now that her sons were away, there was just the girl left, and while she was with Sunil in India, Hima would finally have the mental space to calm down. This would be perfect, for so many reasons.

They put Sunil's brown leather suitcase and Rani's round, pink, plastic one in the car. When Hima dropped them off at the airport, she made Sunil promise not to lose anything. The leather suitcase, the pink plastic case, and the little girl. Sunil said he would do better than that. He would buy a new harmonium, he would buy her all the harmoniums in the world. She glanced in her rear-view mirror at Rani, who was thrilled to have been given a holiday from school.

"Never mind, Sunil," Hima said. "Just be nice to everybody, and be careful."

THE COUNTRY FELT like a weird dream to Rani, full of people who looked like new members of her family. It had a peculiar smell, as if incense was burned everywhere, mixing in with smells of pee, poo, and smoke.

One day her father asked her to wait at a train station, and he left her there alone for so long that she wondered if he was ever going to come back. Another day, they got off a train and her father couldn't remember why he didn't have their luggage. He told her that her mother's sister, Sadhana, would buy her a new outfit, some underwear, and a new toothbrush, but she just bawled.

Her aunt Sadhana and uncle Devdas lived with other aunts and uncles, cousins and second cousins on a sprawling estate with oversized plants and birds, all strange and menacing to her.

An alarming number of people. It was more a community than a home. She was introduced to so many relatives. When she met Sadhana, she burst into tears because she reminded her of her mother. Rani suddenly missed her so much she couldn't stand it.

The food was spicy and it made Rani's stomach hurt. She missed food she could actually eat—at home, the chilis were on a separate plate for her parents, not mixed in. She missed air that smelled of nothing, her bed with the Flintstones sheets, the bathroom across the hall. Her aunt said *now, now, it's only six more days*, but it was seven because of the whole day on the plane.

"Well, maybe Sunilji can get an earlier flight," Aunt Sadhana said, some exasperation in her tone. "Honestly, you should tell your parents that this country doesn't suit you."

She paused and stroked Rani's hair.

"You know, it's funny," she continued, looking into her face. "You are so upset because I look like your mother, but you look a lot like my mother when she was a little girl."

Rani was surprised to hear this. Her tears dried up, and she rubbed her eyes. This was the first time anyone had ever told Rani she resembled anyone at all.

"Can you show me a picture of her?"

"No, I don't have any. There weren't a lot of photographs of people back then. Even in our house, we only had two or three pictures of ourselves as children. And your grandmother—well, this would have been in 1905, something like that."

"So how do you know what she looked like?"

"Well, there was one picture I used to stare at all the time. It was so fascinating to me that long ago, my mother was a child herself. But your mother's the one who could show it to you. My father packed all those old photographs in her harmonium case back when we had to leave. He tucked them under the lining, inside the lid."

"Really? That's so neat! Like secret treasure!"

"Yes, you should ask your mother. I imagine she knows about that."

That evening, Rani and her cousin Sunita were sent to buy 7Up and Coke at a little store. The park they passed on the way had no swings or slides, but there were at least twenty squirrels, ten rabbits, and oh! Two monkeys! She fed them peanuts from a little bag her cousin passed her. Her cousin watched, and then, as four other kids approached, told her to keep walking. The kids were their age but greasy-haired and much skinnier. The kids followed them, talking non-stop in Hindi. Rani asked her cousin what they wanted and her cousin said, "They're begging. Ignore them." She ran ahead of Rani, who lagged behind, staring over her shoulder. The children's eyes were huge in their thin faces. Rani threw the remaining peanuts at them. It made her stomach feel worse when the children suddenly scattered, running to pick them up.

When they got to the store, they couldn't get in because there was an elephant blocking the entrance.

SUNIL'S SISTER-IN-LAW WOULDN'T stop talking. She was giving Sunil a headache. Tell Hima this, tell her that.

"I am sorry, tell her I am so sorry, but Devdas says she should forget this idea. We already have three daughters. And he says there is nothing Indian about yours. She doesn't even speak our language. And he says, when it comes to marrying her off, why not save yourself the whole dowry business and let her marry a *gora*?"

"What's a gora?" Rani said from the doorway. "Is that like some kind of monkey?"

Sunil looked up. What had she heard? No, it seemed she didn't realize they were talking about her.

"It's a white person," he said. "Go play with your cousin."

"RANI," HIMA SAID, waving the blue airmail letter at her. "What is this nonsense about elephants?"

The letter had arrived weeks after they got back. Rani was sitting on the floor at her mother's feet in the living room, working on a jigsaw puzzle of the Taj Mahal, a present from her aunt. Her aunt had attached a note for her mother that Rani was forbidden to read.

"It's true!" Rani said.

"It couldn't have happened," Hima said. "There are no elephants in Delhi."

"It is true! Ask anybody."

"I miss them so much," Hima said. "I wish I could see their faces. My family. Not these elephants you imagined."

"We took pictures," Rani said. "But Dad lost the camera."

She was going to say that, anyway, there was only one elephant, she'd never said elephants. But then she remembered something her aunt had told her.

"I know where there were pictures of your family. Aunty said—"

"Yes, your father told me what she said," Hima said, rising from the couch. She and the couch both made a loud sound like breathing out. She headed to her sewing room, saying she had to finish marking her students' exams.

Face D

5. La chanson de Saraswati (Saraswati's Song)

1996
January

SUNIL COULD NEVER stop marvelling: his daughter a grown woman now. And she was as good as gold. She helped get him in the car, and then, after driving Hima to the airport, brought him back to her house. She even carried his bag and helped him up the stairs. As soon as he limped into the apartment, his granddaughters ran into his stomach like battering rams, shrieking.

"Back to bed!"

It was his son-in-law's voice. The girls ran, giggling, off to their bedrooms. Sunil found Rob and a young woman sitting across the living room from each other. Ah, this was Mélanie. She was sitting inappropriately, bare legs in a lotus position like a sadhu, bare feet on the sofa. Rob got up to greet him and then disappeared into the kitchen to get them both drinks.

"So, Rani tells me you're spreading your wings?" Sunil said to the young house guest.

"Excuse me?"

"You were living at home with your dad but you've flown the coop."

"Flown the coop?" Mélanie frowned. "You mean I've left home? Well, yeah, I'm twenty-one."

Twenty-one and too young to understand the most common of expressions, Sunil thought. Yet so sour. Rani had been sour too, he remembered. He looked at his granddaughters, who had snuck back into the living room and were now lying on their stomachs on the floor, pretending to be fish. He wasn't looking forward to seeing them turn into adolescents.

Or maybe, with this young woman, it was a language thing. Maybe he should try speaking French. He began practicing a phrase in his head but then Mélanie directed a question at Rob as he returned to the room.

"What do *you* do?"

Sunil watched as they gave each other exactly the same slow, sarcastic smile. Whatever it was, Mélanie's tone made clear, it couldn't be cool.

"I'm an anaesthesiologist assistant."

"An anaesthesiologist assistant," Mélanie repeated, separating the syllables carefully.

"It's a mouthful," Rob agreed.

Sunil wondered if she knew what the word meant.

"What does *your* father do?" Sunil asked Mélanie.

"He's a has-been," Mélanie said.

Give her a moment to take it back, or to explain. But his son-in-law broke the silence.

"Ah, grand. And what has he been?"

"He was a rock star," she said. "Have you ever heard of Sensibilité?"

"Oh, that's right," Rob said. "I remember now. Awful name for a band."

The name seemed familiar to Sunil too. He searched his memory, but couldn't find it.

"Yes," Mélanie said. "But, well, it was the seventies."

"True," said Rob. "Funny, I have a vague feeling I've already had this conversation with someone else."

"I guess you don't—"

"No, that's right, I'm the opposite. I'm anti-Sensibilité. I help put people to sleep."

"How? By boring them?"

Rob bristled, and Sunil felt offended too, on his behalf. Sunil wondered, for the first time, if Rani liked her job. Did she like this girl? Was the girl going to be staying long? When was she going to ask *him* about his work? What exactly had she been told about him? Did she know about the hydro-electric dams and the obstacle course that had been his life? He gazed at her, smiling, knowing it was a strained smile at best, feeling the tension in his own jaw. The two of them were not even looking at him.

"Boring them," Rob finally said. "Yes, that's one way. I also use drugs and needles."

"Then you *are* a bit like a rock star," Mélanie said.

Rob raised his eyebrows. Sunil felt he could hear him think, *Really, she has some neck!* He wished Rob would say something, wondered if he should intervene himself. He put his hand up, said, "Uh—"

"No, actually—anyway, my dad isn't like that," Mélanie said quickly. "He's just an old-fashioned drunk."

There was a silence. Sunil looked from face to face. So this was an Asian rock star who sang in French? Then he remembered that Rani had said Mélanie had been adopted from Vietnam. Sunil wondered if he should ask her about her mother now. Was it too late to ask her what her mother did for a living? Yes. Never mind.

"Oh, that reminds me. A drink. That's what I need," Rob said, and went to the kitchen. "Who wants a whiskey?"

"You just had one," Mélanie called, apparently further emboldened by the wall between them. "Are you an alcoholic too?"

"Nah," Rob said, from behind the wall. "I'm just Irish."

Sunil and Mélanie sat in silence, listening as Rob poured himself his drink. Pretty clear that he would be having it standing up, alone in the kitchen. Let this Irishman enjoy his drink.

Sunil waited, hoping Mélanie would ask him a question about himself. Instead, she grabbed the remote and pointed it at the TV. Lucien Bouchard appeared, followed by a scrum. Hobbling along on his one leg. Sunil felt a sharp stab in his chest. Flesh-eating disease. It was so preposterous. Sunil felt it could only be a message to him. Some kind of threat.

He cleared his throat, and ordered himself to be brave, get a hold of himself, clear these thoughts away. Bouchard's amputation had taken place over a year ago. This was no horror movie. He was in his daughter's home. The television was not his. Why would it be sending threats?

"Actually, I'm not supposed to drink," he told the girl, and held his glass out to her. "You see, it interferes with my medication."

She wasn't listening to him or the television. He followed her eyes. Fear seized him again: his son-in-law tiptoeing out of the kitchen, walking along the wall like someone in a spy movie. What was he doing? And then he was startled by a loud roar, and a second later relieved by piercing sounds, squeals and giggles, as Rob gathered both his daughters up in his arms and flung them into their bedroom.

THE GIRLS FINALLY settled, Sunil and Mélanie retired to their respective rooms. Rani took Rob's hand. They looked in on their daughters, and continued through the apartment to their bedroom. Rani caught her husband's whisper: "This should be interesting," he said.

SUNIL GOT UP to go to the bathroom. After flushing the toilet, he filled the glass next to the sink with water. He was about to take a sip when he noticed streaks of almost gummy grease where he was about to place his lips. He went down the hall to get a clean glass but paused when he heard Mélanie's voice, from the bedroom closest to the kitchen.

"So I told him: My little Chicano, you're not getting cheap Chinese labour from me. You have to go down on me too. That's the deal. And you can shave yours first."

Sunil froze, appalled. This wasn't what girls were supposed to be like. They were supposed to be modest, not vile like boys, like his brothers. In his half-sleepy, half-shocked-awake state he felt as if he had stumbled into another horror movie. He continued down the hall to look in on his granddaughters. He imagined Mélanie's bravado spreading like a contagious disease, infecting these sweet little girls. This was the girl who was, according to Rani, so curious about Sunil and Hima's story, but would not meet his eyes or say a word to him. Why? Who was she, exactly? He pushed some thoughts down. No. No connection to his brothers in India. There was no conspiracy. He knew that. But still. You could still distrust someone who wasn't part of a conspiracy, his psychiatrist would agree, and this girl, this stranger, had no business staying in the same apartment as his own darlings, his angels.

MORNING, FINALLY. SUNIL'S leg throbbing, his heart banging as he waited outside Rob and Rani's bedroom for one of them to emerge. Rob, in striped pyjamas, his eyes half-closed. Rob nodded at Sunil, sleepily pointed toward the bathroom and kept walking. Sunil followed along, as fast as his bandaged leg allowed. Excited, but keeping his voice low, he told Rob what he'd overheard. He chose his words with care. He kept staring at him, waiting for his expression to change. But this man really had one of those frozen faces, it seemed.

"I see. She did, did she? I suppose she was referring to her—" he patted his own crotch. "Is that right?"

"What kind of unmarried girl says things like this?" Sunil said. "I don't think Rani knows who she has invited into your home!"

RANI SAT UP in bed.

"Your poor dad," said Rob. "I think this young lass of yours is going to give him a heart attack. Apparently she talks about sex on the phone."

Rani laughed.

"So this means she has friends," he said. "Why doesn't she stay with them?"

Uh-oh.

"She was probably talking to her mother," Rani said. "She told me she calls her up late at night."

"She was saying something like 'I told him, I'm not shaving my cunt for you,'" Rob said.

"Oh my, and my dad heard that?"

"Yes, he told me that girls are not supposed to be vile like his brothers."

"My uncles are vile? Do go on."

But Rani knew he was dying to change the subject.

"So anyway, this was no conversation with her mother."

"Well, she'd say that Jane isn't her real mother," Rani said.

"And why doesn't she stay with this Jane person?"

Well, yes, I was expecting that question.

"Well, I think she'd say they're estranged," Rani answered.

She waved away what Rob began to say next.

"Okay," she said. "I'll talk to her."

RANI WAS SETTING her daughters up with bowls of cold cereal. When she spotted Mélanie coming out of the bathroom, she asked her to join her in the living room for a moment.

"So apparently my dad heard you having a raunchy conversation on the phone."

"What? What was he doing? Listening at my door?"

Rani had to admit that that was a possibility.

"He opens drawers and reads letters too," Rani said. "I just wanted to warn you—about that, and also, if he's a bit strange with you. I think he was a bit shocked by what he heard."

"He doesn't like me," Mélanie said, and pouted in a way that said she was both deeply hurt and completely indifferent. She told Rani that she had sensed his disapproval of her the moment they met. "And you're okay with all that, the eavesdropping and the snooping?"

"Well," said Rani, "he's my dad, and he is a bit eccentric." She wondered if she really wanted to trust this girl with all the details of Sunil's mental health. No. And anyway, that wasn't all it was, was it?

"Okay, well, I'm sorry if he heard something that shocked him."

"Look, he's from a different era, and a different culture. He and my mother knew each other seven years before they got married, but they were virgins on their wedding day."

"You're so lucky to know your parents' story," Mélanie said.

"Well, yeah, but my point is..."

"I get it. Yeah, cultural differences. Pretty different from what I'm used to. Jane is pretty much okay with anything."

Rob wouldn't forgive her if she missed this opportunity to say something.

"How is she, by the way?"

"Fine. Annoying, but fine."

"Yeah," Rani said, pausing before adding, "You know, maybe she's only annoying because she's your mother."

EXCEPT SHE'S NOT *my mother*. Mélanie politely excused herself, saying she needed some air. She put on her coat and went out into the cold Saturday morning. At first, she wandered around the neighbourhood. But she was underdressed, having left her hat and gloves at the apartment. She boarded the first bus she saw and ended up in the stuffy basement of the library again, poring over twenty-year-old newspaper articles in the microfiche room.

She couldn't figure out why she kept hitting a wall. Ever since she'd learned her original Vietnamese name, it had angered her that her parents had, with so little respect for it, mangled it into "Tweetie." But the survival of her name was in itself a miracle. The babies were just piled on planes without any identification tags, she'd read, given away upon landing to whomever had their hands out.

Mélanie had arrived in North America with a picture of herself as a six-month-old baby with a shock of black hair. On the back was her name in black ink and the year: *Thuy Thi Diep, 1975.*

"HOW DOES YOUR MOTHER feel about you wanting to go to Vietnam?" Rani asked Mélanie as they washed dishes together. Sunil was watching TV. Rob and the girls were at the dining room table playing Asshole, whispering the word instead of shouting it, as Rani had instructed.

"She really is very self-absorbed," Mélanie answered. "Anyway, it's none of her business."

"I was just thinking that she could help you out with the plane ticket."

"I'm sure she could. But I don't like asking her for money."

"Is that so bad?"

"You don't understand. She wants my company the way you want the company of an exotic bird in a cage."

Rani nodded.

"That's how I came to be hers in the first place, you know," Mélanie said. "And anyway, I don't want to travel the world. I just want to find my mother."

"You know that could take some time, right?" Rani said gently.

"Yeah, that's what Jane said. She said she'd help me. But of course, she wants something in return."

"The company of her little bird?" Rani asked, feeling she was betraying all mothers, including herself, with those words. She often felt she wanted her kids around her; whether she was *truly interested* in whatever complicated things were going on in their minds was a question she avoided troubling herself with. She just craved their physical presence, like warmth or food. What were Rita and Kira interested in? Establishing themselves as first and foremost in their parents' hearts, as far as she could see. The competition between the sisters half dismayed, half amused her.

"No, she wants me to help move stuff from her house into Serge's," she said.

"So she's sold her house?" Rani asked.

"She's still trying to. Right now she's just sort of emptying it. She wants me to get her stuff, put it in a van, take it to my dad's. I can't rent a van. You have to be twenty-five."

That night, Mélanie descended into what Rob liked to call her "mysterious funk." Rani felt guilty; she put the blame on the questions she'd asked. The girl hated this pressure to be involved in her parents' lives, and was fiercely opposed to having them in hers. But Rani felt she couldn't help it. She was supposed to be a guidance counsellor, but really, she was on the side of the oppressor, the parents. She thought of Serge in his hippie clothes. Hard to see him as an oppressor. That warm feeling again as she imagined his earnestness, the vulnerability in his voice, the love in his smile. But no: apart from being starstruck, imagine her own heartbreak—and especially Rob's—if her own daughters were to grow away from them.

"BUT I DON'T understand," Rita said to Mélanie.

"Me too," said Kira. "Me too, I don't understand."

"Don't you love the mother and father you have?" Rita asked.

It was a drizzly Saturday afternoon and the three of them were sitting cross-legged together on the living room floor.

"Are they bad?" asked Kira.

"It's not about that," Mélanie said.

"Why do you need more parents?" Rita asked. "Won't they just tell you what to do as well? I bet you don't even like it when your parents tell you what to do. You'll have four people telling you what to do all the time."

"Yeah, but at least she doesn't have a big sister," Kira said.

"Maybe she'll find out she has one," said Rita. "She could have this whole other family."

"Maybe they have a dog, and it doesn't like you and it wants to bite you."

"It's not about that," Mélanie said with a slight moan, aware now that the kids were too young for this conversation, but continuing anyway. "You know, if you grow up to be an alcoholic, you can say, oh, that's because of my dad, my dad being Irish and all. Or if your hair is curly, you can say, I got that from my dad. Or your dark brown eyes, well that's from your mother, because she's Indian."

"Mum isn't Indian," Rita said. "She's Canadian."

"Is that what she says?" Mélanie looked into each of their faces.

It was clear Kira was out of her depth but she struggled to say something.

"She's mostly like us," Kira said. "And when we're big, we will be grown-up ladies and we will look like her. Or maybe we'll be alcallics."

"Exactly. And that's what I want to know, about me," Mélanie said.

She resented having to defend herself to these children. Rani had set up this conversation, saying the girls had some questions for her. She sat in wool slippers pretending to read the paper in the opposite corner of the living room. *She really must be getting a kick out of this*, thought Mélanie. The only reason she was there was to save rent money, but maybe it wasn't worth it.

RANI COULD NOT focus on her newspaper. Bits of the living room conversation interrupted her reading at first. Then, a memory and all its brutal power invaded her thoughts: a fall day on Mont Royal, Rita less than a year old, a peeping little chick, her baby hair fine and blond.

An old woman approaching, Rani smiling, anticipating fawning words.

But instead: "What did you do, you dirty brown monkey? Screw a white man so you could have a blond child?" Rob returning from the snack bar just in time to see Rani's shocked face. "What's wrong, Rani? What happened? You're white!"

The memory played over and over. She wished she could press Stop, tape over it with something pleasant, finally erasing it. Her brain did not work the way she wished it did. Why had she let it record this scene in the first place?

MÉLANIE WAS ALONE in the apartment with Sunil now. She'd been pretending to doze on the sofa to avoid having to talk to him. His wife was coming back from India, so he'd be going home this evening. She guessed he figured this was his last chance to do his thing. She watched him, bemused, as he limped around, opened drawers, examined pens, peeked inside envelopes. He even looked under chairs, as if expecting to find listening devices. If Jane and Serge snooped, she'd set a trap. But no, Mélanie reflected, they wouldn't do that; they didn't care enough about her.

Suddenly, Sunil made a surprised, satisfied noise as he pulled a Walkman from a drawer. *Good for you*, Mélanie thought, amused now. He pressed a button, and a low buzz of music reached her ears.

Clarinet, and then—

Ugh.

That. Their double album. *Une convergence de solitudes.* She got up and walked toward Sunil. He acknowledged her with a guilty smile. *Caught snooping*, he must have been thinking. He had no idea. How weird. Rani's dad, doing his thing, comes across her own dad doing *his*. That music carried so many memories for her. The familiar sweetness of the clarinet gave her a sick feeling. Serge's voice. So irritating. She wondered whose Walkman this was. Which one of them was the fan? She hoped it wasn't Rani.

"Silly me. Listening to rock music in the morning."

"I know that band," she told him.

He handed her the headphones. She pressed play, fast forward, play. The whole tape was full of it. A gnawing suspicion of impending hurt. She handed back the headphones.

"There is even a harmonium in some of the songs," said Sunil. "It sounds like my wife's did. It has a bit of a rattle in it. Do you hear it?"

"Not sure," said Mélanie, but she waved away the headphones that he was holding out to her again. She tried to remember if she had ever seen a harmonium growing up.

"You know, I have been trying to find out what happened to that harmonium. She sold it, but she really shouldn't have. It was my fault."

He wasn't making a lot of sense. He looked so sad. Kind of touching, how he trusted her with whatever this was.

"Hey, that's too bad," Mélanie said.

"I would really like to find it for her," he said.

His lips formed an upside-down letter *u*, as if he would start bawling any minute. Such a naked face, like a little kid's. She felt herself melting, was about to offer to help look into it for him when his expression changed, like he'd realized something, and he suddenly asked, "What is this album called?"

"It's—in English it would be, like, *A Convergence of—*"

"I remember now!" Sunil said. "Rani used to listen to this music over and over."

"Really? *This* music?"

How could she!

Overwhelmed by alarm. Ringing in her ears, her head, her chest. And fear, fear of her own rage at this betrayal.

"Yes, yes," said Sunil. "Over and over. Like a crazy person."

SUNIL WAS BACK with Hima. Mélanie had been in a snippy sort of mood recently; at dinner that evening she seemed to be trying to express something through deliberate rudeness. She was playing with her food, making disgusted faces like a baby.

"Is something wrong?" Rob asked. He and Rani had collaborated on the preparation of this meal, Irish steak-and-kidney pie with a crust they'd made from scratch according to his mother's recipe. Mélanie didn't answer, and Rob glared at her, clearly piqued as he watched her lift the pieces of meat out of the shell and place them carefully at the far side of her plate.

"Yeah, fine, just eat the potatoes," Rob finally said.

That was all he said, but the ice in his voice was unmistakable, and after a few seconds, Mélanie pushed her chair back and went to her room without a word.

"Wow!" Rita said. Kira repeated it, and they continued for a few seconds. "Wow oh wow."

"Was she raised by wolves?" Rob asked Rani.

"Something like that," Rani said.

There were different ways to express an imperfect upbringing, is what she said to herself. She knew that she, for her part, had manners that could be described as obsequious, to make up for her own parents' gaffes. They'd had so much to adjust to in Canada, so much going on. She thought of how their habits had embarrassed her, even Sunil's English sometimes. He still called his wallet a "purse" and his underwear "panties," much to Rob's frequent amusement.

MONDAY MORNING, RANI up before everyone else, as usual. So mild these days, maybe cycle to work. She went to the storeroom. The children's bikes were there, but where was hers? She frowned and thought. Rob had once cycled to the metro and forgotten his bike there on the way back, walking home instead. By the time he'd remembered, it was gone. Oh no, had she done the same thing?

She looked out the window. Snow was falling now; she'd take the bus. She went over to the table by the front door and picked up the chipped green bowl where they kept the loose change. No quarters shone up at her, just the dull brown of pennies. She poured some coins into her palm slowly, sifting through them for glints of silver. One nickel, two dimes.

She looked in her purse. She didn't carry change in her wallet. She took out the sole five-dollar bill she found and just stared at it for a moment. *Shouldn't there be more of you?* She returned to the bedroom, picked Rob's pants up from the floor. To her relief, there was enough change for the bus. She put the coins in the pocket of her jacket and looked over at her sleeping husband, rolled over on his side. His eyebrows reaching toward each other, his mouth open. He looked like a man listening to someone, maybe just his wife skulking around the room.

She'd ask the kids in the evening. They might have needed to raid the dish for a bake sale at school.

SIXTY-FIVE BUCKS is what she got for the electric guitar. Twenty for the bike. Plus the ten dollars from the change bowl and Rani's purse. Not worth it, not worth the paranoia. Already convinced that Rani and her husband had discovered the thefts, that the unintelligible drone of sound she had heard from beyond their bedroom wall last night was all about her.

At the library, trying to focus on her research, but the wadded cash in her pocket kept intruding on her thoughts. A paltry ninety-five bucks. Nowhere near the amount she would need for a ticket to Vietnam. She re-read her notes, made herself stare down at the steps laid out on the page, the information she would have to track down for *the basic right of knowing who her real parents were.* She looked around at the other people at the library, anger churning in her gut. She had written these notes after reading an article about an American boy her age who had found his biological parents. Once this boy had located the orphanage and adoption agency, a path had become clear for him. She looked at her notes.

1. your Vietnamese name
2. your adoptive parents' name
3. the orphanage you were from and age on arrival
4. any birth records with names of Vietnamese parents

5. the village, district, or province you were from
6. the year you were adopted, left Vietnam, and what age you were
7. baby photos, distinguishing features

What did she have?
She carefully filled in:

1. Thuy Thi Diep
2. Jane Plant. Serge Giglio.
3. ?
4. ?
5. Ho Chi Minh/Saigon
6. 1975, six months
7. one baby photo

She read on. Sources of information included adoptive parents, adoption agencies, a local state or federal government department that administered immigration and adoption, orphanage papers with signatures, year of your birth and village, people involved in Operation Babylift, the adoption agency that arranged your adoption.

State or federal department. By which they meant the States, and this was Canada.

The library had no answers, of course. Jane had the photo but she always insisted that she didn't remember anything. When Mélanie tried to conjure her early past, an image always came to her of murky water, rather than, say, helicopters and medical personnel. She gathered her papers and left the building. It was almost February; winter was nowhere near over. It had snowed all morning and now the sun was coming out. But the sun had no warmth, just this weak light. She examined the people at the bus stop, their sensible toques and scarves. The long weeks of colder weather that were surely coming were meant for them, not her. It would be warm in Vietnam. She would have to figure it out, how to raise the rest of the cash. Jane would give her the money for a ticket in a heartbeat, but she would want something in return. What might be lying around her house that Mélanie could pawn somewhere? No, not that way. When she'd carried her hosts' bike and guitar off, it had thrilled her. So crazy and dangerous and justified. But the anger she normally felt for Jane had dissipated since she had moved out. And stealing was risky. The thought that Rob and Rani would inevitably discover what she'd done chilled her for a moment. Then she put it out of her mind.

SUCH A SIMPLE thing she needed. Some of the people waiting with her looked like students. The useless courses she had taken; they couldn't help her with anything. If only she could change one tiny law of physics and cross the distance to where she belonged.

As if responding to her impatience, a bus suddenly barrelled into view.

On the way back to Rob and Rani's apartment, she stood, holding onto a pole, gazing around, hating everyone. How many people on the bus had to go to the library to figure out who they were? Her gaze skimmed over the groups of white, French-Canadian students. Then she scanned the bus for people who were obviously related to each other. Two teenage boys, apparently twins, with spiky, super-gelled blond hair. A man with criss-cross cornrows, a little boy who appeared to be his son in his lap. Next to them, a large, older woman in a shapeless coat who seemed to be the boy's grandmother, muttering abuse at the young man. Two boys with side-curls sitting with an older man in a fur cap, all wearing coke-bottle glasses. A brown woman wearing too much rouge, chatting softly with her lighter-skinned daughter. A flash of Rani on the bus that day with the guy in the turban. What had that been about? Rani had seemed so unhappy. It struck her that nobody on the bus really looked all that happy.

And then, walking up the stairs to Rani and Rob's apartment, she remembered her more specific rage against Rani—not a friend, after all, just another crazy fan—and it suddenly struck her as absurd. Her thoughts turned to what she had done, the previous day, when everyone had been out. As she unbolted the door, she recalled her bitter and desperate mood, and felt slightly sick. This was followed by a feeling of apprehension even before she heard Rob's voice, and the actual words he was calling out to his wife.

"Rani, have you seen my guitar?"

RANI THOUGHT SHE KNEW, but didn't want to. Rob seemed more interested in getting her to acknowledge this than actually getting his guitar back. They both knew he could only remember how to play one song, "The Fields of Anthenry"; the performances were sporadic, happening when he was both drunk and melancholy. It was always strange to watch him bumbling around, plugging the thing into its amp, the prongs hitting the side of the socket a few times before finally going in. Then he would kneel on the sofa because standing was too hard, but sitting was a cop-out. He'd strum and sing in his sloppy, inebriated way, his Irish *r*'s curling richly and ringing out. Rani didn't particularly want him to inflict any of this on their guest.

But yeah, it was probably true, what Rob suspected. Mélanie hadn't been able to meet her eyes as she came through the door.

"If you don't ask her," Rob said to Rani in their bedroom. "I will."

There was a knock. Rob opened the door and stood back, waiting.

"I sold it. Your bike too."

The couple looked at each other. What kind of answer was this?

"I'm not kidding. They're in a pawn shop on Masson Street."

"Why are you telling us this?" Rob asked.

Mélanie went to her room. A minute later, she emerged with her knapsack. She removed a card from an outside pocket. She came back into the hall, where they were both waiting for her, and handed the card to Rob. The card gave the address of the pawn shop.

"Are you going to call the police?" she asked.

"Get out!"

Rani was taken aback; she had never heard Rob shout, except in jest.

"I'm sorry," Mélanie said. She moved toward the door. She was in tears as she turned back and repeated her question. Kira and Rita flew out of their room, and both tried to enclose her with their arms, their eyes shut tight. Mélanie stood stiffly in their embrace, and waited for Rob and Rani to answer her.

But Rani and Rob had no words.

A moment later, the anger blew out of Rob, and Rani finally said a soft "No."

Mélanie had already disappeared down the stairs by then.

"YOU NEVER LIKED her at all," Rani said to Rob. "Even before. You must be glad she's gone."

They were talking in the living room after having put the kids back to bed. Rani was sitting on the couch listening to the complaints Rob was finally voicing as he walked around the room, picking up after "that strange young lass." He held up one comb and one hairbrush, both full of hair, three plastic candy wrappers, a cellophane bag containing a few broken peanuts and an alarming amount of salt.

"Not a big fan," he said.

She felt her shoulders relax, a ball of tightness in her chest slowly unravel. Rob was laying down the law now, no more students staying over, no more contact with that strange girl—and she loved him for it. She needed him to keep her grounded. She held out both her arms the way the girls did when they demanded hugs. He bent down, slid his arms around her waist and squeezed her.

"So, you hated her."

"No, it's—" he waved his right hand around, palm up, searching for his words. "Maybe I'm a wee bit Olde World. I don't know. I found her self-absorbed."

"Like…" Rani thought a minute and then repeated a phrase Kira had uttered recently, "'I don't think a day has ever gone by that I didn't sneeze once.'"

"No. Not in a cute way. Mélanie was more of a brat. Rude."

"Oh." This had not occurred to Rani. "I guess I don't see that anymore, or I don't mind it. I see so many students…"

"They're all like this, are they?"

Rani frowned, thinking. She knew what he meant about Mélanie's rudeness, but thought of it differently, found this sass, or bravado, or whatever it was, especially endearing for what it masked. And she loved how the masks kept slipping.

"Well, weren't you self-involved when you were that age?" Rani asked, although she couldn't imagine it. Rob was Rob. He was kind and good.

Rob shrugged. "Beats me. No, honestly, I was a wee bit worried about the effect she was having on the girls. Maybe I just don't want them to grow up too fast."

Grow away, *you mean*, thought Rani. She pictured them now, in the next room, rolled into their blankets like crepes, the soft, steady way they breathed in their sleep. How she and Rob could just go in and check on them anytime they liked during the night. For some reason, no matter the season, Kira's hair was always pine-scented, and Rita's was warm and earthy.

"She swiped my old Walkman too, you know. She probably thought an old fart like me wouldn't miss my music."

An alarm went off in Rani's chest. She crossed the room to check her desk. Her own Walkman was still in the drawer, where she had buried it under a pile of envelopes. Relief. So close to being found out. And she felt protective of those songs.

"You know, at the very least, we should have let her dad know she was here," Rob said, as if reading her mind. "He must have been going out of his mind with worry."

Rani looked at him, surprised. *Of course.*

At work the next day, Rani studied the address and phone number in Mélanie's file.

6. Le pays qu'on choisit
(The Country We Choose)

February

MÉLANIE TOOK THE METRO all the way to Lionel-Groulx, and then a bus to Pointe Claire. She walked three blocks to her mother's house, preparing what she would say. *Help me, I think the police might be after me—*? At six in the evening the winter sky held little light, the moon a thin fingernail-clipping, the streets nearly still. She noticed two people standing in their respective bungalows, looking out their wide living room windows. She imagined they had fear on their faces, like her, but for different reasons. She recalled her father telling her that back in 1980 René Lévesque called the people living here on the West Island, the most Anglo of Québec enclaves, "sleeping cows."

This time around, she knew, all the cows were awake, even now still terrified; the referendum had come so close to passing. What did they imagine was coming? War planes? Agent Orange?

Her thoughts turned again to her own fear, the possibility of being arrested. What an idiotic idea that had been, to raid Rani's storeroom to get closer to her goal of finding her family in Vietnam.

Mélanie wanted to believe that the police *weren't* coming after her. She frantically weighed the probability of each outcome. The guy at the pawnshop seemed sloppy and indifferent, but Rani's husband had been so pissed off. She hoped Jane would help her. It occurred to her that Jane might be happy about this, beyond having her pet back. Maybe she'd be really pleased with Mélanie's deed; didn't she like to think of herself as some kind of anarchist?

WHEN MÉLANIE GOT to Jane's house, there was a shiny car in the driveway. She opened the door and there was a strange woman in the vestibule, her back to her, speaking in a loud voice and gesticulating. The woman glanced over her shoulder, and Mélanie heard Jane say, in a delighted voice, "That's my daughter," whereupon the woman turned back and kept talking. For once, Mélanie thought, no surprise on the stranger's face, no interest at all; it exuded greed, and nothing else.

"These aren't normal times. You aren't going to find many buyers with the PQ still in power. It's up to you. You can make those changes, lower your price, or plan on sticking around a lot longer."

Jane appeared, smiling, from inside the vestibule doorway. She ushered Mélanie in. The woman said she was just leaving, emphasizing her words as if to make clear which option she preferred herself. She looked like an alternative version of Jane, same age, height, colouring and shape, but dressed in an expensive suit, her hair in a puffy do. A love of money: that's where the lack of curiosity came from, Mélanie thought.

"So, you're back, are you?" Jane said as she closed the door.

Mélanie's head began to ache and she was on the verge of tears. But pride kept her from confessing why she was there. She answered Jane with a shrug. She stepped into the living room and looked around. There were no cardboard boxes, but the place looked bare. Jane's paintings and their family photos were gone, and the walls were white now; they had been a sort of turnip-orange for as long as Mélanie could remember. She shivered, and she felt Jane's eyes on her.

"You're not going to sell your house with it looking like this," Mélanie said. "It's so cold."

Jane replied that she might be right. The house wasn't selling. There was no way anyone was ever going to buy a house in Québec in this political climate, and the demands the real estate agent was making reeked of this futility, it seemed to her: empty the house, take down all the pictures, paint all the walls white, reduce it to a shell nobody could imagine living in, halve the price. Jane said she planned to store all her furniture at Serge's house. There was certainly room there, for his house too was a shell, apart from the two rooms where his clothes and instruments lay strewn.

"Tweetie," Jane said. "What's wrong? Are you crying? Is this about your father? Or is this about…a boy?"

"Oh, Mum," Mélanie said, as she covered her face with her hands.

AS MÉLANIE HAD half expected, her mother didn't mind the truth as much as a normal mother, or at least what she thought of as a normal mother, would have.

"Don't worry," Jane said. "The cops aren't after you. They have bigger fish to fry, Tweetie."

Mélanie allowed Jane to lead her to the couch, to hold her and stroke her hair.

"Those people aren't going to call the police, Mélanie. Other people would find that dodgy, you know, someone working as your guidance counsellor housing you at her apartment."

Mélanie shrugged. She was crying now, but this was a release. It was comforting, how sure Jane was. Well, of course, she was older, she knew how some things worked. The police had bigger fish to fry. She could relax.

But here came a sickening wave of remorse as Rani's concerned face popped into her thoughts. So Rani liked that hippie music of her father's. So what? She wasn't exactly the only one. What was she going to do, break into all her music-student friends' houses and steal their guitars and bicycles? And then try to return them before they called the police? Was this how she was going to try to calm herself down, creating problems, piling them on top of one another? That would never help anything. All the grieving and raging and not knowing.

"Come to think of it, don't you find it odd?"

"What?" Mélanie said. And then, "Oh."

"No, Mum," she finally said, pulling a wad of tissue out of the pocket of her jeans, wiping her eyes and her nose. "They're nice people."

"Well, all the more reason they won't call the police on you, then," Jane said. "But you can hide here if you like, just in case."

Mélanie watched Jane's face as she looked around her living room with a wry smile before adding: "If you can find a place to hide."

Mélanie allowed her mother to put a hand under her chin and gaze into her eyes. She knew what was coming next.

"You did this to buy a ticket to Vietnam, didn't you? Why didn't you come to me?"

MÉLANIE USED JANE'S digital typewriter to write to several government departments in Vietnam. Beginning at ten at night—nine in the morning Vietnamese time—she dialled long strings of numbers and finally managed to contact a nurse who worked in an orphanage in Saigon, who contacted someone else, and this person had a look through the records. They did have a record of someone with her name, she said, but that child was sent to parents in the United States, through an American organization. Mélanie was so disappointed that she could barely speak. She thanked the woman, and then rolled off her chair onto her bed, lay on her stomach and wept. Jane was knocking on her bedroom door, but she didn't feel like talking about it.

"All right, love," came the voice on the other side of the door. "We'll talk in the morning."

"SO YOU DID STEAL ME," said Mélanie

"I honestly forgot you were missing that bit of information. It just didn't occur to me." It wasn't stealing!

Mélanie didn't answer. She was waiting, Jane knew, in case more information was forthcoming.

"Can I make it up to you? I honestly didn't know there was—" Jane stopped speaking for a moment, aware that she sounded like a liar. "Is it true, that there is a record of you before you went to America? I'm trying to remember. Everything was a bit slapdash. Look, I'll pay for your flight and I'll do anything to help you find your family." It hurt her to say that word, *family*. The one she had tried to make with Serge was a complete failure.

Mélanie was silent.

"I can pay for your flight, Tweetie," Jane said again.

"You want to come with me." This wasn't a question. Her voice was cold. Jane imagined Mélanie was trying to control her fury.

"This is … It's …" Jane's voice kept breaking. She cleared her throat and began again, a little raspy. *This is what an old broken woman sounds like*, she thought, *a broken, old, wealthy woman who once tried to buy some meaning*. "I'll just pay for your flight. I don't mind. I won't come."

She was sobbing now. Mélanie didn't say anything.

Listening to her sobs filling the silence, Jane was struck again by how much older she had become. The sounds of a tired, decrepit person trying to catch up to a runner decades younger. Mélanie went back up to her room, slamming her door.

WHEN JANE HAD first come to Québec, it had felt incredibly freeing. She could reinvent herself, live according to her own principles, away from the county set, the snobs of her parents' circle. She avoided English people, and even Anglophones, afraid that as soon as she opened her mouth, they would understand exactly who she was. She became a master at hiding herself. Most of the time, Serge and his crowd trusted her, saw her as a kind of pet. She didn't exactly fit in with them. But she could never imagine returning home, where she would be seen as a traitor, to her country and to her class.

But now that she was growing older, she didn't feel at home anywhere anymore. She found herself on a road getting further and further away from the period in her life where her most salient memories still lived, her twenties. She felt as though she was driving away from the world she knew best how to navigate.

It was getting harder to learn new things. She felt one step behind all the time. She asked Mélanie to record the outgoing message for the answering machine. She gave her her digital typewriter as she could not even begin to figure out how it worked. Every time she went to the store to rent a video, she had to remember two codes, one for her membership to the store, and the other for her bank card, only to find, once home, that she was unable to correctly identify the remote control that went with her vhs player—repeatedly confusing it with the phone—let alone *program* the thing.

Mélanie had been happy to have the typewriter, emerging from her customary surliness to thank her.

"What's so great about it?" Jane asked her.

"It's got memory!" Mélanie said.

Jane wondered if this was a joke at her expense.

For it seemed to Jane that she had to resort to extreme measures to remember anything now. She couldn't remember where her things were, things she used every day, like her toothbrush or the teapot. Something else had happened to her brain: listening to phone messages, she was usually unable to process the information. In particular, any numerical information and spellings of names ran by her ears. She couldn't catch them. It was as if her brain was broken.

And there were the problems with clothes. Nothing looked right on her anymore. She would buy a dress because it looked good on a mannequin, and she knew from experience that if it fit a mannequin, it would be made for a slender woman and therefore fit her. But even if it slipped over her head and everything, it would never fit the same way it used to. She seemed to have shrunk a bit, and she had love handles now, despite the fact that she weighed the same as she always had, and moved about as much as she always did. She stared at her reflection in the hallway mirror. There were creases around her neck now, marking her age like the rings around a tree. The clothes didn't match the rest of her; they suddenly looked too feminine and slightly silly, as if made for a doll.

Before she discarded them, she would let her daughter try them on. She knew that these same dresses on her lovely young daughter would somehow just make her beauty shine the brighter.

But as Tweetie grew more beautiful, the angrier and more estranged she became. She had been threatening to go to Vietnam to find her real mum for years; Jane had no idea how many, but it was coming, she could feel it, and maybe she would not be invited along. How painful that would be. She would not be able to stand it.

She wondered where she could go, whether the solution really was returning to England, hiding herself from the world in her parents' huge mansion. Her father was in hospital, her mother had told her the last time they'd spoken on the phone. She didn't seem to know why; in fact, she'd sounded completely barmy. A slight shock as Jane realized: they were both almost eighty.

If she were a different sort of person, she would step up, take control. Try to acquire power of attorney, turn the estate over to a charitable organization. She thought of stories she'd heard of large estates being used to house refugees from Palestine in the sixties, and more recently transformed into rehab centres for young drug addicts and alcoholics. She felt quite sure that she was incapable of doing any of this. There was nobody she could even talk to anymore. Her head was aching. She needed to lie down.

AT SUPPER THAT EVENING, Jane admitted that she didn't remember the name of her friend's adoption agency; nor did she remember Pamela's last name. She did recall the first and last name of a mutual friend of theirs who had remained in England, someone she was sure could jog her memory. Directory Assistance was able to obtain that person's phone number.

She studied the number.

"071," she said. "That's London, I believe."

Mélanie waited. Her face seemed to say, "I've been waiting for twenty years."

"But it's nearly two in the morning there, Mélanie, love. We'll ring her in the morning."

Mélanie was mute. Jane saw both disappointment and faint hope in her face.

The next morning, Jane opened her eyes and met Mélanie's gaze; she was staring at her from the doorway as if she had been willing her to wake up. In her face now, something between impatience and rage.

"Look, I know you've been waiting," she said. "But Tweetie, it's not even light out yet."

Mélanie said nothing, her face still tight with anger.

"Yes, all right, fine," Jane said. It was too early in Québec, but a decent time to call across the ocean. She pulled on her terry-cloth bathrobe, aware of Mélanie's unsparing gaze at her flabby white arms. She guessed what Mélanie was thinking, certainly not for the first time: *not my real mother.* "But Mélanie, you're not going to wait in the doorway. Alicia and I will have some catching up to do. You'll have to be patient."

MÉLANIE WENT to her bedroom. So strange to be back in this room. She felt like an enormous child. As she thought this, she allowed herself to sink into bed and fall back asleep. She had barely slept all night, thinking she had to stand vigil over Jane's bed, to make sure she didn't leave the house before making at least one phone call. The dreams she had now were about malfunctioning phones, wrong numbers, calling Rani by mistake, calling Serge but getting a busy signal.

March

JANE AND ALICIA'S old friend Pamela was travelling in Asia and could not be reached. A week passed. Mélanie taught Jane how to use her digital typewriter. Jane went out one day to run some errands and returned with a damaged black Lab called Bailey.

"I am just fostering him," she told Mélanie, who hadn't asked. "It's just until someone wants to adopt him."

Bailey bit a prospective buyer the real estate agent brought during the first week of March. Jane reluctantly returned the dog to the shelter.

Jane was finally able to reach Pamela, who said that, yes, there were records, that copies were on file at the agency, and that Mélanie's birth mother's name would be on them. At first they were excited, euphoric. Then, as they settled in to wait for these papers in the mail, they grew agitated. A week of gloomy skies, followed by one of freezing rain and flurries, then two more grey weeks featuring drizzle and fog. Both Jane and Mélanie's moods worsened as time went on, stuck in the suburbs in this empty house that nobody wanted to buy. Jane cooked her simple British meals, beans on toast, mac and cheese; they ate their meals together, but in stony silence. Jane registered and resented the recrimination that had returned to her daughter's expression.

The day the envelope arrived, the sky cleared. When Mélanie brought in the mail, Jane complimented her on her colouring, saying her face had the beauty of a warm spring day. Mélanie's cheeks were flushed and she seemed very nervous, but she only muttered that it was still pretty cold. One of the envelopes, Jane saw, was junk mail from another realtor. Mélanie laid this on the small table by the door. The other had her name on it, and American stamps.

Best give her some space. Jane threw on her jacket, stepped into her boots and pushed past her daughter in the vestibule. It would do her good to get some fresh air too. She went through the door and down the front steps, but turned around as she heard Mélanie call her back.

"I'm so nervous," Mélanie said. "Could you stay here—?"

"Of course, sweetheart."

Jane gave her an encouraging smile as she tore open the envelope.

A sharp intake of breath.

And then:

A birth certificate, with the name of her biological mother. Mélanie's eyes filled with tears.

And then:

A form describing a baby's measurements and vital signs.

In a note accompanying the documents, Pamela mentioned a woman in Ho Chi Minh City who had been a matron at the orphanage back then, and whom she thought might know where to find Mélanie's biological mother.

In an awed, shaking voice, Mélanie began to read, "Her name is Annie Hoang. She is in her sixties now. She and I don't understand each other very well. My Vietnamese is gone, and so is her English. But she does speak French."

Mélanie put the note down. Jane picked it up and read the last line aloud.

"Here is her phone number, if you would like to give her a try."

7. Feu de joie (Bonfire)

April

RANI ON THE PHONE. Chit-chat, this and that. And then, before she hung up:

"One of these days, can you tell me about how you and Mom met, and about Partition?"

"Okay," Sunil said. "Whenever you want. When you have time."

He didn't dare push.

He had been waiting for a question like this for years. He felt he understood her better than she did herself, remembered what she couldn't—how, as a tiny child, she had tried to scrub her skin of its colour with soap. As she'd grown older, she'd insisted to him that, unlike her brothers, she was not Indian, as she had been born in Canada. When she was a teenager, if he tried to share his past with her she would turn and walk away, fingers literally in ears. She had been so fierce in her indifference to her Indian heritage—as if distancing herself would change the way she was perceived by other people, make her more acceptable, regular, if not white then at least not foreign. All it had taken to change her attitude, Sunil said to Hima, was for one of the students she counselled to point out that her family had a story and that she ought to be curious about it.

"That was the same girl you met," said Hima.

"I suppose so," said Sunil. "I didn't care for her very much."

Hima was always saying that the student seemed to take up an inordinate amount of Rani's attention. She wondered aloud to Sunil if her daughter wasn't a bit like Sunil, someone who thought too much about one thing, to the point that it started to be unhealthy.

"Is that my problem, then?" Sunil said.

"Yes, I think so," Hima said, patting his hand.

They gave each other wry, gentle smiles.

SERGE HAD BEEN out for a long walk after a night of insomnia. He hadn't been able to fall asleep after an evening out with his friend Alain, Alain's wife, Brigitte, and their daughter, Anne-Sophie, who was about Mélanie's age. The couple had gently brought up a rumour that Serge was composing music again. Some of Anne-Sophie's questions had not sat well with him. What does it feel like, being an aging rock star? He'd bristled. "Do I look like an aging rock star?" He looked like any grey-haired man with a paunch and a moustache, and he hadn't released a record in almost two decades. "But you are composing," Alain insisted.

He had been *thinking* about composing. He had also been *thinking* about giving up alcohol. He ended up drinking five glasses of whiskey that night, and his mouth felt dry and bitter; his head throbbed. At noon he'd gotten up and walked all the way from La Petite-Patrie to Mont Royal, where he stood remembering Jane, when they'd both been young. And the dream he had been so sure everyone shared, of really being able to say *chez nous*. They would get another chance, wouldn't they? The big white dome of the Olympic Stadium caught his eye. No one could figure out what to do about the roof. That place would never be finished. But he still had his dream; hope stubbornly lingered in his heart. He walked home.

JANE CALLED SERGE but got his answering machine. He returned her call when she was out; Mélanie didn't pick up.

"You got a booty call," is all she said. Everything Mélanie said to her that wasn't harsh with rage had this cool flippancy. The closer she got to meeting her biological mother—she had her contact information now, but had to apply for a passport and then a visa—the more nervous Mélanie got, and Jane bore the brunt of her stress. She thought back to the first time she'd held her in her arms. The promise of the baby girl with the pink label, a new beginning fresh from the other side of the world.

"RITA! KIRA! THE bus is here. Where are you?"

Rani moved from the living room window, where she felt, rather than saw, Marie-Claude, the school bus driver, and a dozen or so children peering at her from the road. In the vestibule, one of the girls' coats lay on the rubber mat, three of their rain boots, and both of their little Lion King backpacks.

Rani went to the kitchen and saw that their cereal bowls were empty but that their lunches hadn't been taken from the counter and zipped into their backpacks. She grabbed the lunches and began stuffing them in the bags, all the while pacing the hall and checking their bedrooms. Where could they be?

Marie-Claude honked, twice.

"Do you hear that?" Rani called. "Where are you?"

She was standing outside her own bedroom, the one she shared with Rob, as she said this, and now she heard a low groan and some whispers.

"Girls! Oh, come on now!"

There they were, in their school clothes, lying on either side of their father, their little curly heads barely visible under the sheets, at the level of his shoulders. The bus would leave now, and she herself had to be at work in half an hour.

"Rob," Rani pleaded, "please honey, help me here."

She knew he was exhausted from doing a late shift at Emergency. He slept as if he'd put *himself* under when he came home. Sometimes she thought it was more emotional exhaustion than physical tiredness. He didn't talk about the things he saw, but since what he saw tended to be emergency operations involving children, she could imagine that they would be pretty harrowing. She kissed his head, and then, with regret, pressed his shoulders, nudged him awake and asked him if he could bring the kids to school.

He opened his eyes and gave her a good-natured smile but shook his head no and plunged it back into his pillow. She wondered if it had something to do with how she looked. The last person in 1996 to wear rollers to bed, or so her husband claimed.

"Could you…um, get their coats on, then, so I can get dressed, please?"

"I know!" Rob said, raising his head from his pillow. "I can call them in sick!"

Rani felt a mix of delight and guilt. This Rob would do, stay home with his daughters even though they were only pretending to be asleep, and would both be jumping on the bed in a minute. For her, going to work in the morning after having dispatched the children felt like a release. Work was nothing compared to a day with these monkeys.

A LETTER IN the mailbox. No return address, but she recognized the handwriting. She tore it open, excitedly. Inside, a cheque from Mélanie for a hundred and fifty dollars. A note with the words "I'm sorry" and a simple drawing of a girl in long braids and a conical hat riding a bicycle.

Relief that the bad feelings were over. Also, hope that this meant Mélanie was ready to accept her mother's help, that things were better between them.

An image came to her of the girl standing sullenly before her, a backpack on the ground next to her. Wanting to escape her life, she had said, something to do with both her adoptive and birth mothers escaping theirs. Would she, Rani, ever leave her daughters? No, she wouldn't leave Kira and Rita, of course she wouldn't think of it. But she wished Mélanie, who had felt abandoned by both of her mothers, could know this, that every mother was a person, a person with her own selfish, even ridiculous dreams, every mother felt a little oppressed by her children, every mother occasionally dreamed of running away. This was the only honest and useful thing she could ever have said to her.

But then who was she to say how every mother felt? It wasn't as if she had ever been a normal person. Rani imagined herself running up to Mélanie, joining her in a queue at the airport.

CAKED IN ASHES, Jane stood in her backyard, watching the final blaze. It had taken four. Hands in pockets, blowing some dusty strands of hair out of eyes, wishing she had a cigarette, but then maybe she'd spontaneously combust; she was surely as flammable as her paintings. The fire appearing to make a point about her paintings: *nothing there*. Felt good. The word itself, *bon*fire, couldn't be bad. Emptying all of that space in her house gave her such peace and clarity. This, and not producing and hoarding paintings, was her yoga. From now on, if the urge came back, she'd paint a couple of kites, donate them to a children's organization afterwards. She frowned. Could that work?

The phone rang, startling her.

By the time she entered the house it had stopped ringing. She wiped her hands on her pants and waited.

A moment later, it began again.

"Oui, allô?"

"Mum, hi."

"Oh, hi, love. How are you getting on?"

Mélanie had gone downtown to pick up her passport. Perhaps just calling to say she was staying in town that night.

"Fine, fine. The thing is, I was wondering…"

Or maybe this was about a lift, or a loan.

"I mean, like…" Mélanie said. "Is *your* passport up to date?"

"What?" Jane said. She closed her eyes. Made her voice breezy. "Why?"

"I was wondering," Mélanie started again.

A pause, as if her voice kept snagging on something. And then, "It's just that I'm—"

"Of course—" This was excruciating. Her ballsy daughter, all sass one moment, and then this small, halting voice. How distressingly vulnerable she could sound these days.

"—*terrified*," Mélanie said.

The awkward, heavy way the word landed.

"Of course," Jane said again, "Of course you are. And yes, my passport is up to date."

RANI WAVED AWAY the bills her father was offering her.

"Don't be ridiculous, Dad."

Could she say something like that to him or would it carry too much meaning? She glanced at him. No, oblivious.

"Anything, my dear," Sunil said. "There must be something you would like. How about a nice new coat?"

He was pointing to a display of capes. She supposed these were in right now. Some of the teenage girls she saw at the cégep were wearing them. Not for her, though. In a year, capes would be eccentric again.

"I'm too old for these trendy clothes, Dad," she said.

"Ah, this again," Sunil said. "'I'm too old, Daddy.'"

"Really? I say that?"

It occurred to Rani that she must have used to. *I'm not a baby.* It was normal for kids to say that. Her own daughters certainly did. Maybe for her dad, things that were normal seemed truly remarkable.

He'd tricked her into this shopping trip, claiming he had an urgent errand at Les Galeries d'Anjou and needed a lift. She didn't mind, exactly. It was sweet. Irritating, but sweet.

"Look, we could buy something for the girls," Rani said, after they'd walked around the mall for another ten minutes.

But her dad's face had lost its happy cast.

"I lost my money," he said, opening and closing his hands, something like wonder in his voice.

"But you still have your wallet?" Rani asked.

"I got distracted. I was thinking about something and I got distracted. And I lost my money."

He was looking through his wallet now, disconsolate. Rani carefully led him through the mall to their exit. They crossed the parking lot and got into the car without acknowledging that the shopping trip had been a failure, that they were giving up.

In the car, he put his hand in his other pocket

"Ah, but what do you know?" A bit wry now, at the situation. "Here are the keys your mother was looking for."

"Ah," Rani said. "I have days like that."

Surely everyone did? Or just she and Sunil? Rani caught a glimpse of her own face in the rear-view mirror. Her father's eyes, with that same perpetual panic, surrounded by the rest of her face, always set in that *coping* expression; maybe she got that from Hima, a brave face you put on.

A PERFECT SPRING day. Sunil took Hima's hand as they walked up Mount Royal. Trees in blossom, not too much mud on the ground, even a few blades of green grass poking through here and there. Sunil kissed Hima's cheek and began humming a Hindi song from their youth about birdsong and sunshine. They were approaching the lookout when the fireworks show in Sunil's head began again, suddenly flashing zigzag arcs across his vision. This had been happening on and off for a few days. He had not told Hima about these coloured lights, as he was quite sure they were not real. He would just ignore them. But now something else was happening, the lights were hurting him, shooting him in the head. He turned to Hima and began to ask her if she could see them, but his words would not come out the way he wanted them to.

"Are the lights on?" he asked. No, no, that wasn't what he meant. He tried again. "Can we turn them off?" Oh, why was this happening?

Hima didn't reply. She pulled her collar up on her coat and remained silent, presumably to protect herself from his nonsense. She had good instincts, he thought. She was strong; he doubted if she understood how much he admired her.

"Good," he said.

But that wasn't what he wanted to say either.

He wondered if these were normal side effects of the medication he was taking, along with the drowsiness. *What else do they want to do to you?* a voice asked him, but he silently ordered it to shut up. Hima took his arm then, and gestured back toward their house.

"Shall we?" she said.

He nodded, but a few metres from home he was overcome with dizziness. He shuffled toward a bench where two white-haired men sat, to one side. The world was spinning, and he couldn't walk. Hima tightened her grip on his arm, and tried to pull him upright. He couldn't stand anymore, but he could not sit down either. He tried to lower himself onto the bench but missed and fell to the ground.

8. Une convergence de solitudes (A Convergence of Solitudes)

April

AT EASTER, ROB, Rani and the girls returned from a weekend in the Laurentians to a message from Hima on the answering machine.

Sunil had had a stroke. He was in a coma.

By the time Rani arrived at the hospital, he was dead.

RANI SOMEHOW MADE it back home, reeling from the shock. It had all happened so suddenly. Rob took her hand and told her to take a sleeping pill, maybe some vitamins for her immune system. She went to the medicine cabinet, tears blurring her vision, and began opening the little plastic bottles without stopping to read their labels. There was a bottle that seemed to have belonged to either her father or Mélanie. The prescription label had partly disintegrated from bathroom steam. She shook out a pill and popped it down, telling herself that nothing could make her feel worse, only better.

A childish voice in her head was screaming that she hadn't been a good daughter, hadn't been to see her parents often enough. The guilt was not a surprise. What Rani had never expected was that the news of his death would cause an intense feeling of restlessness.

She decided she would drop in on her mother the next day. But for now, for some reason, she had to go for a bike ride. Right away. She asked the kids if they wanted to come. Rita just stared at her.

"It's raining outside," Kira said.

"Drizzling, yes," she said, "mild for April, though." She was dimly aware that she was speaking strangely. She sounded how she felt: spotty.

"There's slush on the ground," Rob said.

"Well, not on the roads," Rani said. "Rain's washed it away."

She zipped her jacket back up and went outside, ignoring Rob's questions about when she would be back. Forty-five minutes later, Rani was in Laval-des-Rapides. She looked at the wine-red A-frame and marvelled at how, for her, it had always represented her father. It was a neat, tidy little house from the outside, flanked by two fir trees that had never grown as tall as they should have. There was something meek about it. It reminded her of her father's face, always sad, even when smiling.

They had moved many times, but this had been the first house she remembered. On the inside, family dramas that were never properly explained to her. At school, a few blocks away, a few years of torment, hopeful daydreams that life would get better when they moved again, a pattern that repeated itself like long, shifting seasons throughout her childhood.

Now, the living room curtains were drawn. She stood at her old doorstep and looked through the small, diamond-shaped glass panes in the door. A wet breeze blew her hair into her eyes. She pulled her hair back behind her ears and peered through again. She couldn't see a thing.

SIXTEEN HOURS on the plane, terrified. Wanting this for as long as she could remember. She had created so many stories for herself: her mother was beautiful; her father was a French soldier, from Paris. This person, her mother, was about to become real. What if she found Mélanie ugly? She remembered what Rani's kids had pointed out: What if her mother had another family who didn't know about her?

And—this was the thought that accompanied her everywhere, would never leave her in peace—what if her father had been a rapist? What if, when her mother took one look at her, she would remember and find her beyond ugly, purely hateful, the product of a rape?

"You have to be prepared, you know, Tweetie," Jane said into the silence between them.

"I know."

"Not just for a happy ending."

Mélanie groaned. She gritted her teeth. Lucky for Jane, she thought, that she was stuck here on the plane. She so wanted to bolt right now! They had stopped in Vancouver, and then Singapore. If Jane had opened her mouth before

Singapore, she might have fled then; the rage she felt would have been her excuse.

Finally, as her ears began to pop, she saw the moving lights of cars, heard but did not process the captain's announcement. Jane shifted nervously in her seat. They were both dying to get out of the plane; they both knew it would seem like ages before they did.

THE BUS ACROSS the tarmac full of exhausted travellers. Cologne, perspiration, and now the smell and heat of Vietnam. The debilitating wall of sweltering, muggy heat, the smell of ashes and garbage, the noise of hundreds of excited Vietnamese voices.

Ejected into a hall, following the formless crowd, completely confused and enervated, Jane and Mélanie found themselves holding hands.

Ten cubicles at customs, but only two people on duty. Sweating now. When they finally found themselves at the top of the line, Jane let her go ahead alone. The serious soldier, in full Communist garb.

The glare in his eyes as he took her passport, read aloud in English that she was born in Vietnam. He looked up into her face and began firing questions at her in Vietnamese.

"I can't speak Vietnamese."

A look of pure hatred. She was taken aback. She hadn't considered that the official welcome at customs could be like this.

"What is your name?"

She hesitated, was about to answer when he barked another question at her.

"What are you here for?"

He might as well have added "traitor."

OUT THE DOORS, greeted now by the buzz of traffic, urgent shouting, a hot breeze carrying a strong smell of urine. In a taxi, in noisy traffic with vehicles of various sizes: tour buses, cars, scooters, cyclos.

Mélanie's eyes widened as she spotted two riders on a scooter: a little girl on a woman's lap. The woman was in a cone hat, and the child was holding a tall cage containing a bird half her own size.

Past markets, entire city blocks of clothing boutiques, open stalls with shiny things, piles of silk, fish, signs advertising turtle soup, tiger beer, snake blood. Suddenly, as if a page had been turned onto a new reality, tree-lined avenues resembling a scene in Paris, but buzzing with a bewildering level of activity.

A modern hotel with tall glass windows, strangely quiet after the cacophony of the streets. Delicate paintings of rice fields and people in boats, tall orchids in glass vases, a portrait of the president in the lobby—but otherwise, this hush, the air conditioning, the clean, organized plushness of the upholstered furniture. Almost as though they'd left Ho Chi Minh City and returned home. They opened the door to their room and fell upon their beds. They didn't know what time it was; they didn't care. They were overwhelmed, fatigue accounting for a fraction of what they felt. Closing their eyes, they entered their last night of respite.

REPLACING THE HEAVY black receiver. Ten long minutes as they tried to find the street on the map. Stepping outside together into the crushing heat, the noise. From District One, with its authority of cement and glass, back into the shabbier part of the city they had driven through the previous night, the busy crowds, cyclos, scooters, street peddlers, outdoor stalls selling handbags; past doorways of stores filled with tall piles of silk, the smell of fish, the aggressive hawkers trying to sell them everything from cheap trinkets to stinky tofu, war vets begging on the sidewalk. Jane and Mélanie stopped and studied the map, and were soon surrounded by a dozen people who had gradually drifted over and were now trying to peer over their shoulders at where they wanted to go. A shy boy spoke a few words of English that neither Jane nor Mélanie could understand. He gave up with a good-natured smile and indicated to them to follow him. The group moved with him, an amoeba-like blob, though some members gradually began falling away. A right turn, a series of narrow footpaths. Arriving damp with sweat at the orphanage. A man smiled at them and told them in confident English that Annie was waiting for them inside with a letter, *yes, yes, you are in the right place.*

RANI'S COUSINS' HOUSE had been only a few blocks away from this house. As she biked there, a memory came to her of a summertime visit: she and the girls in the backyard swimming pool, bobbing around on plastic floats, when Uncle Krishen asked her if her mother was playing the harmonium these days. She told him she couldn't remember the last time she had seen, much less heard it. He said that it was important for a couple to have hobbies, and preferably hobbies in common. She would have been about twelve. She was surprised that he was being so frank with her about her parents' marriage, as if he thought she could do something about this. Then she'd heard that he and her aunt had separated. She had been shocked, but it seemed that nobody else in her family was. There were murmurs about huge fights about little things. The boys had left with their mother and lost contact with Rani's own immediate family; the girls had stayed here with him. Then they grew up and moved away, and he moved into an apartment.

It had all been…years ago. Many of them.

The pear tree she remembered from her childhood still stood in the centre of the front yard, wrapped in burlap. She parked her bicycle across the street and walked around to the backyard. There was still a lot of snow on the ground here, as if this house had been abandoned by time. She could make out the blobs of shapes under it: the treehouse was still there, as was the swing, and the decks with the picnic tables where they had had their barbecued meals. She could almost smell the tandoori chicken, imagine the chunky blotches of spilled raita on the picnic tables: the one for the grown-ups on the upper level deck, the lower table underneath for the children. She stood on her tiptoes, pressed her face against the kitchen window and peered in. There was nothing to see. The kitchen was bare.

A memory of the smell of Indian spices mixing with the fragrance of Thérèse's various fruit preserves and pies, made from the raspberries that grew in their backyard and in the woods beyond. How she had wanted to live inside this house, belong to this family, when she was small, how she had imagined she would have been so much happier. And yet her uncle and aunt had separated, the children split into two camps.

She dug in her tote bag and fished out her address book. She turned to the page with the address she had copied from

Mélanie's files. She wondered if she would really dare, she felt mad with grief, but not the way normal people felt, she thought. It was as though now that her dad was gone, the craziness was all hers; she could give it free rein.

She calculated: another half-hour bike ride, and it was *almost* on the way home. She got back on her bicycle, switched on the front and back lights, and pedalled toward La Petite-Patrie, her heart pounding. It seemed to her that the drivers she found idling next to her at intersections turned and looked at her. She wondered if her mental state was apparent to them. Or did they just see a brown woman on a bicycle? She decided to take a longer, more meandering route where she would encounter fewer cars.

As she rode through the streets, her thoughts alternately wandered and raced. She wondered if her father had known he was going to die, and if so, if he'd thought about where he was going. She thought of her parents' stories, how they spoke as if the most salient differences that people perceived had to do with whether they were Hindu or Muslim, yet how neither seemed to think about religion itself in a serious way. Her father had other, more unusual, yet, she had to admit, more plausible beliefs. He saw significance in the most mundane objects. His reality seemed lit up with little lights nobody else could see. She wondered about his last thoughts. Had there been clarity?

She came to a soccer field, mostly clear of snow, spotted here and there with mounds of greyish crystals. At the edge of the field, a dozen or so small discs were flying from one point to the other, low, like a new sort of animal, neither insect nor bird. When they reached the opposite side, they all tumbled down together and continued to slide along with the wind. Upon closer inspection: their provenance had been a Dunkin Donuts box. Plastic coffee lids. A dance of plastic lids, that's all this was. She told herself there would be no signs from the heavens today.

She passed two girls overdressed for this mild, wet day in snowsuits, wearing face paint, walking glumly hand-in-hand with their father, who wore sweats and a t-shirt that proclaimed him to be the greatest dad in the world, *Papa numéro un*. Someone playing scales on the piano without much enthusiasm. A fat cat sat under a tree and glared up at a squirrel that was chattering its head off. A school bus had stopped up the road, and she felt the children stare at her through the windows as she cycled by. She remembered being on a school bus, the other children wondering aloud if she was going to lose it someday.

As she got closer to Serge Giglio's street, her heart continued to pound inside her chest like a bird flying wildly in a house, hitting walls and ceilings, trying to find an exit. And now an entrance. She was here. No car in the driveway, nobody in the street. She laid her bicycle down on the front lawn, ran up the steps and rang the doorbell. Probably out— she glanced again at the driveway, and around to the side of the house; there was no garage—but she rehearsed what she would say if he appeared: looking for Mélanie, had she been in touch? She waited a full minute. The front door stared silently back at her.

The way to the backyard was blocked by a locked gate. She went back to her bike, wheeled it down the path, down the sidewalk around the corner to the side of the house, where she leaned it against the back fence. She hesitated and then climbed over, more awkwardly than she would have liked to;

at first, looking at the fence, she'd imagined it going much more smoothly; in her imagination, she jumped the fence, as agile and reckless as a teenager. She walked up the back steps, looking around. Nobody except a squirrel, a few feet away from the base of the steps, its head poking out of a garbage can, and it seemed to her that this creature did stop to give her an incredulous look before going back to the grape it was working on. There was a sliding patio door. The kind that tended to stick, that people sometimes didn't bother locking. She debated with herself for a few seconds. She glanced over her shoulder. Yes, she would do this outrageous thing. She grabbed the handle, pulled it with all her strength. It slid open with a soft swishing noise, and her heart bounced hard in her chest.

The first thing she noticed was a long dining table made of dark heavy wood, and a bowl of mangoes in the centre of it. To the right of the table, a fireplace, and above this, a picture of Krishna on a riverbank, spying on some bathing beauties. When she got over her surprise, she remembered that some-one had told her that story; she thought it might have been her father. Krishna stole their clothes so that the girls came out of the water and searched the bank squawking and naked while he hid behind a tree. It had bothered her that her people worshipped such a cheesy scoundrel. It gave her pause that Serge would have this painting on his dining room wall.

And mangoes. She picked them up and studied their skins. They were hard and green with splashes of red here and there. She thought of her dad, how he would take a ripe yellow mango, cut it into two halves, and then squeeze the juices from each into his mouth. He would have bits of the deep yellow fruit on his hairy arms, down his chin, and on the front of his shirt. He would urge her to try one, pushing a piece in her face, and she would just glare at him and shake her head. She had been intent on being revolted. Only after she'd left home did she start eating mangoes, buying two or three a week, knowing intuitively how to spot and feel the ones that were ripe to eat.

So far, she had been in this house less than a minute but had been reminded of her father twice. What did it mean? Why would it mean anything? Only a crazy person would ask that kind of question. What kind of person would break into another person's house, with no intention of actually stealing anything?

She looked again at the painting of Krishna and the swimming maidens. She stepped from the dining room into the living room. The floor was a mess of papers and books, and an electric keyboard that was not plugged into anything. She looked around the room and spotted Serge's famous twelve-stringed guitar poking out from under a Sherpa jacket on an orange beanbag chair. She tried the jacket on. It stank of cigarettes. It was huge on her. She put her hand in the pocket and found a pen. It leaked ink on her fingers and she quickly replaced it. She picked up the guitar, trembling, ran her left hand up and down the neck, randomly pressing frets as she strummed the strings with her right hand. She spotted a mirror on the wall across from where she was sitting and gave herself a nervous smile. She looked small and ridiculous, like a child playing dress-up. There were blue smudges on the body of the guitar from the leaky pen. She found a tissue and wiped it down.

She was suddenly hungry. She remembered she hadn't eaten since breakfast. She went to the kitchen and looked into the fridge. She had to eat something; she was feeling dizzy now. There were some leftovers of canned pasta in a saucepan. She put the saucepan on the stove, but couldn't wait for the food to heat. She threw the contents onto a plate. It was cold and disgusting. She thought she would throw up. She asked herself what she was doing, what she could possibly be thinking. She began again. Then she gave up, and went to the bathroom, suddenly remembering the pills she had swallowed in her bathroom, wondering if she just needed to vomit. She only managed to spit in the sink. Then her strange energy came buzzing back.

She went upstairs and found Serge's bedroom. The bed was unmade, the floor a mess of cigarette butts and bottles.

An old man still living like a rock star.

Well, she was a bit of rock star, she thought to herself, laughing. High on drugs. She opened the closet and saw very few men's things in there. A pair of jeans on the floor of the closet, a pair of overalls folded on a hanger. There was some kind of Indian tunic, white, light cotton and embroidered, but no pants, no *kameez*. It was the kind of thing that looked great on Serge, but she knew that if she put it on, she would just look more Indian, and poor. There were many dresses, in shiny, pastel fabrics. Rani knew these belonged to his wife, the wife who had left. Rani held a turquoise one against her body and looked at herself in the mirror on the closet door. She thought of trying it on, but suddenly lost her nerve as she noticed a portrait of Shiva watching her from the wall behind her. She left the room, first crept and then ran down the stairs before she let herself out the dining room doors.

THIS IS WHERE *they came and got me. And where my mother left me in the first place.*

Annie Hoang was waiting outside the orphanage. She explained to Mélanie that it was no longer open, that there was a new one, on the outskirts of the city.

"You see, locked," Annie said, trying the metal gate. Mélanie scanned the letter and photographs she had just been given. The sentences were in English. They described the people in the photos. Her family. But what did they mean? She struggled to form the question, but Annie leaned forward.

"Your mother was trying to find you too," she said, in a matter-of-fact voice.

Jane and Mélanie could only gasp in response. Jane put her arm around Mélanie, their eyes filling with tears.

"Okay, are you ready?" Annie said.

Mélanie felt bewildered, overstimulated and tired. Annie walked fast and Mélanie noticed that Jane was having trouble keeping up with her. The noise of the street was deafening—cars honking, engines revving, street vendors advertising their wares, bargaining with customers. She glanced at Jane, who was trying to discourage a stray dog from following her. The dog had buried its head under the cloth of Jane's dress; only its body and four legs were visible as it followed her. Jane finally managed to shoo it away, only to be accosted by a flock of chickens. Annie instructed her to simply walk through the group. She laughed and gestured to her to be more aggressive. Mélanie thought Jane looked like a different person here in Vietnam; her pale skin made her seem vulnerable, even ill.

The air was humid and smelled of barbequed pork and urine; there was an occasional whiff of old fish. Jane and

Mélanie followed Annie through a brick archway, across a cobblestoned courtyard toward a house with a blue-and-white striped awning. A Vespa was parked next to the door. More chickens arrived, seemingly from nowhere, greeting them with a racket.

Annie pointed toward the sky and they walked up a set of stairs, through an open door into a dark apartment. Mélanie looked around. They were poor, she thought. Maybe not by Vietnamese standards, but the room they'd entered had so little furniture—just an old table, with a bed beside it, and one wooden chair—though stuffed with knick-knacks, miniature statues and dolls. There were no panes on the windows; a slight breeze blew through the room and, with it, a smell of incense.

Mélanie suddenly felt shy. Annie called something out, was answered, and as they walked through this room and stepped onto an enclosed porch, Mélanie felt sure everyone could hear her pounding heart. Her own ears seemed to fill with the sound.

"Come and meet your mother," Annie said, as they stepped through the doorway.

She smiled and with a graceful movement of her palms, indicated a woman in a wicker chair, who looked up with expectant, bright eyes.

Mélanie stared at the petite woman, too overcome to move. She studied the woman's short black hair, the lovely red lips, the kind, delicate features.

"Tran Cam Nga," the woman said, pointing to herself. She stood, walked toward Mélanie and gazed into her face.

Their eyes filled as they looked at each other. Tran Cam reached out and placed cool fingers on Mélanie's cheek. They put their arms around each other. The woman seemed so thin and fragile that Mélanie was afraid of hugging her too hard. Tran Cam led Mélanie to a chair next to hers. Mélanie lowered her body onto the seat self-consciously as this woman, her *mother*, reached out again and took her hand.

"I don't know how to say my name," Mélanie said in French, as tears streamed down her cheeks.

"Mélanie," Tran Cam said sensibly, with a laugh. Then she added, "Or Thuy Thi Diep." She had a warm, motherly voice.

Mélanie nodded, trying to control her sobs.

"Your Vietnamese name is like you," this woman, her mother, said in French, speaking slowly. She pronounced it carefully for her again and added, "It means sounds nice, looks nice."

The three slender young men standing against the wall agreed, in American-inflected English.

"Elegant," said one

He leaned forward and said his name, "Nam." This, Mélanie already knew from the letter, was her eldest brother. She was aware of towering over him, and all of these blood relatives, although she was barely five foot four.

"Your name also means 'not fat.'" This was Duc. He had a relaxed grin on his thin face.

He finds me huge. To her, everyone looked emaciated, starved.

"Blue. It means 'blue,' too," said her youngest brother, Minh.

Mélanie looked down at her clothes and laughed. She was wearing a blue blouse, a blue skirt and a pair of blue loafers. *Look at me*, she thought, a little hysterically, *I'm dressed like a Smurf*. She got that from her mother, that monochromic look. *Her other mother.*

She turned to Jane and smiled. Jane's dress, shoes and bag were the same pale yellow. Her hair was its natural colour, light brown mixed with grey. She stood apart from the others, at the door that opened to the porch, shielding her eyes against the sun. She looked apprehensive, and it took her a moment before she focused on Mélanie and returned her smile.

"This is Jane," Mélanie said.

Tran Cam and Jane acknowledged each other. Jane's blue eyes were glistening. She gave Tran Cam a shy, frightened smile. Mélanie thought she suddenly looked much older. Her skin looked blue and grey.

Tran Cam stood up then and walked over to her.

"Thank you, Jane," she said. "For taking care of my daughter."

There was a pause. Jane didn't say anything. She seemed about to cry.

"*Our* daughter," Tran Cam said quickly.

Jane nodded, still too overcome to utter a word.

Mélanie felt wretched for her. She thought of the harsh words she had used, about being stolen from her family; once, drunk and premenstrual, she had called Jane up from Rani and Rob's apartment and accused her of being too vain to bear her own baby. Jane had flaws, but Rani had been right: it was because Mélanie was her daughter that she had been able to see them so clearly, and with so little forgiveness. Jane had always tried her best.

How inadequate, how lonely Jane must feel, standing there now, witnessing the undeniable pull of love between Tran Cam and herself.

"This was your grandmother," Tran Cam was saying, pointing to a small photograph of a round-faced woman with short grey hair and patchy eyebrows. She flipped it over and examined some writing. "Last year," she continued. "She died in January." Her face was both thoughtful and stoic.

"My husband will be home this evening, and you will meet your sister Lan then too," Tran Cam continued. "She is at school right now." She showed her a picture of a child with missing front teeth. Mélanie turned it over. A date was inscribed; the picture was three years old.

"I had her late," Tran Cam said. "I kept trying for a daughter." She blinked away some tears and smiled into Mélanie's eyes.

There was searing joy, joy that felt like pain, spreading through Mélanie's chest, but the other conflicting sensations threatened to dominate. Mélanie felt more conscious of Jane beside her than she ever had in her life. Did she regret never having a baby of her own? She had never asked her, only criticized.

And another thing. She had always imagined that when she found her family, she would feel as if she belonged, because of a strong physical resemblance. Yet nobody here quite looked like her. Her skin colour was deeper than that of the boys, who had freckles and a reddish cast to their skin, like their mother. Tran Cam had red bumps under her eyes, as if she had been crying all these years.

Mélanie studied the four of them, their neat, even-featured, squarish faces, dark brown eyes, the raw hue of their skin, their hair, which seemed wispy and soft.

This husband of Tran Cam's, he's got nothing to do with me. She was sure of this.

"And my father?" she blurted out.

Jane shot her a look, shaking her head.

But Tran Cam just nodded and pulled on the hem of her white skirt. Her face wore a small, unreadable smile.

"It's all right," Jane finally said, clearing her throat, "You don't have to…"

But Tran Cam ignored her. She looked up and addressed the room. "I looked for him," she began. Her eyes fell on her three sons, and then she turned back to Mélanie.

"He was an American soldier," she said.

Mélanie inhaled sharply. She felt reproach in Jane's eyes; whatever goodwill there was quickly fading. Panic now competed with all the other feelings swelling in her chest.

One of them was love for Tran Cam. *My mother.* She was awestruck. It was finally hitting her the way she knew it was supposed to, very hard. *My mother.* She gazed at the middle of Tran Cam's small body. My mother's *womb.*

Jane was right about the biological father. She didn't have to know. This was enough. It would be selfish to force Tran Cam to relive this part of her story.

Her new brothers gave her a polite nod and went inside the apartment.

But after an uncomfortable moment, Tran Cam continued.

"He was a nice boy," she said, and Mélanie heard Jane echo her own quick sigh of relief. "He was all mixed up. Some Cherokee, some Puerto Rican, African, English, Spanish, everything. That's what he told me. He had everything!"

She laughed, paused, and then looked at her lap again.

"After the war, I thought it would be easy to find somebody so special," she said with a wry laugh. "I had never met somebody who called himself 'all mixed up.' I can tell you his name…"

His name!

But Tran Cam met Mélanie's eyes and shook her head. Apology on her face.

No!

"It won't help you. You won't find him."

He's dead. Mélanie cleared her throat, but her question still came out hoarse.

"Why not?"

"Because, my dear Mélanie," she said. "His name is José Rodriguez, and he was from New York City."

Mélanie felt numb. She half heard Jane's short, surprised laugh. Tran Cam got up, disappeared into the apartment and returned a few seconds later with three yellowed sheets of newsprint, printed on both sides. Their jagged edges revealed that they had been torn out of an old phone directory. Six pages chock full of J. Rodriguez's.

"I see," Mélanie said.

"I will tell you about your father," Tran Cam said.

Jane patting her arm now, whispering that she would leave the two of them alone, quietly slipping out of the enclosed porch. Mélanie slowly turned to watch her. Crossing the apartment, stepping outside.

"He was a lovely boy," Tran Cam said. "So special. We were in love. But my parents didn't want us to be together. I was very mad at the time. I think they were afraid I would follow him to America. They didn't want to lose me. I understand. The war was so hard. They wanted. all the family together. All the family together. But they sent you away."

She was crying again now. Neither of them said anything. Mélanie knew the rest of the story, how she had been sent to an orphanage, but that it was supposed to be temporary. Tran Cam had intended to get her out as soon as she could, as soon as she had the means to. But then the Americans took all the babies out of the orphanages, put them on planes, took all those pictures for the news back home.

Tran Cam said she had tried to console herself for years, thinking her daughter would have a better life in America. She was even naive enough to think Mélanie might find her father. Tran Cam paused. Her face collapsed. Mélanie let her own do the same.

"He was very special," Tran Cam said. Quick, staccato words between sobs. "All mixed up. I never met anyone like that."

Mélanie held her arms out and the two embraced again, their cheeks and the tops of their blouses wet with tears.

Tran Cam withdrew from the embrace, wiped her eyes on her sleeve and waved her hand in a gesture that seemed to say, "Enough!" Mélanie let her lead her back inside the apartment. In a tiny alcove to the right of the door was an altar, a wooden shelf holding incense, flowers, and several photographs of various sizes in frames of varying quality.

"Your ancestors," Tran Cam said in a solemn voice. She began to name them all, but soon seemed to realize she was losing Mélanie, who was completely bewildered. She laughed and pointed to the flowers: "*Fleurs-de-lys*. You know?" She plucked one and slipped it through Mélanie's hair, and tucked her hair behind her ears.

IT WAS NINE THIRTY, well past the girls' bedtime, but Rani heard their sleepy voices from down the hall as she came in. She stood at the door to their room. Rob was kneeling at the foot of Kira's bed. They all turned to look at her.

"Mummy," Kira said in a breathless voice. "Daddy says we all die. Do we have to? I don't want to die. I don't want to just lie there. It'd be so boring." She looked down at her blanket, wiggled her toes.

Rita neither chimed in nor argued, for once. She was looking into her mother's eyes with a grave expression.

"Not for a long, long, long, long time," Rani said. "And by the time you are old enough to die, I think the scientists will have figured out a cure."

"A cure for cancer," Rob said.

"No, she means for death. So we don't have to die anymore."

Rani felt Rob watching her but she could only give him a helpless look. It would be nice to have a crutch, a religion to fall back on. For Rob, religion was the same as what it was for her parents, the thing that had torn his country apart, but which he knew was nevertheless an important part of his identity. The last part was harder to shake off, but faith itself would actually be so much more useful.

"So we just disappear," Rita said, staring at the wall in front of her.

"Did Grandpa disappear?" Kira asked, alarmed.

"He didn't disappear, no, and he won't. He's left us his legacy," Rani said. "It's ... I'll explain it tomorrow."

When I've figured out what I mean.

THAT NIGHT, she told Rob a little about her bike trip.

"I went around looking into people's windows like a stalker."

"That's okay," he said.

"But you don't understand. If you'd seen me—"

"You're not crazy."

"I was *acting* crazy."

"Exactly," Rob said. "There's a difference."

What was it about Serge? That bony, kind face, the tragic eyes. His rousing, magnificent music, his unique and disarming voice. He'd looked her in the eyes and told her she radiated beauty; his lyrics told her to be free, when she'd desperately needed to hear those words. A star whose mere proximity had raised her life above the level of the mundane, made her feel unconditionally loved. But this need to feel special. That was like Sunil. The thought rattled her.

9. Coda: Le rythme des marées (The Rhythm of the Tides)

April

AS SERGE WAS about to turn out the lights and get into bed, he was struck with the thought that someone was in his closet. He didn't know where it came from. He thought he smelled a faint trace of Jane's perfume, but he was sure she was not in the room. It was as if whoever was in the closet was stirring up her scent. He unplugged the lamp on his bedside table, wrapped the cord around itself and knotted it. He carried it in his arms as he took a few quiet steps toward the closet. He reached out and turned the doorknob. He expected to hear a rustle or a gasp, but there was no sound. He looked inside. There was nobody there, but one of Jane's dresses was lying on top of his own jeans, on the floor of the closet.

An air current could do this. It was possible. The breeze coming through the window he'd opened that evening, it could stir up a sleeping scent, in this case one of roses and musk, one buried in an alcove or a closet. It could mean something, or nothing, he thought.

With his toe, he pushed a wicker basket along the floor until it sat precisely halfway across the doorway. He memorized its position. If it moved from that position, then it would mean something.

Serge had quit drinking four times since the referendum. He'd been so upset with himself, unable to shake the feeling that he was responsible for the defeat. It had been so close; the fact that he had been sleeping could have sent the wrong message to his fans, the wrong vibe, back through those same waves from the same collective consciousness that he relied on for his own inspiration. Why had he been sleeping? He blamed drink.

For a week, he shook, sweat, shat, and stank. Every night, he had nightmares about falling off the wagon. And then he would. But this time he wanted to make his sobriety stick.

There was a sound that both Jane and Mélanie used to make in their sleep all those years ago, the softest one-note whistle in one nostril, regular, on beat. Serge imagined these little breaths as tiny, drawn shapes, the size of teardrops, mauve outlined in grey. He would go to little Mélanie's bedroom to watch her sleep and listen to her chirpy breath. Then, when he got into bed at dawn he would watch Jane sleep, listening to the same sound coming through her nose. He would fall into a first slumber and wake up a few minutes later to Jane's little noises, reassured.

Now he heard the same sound. He rolled over on his side and reached for her. But there was nobody there. Birds outside his window, cardinals and crows, mocking him. With an ache in his chest he remembered the things she had left in her closet that remained untouched, the things she didn't want, the discarded clothes and shoes.

"HEY!"

When Rani looked up and saw Mélanie standing in her office, she didn't recognize her at first. The young woman was calm and—what was that word?—*radiant*. It was the joy in her face and her voice, Rani realized, that had made her hard to recognize.

Rani stood up from her desk and they hugged. She sat down again and wiped tears from her eyes.

Mélanie's expression became more serious, but no less serene.

"I'm sorry," she said. "I'm sorry about your dad. I saw his obituary in the newspaper. But also, I'm sorry about everything."

"Thanks," Rani said. And after a moment. "What's new with you?"

Happiness filling out Mélanie's face again. Without a word, she passed her a photograph. An overexposed group picture on a dilapidated porch. Mélanie standing next to a tiny Asian woman with a heart-shaped face. They were both smiling, but their faces looked raw, as if they had been crying. There were two skinny youths on either side of the two women, and standing to the side was a white woman, her face in shadow.

Rani asked if the person standing to the side was her mother. The young Englishwoman she remembered whispering to her boss at the restaurant, fourteen years older now.

"Yes," Mélanie said. "Well, *one* of my mothers."

Rani peered at the tiny Asian woman in the picture.

When she looked up again, Mélanie was nodding and grinning.

"That's wonderful," Rani said, and hugged her once more. She sat down again.

"Have you told your father?" she asked after a moment.

"You mean Serge." The grin disappeared. There was something hard in her voice, something of the old Mélanie.

But after a moment, she surprised Rani by saying, "I should go see him now while I have the nerve. Do you want to come?"

"What?"

Rani had no idea what else to say. She looked back at her desk, stamped a form, made a half-hearted attempt at pretence of being absorbed in the task. She heard the challenge in Mélanie's voice.

"Do you want to meet him?"

"Sure," Rani said.

She didn't even feel like a fan anymore. She just felt like a criminal, about to be exposed. When she thought of the strange visit she had made to his house, she just felt sick, confused, utterly disgusted with herself.

They were a rock star family. Surely there were cameras in their house. Maybe Mélanie already knew!

No, she would have said something.

"I was just about to go home," Rani said. She looked at her watch.

"So call Rob and tell him that some student needs a little extra help."

Rani shook her head, but picked up the phone and made the call.

"How are you, honey?" Rob said as she was about to hang up. Rani heard the emphasis in his words. She told him she was fine. "How's it going at the zoo?"

"Oh fine. We're practicing our quacking."

One of their daughters said *quack* into the phone.

"Okay," Rani said as she replaced the receiver. She rose and followed Mélanie outside into the bright spring day.

MÉLANIE RANG THE DOORBELL. An old grey Accord was in the driveway, but nobody answered the door.

"He hasn't gone far," she said.

Rani watched as she used an actual key to open the door.

"It's too clean in here," Mélanie said, looking around. "I feel like playing music these days. I wonder what it means."

Rani found some words. She said what she sincerely hoped was true.

"Maybe it means you're happy."

Mélanie nodded and laughed but didn't meet her eyes.

"Sorry," Rani said, "That was a little..."

"Cheesy? It's okay. I've been having a lot of cheesy moments these days."

Rani looked out the window. Was he coming?

Mélanie went to the piano and sat down on the bench. After a moment, she played a few tentative notes with her right hand, holding her left above the keyboard. Then she lowered her left hand, played a few chords, and abruptly stopped. When Rani began to clap, Mélanie got up from the piano bench, mumbling to herself. Rani wondered if she should say something.

"My father never liked the way I played," Mélanie said. "And his friends said my hands were wrong for the violin."

It seemed to Rani that there was something almost false about this bitterness; there was no conviction in her words. She had just summoned back her resentment.

They stole me. Rani remembered Mélanie telling her that. But you had to forgive your parents. Nobody understood what other people had been through, least of all when those other people were the ones who had brought you up. Mélanie was twenty-one. Still young.

Young enough to go to the kitchen and look through a fridge with a robust sense of entitlement.

Rani kept glancing out the window, wondering if Serge would walk in at any moment. Her head filled with more and more uncomfortable thoughts: she was suddenly aware of her role in all of this hurt, in this estrangement. An enabler, they called it these days. And just what had she been thinking, when she came into his house alone? *Was* she a crazy person, or did she just think she was, because of who her father was? She wondered if her father had been like this, first the craziness, then a moment of clarity. She went to the door and slipped her shoes back on, aware of Mélanie's eyes on her.

"What…?"

"I need to go so you can make peace with your father," Rani said.

The palms of her hands came together and she bowed slightly. The gesture just happened, as if she was channelling someone else's spirit.

"Wow, *that* was *super* cheesy!" she heard Mélanie call out as she went through the door.

MÉLANIE STOOD IN the empty house, studying her father's Hindu paintings. She listened to the silence, felt it entering her, emptying her of the sounds of Vietnam—the long-haired girls sounding the horns on their motorbikes, the loud gossip of the women at the market in their little cone hats, sitting in their bright plastic chairs, selling spring rolls, the little man with his cart singing about hot buns at five a.m. She already missed the constant flow of people, the movement and energy, the smells of garlic and fish broth.

The urge to play music returned. She sat back down at the piano, played a chord with her left hand, her thumb and pinkie alternating, searching for the rhythm her body felt. She let the chord travel up and down the keyboard. A few tentative notes with her right hand as she began to hear a melody. She marvelled at how the music flowed from her mind to her fingers.

I can do this! She closed her eyes, afraid to break the spell. Her fingers suddenly seemed to know how to find the right notes. The simple melodic line began to develop into something lovelier and more complex. The song was composing itself! She couldn't stop playing, even as she heard her father open the door and enter the house.

HIS DAUGHTER'S BODY swaying, the pulse of the bass line holding her to the music. Turning, looking at him, grinning. A few more moments of this miraculous music.

And then here she was jumping up from the bench and throwing her arms around him, around his skinny, haggard self.

"Papa."

"PAPA, DID YOU EVER have a harmonium?"

Serge gazed at Mélanie, let his eyes linger over her lovely face, and then looked away, afraid to spoil the moment.

"Uh, yeah, I did, I think, for a few years. We used it on *Une convergence de solitudes*. It had this wonky sound, but it was kind of cool."

Mélanie watched her father's face as his mind left the conversation to listen to some remembered sounds. Until recently, she'd hated it when that happened. Now she found it…*kind of cool*. A smile broke out across her face.

"What happened to it?" she said after a moment.

"No clue." He gave an exaggerated shrug and a dopey smile. He turned away and poured himself some tea, his hands shaking slightly.

"**DO YOU REMEMBER** where you got it?"

Serge rubbed his temples as he stared straight ahead of him, trying to think straight. He shook his head.

"We couldn't use it on the second album. It was just too broken. I thought it'd be easy to fix, like an accordion."

"But do you remember where you got it, or what happened to it?"

"No. I remember we were still thinking of using it when we were going to record, I think it was our last album, and it just wasn't working and someone, Hugo, maybe, said he wanted to try and fix it. No, it wasn't Hugo. Maybe it was me. I think I did bring it home, and tried to fix it."

"And who bought it in the first place?"

"Maybe Marc," Serge said. She wasn't going to let this go. He laughed. "Or no, was it that guest sax player we recorded with the first time who sold it to us? No idea what his name was. Oh, we must've just given it back to him. I really don't remember."

He looked around his living room, as if he thought it might be hidden under a piece of clothing, or behind a plant.

His hands continued to shake, but it made him happy; it was proof he hadn't had a drink in a while.

"Why, do you think you saw one here at some point?" he finally asked.

"Maybe," Mélanie said, shrugging. "I told someone that. He was looking for this harmonium that used to belong to his family. They sold it in the seventies."

"That was a long time ago, Tweetie," he said. "You could tell him that he might be able to find one in a pawn shop."

"No," Mélanie said. "It doesn't really matter anymore."

HIMA'S HAIR WAS very sparse now but dyed a defiant black. From the time Rani was fourteen and Hima forty-eight, her mother had been slightly shorter and wider than her. In the past few years she had dramatically shrunk; she was barely over five feet now. As a small child Rani had worshipped her beauty and wondered why she didn't resemble her at all. Hima was Indian, but the fold of her eyelids, the delicateness of her features, the sculpted appearance of her cheekbones made her exotic even back in India. She told her daughter that she was always teased, yes, like Rani, for looking different.

"They called me 'Nepalese girl,'" Hima said. The way she spit the words out, it was clear she'd taken it as an insult. "But they couldn't do anything serious to me. I had plenty of brothers and sisters at school, and we all had the same face."

"You were never alone," Rani said.

"No," Hima agreed. "But I didn't always particularly enjoy the company I had, four brothers and two sisters. My sisters, especially, were such pests. They would invade my closets, steal my clothes. They would make such a mess."

Rani wished she could find the harmonium case with all those photographs so that she could picture these young siblings. As a child she had been envious of Hima with all her sisters, convinced her life would have been much easier, and less lonely, with a permanent close friend, a friend who resembled you: this is what a sister was, she felt. She remembered meeting one of her aunts, how her resemblance to her mother had shocked her, made her cry.

They were going through Sunil's things. There was a red shirt on a hanger. Rani paused. She could see him in this shirt, in her memory. She touched its cloth.

"Take it," said Hima. "Red is your colour."

"What? How could I wear this? It's a man's shirt, about ten sizes too big."

But she held it in front of herself on its hanger all the same, and peered in the mirror on the door of the wardrobe.

"Oh, all the ladies are dressing like that now," Hima said. "Just put it on. You'll see."

Where did she get that confidence from? And that sang-froid? Was she going to cry at some point? It was pretty clear she would not be wearing white or shaving her head, not this Indian widow. But if Rani lost Rob, she reflected, she would be a puddle on the floor. She would not be standing in front of her husband's wardrobe distributing his clothing, giving fashion advice.

Rani's eyes fell on a magazine on the floor of the closet.

"What's this?" she asked.

"Oh, it's the community newsletter. Every time someone dies, they have a feature on the person. You find out all kinds of stuff about people. Secrets sometimes."

"They write obituaries? Who? Who writes them?"

"I guess some family member. Some younger family member. I don't know whose idea that was. Long articles, several pages long. The funny thing is, they're not always all that flattering."

Rani sat down on her mother's bed.

"But they are interesting, that's for sure," Hima said.

"You know, I could write one about Dad if you want."

"He'd probably like that," Hima said with an uneasy laugh. "He really wanted to be famous."

They sat in silence for a moment.

"He wrote a book, you know."

"No kidding?" said Rani. "About what? Being pioneers in the Indian community?"

She wondered if she sounded sarcastic, even to herself.

"No, about engineering," Hima said in a flat voice.

Rani felt her own interest slipping away.

"A long time ago, when he first came," Hima said. "He wrote it at the same time as his Master's thesis. He was always saying, 'There's so much water. It's a waste not to harness its power for energy.'"

"Hydroelectricity."

"Yes. And they did construct them, you know, the dams he was talking about in his book."

"Wait, you're saying that was his idea? Hydroelectricity?"

"He didn't invent hydroelectricity. There were already dams. But he was always pushing this idea on anyone who would listen that there was a lot of room for development. I know he showed the book around, to his bosses, and then to a publisher, but nobody wanted it. He was very young, he had this big accent..."

"The dams they developed... those couldn't have been his idea."

"I don't know. We can't ask him now." Hima said with a shrug.

"We should've asked him before."

"Yes, he would've liked that. You know your dad. He would've liked some recognition."

"But Ma, was he really a genius, like he thought he was?"

Hima winced.

"I'm sorry. I mean...Where *is* this book?"

"I threw it out," Hima said, her voice soft but firm. "So, if you want proof..."

"Yes?"

"There is no proof." Hima said. "Your dad was a smart man. This province, they liked his intelligence and his ideas, but they could never credit him. You know, so much politics around energy. He was, like I said, this Indian man with a big accent. He used to say, when he met people for the first time, 'Hello, my name is Sunil. I am Indian. From *India*. I'm the guy I believe you are looking for.' I don't think they liked that very much. Anyway...he had a big ego, he needed a lot of attention, and it made him crazy."

Rani wondered what her parents had talked about, in their bedroom, when nobody else was around. They had shared a language, one they'd never shared with her, and it seemed as if her whole life they'd tried to shield her from so much of who they actually were. Her father had a sense of humour? An awareness of politics and history? That was news to her. Her brothers must have known a little more. She remembered something Ramesh said he'd been told by their father: "You have to be ten times as good as a white person to make it here. So, work ten times harder. But be careful. It can make you crazy."

FOR THE NEXT few days, Rani spent her lunch hours on the phone with Hima. The conversation would begin with whatever was worrying her. Rani would listen patiently but with half of her attention, waiting for the moment when the interview could begin.

"You know, I need to ask you some more questions about your early life with Dad, for this obituary. How many months pregnant were you when Dad sailed to Canada the first time?"

"Eight, eight and a half months."

"That must have been scary for you. How did you feel?"

"I was with my family. I enjoyed being home. I had a lady doctor, and an aya…"

"But still…" Rani said, and then stopped. She realized she wasn't going to get anywhere. Feelings were taboo, she supposed. "And do you remember anything…more concrete… about the people you met at the time, or the apartment you lived in?"

"Well, I have to tell you, these details you're asking me, so boring to read. When I read, I skip over those details. I feel the writer's wasting my time."

"I'll make it interesting."

"You want secrets," Hima said.

Rani wasn't expecting this. She held her breath.

"Here's something for you," Hima said. "At one point in the last year or two, we were always having fights. He said I wasn't a good wife, that I hadn't made sacrifices."

Rani was shocked. She couldn't think of anything more preposterous. There was a silence, during which the two women rubbed over this wound together, angry at a man who had died.

"Like when I went back for my nephew's wedding," she said.

"Really?"

"Sunil said, he always said I should have stayed home with him. He said, What kind of wife leaves a man who just had an operation?" Hima's voice was weak. It was a new, hoarse voice, with an old crust inside it.

"What kind of husband leaves his wife when she is eight months pregnant?" Rani blurted out angrily. And then, a memory and more bitter words came to her: "What kind of husband throws his wife's harmonium out into the snow?"

"SO YOU'RE FAILING your first year of cégep," Rani said as she pulled up a file on her computer.

The blond boy didn't answer. He wore a sarcastic smile, a hoodie, jeans and sneakers.

They both waited for the other to break the silence.

"Do you *want* to fail cégep?" Rani asked. She read his marks. It did not appear as though he had been doing a shred of work.

The boy shrugged.

"So, what are you doing here?" Rani asked.

The boy gave a nasty laugh.

"What am *I* doing here?" He leaned forward. "What are *you* doing here? What are you doing in my country?"

Rani was shocked. She didn't say anything at first. This kid was troubled. He was possibly insane. His question so absurd, in the given political context. An Anglophone challenging another Anglophone to her right to be in the country, whatever that meant. Before she spoke, she forced herself to look him in the eyes, and smile a little.

"You know, I was born here, but whenever people say stuff like that to me, challenge the right of immigrants to be here, I tell them about my father," Rani heard herself saying. "My father was a brilliant engineer. He designed all the hydroelectric dams in Québec. Your cheap hydro bills? You should thank him for them. He was a genius. Everyone used to fight over him. They all wanted him to work for their government. His brothers were *super* jealous of him. You have no idea…"

Her heart suddenly so loud in her ears, her face burning. She was making it up as she went along and his amused expression, his glinting green eyes, told her that he knew. But then he was a kid, a troubled kid. This was how he responded to everything.

May

ONE LUMINOUS SUNDAY morning Jane received a ton of earth and half a ton of stones. She spent an hour shovelling the dirt into the wheelbarrow. Then two more hours to fill the accidentally beautiful boxes she had made from the remnants of her broken deck. She worked doggedly, wiping the sweat from her forehead once in a while with hands black with dirt.

She looked up and saw Mélanie standing at the window, caught her eye, waited until she came out to help. Together they made a path with stones and put smaller ones around the flowerbeds. In the beautiful wooden boxes, they planted chives, coriander, thyme, oregano, radishes, tomatoes, lettuce, and spinach. They planted some string beans in pots, raspberry and blueberry bushes, a Japanese dappled willow, some Green Velvet boxwood and a small cedar tree. Jane took an axe and chopped up the For Sale sign that stood, ignored, on the front lawn. She used the picket as a tutoring stake for a rose bush. The plasticized sign became an improvised doormat on which they left their muddy shoes before entering the house.

ON HER WAY to Hima's after work, a block from the college, Rani recognized the sounds of her parents' language and looked up to see a stunning beauty with shining dark eyes, skin the colour of chai, turning at the top of a winding staircase, calling to a young man on the sidewalk below. Rani recognized the word for keys: *chaambiyaan*. Another word came to her, trying to take its place, *chiavi*, the word she had learned in Italian class, back in cégep. Ah, but it was time she learned a little Hindi. The husband threw the wife his keys. The loud clank as the woman caught them, then the jingling as she shook them with triumph, reminded Rani of her mother, in joyful moments, the constant music of her bangles. Rani strode along, glancing at them, trying not to stare, but also to make out more of their conversation. *Ek minute*, the wife shouted over the wind, which had begun to roar through the elm trees on either side of the door. *One minute*. Rani imagined going into their house, creeping along the hallways, examining their things. Would the house smell of incense? Of ginger and cumin, fried in ghee? She realized that her fantasy had changed; her curiosity was moving in a different direction.

HE ENTERED a restaurant where she was having dinner with some of her colleagues. None of the others at her table turned around, although he caused a stir amongst the Francophone patrons. He was wearing a Stetson and a long trench coat. It was a blustery evening, and when he came inside it seemed as if the wind had blown him in. The dark circles he'd always had under his eyes had become dark puffy bags, but he seemed cheerful enough.

Rani gazed at the man in the doorway as he scanned the long dim room. He noticed her direct stare; as their eyes met a thrill shot through her. A word came to her: *swoon*, although she didn't quite feel dizzy. He acknowledged her with a curt smile and put a finger to his lips. Then he comically crouched and mimed sneaking away as he headed to join his friends.

During his band's heyday, his hair had been long, fine, straight, and brown. It was shorter now, grey, and somehow thicker. Rani thought about telling her friends about the musical god who had just entered the restaurant, but no, they wouldn't be interested. And anyway, she was mute with amazement. After all that had happened, here he was. She had to talk to him. She had to introduce herself to him, tell him about her link to his family, explain how she had always loved and worshipped him as a teenager, and how he had changed her life. He wouldn't remember their brief encounter, which had been like this, strangely personal, across a space full of strangers—but she'd remind him, tell him the whole story. She wondered how she could discreetly slip away and approach him. At other tables, people were staring at him and speaking loudly. But she was the one he needed to hear from.

An odd thought came to her: her father would understand.

She got up and walked toward him. Gold light streamed through the restaurant's hanging lamps. A waiter carrying drinks squeezed by her. Everything seemed very loud now, her heartbeat, and the sounds of cutlery clanking against plates, a chair scraping back along the floor.

She walked past his table, brushing against his elbow as he stubbed out a cigarette. She glanced at him—he was oblivious—as she quickened her pace, continued on, and headed toward the restroom. She opened the door, stood in front of the mirror, and, seeing her reflection, felt relieved and pleased; she was suddenly overwhelmed with a sense of her own amazing good fortune. Her head filled with all the people she loved and who loved her back, the miracle of it, the variety—her witty, low-maintenance husband, her fierce, unbreakable mother, her daughters with their impossible innocence, their wide, thoughtful gazes, their uncommon beauty and affectionate hearts. Lovely, tormented Mélanie, whom, it occurred to her now, might have once longed to belong to her, be *her* adopted daughter. All these people, so vibrantly present in her life, now. The man in the hat with the tired, lined face didn't matter. The bleakness of this realization threatened to roll over her feelings of exhilaration, as it struck her that nothing she felt now had anything at all to do with him. The uselessness of it all, not just this, the rest too, all the beauty, even the wonder of love: it was just one life, so particular, fleeting and insignificant in the grand scheme of things. These great tidal waves of emotions and insights would rise, converge, carry each other away, feelings would recede, be replaced, rise again; moments of shining clarity and shimmering excitement would fade: an unremarkable state of mental instability which belonged to everyone, whether lucid or insane.

It was just life, but really, it was enough

Acknowledgements

FIRST OF ALL, I have to say that I would never have had the confidence to even try to write a novel without the encouragement of Dimitri Nasrallah.

Next, I would like to thank the Canada Council for the Arts and le Conseil des arts et des lettres du Québec for their generous financial support.

I am grateful to the many readers who offered valuable advice upon reading earlier versions of this book: Michael Belcher, Zsuzsi Gartner, Dennis Bock, Debra Nails, William Levitan, Andrew Katz, Gina Heiserman, Nathan Elliott, Leila Marshy, Linda Leith and Elise Moser.

Thanks to Usha and Virinder Dhir, and especially to Kailash Anand for helping me picture Partition-era India.

I am deeply indebted to Cath Turner for sharing her story of adoption, to Ann Elsdon for her musings about Jane, and to Ariane Vu for her vivid recollections of Vietnam.

To Christine Finlayson: thank you so much for the peace of your cottage and for your incredible kindness.

To my wonderful publishers, Hazel and Jay Millar, and to the fantastic editors they brought on board, Meg Storey and Melanie Little: thank you so much for the work you did on this book. It would have been a very different novel without Meg's deep insights and all your careful edits.

And to Frédéric Samson, my amazing husband, amateur psychologist, 24-hour tech support and in-house editor: I am beyond grateful. I still can't get over my luck.

CREDIT ALEXIS LAFLAMME

ANITA ANAND IS an author, translator and language teacher from Montreal. She is the winner of the 2015 QWF Concordia University First Book Prize for *Swing in the House and Other Stories*, which was also shortlisted for the 2016 Relit Award for Fiction and the Montreal Literary Diversity Prize. Her translation of *Nirliit*, by Juliana Léveillé-Trudel was nominated for the 2018 John Glassco Prize. She has also translated Fanie Demeule's novel *Déterrer les os*, known in English as *Lightness*.

Colophon

Manufactured as the first edition of
A Convergence of Solitudes
In the spring of 2022 by Book*hug Press

Edited for the press by Meg Story
Copy edited by Melanie Little
Proofread by Charlene Chow
Type + design by Ingrid Paulson

Front cover image © Claudio Divizia/iStockPhoto
Inside cover image © Béatrice Prève/iStockPhoto

Printed in Canada

bookhugpress.ca